ALSO BY ANNETTE MEYERS:

The Big Killing
Tender Death
The Deadliest Option

BLOOD

ON THE

STREET

....

ANNETTE MEYERS

A PERFECT CRIME BOOK

DOUBLEDAY

NEW YORK   LONDON   TORONTO   SYDNEY   AUCKLAND

A PERFECT CRIME BOOK
PUBLISHED BY DOUBLEDAY
a division of Bantam Doubleday Dell Publishing Group, Inc.
666 Fifth Avenue, New York, New York 10103

DOUBLEDAY is a trademark of Doubleday, a division of
Bantam Doubleday Dell Publishing Group, Inc.

Grateful acknowledgment is made for permission to reprint from *The Poetry of
Robert Frost*, edited by Edward Connery Lathem. Copyright 1923, © 1969 by
Holt, Rinehart and Winston. Copyright 1951 by Robert Frost. Reprinted by
permission of Henry Holt and Company, Inc., and Jonathan Cape Ltd.

BOOK DESIGN BY TASHA HALL

Library of Congress Cataloging-in-Publication Data
Meyers, Annette.
    Blood on the street / by Annette Meyers.
        p.   cm.
    "A Perfect Crime book."
    I. Title.
    PS3563.E889B58   1992
    813'.54—dc20   91-43064
                                              CIP

ISBN 0-385-42376-4
Copyright © 1992 by Annette Brafman Meyers

June 1992

1 3 5 7 9 10 8 6 4 2

First Edition

FOR KATE MICIAK

My thanks to Donna Aceto, Henry Asher, Carol Bullard, Dolores Bullard, Richard Feldman, Joan Fisher, Kevin Jennings, Myron Kalin, Marcia Lesser, Michael Levy, M.D., Detective Tom Natale, NYPD, Detective Ray Pierce, NYPD, Linda Ray, Jane Rocks, Cathi Rosso, Chris Tomasino, the Central Park Conservancy.

And always, Marty.

STREET JOKE 1

Did you hear the story about the woman who was married three times but was still a virgin?

Her first husband was a minister who prayed all the time so the marriage was never consummated.

Her second husband was an alcoholic and all he did was drink.

Her third husband was a stockbroker. All he did was sit on the edge of the bed and tell her how good it was going to be.

STREET JOKE 2

A stockbroker dies and arrives in Hell. He knocks on the door. The door opens and he's told it's a mistake. It's not his time. He hears disco music in the background and begs to see what's happening inside before he goes back. "Oh, very well," the doorkeeper says, and he opens the door. The stockbroker sees half-naked men and women having a great time dancing to wild disco music.

Five years later he really does die. When he gets to Hell, the doorkeeper opens the door and all the fires of Hell surge out. No disco music, no naked dancers.

The stockbroker insists there's been a mistake and demands to see the Devil. "Where is what I saw? Why is it different?"

"Oh," says the Devil. "Then you were a prospect, now you're a client."

1

·······

Following Smith's haphazard instructions, Wetzon walked along Barrow Street in the West Village, crossed Hudson, walking west toward Greenwich. She passed a gated park and checked the house numbers. It had to be around here somewhere, because a black limousine was parked in front of a fire hydrant across the street.

Almost as if she'd willed it, a short, compact man with razored brown hair, dressed in a Paul Stuart navy pinstripe and carrying an attaché case, came out from between two ivy-shrouded brownstones. He nimbly forded the century-old cobblestones on his shiny black wing tips and got into the limo. The door closed with that dead sound perfectly fitted doors make. Motor purring, the limo pulled away in the direction of Washington Street and points unknown, its windows anonymously dark. Ominously dark. There was something creepy about—

A brown squirrel popped out of the flower bed surrounding an ancient city oak, and Wetzon jumped, almost stumbling.

"They do that all the time. They wait for someone to come along." The man wore tight jeans, an even tighter cut-down T-shirt, and a small gold hoop in his right earlobe; a ring of keys dangled from his belt hook. His amused eyes followed the frisky squirrel up the oak tree.

Wetzon laughed. "New York squirrels." But no doubt about it, she was jumpy. She looked up at the squirrel, who chattered at her boldly. The leaves of the tree were beginning to turn a ruddy gold. She'd always loved the changing seasons in New York, but this time the coming of fall made her sad. She walked a few paces. Now, where had the man in the business suit come from? The sidewalk was uneven, bulging slightly, because the root of the tree had stretched out, demanding space under the cement. A true New Yorker, she thought.

"If you're looking for Judith," the man with the earring said, "she's behind the next house. Turn down the alley. You'll see it."

Startled—she'd quite forgotten him—she felt her face go hot. "Thanks," she said, avoiding his eyes. This was too embarrassing. How had she let Smith talk her into this? There it was. An alley not big enough for a car, about the size of a bike path, paved in flag stones.

No sun here except at midday, and it was long after midday now. She shivered in her black-and-white-checked suit and pulled the leopard silk scarf up around her neck, glad she'd switched her closets to fall-winter.

The alley had a dank, mossy essence. Her heels sounded extra loud on the flagstone as she hurried down the narrow walkway, then emerged into a clearing filled with late-afternoon sunlight. The backyard of the brownstone held a cottage of two floors, shaded by a giant elm. White paint clung unevenly to weathered wood. The window trim and door had once been green. Herbs grew in small, cared-for clumps, protected by chicken wire, and the air smelled of sage and thyme.

Looking at the shabby cottage, Wetzon wondered if the fire department knew about it. It had to be a firetrap, all wood. She'd heard about these outbuildings around the city before, but she'd never seen one. They didn't appear on rent rolls or tax rolls. They just didn't exist. And yet she was sure Con Edison provided electricity, and New York Telephone, phone service. One giant hand in this tremendous bureaucracy never informed the other.

A small, tacked-on-later Victorian cupola guarded the front door, its wooden lace almost bare of paint but cluttered with ivy. There was a modern metal doorbell with an intercom to speak into, under a taped-up note in red crayon that read: "Ring Once, Then Announce Yourself."

She stopped, her finger poised near the bell. She still had time to turn around and hotfoot it out of there. But no, she'd been promising Smith for months and ducking it. And it was, after all, a birthday present.

Smith had wanted to come along—to make sure she got there, no doubt. It had taken all of Wetzon's incredible powers of persuasion to keep her away. They'd agreed to meet later for dinner at Quatorze on Fourteenth Street at seven o'clock.

Oh, what the hell, she thought, and pressed the bell. The intercom crackled. "Leslie Wetzon," she announced crisply. She put her hand on the door handle and pressed as a buzzer sounded. The door opened and she stepped into a tiny, low-ceilinged living room with a cracked and scarred marble mantelpiece over a blackened fireplace. A gigantic TV on a rolling cart was the most important item in the room, which was, otherwise, incongruously, decor by Conran's.

The aroma of chili wafted in from the left, and she could hear someone in the kitchen talking. "Just a minute, please," a male voice called. Her stomach growled.

The owner of the voice appeared almost immediately: a man, thirty-something, wearing an apron over walking shorts and a plaid shirt. His dark, kinky hair was tied back in a ponytail. He was wiping his hands on his apron.

"I'm sorry, Ms. Wetzon, but Judith is meditating." He pronounced it "Judit," in a clipped New Yorkese street accent. He looked at his watch. "Do you want to have a seat?" He indicated the TV room. "She'll let us know when she's ready."

How? Wetzon wondered. *Oh sure, mental telepathy*. She smirked, eyeing the narrow staircase with its threadbare carpet. Rubber treads had been nailed down over the carpet shreds. What the hell was she doing here anyway? Okay, she'd be a good sport. She sat down on the love seat in front of the TV. The floor of the cottage sloped, making the love seat slope. She planted her feet firmly on the floor to keep from sliding off. She felt as if she were in one of those nasty fairy tales, Hansel and Gretel about to meet the witch.

A phone rang somewhere, and she heard the answering machine pick up. It was a Panasonic like hers; she could tell by the parade of cute clicks. But no, this one had a tinkle bell at the end of its serenade.

"Ms. Wetzon."

She looked up.

"Judit will see you now. Just go on upstairs. It's the door on the right."

Wetzon didn't know what she'd expected, maybe a gypsy with a lot of colorful scarves and beads, but Judith looked as if she'd just come from Bloomingdale's active sportswear department. She was a woman with soft, rounded edges, thick chestnut hair governed some-what by a black hairband. She wore loose black leggings and a baggy wine silk shirt. And black Reeboks that looked like space shoes. Only her earrings spoke of other dimensions, huge blue metal moons that hooked through long thick lobes and grazed her shoulders. Her eyes were dark behind slightly tinted red-framed glasses.

"Close the door, Leslie Wetzon," Judith said in a husky voice but with the same New York street accent of her companion. She was seated at a rickety card table covered in an old linen tea cloth. A large octagonal mirror lay flat on the tabletop. An empty chair stood half turned toward Wetzon. "Sit, please." She was wearing a smoky topaz emerald cut-ring on her right hand, and on her wrist was one of those stupid Cartier love bracelets that you needed a special screwdriver to remove.

"Gimme your hand," Judith said.

Wetzon settled into the chair and extended her hand. Judith's was dry and warm. Wetzon's was cold. Judith closed her eyes.

This is silly, Wetzon thought. So why was her heart pounding? Her hand tingled with a warm current. Their hands were reflected magnified in the octagonal mirror.

"You have a strong will, a long life line," Judith murmured. "You are air." She opened her eyes. "Aquarius."

Yeah, big deal, Wetzon thought. *Smith gave you to me in January for my birthday.*

"In one of your other lives, you were a prima ballerina."

Not a bad guess about a woman who wears her hair in a dancer's knot on top of her head, Wetzon thought.

"In this life . . . you do not dance now. You are very successful. Money. I see a lot of money. Friends . . ." She paused.

A little stab of hunger caught Wetzon under her rib cage and distracted her.

". . . difficult relationship. Fighting . . . a separation."

"Smith and I always fight."

"This is a man."

A man? Did she mean Silvestri?

"Awg—" Judith's hand turned to ice. Her mouth twisted.

"Blood!" Judith released Wetzon's hand and backed her chair away from the table.

Wetzon looked at her hand. "Blood? Where?" There was no blood.

"Where?" Judith sounded dazed. Her eyelids closed. "I'm . . . sorry. Come back another time."

This was nuts, Wetzon thought. The psychic had sunk into some kind of stupor. Wetzon rose, settled her purse strap on her shoulder, picked up her briefcase from the floor.

"Be careful," Judith muttered.

Hand on the doorknob, Wetzon tried again. "I don't understand. I'm sorry. Where do you see blood?"

Judith didn't respond.

Wetzon shrugged and left the room, going down the stairs. She could hear Judith come out of the room and felt her presence on the top of the stairs. Wetzon stopped and looked back.

"On the street," Judith said. "I see blood on the street."

have a wee drinkie problem? If so, would you kindly stop it for six months, old sot?' "

Smith grinned at her suddenly. "There, I know you can do it. Anyway, I'm working on something *really* big." She held up the palm of her hand. "No, don't ask me. If I land this client, we'll ride right through the recession in a Rolls."

"I certainly hope so. The phones have not been ringing off the hook lately." She smiled and leaned back in the garden chair, feeling the ironwork Victorian floral pattern on her back through her blouse. "On the other hand, the Langfords are about to accept at Shields Kaufmann and Brian Middleton is starting at Loeb Dawkins today."

"How lovely," Smith purred.

They were interrupted by a preppy young man in a crew cut. Their assistant, B.B., short for Bailey Balaban, opened the door and said, "Twoey for you, Smith."

"That's Mr. Barnes to you," Smith snapped. "Show some respect."

"But he told me to call him Twoey."

The look Smith gave him was scathing, and he escaped into the office as if afraid to turn his back to her.

"Gawd, Smith, do you want to drive B.B. to Tom Keegen, too?"

Tom Keegen, their major competitor, had stolen away their previous associate, Harold Alpert, and Wetzon was certain that Harold wouldn't have gone if Smith had treated him better.

Smith ignored her and took a final gulp of water. She rose languidly, running her fingers through her short dark curls. She had a model's figure, long and lean, olive skin and high cheekbones that set off almond-shaped eyes, and a great metabolism, which was a stroke of luck because she didn't believe in exercise.

What Smith and Wetzon did was mysterious, in the best sense of the word, and therefore, it was glamorous. They saw themselves as detectives, searching out the best candidates for the positions their clients had to fill. It seemed appropriate that even the biographical profiles they filled out for each prospect were known as "suspect sheets."

The Street called them, and those like them, headhunters, and they didn't mind. Away from the Street, recruiting professionals were executive recruiters or search consultants, and "headhunter" was a derogatory term. But the Street admired toughness and rewarded piracy. Anyone who could "get away with it" was respected.

And their clients were not ordinary businesspeople; they were the movers and shakers of the all-powerful financial community. The Street, with a capital *S*.

While Smith and Wetzon were not truly insiders, they were not outsiders either. Thus, they were in a perfect position to see every problem objectively and give the client an overview.

They were truly an odd couple. Smith had come out of personnel, and Wetzon had been a Broadway chorus dancer. That together their names were memorably similar to the gunsmiths' served only to amuse them, but they used it to enhance their singularity. They were women in a man's world.

They worked out of a small office in what had been a one-bedroom apartment in a converted brownstone, between Second and First Avenues, on Forty-ninth Street. It was ground-floor space, the back door opening onto a modest garden.

They'd been together almost eight years and had done extraordinarily well, through feast and famine on the Street. Smith concentrated on business development—bringing in clients—and Wetzon recruited brokers, the division of duties coming mainly because Smith loathed brokers. "Scum" and "dirtbags" were her kindest terms for them.

At the time of the stock-market crash in October of 1987, and for almost two years thereafter, business had been incredible. Then the real impact of the loss of the retail investor began to be felt on the Street, and in the downward slide of capital base, bankruptcies, mergers, and buyouts ensued. The refrain "the check is in the mail" was heard throughout the land.

The shape of Smith and Wetzon's business had changed gradually. They found they were in demand for a fair amount of management consulting, fees paid with a sight more regularity than were those for headhunting, thank you very much.

Wetzon sighed and looked out at their garden. It had been completely replanted and repaved with bricks, and like the phoenix, had risen resplendent from the explosion that had destroyed it the previous summer. She gathered up the detritus of their lunches and disposed of everything in the plastic garbage bag in their bathroom.

"Of course, Abe," Smith was saying into the phone in the professional voice she saved for only the choicest clients. "I'll get our proposal off to you by the end of the week." She winked at Wetzon and gave her a thumbs-up sign.

Abe could only be Abe Bloom, chairman of Cooperman Bloom Securities. Was this the big new client?

Wetzon looked at her watch and then at the Andy Warhol pencil drawing of a bankroll of dollar bills, which she and Smith had paid for with their first fee. She saluted it. Time to start dialing for dollars. She picked up the phone and called Brian Middleton at Bliss Norderman.

"Mr. Middleton's office."

"Mr. Middleton, please."

"He's not in today. May I help you?" The woman's voice gave nothing away.

"No, thank you. I'll call tomorrow." So far, so good, Wetzon thought. That's what they usually said when someone has resigned. A manager generally gave out the resigned broker's accounts to his favorites in the office and kept some for himself, so by not telling the truth—that the broker had resigned—he was buying some time.

With the eraser end of her pencil, she punched out the number for Simon Loveman, the manager of the Loeb Dawkins office where Brian Middleton was now going to be making his home.

"Simon Loveman's office."

"Hi, Joyce, this is Wetzon. I'm just checking to see if everything went all right with Brian." The line seemed to go dead. "Hello, Joyce?" Something was wrong—Wetzon's mental computer sent out an alarm: *Error, error, error.*

"I'll put Simon on."

Uh-oh. Wetzon's mental alarm went into overdrive.

"Yeah." Simon's voice was cold and angry.

"Simon, Wetzon here. Has something gone wrong with Brian?"

"You tell me."

What a strange thing to say. "Okay, switch me over."

"I don't think that'll do much good."

"Why?" What was wrong with everyone?

"Because your prima donna was a no-show this morning."

3

■■■■■■■

"This can't be happening." Wetzon's hand was frozen on the receiver.

"What can't be happening?" Smith asked without turning to look at her. She was staring at herself in her hand mirror. "Damn, another gray hair. Ouch." She pulled it out.

"Brian Middleton. Bliss Norderman says he's not in today, and he never showed at Loeb Dawkins."

"Oi." Smith swiveled in her chair, dropping her mirror on her desk. "How much production?"

"Three quarters of a mil. He was supposed to resign first thing this morning and go right over to Loeb Dawkins so they could get clearance today." Wetzon's fist came down hard on her desk top and dislodged the marble peach paperweight that Laura Lee Day had given her. "Dammit!" She caught it on the roll and kept it in her hand, absentmindedly stroking its rough texture. "He couldn't have gone somewhere else. I spoke with him last night and everything was set."

"Let's not panic," Smith said, panic in her voice. "This is a big fee, and we haven't lost it yet. Call him at home. Maybe he's sick."

Wetzon shrugged. That was hardly likely, and Smith knew it. "Okay, what the hell." She punched in the numbers and listened. At the fourth ring the answering machine clicked on, then *Twin Peaks*-y music throbbed, followed by Brian's voice asking for a message after the beep and ending with the suggestion to "think peace." She felt like howling at him, but she didn't. It would be decidedly unprofessional. So she said, with just the right tone of cool urgency, "Brian, this is Wetzon. Where are you? Please call me." She left her office number and her home number and hung up. "I don't know," she said to Smith.

"That low-life sleazebag went somewhere else." Smith was heating up to a boil.

"Maybe, but it's a little hard to believe. Brian put in so much time getting this move right. Hell, *I* put in so much time getting this move right."

"I can't believe you still think they're going to do the right thing. May I remind you about Fran Berman?"

Wetzon held up the palm of her hand. "No, please." Fran Berman had resigned and was packing up her car on Water Street, on her way to Wertenheimer, when she bumped into a broker she'd once worked with who was now at Dean Witter. A half hour later, Fran Berman was a Dean Witter broker. What did it matter that Wertenheimer had printed up business cards and spruced up an office? What did it matter that she had a handshake agreement with the manager? And insult to injury, she'd never bothered to call Wetzon or the manager at Wertenheimer to say she wasn't coming. She'd never even apologized. Wetzon sighed. "When God gave out manners, I guess he left out a lot of stockbrokers."

"Humpf." Smith picked up the phone. "What's the scum's number at Bliss Norderman?" Her long fingers danced across the digits as Wetzon called out the numbers. "Mr. Middleton, please, dear." Pause. "Oh, well, then, I'll call tomorrow." She raised a finely brushed eyebrow at Wetzon as she hung up. "He'll be in tomorrow. Ha! Try him at home again."

Wetzon heard the numbers go through and was rewarded, this time, with a busy signal. "Either he's there or someone else is trying to get in touch with him."

They looked at each other. Smith said, "Where does the rotten scum live? Still in that town house on the Upper East Side?"

"No, he and Rona split, don't you remember? She's got the town house, the baby, and the nanny—"

"And he got the business."

Rona Middleton had been a stockbroker and had built up a nice book. Brian had been a slip-and-fall lawyer. Rona had brought her husband into the business, got him registered, and they began working together. When Rona got pregnant for the first time—at the age of forty—her concentration transferred to her pregnancy and Brian serviced the accounts. The plan had been for both of them to move to Rosenkind, Luwisher. Rona would go first, then three months later Brian would join her. They'd agreed to tell everyone they were splitting up their business. Their manager would not give out Rona's accounts, because Brian would have them. But as soon as Rona settled in at Rosenkind, Luwisher, Brian announced he wanted a divorce. He'd never had any intention of moving. In the fallout, most of Rona's clients had stayed with Brian.

"I feel for her. She's struggling. He took an apartment on the West Side. Seventy-ninth Street near Columbus. I ran into him on the coffee line at Zabar's last week." Wetzon's eyes drifted down her schedule. Lots of people to call, but no appointments. She tried Brian again. Still busy. She pushed back her chair. "I'm going up there and waylay him. I don't want to take a loss here."

"I'll come with you." Smith rose and checked herself out in the full-length mirror on the inside of their bathroom door. She gave her reflection a seductive smile.

Well, thank you very much, Wetzon thought, slipping into her jacket. She said, with more acerbity than she intended, "I don't need an escort."

"I'm protecting our investment, sweetie pie. Besides, I have a five-thirty at Enzo, who, if you remember, is on Central Park South, then dinner with Twoey—"

"Spare me the itsy-bitsy, minute-by-minute of your schedule." She was usually able to let Smith's eccentricities roll off her back, but not today, and worse, she hated when Smith was proved right in her low opinion of stockbrokers. Because the truth was Wetzon liked most of the candidates she worked with. They were talented, dramatic and egocentric, and insecure—just like the people she'd worked with in the theater when she was a Broadway chorus dancer. And Smith made sure to needle her whenever something happened that proved Smith's thesis.

Peeved, and feeling childish because of it, Wetzon put three suspect sheets into her briefcase. She'd call them later. Some brokers, concerned about confidentiality—it was almost impossible to keep anything secret on the Street—preferred calls at home. "Well, come on, then," she drawled to Smith, making an effort to recapture her good humor, "let's get outa here."

In their small reception area, which had been part of the original kitchen, there were three upholstered chairs, the coffee machine on a side table, and a desk. The desk had first been Harold's, their general assistant, then B.B. had sat there for two years while he worked as a cold caller and general assistant, and Harold had become an associate.

Last year, after the duplicitous Harold Alpert left them, they'd moved B.B. into the cubbyhole office that had been Harold's, and began to interview replacements for B.B.'s old job. It had been a fiasco. They'd hired people who never showed up, and the ones who did, never lasted more than three or four weeks. The desk now belonged to Max Orchard, a round, balding, sixty-six-year-old retired accountant who wore gum-soled shoes. He worked part time Mondays, Tuesdays, Wednesdays, and Thursdays, and didn't want full time.

Smith had resisted hiring him, but they'd been so desperate, Max was given a shot. After four months, even Smith had to admit he was effective, and even better, reliable. They paid him ten dollars an hour and gave him five percent of the fee they earned on each placement generated by one of his prospects. Three such placements had panned out in the short time he'd been with them.

But today was Friday, and Max was not there. On top of his desk was a neat, fat blue folder in which he filed suspect sheets by area of the country. On his blotter was a monthly calendar with appointments blocked out.

"Anal obsessive," Wetzon heard Smith murmur. Smith was very into psychological jargon since she'd been in therapy.

"Lock up, B.B., and have a nice weekend," Wetzon called. "Leave any crisis messages on my answering machine."

They found a cab easily on Second Avenue and rode west through the Park on the Seventy-ninth Street transverse. It was five o'clock when the cab dropped them on the corner of Columbus and Seventy-ninth Street.

The sky was a perfect robin's-egg blue dappled with little cotton fluff clouds. An unseen skywriter had drawn white dragon's breath in two slowly dissipating lines across the roof of the sky.

"I only have fifteen minutes," Smith said, irritated. "Where is it?"

It had been a mistake to let Smith come along. Steamed, Wetzon pointed to a brown brick apartment building that probably dated back to the 1930s. Brian was subletting an apartment "as far away from the bitch as I can get," he'd told Wetzon. She checked the scrap of paper on which she'd noted the address. Apartment 8B.

Lit only by two deco sconces, the lobby was typical of West Side buildings: marble, leather chairs, wooden benches. Sunlight filtered through the beautiful stained-glass windows that faced the street. Across the lobby and up two steps was the elevator in an elegant, highly polished framework of deco-patterned brass.

An empty chair sat facing the elevator, the *Daily News* folded open on it. No doorman was in sight, so maybe this was a manned elevator building.

"Don't you love the security?" Smith pressed the elevator button impatiently. The arrow above the door crept counterclockwise to 1 and the door slid open. It was empty. The women stepped into the car and got off on the eighth floor.

In front of 8B was a large cowbell, but there was no need to ring it. The door gaped open.

4

....

An overweight apparition in big sunglasses and a floppy-brimmed straw hat, a wild print dress, and high red Reeboks came barreling out the door carrying a Big Brown Bag shopping bag.

Taken by surprise, Wetzon stepped back and bumped Smith.

"Ouf," Smith said.

The woman ignored them and closed the door to 8B.

"Who are you?" Smith demanded, giving Wetzon a nudge.

"Isn't this Brian Middleton's apartment?" Wetzon saw the woman had a slim, smooth neck. She was younger than she appeared.

"*Por favor*, I the maid," the woman said in a thick Hispanic accent. "He no *aqui*." She slipped past them and pressed the down button of the elevator.

"Are you sure?"

The dark glasses were mirrors, reflecting them like moving pictures. "I sure."

"Do you have any days free?" Smith asked.

"Smith!"

The fat woman swiveled her head slowly to Smith and coughed as the elevator door slid open.

They stepped on the elevator after the maid.

"Don't 'Smith' me. I could use a new maid. Delilah's gone to live with her daughter in Philadelphia." She turned to the woman. "Well, do you?" The woman shook her head emphatically. Smith sighed. "It's so hard to get good help now."

The woman rushed out of the elevator clutching her shopping bag and left the building ahead of them.

"You have no class, Smith," Wetzon said.

"I've told you time and again, sweetie, you must seize the moment. You rarely do, that's why you—"

"Enough! Truce!" Wetzon held up her hand. She was in no mood for a lecture on her life, least of all from Smith.

"What a waste of time," Smith said. She looked at her watch. "I'm going to be late. I don't know why I let you talk me into your little adventures." She laughed lightly when she caught Wetzon's glower. "Are you coming?"

"Don't let me keep you."

Wetzon was shrugging off Smith's indignant "humpf" when a door opened in the rear of the lobby and a swarthy human bulldog appeared. He was in half uniform, dark pants with a dull gold strip up each leg, no jacket. An invisible cloud of garlic armored him. He planted himself heavily in the chair facing the elevator and picked up his *Daily News.* He looked over at them without curiosity, then went back to his newspaper.

"Have you seen Mr. Middleton?" Wetzon asked.

He shook his head. "Not today, lady." He didn't get up.

A pregnant woman came into the lobby pushing a stroller loaded with grocery bags with one hand, a boy of perhaps three years toddling beside her, trying to avoid her other hand. Now the doorman rose and dropped his newspaper on the chair.

As Wetzon left the building, she saw Smith getting into a cab on Columbus. She quickened her steps, but the cab took off. Oh, well. Smith would get over it. And so would she.

Damnation. She'd kill Brian if he'd gone to another firm. But nothing could be done till he surfaced somewhere. No sense in jumping to conclusions yet.

She saw the fee slipping from her grasp. Money was tight. The maintenance on her apartment had gone up twice in the last eighteen months, and now there was an assessment for the new elevator.

She crossed Columbus and walked, balancing carefully in her narrow heels, on the cobblestoned sidewalk behind the Museum of Natural History. A thin, black iron fence closed in the small park, known here as Theodore Roosevelt Park and running up to Eighty-first Street where it became Margaret Mead Green, named for the anthropologist who'd had an office for much of her career at the museum.

To her left, cars were parked in front of meters; to her right stretched the park grounds. On benches along the outside fence was a colorful mixture of residents, tourists, and the homeless. She had come to know that there were several categories of homeless in the city. One was the truly homeless. People burned out or destitute because of job loss. Then there were the derelict homeless: the disturbed, the addicted. And last, the professional homeless, who made a career out of begging and hanging out, who would not take a job if it were offered, preferring the nomadic and often lucrative life of the streets. The parks and benches and subways had become home to all categories.

She passed a woman, made rotund by myriad layers of clothing, who had set herself up on one whole bench, with seven or eight swollen shopping bags around her. She was eating a burrito and drinking Evian water from the bottle.

Huge sycamores, their leaves burnished gold and red and rust, hid much of the rear of the museum so that only the circular turret and empty windows could be seen from where she walked. Across Columbus Avenue were three big white trailers parked one after the other. In all likelihood, a movie was being shot somewhere nearby.

As she came toward Eighty-first Street, she saw several people moving into the Green at a fairly fast clip through the two stacks of massive gray stone that marked the entrance to the Green.

"Help!" someone shrieked.

"Get an ambulance—"

Wetzon stopped. In the park, people and dogs were congregating around a tree. On Columbus Avenue, bus and car traffic moved steadily downtown. They were probably playing a scene around that tree. She had never been a New Yorker who gawked at movie stars; she never hung around accidents or arrests. She never followed fire engines. She would, in fact, rather not be involved. So why was she heading through the entrance toward the crowd around the tree?

The pathway was a three-way fork with one path going off sharply to the right, benches on both sides, each territorially occupied by a homeless person. Two dogs chased each other, making circles around the grass. A huge, gnarled oak tree stood in the center of the two-way fork just ahead, its leaves rustling in the light breeze.

People were milling around a man in running shorts and T-shirt sitting under the tree. She saw someone with a bullhorn. This had to be a movie. The man appeared to be ill or dead. Wetzon slowed her pace. A woman leaned over him, seemed to be talking to him. Somewhere in the distance came the pulsing sound of a siren. A man in jeans was taking pictures with a hand-held camera.

Two actors in police uniforms, a man and a woman, made the turn into the Green and passed her, going right up to the man under the tree. The other woman stood back as the policewoman spoke to the man under the tree, but he didn't move. The policewoman took his wrist, obviously searching for a pulse.

Wetzon came closer, standing on tiptoe to see over the crowd. The man's face was beautifully made up to show a mottle of swelling and bruises.

The actress playing the policewoman dropped the man's wrist, and the movement unbalanced him. He tipped over on his face. There was a collective gasp from the crowd. The back of his head had been crushed like an eggshell.

Wetzon stood frozen in place. She had caught just a glimpse of the man's face, just enough, before he fell over.

Brian Middleton.

The body rolled over, faceup. "My fucking back just went out," it said.

"Cut!" someone shouted.

5

·······

Sigourney Weaver and Robert De Niro were standing near the entrance to Margaret Mead Green, heads bent, getting instruction from a small, slim woman in jeans whose mass of curly red hair threatened to obliterate her face.

What the hell is the matter with you? It was getting so she was seeing bodies under lettuce leaves. Any fool could have seen the body under the tree was an actor. Why would she think Brian was dead anyway? It was that damn psychic Smith had sent her to three weeks ago. That's what it was. Judith had given her the willies. Blood on the street, for godsakes.

Enough of that. She stopped in front of Endicott Booksellers to look at the window display featuring a huge picture of mystery writer Sara Paretsky and all of her books, hard- and softcover, starring her tough woman private eye, V. I. Warshawski. Wetzon had devoured every one of the books. A notice in the window said that Paretsky would be reading from her latest at Endicott the first week in November. She made a mental note to write it in her calendar.

A translucent bubble exploded in her face, and another floated past, and another, as the breeze shifted and the sitting teddy bear in front of Penny Whistle Toys, set on automatic, blew bubbles at the world passing by on Columbus Avenue. Two children in strollers reached greedy mitts upward to catch the bubbles when their mothers stopped to talk.

Daylight was fast receding, and the streetlights came on. Wetzon sighed and moved away from the bookstore.

"Miss Wetzon . . . Leslie."

She stopped and looked around. A broad-shouldered man in a light-gray pinstripe had emerged from the bookstore. He called her name again.

She should know him . . . but who was he? She smiled at him blankly, searching her memory, and accepted his proffered hand. Lots of dark-gray hair and ironic humor in his eyes.

"You don't know who the hell I am," he said, his amusement reaching his mouth. He held on to her hand.

There was an assurance, a certainty about him, and Wetzon felt a small rush of adrenaline. "Of course I know who you are." Her mind was dancing a dervish. He had the kind of smile that enveloped. Nothing enigmatic about him. Ah . . . yes. He was that highly re-spected labor leader she and Smith had met last year when he was serving on the board of directors of Luwisher Brothers before its merger with L. L. Rosenkind. Twoey's friend. "You're Alton Pinkus." *What a good head you have, Wetzon,* she congratulated herself. She gave her hand a small tug, but he wasn't letting go.

"Very good." He was balancing a book-thick paper bag under his arm. "Do you live around here?"

"Eighty-sixth. How about you?"

"Eighty-first. The Beresford. We're neighbors." He continued to study her with his warm brown eyes. He was making her feel awkward, like a teenager, for some reason. "Perhaps we can get to-gether for a drink . . . or dinner," she heard him say.

"I'd like that." *What am I saying?*

"I'll give you a call. Are you in the book?"

"No, I'm not. If I might have my hand back, I'll give you my card." That seemed to amuse him even more. Unsettled by the fris-son of guilt that ran through her, she scrawled her home number rather defiantly on the back of the card and handed it to him.

"How about Sunday night? We can have an early dinner . . . about six. Café des Artistes."

"Okay," she said hastily. "I'll meet you there." She gave him a quick wave and hurried up Columbus. At Eighty-second Street, wait-ing for the light to change, she sneaked a look back. Damn. He was standing there watching her. He waved, and she gave him a small salute.

Merde, she thought. What was she getting herself into? This was all Silvestri's fault. He was in Quantico, Virginia, at the FBI Academy, taking a course in psychological profiling. It was an honor to be chosen to go, but the course ran nine months, from September through May, and although it was a five-day, Monday-through-Friday week, from eight to five, the students lived in a dorm and a lot of them stayed down through the weekends. Something to do with bonding.

She'd taken the Metroliner down last Saturday and stayed at the Watergate Hotel in D.C. They'd gone out to dinner with another couple, both of whom were at the school; Wetzon had felt like an outsider.

Harry, her new doorman, rushed to open the door almost as if he'd been watching for her. He seemed all hyped up about something. "Good evening, Ms. Wetzon." He was standing in her way, not letting her by. "There's a cop here to see you," he whispered. "He showed me his badge."

Oh, how nice, Silvestri was surprising her. He had come for the weekend. But why hadn't he gone right up?

Harry stood aside then, and Wetzon walked into the lobby. A man, his bulk crammed into a brown suit, rose. He was somewhere in his late thirties with a neat black mustache, a yellow oxford cloth button-down, and red foulard tie. His hair was dark, his sideburns a fraction too long. Certainly not Silvestri.

She came toward him, puzzled and slightly disappointed. "I'm Leslie Wetzon. You were looking for me?"

"Detective Robert Ferrante, Central Park Precinct." He flipped his ID and she read his credentials.

Now Harry was paying more attention to her and her conversation with Detective Ferrante than he was to the other tenants as they came home.

"What is this about?" She'd like to get their conversation away from nosy Harry. "Do you want to come up?" she asked, wishing Ferrante would say no.

"Excuse me," Ferrante said. He touched her elbow lightly and they escaped from the doorman by going out to the street. "We'd like to see if you can identify someone, if you could—" His eyes flicked a fraction, and she turned and saw a second detective leaning against the door of a double-parked car, arms folded. He was young, his skin a dull charcoal.

She looked back at Ferrante. "I'm confused. Where do you want me to go?"

"The medical examiner's office."

Her stomach flip-flopped. "Who?" She shook her head. "What a stupid question. I'm sorry. Give me some background."

"Two nurses from Mt. Sinai went out to eat their lunch in the Conservatory Garden on 104th Street and found a dead man on a park bench. Maybe six feet, reddish hair. Looked like a mugging victim."

"How was he killed? What time?"

He raised an eyebrow at her, and moved aside to let a woman come out on the street from the private entrance of a dentist's office.

"I'm not stupid, Detective. A good friend of mine is an NYPD detective, too—Silvestri—he's with the Seventeenth. And I worked for the department as a consultant last year. You can check me out with the Chief's office."

Ferrante didn't even blink. "We have the vic on ice. There'll be an autopsy, but before that we want a solid ID."

"What do I have to do with it? Why me?"

"I called your office, and the guy there gave me your number."

"Detective Ferrante—"

"Ms. Wetzon, the victim had nothing on him, no wallet, papers, or ID. Just your business card."

6

· · · · · · ·

"How was he dressed?" Wetzon asked, but her mind was swinging back and forth in great arcs. *Don't presume. It didn't have to be Brian. It could be anyone.* She passed her card out indiscriminately, hoping to get referrals, and it had always worked well for her.

Ferrante gave her the eye again. He was resting his big arm over the back of the car seat. "Expensive suit, white shirt, yellow paisley silk tie, good shoes . . . suspenders."

Emile Martens, the black detective who was driving, snorted.

"What time do you think it happened?"

"He was cold and stiff. Somewhere between five A.M. and nine, maybe."

It couldn't be Brian, she thought. He lived on the West Side. Both his old firm—Bliss Norderman—and his new firm, Loeb Dawkins, were in midtown, one on Sixth Avenue and the other on Park. So the Conservatory Garden at 104th Street and Fifth Avenue was hardly on the way to anywhere.

Friday night, and rush-hour traffic down Second Avenue was clogged. Cars were creeping toward the Fifty-ninth Street Bridge and the Queens Midtown Tunnel for the commute home to Long Island or the weekend house in the Hamptons. They were having a glorious Indian summer, and New Yorkers streamed out of their pueblos toward the sea. Like so many lemmings, she thought, closing her eyes and leaning back. Her stomach alternated between sudden leaps and hunger pangs. She'd seen enough dead bodies.

A thud on the roof made her eyes open. A revolving red light radiated from the top of the car onto everything around them. Crawl space began to appear in front of them. A siren burped on and off and Emile moved the car forward and began to weave in and out of traffic lanes, circling over to First Avenue and finally stopping in front of a stone building on Thirtieth Street. It was the neighborhood of University Hospital, and one was likely to see interns and residents, nurses and aides in their hospital whites or surgical greens, mixing with regular residents. Most New York hospitals maintained fairly inexpensive living quarters, giving their employees a break, compared to what it cost the average New Yorker to live.

The building had a name printed on the metal awning over its entrance: DEPARTMENT OF FORENSIC PATHOLOGY.

On the sidewalk, Ferrante and Martens presented credentials and spoke briefly to the security guard, who warbled into a walkie-talkie. A few minutes later a young Asian man in whites, whose name tag said "Dr. Michael Reyes," came up the stairs and led them down into the basement. All except Wetzon. She was Velcroed to the floor. Looking down the stairs, she felt a shiver of dread. It was going to be someone she knew, and she had the irrational thought that maybe she could put it off. Let them go ahead. She would wait here.

"It's okay, Ms. Wetzon." Martens had come back up the stairs and was standing three steps below her so they were on eye level. He had melting chocolate eyes. "These things are never easy, but you're our best bet. He might have a worried wife and kids somewhere . . . Okay?" When she nodded, he added tersely, "And breathe through your mouth. You won't like the smell."

Ferrante had disappeared below, and when Wetzon reluctantly followed Martens to the bottom of the stairs, she saw Ferrante talking to a pale, attractive woman who wore a cream knit dress under an open white lab coat. She was introduced as Dr. Jennie Vose, the assistant medical examiner.

Built into the near wall was a window that looked in on a room containing built-in floor-to-ceiling steel filing cabinets with huge drawers.

Ferrante said, "We're just going to slide him out, Ms. Wetzon, and uncover his face. Take a good look. You ready?"

"Yes."

"Go, Mike," Ferrante said to Dr. Reyes, who went into the filing room with Dr. Vose.

Mike pulled the handle on a drawer and it started to open. Dr. Vose peered in. She shook her head and pointed to another drawer.

Oh, God, Wetzon thought, taking air in short gulps. Her whole body was quivering, turning to ice. She felt Ferrante's hot breath on her ear and closed her eyes.

When she opened them, the next drawer was partway out. She saw the outlines of a face under the white cloth. Somewhere in the depths of her soul she crossed her fingers. Let this not be anyone she knew.

"Now, Ms. Wetzon." Mike flipped the cover from the face and Wetzon forced her eyes downward.

She saw reddish-brown hair, squared jaw, red and purple mottled skin. Bare shoulders and curly red chest hair. Mouth contorted in a silent scream. One eye, raccoon-marked; the other—oh, God—*Cover his face. Cover his face!* her mind shrieked. Hands up to protect herself, she heard her own strangled cry and stepped back into Martens.

"You know him?" Ferrante demanded.

She closed her eyes and breathed in sharply through her nose, forgetting instructions. Dead animal smells mixed with antiseptic. Biology lab, the frog pinned to the dissecting tray. Her groan was inadvertent. *Grow up,* she commanded. *Grow up!*

"Who was he?" Ferrante sounded impatient.

Wetzon looked at the face again. Even through a window, viewing a body on a slab was horrifying. He was naked and vulnerable. His left eye was blown out. Where it should have been was a double ring of two different shades of dried blood, pieces of bone, gook, and other things she didn't want to give a name to. A black ribbon of caked blood came from his right ear.

"It's Brian Middleton," she said.

7

·······

"Brian never showed up at his new firm this morning," Wetzon said. She was sitting in a waiting room of sorts, on a plastic chair, sipping orange juice from a Styrofoam container that Jennie Vose had supplied from her private refrigerator. Which made Wetzon wonder whether organs and other things sat on the shelves in mason jars next to orange juice and English muffins. Her hands shook, and a trail of orange liquid slipped over the lip of the container and dribbled through her fingers.

"What exactly do you do?" Martens was writing everything down in a small black notepad.

She felt a kind of déjà vu. Silvestri had asked her the same question when they first met four years ago after Barry Stark was murdered. "I'm a recruiter, a headhunter. I persuade stockbrokers to move from one firm to another."

"You're a personnel agency."

"No. We don't have to be licensed as personnel agencies do. We get paid a percentage of the broker's gross commissions. Brian was one of my hires. Or rather, he would have been. He was to have started today at Loeb Dawkins."

Ferrante had gone uptown to get Rona Middleton. She was next of kin. They were separated, not divorced yet.

"He didn't call?"

"No. He just didn't show. I spoke with him last night about nine-thirty. Everything was cool. I can't figure what he'd be doing in the Conservatory Garden," she said. "Especially on the day he was to start a new job."

"Did he have a girlfriend over there?"

She shrugged. "I wouldn't know." She finished the juice and tossed the container into a nearby brown plastic waste receptacle. Just like the big fee they now didn't have and never would have, she thought. Smith would be wild.

"You want to give us a guess on time of death, Doc?"

Jennie Vose frowned. "Don't hold me to it. I'd say maybe seven, seven-thirty A.M."

"Look," Wetzon said, "why would he go out for a walk in an isolated section of Central Park at that hour?" She stood and stretched her legs. She was getting stiff. "And in serious clothes. It doesn't make any sense to me. Brian wasn't stupid . . . but he always carried a lot of money on him." She remembered having lunch with him and then his walking her into Tiffany's and peeling off wads of bills for a tennis bracelet for Rona. All diamonds. All retail. Top dollar. And she'd thought at the time that neither she nor anyone she knew would ever buy jewelry retail. New Yorkers just didn't . . . not even to show off.

Rona. Rona would get the business now. Clients feel safer with people they know. They would all come back to her. Rona would do well in her first year at Rosenkind, Luwisher, and Smith and Wetzon would do well because their compensation agreement with Rosenkind was based on Rona's future production. That would please Smith no end.

And what about you, you mercenary bitch, she asked herself. She couldn't put it all off on Smith. Leslie Wetzon liked making money, too. No doubt about it.

Dr. Vose excused herself, and Wetzon sat down and looked at Martens.

"You want some coffee?" Martens said it so halfheartedly that she laughed.

"No, thanks." Hunger had become a dull ache. Her head was throbbing. "I've never been to the Conservatory Garden," she said.

"Nice place. Peaceful." Martens rose and began pacing. He was antsy, a tall, angular African-American whose bearing and grace, not to mention bone structure, made him look like a Masai warrior in Western garb.

"Is Martens a French name?"

"Yeah. Somewhere way back. My grandparents came from Martinique." He came to a stop in front of her. "You said he was supposed to start a new job today?"

"Yes. And he would have collected a big upfront check for two hundred and twenty-five thousand dollars once he was on board."

A long whistle squeezed through Martens's teeth. "Was that a secret?"

"No. Everyone involved knew. Actually, everyone on the Street knows what the deals are."

"But he didn't collect it because he didn't start."

"As far as I know. I've never heard of an instance where someone collected a deal before he started."

There was no window in the room, and Wetzon began to feel claustrophobic. Her suit jacket weighed down on her, and her face was numb.

A phone somewhere close, perhaps the next office, began to ring. She counted twenty before someone finally answered it.

"Excuse me." A young woman in a lab coat stood in the doorway, her hair braided in a coronet on top of her head. Her glasses clung to the top of her nose. "Detective Martens? Ms. Wetzon?"

Martens stopped pacing. "Yeah?"

"You're both wanted downstairs." She nodded at them distractedly and left.

Wetzon followed Martens to the lobby, where Rona Middleton greeted her with an hysterical shriek and threw herself into Wetzon's arms, a highly difficult feat because Rona was a big woman and easily a head taller than Wetzon, closer to Smith's height. Rona was an athlete, an avid tennis player and a fanatical jogger. Her muscles had muscles. She did five miles a day around the reservoir, or she hated herself, so she said. She wore her hair in a short, boy's cut, shingled up the back, with a shock of blond curls from the top of her ears to the top of her head, not the most flattering do for a long, lean face.

"I can't go down there without you." Rona squeezed Wetzon's hand so hard, Wetzon winced. "You've got to go with me."

Wetzon's stomach did a forward roll. She couldn't.

Ferrante's eyes told her, *Let's get this over with.*

So it was down the stairs again. Breathe through your mouth. The memory of the smell was enough to make Wetzon gag. She held

Rona's freezing cold hand as the cloth was once again drawn back, and Brian lay there in his long sleep.

"It's Brian. My husband, Brian Middleton," Rona said calmly. She withdrew her hand from Wetzon's. "The shit finally got what he deserved."

8

■■■■■■■

Rona was wearing a white Elisse jogging suit and Avias. Small gold hoops pierced her earlobes, followed by two pearl studs on the rise. No rings on her fingers, no other jewelry. She must have been on her way out to do her five miles. Dark eyebrows, dark lashes, slight tan, red gash of a mouth. A quilted Chanel shoulder bag—the real thing, not a copy—hung from her shoulder on a dainty gold-and-leather chain. But dainty was not the word for the Rona Middleton facing Wetzon. There was something tough and uncompromising about her that Wetzon had never perceived before.

Ferrante gave Wetzon a silent order by making eye contact and jerking his head toward the door.

"Watch your mouth, Rona," Wetzon said sotto voce, but Rona wasn't having any. She wore triumph like a banner as she turned to leave. *Oh, Lord*, Wetzon thought. *I hope she has an alibi*. Wetzon could just hear Smith if Rona were to get arrested for Brian's murder and there'd be no fee on Rona's production either.

"Leave him out," Dr. Vose said. "I'll do it now. You might want to hang around."

Not on your life, Wetzon thought, gearing to make a break for it.

"Don't push, Wetzon," Rona said. "You're walking on my heels." She bent to slip her heel back into her jogging shoe, and Wetzon saw a purplish bruise on her leg between her white sock and her pantleg.

"You want to hazard a guess about cause?" Ferrante asked the assistant M.E.

Cocking her ear, Wetzon stayed put, letting Rona go on up the stairs.

"Sure. I can give you a guess, but again, don't hold me to it. I'd say he had quite an earache."

An earache?

"An earache?" Ferrante gave voice to Wetzon's thought.

"Yes. Caused by a small-caliber gun pressed to the ear. A .32, I'd say."

"I thought you were in such a rush to leave, Wetzon," Rona proclaimed from the top of the stairs. "I'm going to make a phone call." She disappeared from Wetzon's view.

Wetzon hung around for a few minutes at the foot of the steps, but heard nothing further. She found Rona in the small waiting room off the lobby talking to Detective Martens.

"It was a legal separation. I've said only two words to him in the last four months. 'Drop dead.' How obliging of him. Megan, my little girl, is eight months old and doesn't even know she has—*had*—a father." Seeing Wetzon, Rona waved a hand in her direction. "Ask Wetzon. She knows what I've been through. The shit refused to pay support for his only child."

Martens was listening politely and making notes in his notebook. "When did you see your husband last, Mrs. Middleton?"

Rona shrugged.

"She's tired and a bit distraught, Detective," Wetzon offered, trying to keep Rona from saying too much.

"I'm nothing of the kind, Wetzon. This is exhilarating. When did I see the turd last? I don't remember. It's been months, I'm sure."

"And this morning? Where were you between, say, between five and nine?"

"You have to be kidding," Rona exploded.

Wetzon raised her eyes heavenward. *Thank you, God.*

"You think I did it? Oh, puh-leeze. Do you believe this, Wetzon?"

"It's procedure, Rona. Just confirm where you were and then we can go. Right, Detective?"

Martens nodded. "For now." He waited, pen poised, for Rona's statement of her whereabouts.

"Okay, okay, well, let's see. I woke up at five as I always do, showered, dressed. Then Megan and her nanny and I had breakfast together, as we do every morning. I usually leave for the office around seven, and I'm in by seven-thirty. I thought he was mugged?"

"This is just routine, ma'am. We'll know more after the autopsy."

"Ugh. I don't want to hear any more. Have you had dinner, Wetzon?" Rona took her arm.

Ringo was beating a solo in Wetzon's head, and she was starving. She shook her head slowly.

"Good. Let's go get something to eat. I'm famished." Rona looked down at her running costume. "Someplace informal."

"I think I should go home," Wetzon said, but her stomach reminded her there was nothing in her fridge except nicoise olives and half a tomato. Without Silvestri around, she forgot about having food in the apartment. She certainly was not about to cook a meal for one, so when she had dinner at home, she dined splendidly on bagels with a choice of topping. But she didn't even have a bagel in the freezer.

"I know—" They were on the street, having declined Martens's offer of a lift. "Let's go to the Carnegie."

"The Carnegie." Wetzon smiled. Why not? She hadn't been there in ages.

There was a short line in front of the Carnegie Deli on Seventh Avenue and Fifty-fifth Street, and it would get longer after the theaters let out, but now it was moving fast. The deli counter was jumping; waiters were pushing, demanding attention, while customers waiting for take-out orders grew restless. The rest of the restaurant was moderately crowded, but the noise might have been coming from a football stadium. It was bedlam. Everyone was shouting.

They were led to a table in the rear.

"Look who's here," the man at the table said.

"Good grief." Wetzon found herself looking at Twoey and Smith. "We have to stop meeting like this."

"Oh, for pity sakes." Smith was halfway through an enormous Reuben.

"Do you know each other? This is Smith, my partner, and this charming man is Goldman Barnes Two. Rona Middleton."

Twoey smiled at Wetzon and nodded to Rona. "We've met." Twoey was a managing director of Rosenkind, Luwisher, where Rona was a broker.

Smith frowned. Taking stock of Rona's jogging clothes and

Wetzon's suit, she said, "Hi, Rona." She folded her eyelids into slits and put down her fork. "Should I know something?"

Damn. Wetzon saw this was going to be tough. She spoke fast and got it out quickly. "Brian was mugged and murdered this morning in Central Park."

"Brian? Brian Middleton?" Smith shrieked, and even in the blare of conversation and clattering of dishes, people looked over at their table.

"The husband," Wetzon explained to Twoey, who looked taken aback by Smith's reaction.

"The *ex*-husband," Rona corrected. She'd sat down next to Twoey, picked up the menu, and was studying it.

"I'm so sorry." Twoey had a platter of potato pancakes with sour cream in front of him. He'd put on some weight since he'd been seeing Smith, probably because Smith had that enviable metabolism and indulged it.

"Wetzon . . ." Smith muttered.

"Right," Wetzon whispered. "No fee for us, old dear." She stared hungrily at the huge plate of french fries between Twoey and Smith, then filched one and ate it. It was deliciously greasy and salty.

"How, pray tell, did you get involved, or is that a dumb question?"

"The police were waiting for me in my lobby after I left you tonight. The only thing Brian had on him besides his clothes was my business card. They thought I might be able to identify a mugging victim."

An ancient, slow-moving waiter in a shiny black suit, a white linen napkin over one arm, seemed to be making his way in their direction. His progress was mesmerizing; he was moving like a rusty-jointed Tin Man.

"So what I can get for you?" he asked in a weak voice. He looked as though he would never make it back with their food.

"I'll have what she's having," Rona said, pointing to Smith's Reuben, "and a Diet Coke."

"Corned beef hash with one poached egg, black decaf." Wetzon knew she'd ordered the best thing on the menu at the Carnegie. It was like a trade secret, and the enormous choice on the menu never tempted her away.

"I'm sorry about this, Rona," Smith offered glumly, but Wetzon understood the subtext. Brian was a big ticket that they'd lost. Sooner or later, Smith would figure out that Rona had a shot—*a shot?*—at getting Brian's book, since most of it had been Rona's to begin with.

Wetzon picked a sour tomato from the stainless-steel pot on the table and bit into it, inadvertently splashing Smith, who looked daggers at her.

"Thank you, Smith, but we all know what a shit he was, so let's not wallow in grief here, if you don't mind." Rona made a small cutting gesture with her hand.

Twoey's eyes blinked behind his gold-rimmed glasses. Rona sounded pretty callous, but then, Twoey should be used to it because Smith was not that different, unless, of course, Smith was not showing Twoey that side of herself.

Smith smiled suddenly, a radiance.

There, she'd put it together.

"Ah," Smith said. "Dear Rona, what a shock for you." She picked up her fork and dug into her Reuben with gusto. "And how are you doing, sweetie?" she said to Wetzon, but her eyes said, *We will see some money on this after all.*

Wetzon nodded, responding to what Smith didn't say aloud. "Rona and I had to identify him." She watched the passage of the ancient waiter and their food, which was fraught with potential disaster from diners and other waiters, but miracle of miracles he made it through and with tremoring hands meticulously cleaned the edges of their plates with his linen napkin and set their orders and the check on the table. A third of Wetzon's coffee was in the saucer. She poured it back into the cup.

"How hideous," Smith said, referring, Wetzon assumed, to the fact that she and Rona had to identify the corpse and not to Wetzon's coffee procedure, but she couldn't be sure.

"Oh, I don't know," Rona said. "Black and blue and dead suited him, rather." She looked pleased, and attacked the Reuben with a vengeance, letting her left hand feed her while gesturing almost continuously with her right. "Come to think of it, how did he die? They never told me." Now she looked annoyed.

You never asked, Wetzon thought, remembering the trail of blood from Brian's ear and Dr. Vose's remark about the .32. She took a sip of the coffee, then stuck her fork into the egg yolk, breaking it, watching yellow blood run in rivulets over the white, mingling with the chunks of corned beef and potatoes. The image was so grotesque that she set her fork down.

"Sweetie pie," Smith was crooning to Rona, "just tell us how Wetzon and I can be of help." She reached for the check. "We'll take care of this, of course."

"You can get me a copy of Brian's book."

"No," Wetzon said. "There's no way. It's up to Simon Loveman at Loeb Dawkins. He's got Brian's copies of statements. I think he'll give the accounts out to brokers in his office."

"Wait a minute—" Smith pointed her fork at Wetzon.

"No, Smith. Rona, you *know* Brian's book. Most of it was yours to begin with. Prepare an attitude, then get to them, because sure as hell, Bliss Norderman will also give out his accounts the minute Tony hears Brian's dead. And don't forget, Brian's assets are still sitting at Bliss because the transfers couldn't go through until he was formally at Loeb Dawkins."

Rona pushed her chair back. "Excuse me a sec."

"We'll do all right," Smith said the minute Rona was out of hearing. "Not great, but okay."

"If she can get those accounts, and I think she will. We're going to eat off a dead man's back."

"Give me a break! Did you hear her, Twoey? Miss holier-than-thou here? This is business. What do we care if any of them live or die? The important thing is do we get paid."

"Classy, Smith."

Smith smiled benignly and handed the check to Wetzon. "Pay this, sugar. I don't have any cash with me."

"You never do."

Twoey ate the last of his potato pancakes and grinned at them. "Cool it, men. Your quarry is about to return."

Rona sat down again. She'd redone her lipstick and combed her hair. "You've been very helpful, and I thank you." She turned to Wetzon. "When you mentioned assets, I just wanted to confirm something I was almost positive was in our separation agreement." She raised her glass of Diet Coke. "I'd like to toast my dearly departed ex. Come on, drink with me."

"Did I miss something?" Smith murmured, raising her club soda.

Rona continued, "In death the louse has finally done the right thing. Our agreement as written says that if Brian should die before we are divorced, all of his real assets, his possessions, his bank accounts, everything, come to me."

9

·······

Her apartment was dark and still. "Lights up," she said, touching the switch on her right, and the blue and gold globes of the art-glass chandelier flooded her foyer with warm light.

Beloved objects: the drunkard's path quilt on the wall, the white slat bench from her childhood on the farm, the pie safe with its pierced tin face.

She double-locked the door and dropped her purse and briefcase on the floor. It had been an utterly exhausting evening.

In her dining room, which doubled as her studio, the little light on her answering machine was blinking, two messages. She pressed the replay button and stared across at herself in the wall of mirrors behind her barre. She looked slightly faded, blurred around the edges, no longer sharply defined.

Hi, Silvestri's taped voice said. *It's ten o'clock Friday night. I'll be in Atlanta, so you won't be able to reach me.* That was it. His words sounded cold and formal.

"Dammit," she said aloud. "Might just as well have been a call from my brother, if I had a brother."

The machine beeped, another message. *Les? It's me again. I miss you.* He cleared his throat. *Why do I feel you're flying by the seat of your pants again? Whatever it is, stay out of it.* The answering machine reset itself and clicked off.

"Up yours, Silvestri," she said, giving him the finger. What did he think? She couldn't get along without him?

She pressed the button that cleared the tape and kicked off her shoes, flexing and pointing her toes. She opened a window and closed the blinds, then took off her skirt, jacket, and blouse, laying them on the dining table. At the barre she did a warm-up workout in her underwear. She finished with a deep curtsy, acknowledging phantom applause and accepting imaginary bouquets.

She rose and turned out the lights in the foyer, in the dining room, showered, and lay on her bed in the dark listening to the night sounds in her building. She heard the last garbage collection, the elevator, her neighbor coming home. Her refrigerator, the wind *tap-tap*ping on her wooden blinds through the open window.

She was like a walnut shell without its meat, because she'd gotten used to her life with Silvestri. She had grown dependent on him, and she hated the way she felt without him. As if there were something missing, that she was incomplete.

But you love him, you dope, she thought, entering into a dialogue with herself.

Yes, but when you love someone, you cede control.

Are you some kind of control freak?

No. Yes. Dammit all, maybe.

How would you feel if you were married, then? Would it change any-thing?

Oh, God. She slid under the covers and pulled them over her head. It had all been so simple before Silvestri; now it was so compli-cated.

She closed her eyes. Think about something else. Think about your premonition that Brian was dead, even murdered. Premonition, nothing. Anyone who doesn't show up on his first day where he's going to collect two hundred and a quarter big ones *has* to be dead.

She was wide awake. So it was going to be that kind of night, was it? She sat up and put on the light. Her little digital clock radio said 12:30. Hell, it was Friday night. She could sleep in tomorrow. Friday night. It wasn't as if she had plans. The only thing on her schedule was dinner with Carlos. They'd met in a dance class when she'd first come to New York and had danced in the chorus of one musical after another until Wetzon, not fancying herself as an aging chorus girl, had called it quits and formed a partnership with Xenia Smith to recruit brokers for Wall Street.

Carlos had gone from Princely Service, his successful sideline cleaning business, where he employed out-of-work dancers—gypsies —to clean apartments all over the city, to Broadway choreographer. And their friendship had only deepened over the years.

She had just finished the third chapter of Jack Finney's glorious *Time and Again*, when a big wet spot appeared on her page, then quickly another and another. What the hell . . . ? She looked up at her ceiling and a blob of water landed on her nose. Serious water then began to leak through a crack in her ceiling and through the top of her ceiling fan.

She leaped out of the bed and frantically began pushing the bed out of the way with such force that she knocked over the small sewing table on the other side. And in the nick of time, too, because a big chunk of plaster slammed into the section of the floor where the bed had been, where she had lain.

Screaming in fury, she edged around the waterfall to her bathroom. Water was pouring through several areas of the ceiling. She grabbed her robe from the door and her makeup box and ran for her intercom, parking the Lucite box on the floor near her feet.

She pressed the button on the house phone rapidly two or three times. Four times. No response. *Think, think.*

The elderly couple above her were in Florida, but someone was staying in the apartment. A grandson or something. Wetzon pulled on her terry-cloth robe, which one could hardly call dry, stuck her feet in her shoes lying where she'd left them in the dining room, and raced up the back stairs.

Hard rock music thumped a pulsing heartbeat through the door. She could hear water running. She rang the bell. Heard nothing. Rang again, furiously, three, four, five, six, seven—the rock music stopped. She began pounding on the door. "Turn off the goddam water!"

Behind her, a door opened and a sleepy neighbor stuck her head out. "What's the trouble?"

"I've got Niagara Falls in my apartment because this fool must have gone to sleep with the tub water running." Wetzon punctuated each word with a thump on the closed door.

Then she heard an exclamation and running footsteps. The sound of flowing water stopped. He never came to the door.

"You can sue the shit out of them," Wetzon heard her neighbor say enviously as she ran down the back stairs.

Her apartment was a mess. Water had come through the ceiling in her dining room and had even puckered a huge corner of the living-room ceiling, from which plaster was flaking like snow. She threw her arms up and howled.

The doorbell rang and she flung the door open in a fury, expecting the culprit. It took a moment to recognize the angry face of Roger Levine, attorney, president of the co-op board and her directly-below downstairs neighbor. He was wearing jeans, an Izod shirt, and Weejuns without socks.

"Don't say a word," she warned as he opened his mouth. "It's that asshole upstairs. Come on in and see for yourself." Anger and frustration made her gasp for breath as she stamped down the hall, splashing through the overflow. "Look, just look at my beautiful apartment."

He followed, somewhat mollified. When he saw her bedroom, he ordered, "Unplug your appliances and take Polaroids of everything. I've got water coming through my ceiling fixtures, but you've got a disaster."

They went back upstairs together and pounded on the door, but couldn't raise an answer. "See what I mean?" Wetzon sniffled into a ragged tissue.

Levine banged on the door one last time. Then he said, "Fuck this. Let's get Albert up here."

An hour later Wetzon was sitting in Roger's apartment with his wife, Holly, a drug analyst with Smith Barney. There was an untouched cup of coffee in front of her. "I'm really sorry about this."

"Forget it, Leslie. It's not your fault," Holly said. She was five months pregnant and just beginning to swell out under the tie belt of her robe.

"Yeah," Roger added. "We're not too bad, but your place is a horror."

Tears rolled down Wetzon's cheeks, etching wet salty trails in the grime.

"Oh, Roger," Holly murmured.

"It's true though, Holly. I'm going back upstairs and move things out of harm's way. And pack what I need so I can live in the living room until everything is repaired."

"I hate to say this, Leslie," Roger said, "but I think you should move out until everything is fixed. The ceilings could come down on your head. It's too dangerous."

"Oh, I'm sure I—"

"Do you have a place you can stay?" Holly asked.

"I suppose so." She thought, *Smith? Carlos?* He was staying at Arthur's, but he'd sublet his apartment in the Village. Silvestri's apartment in Chelsea was empty, maybe, but was it livable? She'd never even been there. He used it for his poker nights. Laura Lee? Wetzon hated the thought of living in a strange place. She loved her home.

She climbed the single flight back up to her apartment. Albert, the super, was just leaving. "What do you think, Albert? When can you fix my ceiling?"

He shook his head. "It's a big job, and it's got to dry out first. Maybe three, four weeks minimum. You can't stay here."

"I can stay in the living room, can't I?"

His brow furrowed. "If it were me, I wouldn't. That ceiling in the bathroom isn't going to make it. . . . You could get hurt."

Her low moan was spontaneous. Albert patted her shoulder awkwardly, then left her. She closed the door and screamed.

Pull yourself together, Wetzon. Somewhere she had leftover plastic drop sheets she'd bought when they'd chopped up her bedroom ceiling to install the fan.

She stripped her bed and covered the mattress with plastic, then right-sided the old single-drawer sewing table that was on Silvestri's side of the bed. Good thing Silvestri wasn't here. Half the contents were on the floor. She picked up a stack of wet papers, newspaper clippings, and a soggy notebook. Two paperbacks fell apart in her hands. There was a drenched box containing a tiepin, a snapshot of the two of them taken last summer on the carousel in Central Park. Two handkerchiefs, neatly folded. She sniveled into one.

A leather box was wedged into the back of the drawer. She pulled it out and unzipped the cover. Nestled in a black velvet cutout frame was a small gun.

10

·······

The night was spent ranging from room to room collecting what she would need or wanted to protect, preserve. Water had seeped through the ceiling of her wall of closets in the bedroom, but the upper shelves where she stored extra pillows and blankets had absorbed most of the moisture, and her good clothing wore plastic dry cleaner's covers.

Sitting on the floor of her foyer, she read the incomprehensible directions translated from Japanese to English by way of Korea, and assembled, after three false starts, the portable metal coatrack that she usually kept in its box in the hall closet. She'd bought it when her bedroom closets were being built and had never used it again.

With her clothes hanging safely on the rack, she began on her shoes, which were stored each pair in its own box. Almost every box was soaked. She stuffed each shoe with towel paper and threw the boxes into a humongous garbage bag that Albert had brought up.

At four o'clock in the morning she stopped and inspected the wreckage. The copper-stock pots she used as wastebaskets were in various places where the dripping continued. Towels covered her floors, soaking up moisture. The ceiling over her tub had come down, into the tub.

She put on white leggings and a bulky red cotton sweater and lay on her sofa under her old baby blanket with the cowboys on it she'd found on a shelf in the hall closet. Her bookshelves were safe, because they were on the wall farthest from the bathroom. She stared at the clutter on the floor-to-ceiling shelves, her eyes swimming. If she closed her eyes, she might just make everything disappear. It could all have been a hideous nightmare. She closed her eyes.

Water splashed across the raked deck, and everyone stopped dancing, just like that, and looked at one another. They were doing *No, No Nanette* at Jones Beach. There wasn't supposed to be water on the dance floor. A mighty swell, and the floor heaved under them and the deck tipped over and spilled them into the ocean.

"I'm too old for this," Wetzon screamed, getting a mouthful of salt water, struggling with the sea.

"Stop fighting and float," Alton Pinkus suggested in an amused voice. He was treading water beside her. "Nothing bad is going to happen to you."

"Listen to him, Les," Silvestri called from a great distance. "You can't control everything."

Oh, yes I can, she thought, but she thrust her legs out and let the water buoy her. The sun shone warm on her face, and it came to her that if she only had sunblock, she could stay like this forever. No responsibilities, no decisions. She turned her head slightly to thank Alton, but he wasn't there. A body lay floating facedown next to her.

Dead man's float.

The dead man lifted his head. It was Brian Middleton with a death grimace on his face and water spilling out of a hole where his eye had been. His extended hand touched hers. He was giving her something, pressing it into her hand. A gun.

"No, no!" She flung it as far away from her as she could, but the effort disturbed her balance and she began to sink . . . thrashing. . . . Her ears were buzzing, buzzing. What was buzzing?

She opened her eyes. She was lying on her sofa. Her doorbell was buzzing. The sun was coming through her living-room blinds warming her face, and water was dripping on her from her living-room ceiling.

"All right, I'm coming." She rolled off the sofa, stuck her feet into her Keds, and let Albert, Bob, the handyman, and Mike DeVota, the representative of the building's managing agent, in to survey the damage. Albert handed her the *Times* from her doormat.

Her kitchen was miraculously untouched. She put up water and measured coffee into a filter. After the men left, she sat on the stool in the kitchen and opened the newspaper, looking for something on

Brian's death. She found it in the Metro section under the headline "Stockbroker Slain":

> A STOCKBROKER WAS SHOT TO DEATH FRIDAY MORNING IN THE CONSERVATORY GARDEN IN CENTRAL PARK, POLICE SAID. BRIAN MIDDLETON, 45 YEARS OLD, OF 100 WEST 79TH STREET, A FINANCIAL ADVISER WITH BLISS NORDERMAN, WAS FOUND AT 12:30 P.M. SITTING ON A PARK BENCH ABOUT 10 FEET FROM THE ENTRANCE TO THE GARDEN ON FIFTH AVENUE, THE APPARENT VICTIM OF A MUGGING. HIS WALLET, MONEY, AND JEWELRY WERE NOT FOUND.
>
> ASSISTANT CHIEF GARLAND P. HOWITZER, COMMANDING OFFICER OF MANHATTAN DETECTIVES, SAID MR. MIDDLETON APPEARED TO BE THE VICTIM OF A ROBBERY. "HE PROBABLY RESISTED," CHIEF HOWITZER SAID. INVESTIGATORS SAY THEY HAVE NO SUSPECTS IN THE KILLING AND THAT NO WEAPON WAS RECOVERED AT THE SCENE.
>
> MR. MIDDLETON WAS A GRADUATE OF WESLEYAN UNIVERSITY IN CONNECTICUT AND FORDHAM LAW SCHOOL. HE WAS MARRIED TO THE FORMER RONA WALSH, ALSO A STOCKBROKER, AND LEAVES AN EIGHT-MONTH-OLD DAUGHTER, MEGAN.

Chief Howitzer? The big gun. *Very funny, Wetzon,* she told herself. Get a grip, her friend Laura Lee would say. Putting the newspaper aside, she poured orange juice into a glass and took her C's, E's, calcium, and beta carotene. She sipped her coffee and concentrated on getting herself organized.

First, call Carlos. Not Smith. Smith would insist she move immediately into her son Mark's room, but on careful consideration and gut instinct, Wetzon knew this was not the option of first choice. Even if Smith spent most of her weekend time with Twoey, she'd be in her Seventy-seventh Street apartment during the week, and living with Smith was a nightmare she wasn't about to wish on herself. Smith was too chaotic, too eccentric, and too controlling to be anyone's roommate, particularly Wetzon's.

She picked up the phone, punched out Arthur Margolies's number, put the receiver to her ear, and heard nothing. No dial tone, no crackling. Nada. Dead. Water must have gotten into the wiring. Oh, hell. It was too early to call Carlos, anyway. He lived on theater time.

Her big suitcase was all the way in the back of her hall closet. Hadn't used it since the road company of *Chorus Line*. She pulled it out and laid it on its side, unzipped it, and threw the flap back. Her theatrical makeup in a blue metal toolbox, balls of yarn and a half-finished sweater still on circular knitting needles. She fitted it against her breast. Hmm. Not bad. Damn. What was she thinking? She dropped the sweater on the floor and pulled out two worn white face towels with the hotel names faded to oblivion. An old black leotard. Dirty, worn, silver jazz shoes. She held up a pair of black tights with a hole you could run a fist through. When she opened the makeup case, it gave off greasepaint odors and something rancid. The jar of cold cream, half spent, had turned sour. A wave of nostalgia hit her, and she sat back on her haunches brushing away tears with her fingertips. She sighed. *Come on, you silly twit.* What was there to be nostalgic for? Sore muscles? Shows closing on opening night? Crummy hotels, bad food. Injuries. Unemployment. Open calls. Yes. And close friends, late dinners, fabulous costumes, the joy of getting the new combinations, the exquisite pain of opening nights. The camaraderie.

She sighed again and dumped everything in the garbage bag. So much for her past life. She stared at the bag for a long minute. No.

She pulled out her jazz shoes and slipped them on. In her head she heard the first thrilling notes of "Cool." Then, snapping her fingers, "easy does it," she did as much as she could remember of Anybodys, the tiny scamp from *West Side Story* who wanted to play with the big guys, dodging her clothes rack and suitcase.

As Anybodys, she was tough as they come. Much tougher than Leslie Wetzon, for sure. Anybodys danced over the towels right into the mess of Wetzon's bedroom, right over to the sewing table, reached into the drawer, lifted the gun in its pouch, danced back to the foyer, and dropped the gun in the suitcase.

It was Wetzon who went downstairs to call Carlos.

11

·······

"Fuhgeddaboudit!" Wetzon told Smith, who was insisting—surprise, surprise—on putting her up in Mark's room. She'd left word for Carlos on his answering machine that she had an emergency and was on her way over.

"We could have so much fun being roomies. Come on, sugar-plum." Smith was salivating for the chance to get her hands on Wetzon's life.

"No way." Wetzon shook her head emphatically at the skinny black woman in dirty sweatshirt and ragged jeans, rubber thongs on bare feet, who was shoving a paper cup at her. The woman babbled something at her through crooked teeth, then gave up and went after a stately old lady in a stunning black-and-white suit, a black hat on her head with a jaunty polka-dotted band. Her hands in white gloves carried no purse. Saturday morning, the Jewish Sabbath, she was probably going to one of the synagogues in the neighborhood.

"You could come up here and spend the rest of the weekend." She'd called Smith collect at her Connecticut house from the pay phone on the corner.

"Can't. I've got a mess to clean up here."

"Humpf. Then let's have dinner tomorrow night. Dick Tracy's still in Washington, right?"

"Right. Dinner's fine—oops—no, it's not. . . . Oh, dear." She'd just remembered her date with Alton Pinkus. She'd have to break it. No. Why should she? They were to meet at the restaurant anyway.

"Hello? Wetzon? Are you there?"

"I can't, Smith. I have . . . er . . . uh . . . dinner plans." She could hear Smith's mind mulling over that one.

"You have a date." It was an accusation.

"No!"

"You do. I know. You can't keep anything from me. The tarot showed another man, an older man. Who is it?"

"My grandfather. I have to go. There are three people dying to use this phone."

"Wait a—"

Wetzon hung up. There was no one dying to use the phone. She'd wanted to tell Smith about Alton, but Smith would make such a big deal of it.

She strolled down Eighty-sixth Street toward Broadway. It was a crisp, dry autumn Saturday. Hard to be depressed on such a day, even if your apartment was flooded and you had to move out. Joggers were out in force, as were young mothers with children in strollers. The sky was a deep, cloudless blue, not one streak of haze anywhere. From Broadway and Eighty-sixth Street, she had a clear view of the Hudson River across to the cliffs of New Jersey.

Arthur Margolies, Esquire, owned a five-room apartment in a smart old West End Avenue building. The rooms were enormous by comparison to Wetzon's, the windows broader, taller, the tone, tonier. The building had the full complement of doormen and elevator men in musical-comedy uniforms.

"They just got back," the doorman said, announcing her.

"They just got back," the elevator man said, taking her up to the tenth floor.

As she walked down the hall, the door to Arthur's apartment flew open. "Birdie!" And dear, wonderful Carlos gathered her in. A fashion plate in tennis garb, he wore a white cable-stitched pullover casually on his shoulders, sleeves tied loosely in front. "What's wrong?" He held her at arm's length and studied her face.

They were exactly the same height, both slim, but he was as dark as she was pale, black hair, mischievous jet eyes. The diamond stud in his left earlobe glittered against bronze tanned skin.

She felt her face begin to crumple under his scrutiny. She looked down and focused on the tennis racquets leaning against the big oak umbrella stand. She saw Arthur's concerned face materialize behind Carlos and choked up.

"Oh, dear heart, please tell Carlos what happened. Did somebody die? Your partner, perhaps?" He said it hopefully. Smith and Carlos had always loathed one another.

She gave him a measly punch and, half laughing, half crying, burbled out pieces of it between sobs, and soon found herself sitting in their huge kitchen sipping hot chocolate.

While Carlos dictated, Arthur fussed over a yellow legal pad. "First," Carlos said, "Princely Service is sending two Hazels over to your apartment at twelve. They will bring a U-Haul. They are going to pack you up and move you down to Tenth Street."

"Tenth Street? Your place?"

He nodded. "My sublet moved to the Coast last month. He thinks he's going to be the next Rock Hudson. God save us." Carlos fluttered his long dark lashes and rolled his eyes heavenward. "I had it cleaned and painted and was just going to show it again, Birdie, so it's yours for as long as you need it."

"Oh, Carlos, you're the best." She gave him a hug.

"Don't I know."

"Insurance," Arthur said.

"I've got a homeowner's policy. Do you have a camera? I'm supposed to take pictures."

"My Hazels will do it. Not to worry. Write that down, Arthur."

"Telephone. What will I do?"

"We'll get it repaired later. Right now, we'll have call forwarding to my number on Tenth Street, and my answering machine is still hooked up there."

Carlos had bought his loft apartment in the Village when Princely Service began to be profitable. It was a huge one-bedroom on tree-lined Tenth Street, west of Hudson. It consisted of a big, open kitchen, designed for cooking, with a long maple trestle table that could seat twenty, down the middle. The bedroom was gigantic and comfortably held a king-sized bed, with a profusion of pillows, linen designed by Ralph Lauren, an armoire for giants, a double bureau in the Herman Miller design of the '50s. On the floor was plush wall-to-wall carpet in a creamy terra-cotta. A spacious dressing room with a hardwood floor held a freestanding barre, lined up in front of a wall of mirrors.

The living room was an Olympic expanse, decorated English informal with a flat woven carpet, big overstuffed chairs in ruddy chintzes, and two fat garnet sofas at right angles. A gleaming baby grand piano wore a paisley shawl. On tabletops everywhere were what Carlos called his *chotchkas*, mementos of shows, road tours, photographs, opening-night presents, the heady accumulation of the theatrical life.

By the time she got there, her clothes were hanging in the closets. Her suitcase stood at the side of the bed. She'd get to it later. She changed into black leather pants and a red silk shirt, put her feet into laced-up boots, and gave herself up to Carlos and Arthur.

They took her to John Clancy's for dinner and plied her with oysters on the half-shell. Seated in the step-down dining room with the whitewashed brick wall amid the jolly noise of happy diners, they feasted on swordfish grilled over mesquite and shared the chocolate mousse cake, which was too rich by far for even two people. And Carlos presented her with a set of house keys in a Gucci holder.

After dinner, at her insistence, they deposited her back in the vestibule of her new home with the Sunday *Times*, and she took the elevator to the fourth floor and let herself into the apartment. Light spilled down from the small art deco chandelier in the broad slate-tiled foyer. A cinnamon and vanilla potpourri scented the rooms.

On the kitchen table, leaning against a huge Lalique bowl, was an envelope of photographs with a note from Carlos urging her not to look tonight. Her fingers worried with the flap, but she set it down unopened. She was exhausted. She left her clothes on the bedroom floor and took a bath in Carlos's majestic black-marbled and mirrored bathroom, letting the Jacuzzi soothe her aching muscles.

She felt like a new person when she came out wrapped in a sarong of one of Carlos's bath sheets. He always found the softest towels. She stretched out across the bed and looked up at the ceiling. High up were the pipes and the vast sprinkler system distinguishing the loft from an apartment.

Something flashed across her peripheral vision. She turned her head and saw the answering machine was blinking at her from the skirted table next to the bed. Calls for Carlos, his departed tenant, perhaps for her. She sat up, crawled to the far side of the bed, and pressed the replay button.

Babycakes, where are you? Smith, sounding breathless. *I've been trying you all day. I* must *talk to you.*

Beep.

Leslie, this is Roger Levine. Please call me at your convenience. He left his number. She'd call him tomorrow.

Beep.

Sweetie, this is not funny. Call me. I'm worried *about you.* The voice faded, but Wetzon heard Smith say, *This is so typically selfish of her.*

"Grrr," Wetzon growled. "Call you? In your dreams, baby-cakes."

Beep.

Wetzon, this is Rona. Rona's voice was tense. Ice rattled against glass. *Please call me tonight, if possible, or tomorrow. Something unexpected has come up.*

12

·······

Her perception on awakening was of another dimension, and as she lay there she had no sensation other than tranquillity. The bedroom windows (there were six in all) faced south and west, so it was still too early for direct sunlight. The landscape, although unfamiliar, was rather like being in a secret garden.

She limbered up at the barre and took a leisurely shower. In the freezer she found a bag of coffee beans marked "Decaf" in pencil. On a shelf, a coffee grinder, filters. Carlos's machine was electric, and soon it was dripping luscious-smelling coffee into its fat-bellied pot. She felt entirely detached from what had happened, almost as if she were in a hotel. And she didn't even care that she hadn't read the Sunday *Times*.

It was after ten when she came down to earth and remembered to call Rona.

"Can you meet me for a drink this afternoon?" Rona was brisk and cool. "Actually, I'd like both of you there."

"Both? You mean Smith, too?"

"Yes. I'll have the transfer papers for you to sign."

Transfer papers? What was she talking about? "Rona, I'm sorry. I'm a little confused. What transfer papers?"

"I'll need both yours and your husband's signatures, because it's a joint account." There was an edge in Rona's voice.

Huh? It took Wetzon only a second. "You're not alone."

"That's right."

Wetzon chewed her lip. "Smith's in the country. I don't know if she'll be back tonight or tomorrow morning. What about holding it till the morning?"

"No!" Rona was vehement.

"All right. How's four o'clock? I'll see if I can get Smith back here."

"Fine. The Mark."

Wetzon punched out Smith's number, fully expecting a tirade. Smith did not disappoint her.

"You are the limit, Wetzon. People do worry about you, you know. You don't care. You only think about yourself."

"Excuse me? I suppose it was *your* apartment that was flooded and *your* ceiling that fell in?"

There was a pause. "See. You do that all the time. You always turn things around to suit yourself."

Wetzon hung up on her.

The phone rang.

"Hello."

"We were cut off, sweetie pie. Your phone must be water-logged."

"We were not—" *Oh, screw it,* she thought. It was like trying to have a conversation with a bowl of chili.

"Are you in your apartment, sugar?"

"No, Smith. Read my lips. I had a major flood. My apartment is unlivable."

"Oh, you poor baby," Smith cooed.

"No, don't do that, Smith, because I'll come apart, and I hate feeling sorry for myself." She said with determination, "This is just a minor blip in an otherwise perfect life. I'm in Carlos's apartment in the Village. I've got call forwarding."

"Carlos! You're staying with *him* and not me?"

"Will you stop that, please?" The feud between Smith and Carlos was unrelenting, no holds barred. He called her the Barracuda and she called him the Degenerate. Carlos blamed Smith for Wetzon's defection from the theater and felt that Smith was selfish and self-serving, while Smith was homophobic and resented Wetzon's affection for Carlos and was always trying to undermine it. Which was truly an impossible dream. But that didn't stop either Carlos or Smith from taking pokes at one another as Wetzon struggled to keep the peace.

Since Carlos had become a successful choreographer and a celebrity, Smith had somewhat tempered her abuse of him whenever his name came up. She now called him "that gay person."

Carlos was vain and self-centered, too, but for those he cared deeply about he was loving, generous with his talent, his attention, and his money. He was Wetzon's best friend.

"Is it Jake Donahue?"

"What are you talking about, Smith?"

"Your dinner date tonight."

Wetzon groaned. "Will you stop? I called you because Rona wants to see us this afternoon for a drink. She insisted on both of us being there."

"Rona Middleton? What for?"

"If I knew, don't you think I would tell you? I don't know. Someone was with her, so she was talking as if I was a client. She left a message for me last night that something important had come up." When Smith didn't say anything, Wetzon said, "I made it for four at The Mark and told her I wasn't sure I could get you. So if you don't want—"

"Of course I'll be there." Smith was suddenly so agreeable that Wetzon wondered what was up.

"Is everything all right with you and Twoey?"

"Perfect." She said it quickly, spitting it out. "It's just that Janet is coming in from Paris this afternoon and Twoey has to go out to Kennedy to meet her." She didn't bother keeping the resentment out of her voice. "He's having dinner with her tonight."

Janet Barnes was Twoey's mother, a still-beautiful, domineering, redheaded widow. Last year, when they'd first met Twoey, Wetzon had warned Smith that he was mother-led, but Smith had brushed it aside, declaring she could handle Janet. She'd flipped out over Twoey and had dumped Jake Donahue for him.

"Without you?"

"My choice."

Wetzon wondered. "I can meet you at The Mark."

"I have my car," Smith said. "Will you be in the Village? I'll pick you up."

"I'm going up to my place to see what else I can salvage. You can pick me up there if you want to."

"I hope this thing with Rona is not something that's going to cost us money." Smith sounded worried.

"You and me both."

"Is it someone I know?"

"Will you quit?" Wetzon laughed. "You're like a little kid." Smith wouldn't quit till she found out about Alton Pinkus, but Wetzon had no intention of telling her. At least, not yet.

She hung up and got back into bed with *The New York Times Book Review* and another cup of coffee, but she didn't get past the first page because Carlos called, checking up on her. Then it was noon and she couldn't waste any more time.

The big suitcase had to be unpacked, her lingerie and sweats put in the empty bureau drawers. When she reached the bottom of the suitcase, she found the black leather box containing the gun and sat on the bed and stared at it for a moment. It went into the drawer under her panty hose. Knowing Silvestri, it wasn't loaded. Nothing to worry about. Besides, she wouldn't know how to check it anyway.

She dressed in her black leather pants and red silk shirt, put a bit of gray shadow on her eyelids, some blush on her cheeks. A neutral lip gloss. Brushed out her braid and rolled her hair up into her usual dancer's knot on top of her head.

The phone rang. Should she let the machine catch it? She did.

Hi, there, came a voice, only it came out *Ha, thar. I surely think I must have the wrong number.*

Wetzon grabbed the phone. "Hold on, Laura Lee."

Her friend Laura Lee Day had come to New York a decade ago to be a concert violinist and, having to support herself, took a job with Merrill Lynch as a stockbroker. Wetzon had met a lot of stockbrokers who were or had been musicians. It was a strange combination: music and finance. When Wetzon got Laura Lee's name as a confidential referral, she'd cold-called her and they'd become acquaintances, and then friends. Wetzon had moved Laura Lee to Oppenheimer, where she was a top money manager. She was even managing Wetzon's money.

Because of her classical music background, Laura Lee attracted successful people from the arts and had built a broad, if demanding, client base. As with many successful financial managers, for many of her clients she had become more than a financial consultant. She

fulfilled the various roles of mother, sister, friend, and even therapist.
She was godmother to her clients' children and peacemaker between
clients who divorced. It took its toll on her, but Laura Lee's good
humor always bubbled close to the surface, and she rarely let most
situations get to her. The stock-market crash in '87 had so freaked
her and everyone connected with the market, there was nowhere to
go, she said, but up.

"Who is the charmer on your answerin' machine? What haven't
you told me, darlin'?"

"Nothing, only that I was flooded out of my apartment last
night, and for the duration, I am living in Carlos's loft in the Village,"
Wetzon said. "And don't say I could have called you, please." She
heard the defensiveness in her voice, and kicked herself. That's what
Smith always did to her.

"Far be it from me to criticize, darlin', but you are actin' unchar-
acteristically cranky, so it must have been truly terrible."

"Truly. The idiot upstairs fell asleep and let his tub overflow. I
had Niagara Falls. I've got to get someone to give me an estimate.
Oh, shit, Laura Lee."

"Get a grip, darlin', it'll be okay. Think of the fun you'll have
redecoratin', and I'm here to tell you your accounts are up thirty-two
percent this year, so you can spend—"

"Oh, who cares, Laura Lee? Who cares?"

"Darlin', let me ask you somethin'. Did you get injured in this
flood?"

"No, but—"

"Do you have a life-threatenin' illness?"

"No."

"Need I say more?"

Wetzon swiped at her eyes and sighed. "Oh, you're right, of
course. You're right. I've just had two really bad days, which began
when my next big placement got himself murdered the morning he
was supposed to start at Loeb Dawkins."

"Oh my, Brian Middleton. Was he yours?"

"You knew Brian, Laura Lee?"

"I met him once. Recently, too. And to tell the truth, darlin', I
wasn't impressed. I don't like to speak ill of the dead, but what a
sleaze. He was interviewin' here, through another headhunter. And

you know how they like to parade li'l ol' me past these prospects. Anyway, they brought him in to say hi, how're you."

"Wait a minute. Did you say he was working with another head-hunter? Which one?" Why did this always shock her? *Get real*, she told herself. They worked with other headhunters. Don't take it personally. But she did.

"What's his face . . . you know, Harold somethin' or other. The one who works for Tom Keegen, who used to work for you."

13

·······

She stopped at Zabar's for a couple of choc-
olate croissants and a pound of decaf Colombian beans, then made a
beeline for her apartment building.

After collecting her mail, she buzzed Roger Levine's apartment
from the downstairs intercom. "I'll be upstairs salvaging what I can,"
she told him.

"Be careful. The ceiling in the bedroom could cave in anytime.
I'll be up to talk to you. How long will you be there?"

"About an hour, maybe more." She calculated that that should
do it. She could park some bags in Smith's apartment and pick them
up afterward, take a cab back to the Village, change for dinner, and
take a cab back up to Café des Artistes. Whew!

She told Julio, the Sunday doorman, to send Smith up without
announcing her.

The Sunday *Times* lay on her doormat. She picked it up and
unlocked her door, opening it tentatively. The scent of ammonia
tainted with mildew assaulted her. Although the destruction was organized, thanks to Carlos's Hazels, it was much worse than she'd
remembered.

Her carpets were gone, so the damage to her floors was exposed,
white stains and buckled parquet. In the living room, her furniture
had been piled under the only spot where the ceiling hadn't puckered
and cracked. Everything was neatly covered with plastic drop cloths.

On her kitchen counter, tucked under a coffee mug, she found a
cleaning ticket for the carpets. She made a pot of coffee before she
ventured further.

Plastic also shrouded her bedroom furniture, and here, too, the oak flooring had buckled. The cost of new flooring would be staggering.

She pulled a worn suitcase and a huge canvas shopping bag from the hall closet, unloaded the old sheets and blankets stored there, and packed as much as she could fit of what remained of her clothing. A half-dozen pair of shoes went into the Zabar's shopping bag along with what had been on top of her desk.

The doorbell rang, and she squished back down the hall on sodden floorboards to let Roger in. He looked around glumly. "Ah . . . Leslie . . . the building, as you know, is insured when it's our fault, but this is not—"

"What is *that* supposed to mean?" She stood with her hands on her hips, not at all liking the way this conversation was going.

"Well, it means we'll help you work this out, Leslie, but it is between you and Mr. and Mrs. Muscat. And also, me and the Muscats. You and I seem to be the only ones affected. I've talked with them in Florida and they've agreed to assume responsibility, so that is something. And they do have an insurance policy. I think we can work it out satisfactorily, but my feeling is that we'll have to get the work started and then bill them accordingly."

Why did lawyers talk so much? Somewhere buried in all that language was a warning; Wetzon was certain of it. "Listen, Roger, do you want to talk about what new oak flooring costs?"

He shrugged.

"Am I going to have to sue them? You're the lawyer. Tell me the truth."

"I don't know, and that's the truth, Leslie." He managed to look everywhere but at her. "After all, we have to live together here. We want to be good neighbors."

"That's bullshit, Roger, and you know it. Being a good neighbor stops when your neighbor has damaged your property and made it unlivable. Okay, I'll get some legal advice. And my insurance people have been notified. They'll have someone up here tomorrow to look around."

"Oh, my Lord!"

Wetzon spun around and Roger jumped. "Oh, my Lord," he echoed.

Smith stood in the doorway in a black stretch cat suit over a gold silk turtleneck, looking tall, sexy, and absolutely gorgeous. She had one of Calvin's short quilted jackets under her arm.

Levine was bowled over. His mouth hung open.

"My partner, Xenia Smith," Wetzon murmured.

"Charmed, I'm sure," Smith drawled, like a character out of *Private Lives*. She batted her eyelashes at Roger and offered her hand.

"Delighted." Roger was plainly in *Private Lives*, too. He took her hand and held on to it a trifle too long, then cleared his throat and tried halfheartedly to pull his eyes back into their sockets.

"Oh, fuck." Wetzon withdrew to the kitchen and poured herself a cup of coffee. As she put the croissants on a plate, she heard the outside door close.

Smith bustled into the kitchen with "What a charming man."

"He's married to an analyst with Smith Barney, and she's pregnant." Wetzon took another cup from the cupboard, banged it down, and poured coffee for Smith. She felt belligerent. And short. Sometimes she felt if she were just two inches taller, she could handle anything. . . .

"What do you take me for?" Smith reached for a croissant. "Mmmm."

Wetzon took a sip of coffee. "I'm not going near that." She gave Smith a severe look. "What's with you and Twoey?"

Smith grinned at her. "I have to keep my hand in, hone my skills, so to speak. You never know, do you? Besides, a little flirt now and then never hurts anyone."

"Oh, I give up."

"What you'll never understand, sweetie, is that we women have to use everything, and I mean *everything*, we have to compete in their world."

"That is so depressing. I want to go back to the theater."

"There's nothing to go back to."

"Oh, Smith, that sounds so final." Wetzon sniffed. Smith was right.

"Let's be realistic, sugar. Would you like to know why we've been as successful as we have?"

"One way or the other, I'm sure you're going to tell me."

Smith ignored her. "It's because we're good, but it's also because we're women and we're a token. They can show us to the affirmative-action people and say, 'Look how gender-blind we are. We deal with a company owned and operated by women.' "

"Now you've thoroughly depressed me. And furthermore, you know how much I hate when you do that sexual tease."

"So?" Smith smirked at her. "Your apartment is depressing, but our situation is not. We can't win on their ballfield, playing by their rules, so I make up my own and force them to play by ours. My motto is: Confuse them with sex and make an end run for the goal. Stick with me." She winked at Wetzon and took another bite of her croissant.

Wetzon poured herself more coffee. She might disagree with Smith's tactics, but could she say Smith was entirely wrong? Women on Wall Street had no old-boy network, exchanged no confidences over urinals, and didn't do business in the clubhouses and on the golf links. So what was left?

They packed Wetzon's bags into the trunk of Smith's Jag and drove over to The Mark, where Smith found a parking place on Seventy-seventh Street almost at once. At ten to four they were sitting at a table in Mark's Bar, Smith with her Lillet and Wetzon with Pellegrino.

"Something stronger might be in order," Smith said.

"I'll have a beer later."

"Ah, yes. The mysterious dinner companion." Smith reached into her boot and brought out a tarot card. "The King of Cups," she said. She held it up to Wetzon.

"What the hell is that supposed to mean?" Wetzon grumbled.

Smith gave her a long-suffering look. "Your dinner companion. A kind man, an intelligent man, a leader of men—and women—well-respected." She paused and rolled her eyes. "An *older* man."

"Put that damn card away, Smith." Wetzon felt herself flush up to her ear tips. "Here comes Rona."

And indeed, a very determined Rona Middleton was striding toward them, and she wasn't alone.

14

·······

The woman struggling in Rona's wake was short and a bit pudgy, definitely pear-shaped. While Rona made a statement, albeit an overstatement, this woman disappeared into the woodwork. She was about Rona's age but wore no makeup, and her skin was sallow; one infinitesimal chin buried in a second, fleshier. Straighter-than-straight brown hair with no body whatever and cut badly, perhaps by herself with manicuring scissors. Bangs hung limply to midforehead over myopic brown eyes behind clear-rimmed glasses. Brown tweed skirt, brown blazer, white cotton blouse with a schoolgirl collar.

"This is Penny Ann Boyd," Rona said, with a withering glance at her drab companion. Poor Penny Ann's rounded shoulders slumped.

"Penny Ann Brown?" Smith's smile was artless.

"Boyd," Wetzon said, kicking her under the table.

"Well, don't stand there. Sit down," Rona commanded, dropping into the closest chair. She was casual in washed silk blue jeans, a mauve turtleneck, cowboy boots. Her blond curls fit like a pot cover on top of her head, and the expression on her gaunt face was angry. "Barbie is parking the car."

Thrilling, Wetzon thought. *A meeting of the girls' basketball team.*

"Weeeell." Now Smith's smile was silky. "Why don't you tell us—"

Rona beckoned to a passing waiter. "A martini—very dry." She pointed to Penny Ann. "She'll have the same."

"Oh, no Rona, I couldn't . . . not with the Valium . . . and all . . ." Penny Ann's voice was as pallid as her skin.

"Well, order something," Rona said impatiently, "so we can get on with it."

"Tea with lemon, please." Penny Ann's lips trembled. The poor thing looked scared to death. Of Rona?

A pretty woman in a black leather bomber jacket and a long swinging black skirt was heading toward them. Her hair was a wild cascade of red curls, and she had the fragile pink complexion of some redheads. She shook hands firmly with Smith and then Wetzon, saying, "I'm Barbara Gordon." Surrounding pale-green eyes were fine white rims. Wild-animal eyes, wolf eyes. "Rum and Coke," she told the waiter, and sat down next to Wetzon. She emitted a faint woodsy perfume.

When the waiter left, Rona looked at Penny Ann. "Tell them."

Penny Ann mewed before she spoke. It was disconcerting. "It's . . . I mean, my . . . it's about my . . . daughter. Tabitha Ann."

Smith choked, put her hand over her mouth, and cleared her throat, using the motion to cloak her roll of eyes at Wetzon. "Please go on, dear," Smith said sweetly. "My allergies . . ."

Barbara Gordon lowered her eyelids halfway and stared at Smith. She was onto her.

Wetzon turned her attention to something in her purse. Smith was going to set her off in an avalanche of giggles if she kept this up. She pressed her lips together and gave Smith another nudge under the table. Barbara Gordon was no fool.

The waiter brought a cup and saucer, a small teapot, a dish of lemon slices and Rona's martini, Barbara's rum and Coke, set everything up, and left them. The gin vapors intruded. Wetzon was straightaway nauseated, she and gin having disagreed many years ago after she'd had her first cocktail, a pink lady.

"Tabby Ann's run away!" Penny Ann was obviously dismayed by the force of her exclamation. She looked from Rona to Barbara for help.

Rona dug her olive out of the glass and gnawed at it. She was silent.

Barbara leaned behind Rona to pat Penny Ann on the shoulder. "Don't lose it, Penny Ann."

What the hell did this have to do with them? Wetzon thought. And Smith nodded, picking up on her mental trail.

"God save us, Penny Ann, you are hopeless." Rona took a swallow of the martini. "Tabitha Ann happens to be my godchild."

Tears rolled out from under Penny Ann's glasses.

"Oh, Rona, go easy on her," Barbara said. She'd slurped up the rum and Coke awfully fast.

"What does this have to do with us?" Smith looked pointedly at her watch.

"Brian stole our money," Penny Ann began, and stopped when Rona raised her eyes to the ceiling and groaned. "After Wilson died." Penny Ann began to make gulping noises.

"Oh, dear God," Smith said. "She's hyperventilating."

Wetzon patted Penny Ann's hand. "Just relax. You're with friends." Smith whacked her under the table.

"Wilson had a brain tumor and was dead six months after he was diagnosed," Barbara said.

Rona added, as if to mitigate her involvement, "When Penny Ann got her settlement, I was having Megan. . . ."

"I gave him my money to invest for us. For our security. For Tabby Ann's college . . ."

"How much was it?" Wetzon asked. Brian was a piece of work.

"Two hundred thou," Rona said. "The dirtball put it in stock-index options. All she has left is about fifteen thou, and that's after taking out a second mortgage on the house."

"You gave him discretion?" Wetzon was incredulous. Why did people do that?

Penny Ann whimpered. "I just signed the papers he sent me. I didn't know. I told him to put it into something conservative. He was Rona's husband, and he was a lawyer and everything. I didn't know."

"Well, you should have asked," Rona said. She scowled at Wetzon. "Giving discretion is fine. You just have to know the person you're giving discretion to."

Wetzon disagreed, but kept silent. Rona was a client. As much as she loved and trusted Laura Lee, Wetzon would never abdicate responsibility for managing her own money. She worked too hard to make it. Yet that's exactly what people did. And not just naive people and first-time investors. One was constantly reading about movie stars and celebrities who had handed their money over to trusted counselors, even relatives and spouses, to invest and were taken to the cleaners. It was really interesting. People loved having money, making money, but didn't love dealing with it. It was almost as if it was gauche—or too dirty for the Protestant ethic so ingrained in these here United States of America.

"I trusted him," Penny Ann whined. "How could I have been such a fool?"

"I trusted him, too," Rona said matter-of-factly. She signaled with her finger for another martini.

"What are you doing about it?" Smith asked. "Have you filed a complaint?"

"It's done," Rona said. "It went into arbitration."

"Arbitration," Penny Ann said bitterly. "That's when friends of brokers and brokerage firms sit on a panel and decide if the complaints are valid. How fair is that?"

"You couldn't sue?" Wetzon asked.

"It's not that simple." Barbara waved her empty glass to the waiter for a refill.

"I signed an arbitration agreement in all those papers." Penny Ann seemed to cling almost lovingly to her portrayal of herself as victim. "I didn't know I was signing my rights away."

"Oh, please," Rona groaned. "You are responsible for yourself. The Supreme Court barred most lawsuits against brokers, especially if the arbitration agreement had been signed when the account was opened, because there were so many frivolous lawsuits."

"But, Rona," Penny Ann mewed faintly, "the print is so small and the wording is so involved. And Dr. Jerry told me you can't open an account with most quality brokerage firms unless you sign that agreement."

Who the hell was Dr. Jerry? Wetzon put a smoked, salted almond in her mouth. She was tired and having trouble concentrating.

A rum and Coke refill for Barbara arrived with Rona's martini, and the empty glasses were whisked away. No one else was having seconds.

"The arbitration usually goes against the broker," Rona snapped.

"Well, this time it didn't. Brian won and Bliss Norderman won. And I lost."

"Penny Ann," Rona said wearily, "I'm sorry, but you did get a settlement." Penny Ann's mouth twisted into a sneer. "You did." Rona looked at Smith and Wetzon. "Bliss Norderman assigned her and Tabby Ann each annuities of ten thousand dollars."

"But that only comes to twenty thousand dollars, and meantime I have a second mortgage on my house and I have no money, no income. . . ." Her little voice was plaintive.

"You might get a job," Smith suggested. If she were a smoker, she would have blown smoke in Penny Ann's face.

Rage flashed quickly across Penny Ann's dull eyes and was gone in a moment. Then she said the wrong thing, and to make matters worse, she said it primly. "You don't understand what it's like being a single parent."

"Oh, don't I?" Smith was breathing icicles.

Penny Ann gaped at Smith. "I'm sorry if I've offended you. Tabby Ann is sixteen."

"My son Mark is also sixteen. He's at Groton."

Barbara was chewing on the ice in her empty glass. She had scarfed up the second rum and Coke faster than the first, but except for small red blotches on her cheeks, there was no evidence of inebriation. Rotating the ice shards in her mouth, she said, "It's not exactly easy raising children when there are two parents."

I'm the childless woman at the table, Wetzon thought suddenly. *Does that upset you*, she asked herself, looking inward. She couldn't answer. Lately everything upset her. Instead she said, "This Peter Rabbit talk is all very nice, but can we get to the reason for this meeting?" The other four women looked at her. *Damn it all*, she thought, *I sound like an irritable old maid.*

"Tabby Ann has had some emotional problems," Rona said, and Penny Ann mewed again. "Do you want to talk?"

Penny Ann shook her head. She squeezed a slice of lemon into her teacup and poured. It was probably cold.

"She was obsessed with Brian."

"Who was?" Smith frowned.

"Tabby Ann," Penny Ann said. "He led her on. I didn't know until I read her diary."

"Was Brian Middleton having an affair with your daughter?" Smith asked. Her eyes sparkled with interest.

"No . . . yes . . . no . . ." Penny Ann said.

Rona sighed. "We don't know. She was underage, of course, and I didn't think he could be that much of a prick—"

"There are the papers, too," Penny Ann said. Again she looked at Rona.

"What papers, for pity sakes?" Tolerance, which Smith was always short on, at last had fled.

"My private papers relating to the arbitration. They're missing."

"Now, Penny, you've probably just misplaced them," Barbara said smoothly. "It's Tabitha we're really worried about."

"You say she's run away?" Wetzon still couldn't figure out what this had to do with her and Smith. She looked over at Smith, who wasn't bothering to keep the bored expression off her face. "When did you see her last?"

"Um . . . she's been gone almost a week," Penny Ann said.

"A week!" Smith exploded.

"It's not what you think. She's done it before. She stays with the Maglias sometimes. They have a ten-year-old daughter she baby-sits."

"The Maglias? Tony Maglia, the manager at Bliss Norderman?" How complicated, what with the arbitration and all. None of this was making any sense.

"And she used to stay with Brian, of course."

Wetzon looked at Rona, who shrugged. This meeting was turning surreal.

"It was suggested that you might—" Penny Ann stopped and looked at Rona.

"Suggested by whom?" Wetzon asked.

"Dr. Jerry said—"

There it was again. "Dr. Jerry?"

"Dr. Jerome Gordon," Barbara said. "Actually, I'm standing in for him this afternoon. He had a speaking engagement in New Haven. He's my husband."

"And our therapist." Rona tapped Barbie's hand and smiled.

"Our? Yours and Tabby Ann's?"

"Rona's, too, and Brian's."

Wetzon felt rather than saw Smith pop alert. "Dr. Jerome Gordon?" Smith said, narrowing her eyes. "You don't mean the one with the radio show in Connecticut, 'Ask Dr. Jerry'?"

"Yes. Dr. Jerry suggested that you have connections. He read about you or heard about you. He said you might be able to help me find her."

"I'm afraid there's been some sort of misunderstanding," Wetzon said. "We are not detectives. You have to be licensed to be a detective."

"Hush." Smith held up her hand. "Let me think. We are consultants. We handled the Goldie Barnes case. That's probably where Dr. Jerry heard about us." She paid no attention to Wetzon's foot rapping hers. She smiled. "You can hire us as consultants."

"I think it would be better if you told the police that your daughter is missing. We have no experience with runaways." Or kidnapping? Wetzon's brain whirled.

Penny Ann looked panicked. "I couldn't do that, I just couldn't. The police are going to think she did it, that she killed him."

"Oh, come on now. That's not realistic. It was a mugging, wasn't it?" Smith glanced at Wetzon.

Penny Ann lifted her plump little chin, from which a fat teardrop teetered. "Tabby Ann's diary said she was meeting Brian in New York Friday morning at the Conservatory Garden."

The teardrop splashed into her cup.

15

·······

"Our consulting fee is fifteen hundred a day, plus expenses," Smith said. "How do you propose to pay us if you have no assets?"

Both Penny Ann and Barbara looked to Rona.

Rona said, "Jerry and the group. We're chipping in. We'll be responsible. But that's too high."

Wetzon tried again. "This is really a problem for the police, don't you think? A missing child . . ."

This time it was Smith who kicked Wetzon. "What Wetzon means is our expertise is in financial matters. But, of course, we do have our sources within the police department. . . ." Smith paused as if to let the import of her suggestion sink in.

"Oh we do, do we?" Wetzon murmured.

"Tabby Ann worked for Brian all summer, as an intern. She saw things and heard things."

"What are you talking about, Penny Ann?" Rona demanded.

Penny Ann burst into tears, bawling loudly. The elegant clientele in Mark's Bar took notice.

"Stop that, please," Smith ordered. She shook her finger at Penny Ann. "I will never be able to show my face here again."

Penny Ann looked stunned, but she stopped crying, took off her glasses, dried them, dabbed at her eyes, reset her glasses.

"We want two days in advance before we start."

"This is a little different from a consulting project for a major brokerage firm, Smith." Rona made a motion to Barbara, who took out a blank check from her bag. "I'm suggesting a short, quick investigation with a short, concise report. Five hundred."

"Seven fifty." Smith smiled. "Because it's you, and you're a friend."

Rona threw Smith a cynical look, then nodded to Barbara.

"Make it out to Smith and Wetzon, dear," Smith said.

"Let's get this straight," Wetzon said. "You want us to find Tabitha Ann in this city of a hundred million people?"

"And my papers," Penny Ann said, biting nails already bitten to the quick. "Dr. Jerry felt that it would be easier for people like you to get information than the police."

Yes, people like us, Wetzon thought, *are very good at getting information.* "Look, Penny Ann, we're not going to take your money if we can't help you." Smith's fingers clamped down on her thigh, and Wetzon gave up. "Let's give it a week, okay? And we'll see what we can find out."

Smith beamed and took the check from Barbara. "I'll do up a little letter agreement. Who gets it?"

"I do." Penny Ann gave them an address in Redding, Connecticut, which Smith entered on a cocktail napkin with Wetzon's pen. "We're practically neighbors," Smith said. "I'm in Westport."

"Do you have our card?" Wetzon handed Penny Ann a business card and gave another to Barbara, who was fidgeting with her handbag. Short attention span.

"I've got to go." Barbara stood abruptly, bumping the table. The glasses teetered and liquid sloshed. "Penny Ann?"

"Wait, please. What does your daughter look like? Do you have a photograph?" Wetzon took her pen back from Smith and opened her Filofax, flipping through it to a blank page.

"She's beautiful," Penny Ann said. She fumbled in her purse.

"She's fat," Barbara said.

"Baby fat." The photograph Penny Ann handed to Wetzon was of a young woman in a floppy straw hat sitting on a beach towel. She was wearing a very scanty bikini from which flesh spilled dangerously.

"Ugh." Smith coughed, taking the photograph from Wetzon and holding it as if it were contaminated.

Wetzon nudged Smith with her knee. "What was she wearing when you last saw her?"

"I don't know."

"You don't know?" Smith spoke the words, stretching them out in disbelief.

"Well . . ." Penny Ann was flustered. "Her Reeboks are missing, but her clothes . . . I don't know . . . I wouldn't be able to describe . . . they're so weird."

"Okay," Wetzon said. "White Reeboks."

"Red."

Smith and Wetzon looked at each other. *Red Reeboks.*

"How is she with accents?" Wetzon asked.

"Accents?"

"Come on, Penny Ann," Rona said impatiently. "You know she's a good mimic. Why are you asking?"

"How about Spanish?" Smith said.

"Umm, her au pair was Spanish. She can speak a little."

"And imitate a lot," Rona said. She got up, joining Barbara, who looked as if she was going to bolt momentarily. Rona motioned to Penny Ann. They shook hands all around. "You'll keep us informed."

"The diary," Wetzon said. "I think we should have it."

"Good thinking," Smith said, patting Wetzon on the thigh this time.

"Gosh, I don't know," Penny Ann said at a funereal pace. "I'll talk to Dr. Jerry. Don't you think I should talk to him, Barbie? He'll know what to do."

Smith rolled her eyes. "You read it, of course."

"Well . . . um . . . I skimmed it." She stared at Smith, trying to figure out if criticism was implied, then said, defensively, "I'm her mother."

"I'll get the car and meet you in front," Barbie said.

"Let's go, Penny Ann." Rona gave her a push. "We'll see you get the diary."

"Fed Ex to the office, please," Smith said, not looking up.

"Start with Maglia," Rona said. "You understand why we can't?"

"Not really, Rona. If she were my daughter, I would have been in the city talking to everyone she knew."

"I would have alerted the police," Wetzon added.

"You don't understand how vicious this all got. Tony was furious when I left Bliss Norderman. He tried to destroy my reputation.

They've been really good to me at Rosenkind. Brian wrecked Penny Ann's life, not just with the mishandling of her money, but with Tabby Ann. The arbitration was awful for her."

"So terribly sad," Smith intoned. "We'll do everything we can to help. Won't we, Wetzon?"

"We'll certainly try—"

"Trust us," Smith interrupted, putting an end to the conversation.

"You'll keep me informed." It was a throwaway. Rona caught up with Penny Ann at the entrance to the bar.

When Rona and Penny Ann were out of sight, Smith and Wetzon shook hands.

"That's the easiest money we're ever going to earn," Smith said.

"We're such hotshots, I hope we're right."

"Who else could it have been? That was no maid at Brian's apartment, of that you can be certain. I *knew* that accent was phony."

"You're just miffed because you couldn't get her to work for you."

"Very funny, I'm sure." Smith fluttered her fingers at a passing waiter. "Check, please."

"Could she have been living with Brian, Smith? He knew how old she was. Of course, it might not have been sexual. . . ."

Smith's left eyebrow rose an inch. "Oh, for pity sakes." She pulled the check from the waiter's hand and thrust it at Wetzon. "I hope you're keeping track of your expenses."

"Which I am incurring for both of us." Wetzon returned the bill to the waiter with her American Express card. She looked at her watch. "God, it's after five. I've got to go down to the Village and change for dinner."

"I'll drive you," Smith said when they came out on Seventy-seventh Street. "You might feel so grateful that you'll tell me who you're having dinner with."

"Whom. What we really should be doing is checking out Brian's apartment."

"Ummm," Smith said, negotiating a turn onto Tenth Street by cutting off a yellow cab. Brakes squealed and the cabdriver, a wiry Pakistani, leaped from his cab and screamed incomprehensible insults, all the time waving his arms at Smith, who gave him the finger through the open sunroof of her sable Jaguar.

"I wish you wouldn't do that," Wetzon said wearily when they came to a stop in front of Carlos's building. "Someday someone's going to take out a gun and shoot you. And me."

Smith grinned at her. "This country is altogether too open to the Third World. They should go back to where they came from."

"Of course you'd say that, you bigot."

"Why should I disappoint you, sugarplum?" She pulled Barbara Gordon's check from her pocket. "Look at this. Barbara Orlofsky Gordon."

"So?"

"If she's one of the liquor-dynasty Orlafskys, she's an heiress."

"Meaning?"

"There's a lot more where this came from." Smith was chortling.

Wetzon eyed Smith with suspicion. "And you are altogether too good-humored. What are you up to?"

"Mmmm, well, I thought I might take a quick tour of Brian's apartment and see if I can catch our missing little pussycat."

16

. . . .

Wetzon stood on the park side of West Sixty-seventh Street and watched the little red taillight of Smith's Jaguar slide smoothly through the moderate Sunday-evening traffic and disappear. Smith was absolutely thrilled with herself, Wetzon knew for certain, because she was getting up to her elbows in a murder and was going off on her own to do some "detecting." The Pussycat Caper. Ha!

And when Smith came up with Tabby Ann Boyd, Wetzon knew who would take all the credit for it. Truth was, she should have gone with Smith. She had no business having dinner with Alton Pinkus.

Behind her, Central Park smelled lushly damp and mossy, the fallen leaves degenerating into compost. The lights strung on the trees around Tavern on the Green made this setting a fairyland at evening. Joggers passed her, singly and in twos, entering the park, heading uptown for the track around the reservoir.

Wetzon sighed. When the light flashed green, she crossed Central Park West. The vanishing sun cast Lincoln Center in gold leaf, in ONE, before a curtain of dark-blue sky. The specific, almost spicy, odor of wood fires, dried logs burning in real fireplaces, filled the air. A sure harbinger of winter.

Halfway down the block in a wonderful old turn-of-the-century apartment building known as Hotel des Artistes, now an expensive co-op, was Café des Artistes. She hadn't been to the restaurant in years, but it had changed not one iota. Dark wood walls glowed with the satin patina of age. This, plus leaded-glass windows and the famous beaux arts murals of Howard Chandler Christy, contributed to the feeling of stepping back into a more gracious, more civil time. All of the beautiful naked ladies in the murals were said to be the actress Marion Davies, longtime mistress of William Randolph Hearst.

It was early, so there were a few empty tables. An elderly couple were waiting at the reservations desk, chatting with an ebullient young man. The woman was tiny in a navy Adolpho suit with white trim, her back rigidly straight. She was perfectly coiffed, tinted in the blond color that women of a certain age seemed to prefer and then sprayed in place for life. Wetzon patted her topknot and made herself a mental promise she would go gray gracefully and without hair spray.

The woman's companion was half a head shorter, a frail man with an osteoporosal hunch and a tremor in his hands. They must be regulars, because the maître d' asked after their children and grandchildren as he whisked them away into another wood-paneled room.

Wetzon stepped up to the desk. "Mr. Pinkus," she said. Behind her were two couples, older men with much younger women. The women were modishly dressed in cashmere and silk, hem lengths that stopped about four inches above slim knees. Their escorts were both tall, white-haired, and distinguished, one deeply tanned as if he'd just stepped off his yacht. Was this a place, she wondered uneasily, where older men brought young women?

"This way, please, Ms. Wetzon." Caught off guard, Wetzon turned to see the maître d' waiting for her.

She followed him up a flight of stairs to the bar area, which had a decidedly '20s quality and was peopled with attractive, clever types that might have stepped out of an F. Scott Fitzgerald novel. Alton Pinkus was sitting in a booth just past the bar talking to a distinguished, balding man, compact in a good tweed sports jacket. They both rose to greet her, and Alton introduced her to George Lang, the owner of Café des Artistes. She shook hands with Lang, who was at once called away by the maître d'. And her hand was quickly swallowed by Alton's great warm paw. He waited till she was seated, then asked, "You're drinking?"

"Amstel Light." She had hardly gotten the words out when it arrived.

"You have gray eyes," Alton said. "Why did I think blue?"

He seemed to want an answer, and she was unexpectedly tongue-tied. *Damn you, Silvestri*, she thought, flustered. *What the hell is the matter with you, Leslie Wetzon?* she asked herself. In her mind she heard Laura Lee shriek, *Get a grip!*

She was saved by the maître d', who announced that their table was ready, and they rose and traveled back down the stairs into a large crowded room, passing an amazing buffet of appetizers and a cornucopian dessert display. The leaded windows were almost obscured by plants, couples sat tête-à-tête, all observed somewhat cynically by the Christy nudes in their pastoral setting.

"We could have stayed upstairs, but I rather thought you'd like this room. I do."

They were seated in an almost-private corner, her back to the greenery-covered window, Alton opposite. Her hardly-touched beer had somehow miraculously appeared on the table, along with Alton's glass of what looked like Scotch.

A waiter approached with two huge menus and asked Alton if he wanted another drink. He shook his head and ordered a bottle of Pellegrino, looking to Wetzon for agreement. "Mineral water is fine," she said. She felt like a stranger to herself, as if the real Wetzon wasn't sitting here, that some part of her had spun off and established itself, like a clone, and she was simply observing.

". . . wine with dinner," Alton was saying. "Is that all right?" He was waiting for her answer.

"If it's white and dry."

"We'll make sure it is." His eyes were medium brown with darker edges, heavy lidded beneath unruly gray brows.

The waiter reeled off the specials, then discreetly withdrew to let them decide.

"Everything sounds wonderful," she said, listening to the warm hum of voices around her. "I'm much better when I have only a few choices." She hid her face behind the immense menu. It was daunting. This whole situation was daunting. He obviously liked her, and she didn't know what to do with herself. Why was it so easy for her to talk to strangers but the minute there was the suggestion of intimacy between her and a man, she became an inarticulate idiot? She had felt safe with Silvestri; now she was adrift.

Sighing, she stared at the words on the menu, not seeing them, until Alton gently took the menu away from her and folded it.

"Would you like me to order for you?"

She nodded, feeling her cheeks blaze. "Something from the sea, please."

He ordered the four kinds of salmon appetizers, then grilled swordfish with tomato olive coulis, and a 1963 Montrachet. When the waiter left them, he asked, "How'd I do?"

"Great." *You've gone monosyllabic, Wetzon.* She settled back in her chair and let herself smile at him. *Be cool.* Hunger gnawed at her, and with a ridiculously tremulous hand she plucked a piece of toasted bread from the bread basket and broke off a chunk, busying herself with buttering it. When she looked up, he was smiling at her, and she flushed again. "Don't do that," she said.

"Do I make you nervous?" He, for one, was having a good time torturing her.

"Nervous? Me? Oh my, no. Of course you make me nervous." She stared at the Chinese figures in a repeat pattern on his tie, refusing to look into his eyes.

The waiter returned and displayed the wine bottle; Alton nodded. The bottle was opened with a flourish, and a splash of wine was poured into Alton's glass. After he tasted and approved, the waiter filled both glasses and slipped the bottle into the cooler next to the table.

"To beginnings," Alton said, raising his glass.

Oh, no, Wetzon thought. She said, "To world peace and long life and renovated apartments." She grinned at him and took a sip of the wine, closing her eyes. It was lovely, sophisticated. And romantic, like the restaurant. "Oh, dear," she said, opening her eyes, and there he was, smiling at her again.

"It *is* nice, isn't it?" He was wearing a gray flannel jacket and a white shirt, open at the collar, and he, or the beer or the wine, was making her heart catch.

"Who are you, Alton Pinkus?" she asked suddenly, setting her glass down. "What am I doing here having dinner with you?"

He didn't look the least bit surprised by her outburst. In fact, he looked pleased. "Born 1936, New York City," he said, counting facts off with his fingers. "Columbia, class of '56. Captain, U.S. Army. Harvard Law School—"

"Impressive CV, but—"

"Married to Tessa, 1960," he continued. "Three children, all grown and self-supporting. Tessa died four years ago."

"I'm very sorry."

"So am I. You would have liked each other."

"Alton, good to see you." A dark-haired man in his forties, his huge mustache covering his upper lip, clapped Alton on the back. His eyes flicked over Wetzon. He stood aside to let the waiter serve their dinners, but he didn't leave.

"Charley, how are you?"

"Karen," Charley called to a salt-and-pepper brunette who had gone ahead of him. "Look who's here."

Wetzon was introduced, then Charley and Karen moved on to their table.

The food, the wine, the romance of the restaurant were bewitching, and she found herself colorfully describing the nightmare night of the flood and moving to the Village, laughing, making Alton laugh. He had a wonderful laugh: he threw his head back and committed himself in a big way.

They were interrupted three more times by people she didn't know, once by the director of the Metropolitan, whose name she recognized, and finally by Ed Koch, an ex-mayor of the city, who heartily recommended The Great Bonaparte for dessert.

Wetzon had a glow on. She lost pieces of conversation. The wine had gone to her head. The Great Bonaparte, which proved to be a mountain of puff pastry, lemon curd, strawberries, and whipped cream, arrived with two soup spoons. Decaf espresso for two. Alton let her eat most of the concoction, but there hung between them a cobweb of shared intimacy over an over-the-top napoleon.

"This is mad," she murmured. The wine made her smile; the smile turned to a yawn, shattering her decorum.

"I should get you home," he said, not moving.

"I'll take a cab," she said. She didn't move either.

He signaled for the check.

"What do you do, Alton? You're too young to be retired." She gazed at him through wine-besotted eyes. He was very nice, if a bit blurry. She felt another yawn coming and covered her mouth.

He signed the back of the check and handed it to the waiter. "I keep busy. I run four miles a day. I'm writing my memoirs." He smiled. "I'm still called upon to speak now and then. I'm on several boards . . ."

"Yes, the late Luwisher Brothers was one."

He nodded. "And I'm part of a pool of people who are called to sit on arbitration panels."

Wetzon blinked. Had she heard right? "Did you say arbitration?"

"Yes." He rose and gave her his hand.

"In what industry?"

"Yours."

17

·······

Carlos's apartment was cold and still, but not unfriendly. Just not hers. Wetzon closed the windows and put the thermostat up to get the chill out. Apartments in the newer buildings and the expensive renovations had their own thermostats, a luxury particularly at this time of year when the temperatures did not go down quite low enough to warrant the use of expensive heating oil.

She hung up her clothes and wrapped herself in her white terry-cloth robe, then scrubbed her face and took down her hair. It came to the middle of her back. Laura Lee was always after her to cut it off. She stared at herself in the mirror. "You haven't got the guts," she said out loud, and braided it into one loose braid, tying it off with a band. It was all a smoke screen to keep her mind off the evening.

The answering machine was telling her there were five messages. Five. One would be Silvestri, and what was she going to say to him? Did he think she should sit home and wait for him to come back? She felt defensive, angry, as if she had somehow done something wrong. But she was hungry for companionship, for conversation, and, she admitted to herself reluctantly, the physical presence of a man. *Come off it, Wetzon, you miss the sex.*

She had sort of slipped into the dinner with Alton, and it didn't have to go further. But she knew it very well might if she continued to feel so abandoned. And Alton liked her, and his approval was flattering. So there it was.

The first message was from Carlos, and the surge of relief she felt clogged the traffic from her ears to her brain, and she had to play it back. *Hi, Birdie, just checking. What are you up to, you runabout you?*

You're going to get a call from one Louie Armstrong, who's going to make everything nice for you again.

Beep.

Smith: *Bad news, sweetie. The kitty is playing elsewhere.* Pause for affect. Smith was really enjoying the cloak-and-dagger stuff. *But she, or someone, went through the place with a fine comb. Call me, even if it's late.* She laughed an evil laugh. *I want to hear about your big, hot date.*

"Sure, right away," Wetzon told the machine.

Beep.

Hi, Les. Sorry I missed you again. Silvestri sounded annoyed, and he emphasized *again* as if it was her fault she was not at his beck and call. He left the number in Virginia.

Beep.

Ms. Wetzon. Detective Ferrante. Central Park Precinct. Would you call me? He left his number.

Beep.

Detective Ferrante again, Ms. Wetzon.

"Oh, leave me alone! All of you!" Wetzon found herself yowling. She jumped into bed and pulled the down quilt up over her head and breathed warm air into the dark cocoon.

She had enjoyed herself tonight, enjoyed Alton's company. She'd been dazzled up to spillover by the illusion of reflected fame. Alton Pinkus wore power casually. It was seductive. And lying there in the warm darkness, she suddenly understood Smith's attraction to these men. And to think, she had put Smith down for this—it had seemed so shallow. Now here she was doing the same thing. No wonder she felt scummy.

When they emerged from the restaurant, Alton had taken her arm, tucking it into his, and said, "I'll drive you home."

"No, I mean, it's all right. Really. I'll take a cab." She'd stammered, wondering what she'd do with him if there should be a parking place in front of Carlos's building. Would she have to ask him up? And then what would happen?

"Okay." He was looking down at her gravely, as if it really was okay.

I'm making a fool of myself, she thought.

"I'd like to do this again," he said.

A fine mist was dancing in the splash of light from the street lamp. It dappled his face.

She'd turned to him then. "There's—I have—I'm—I am in a relationship."

He didn't seem either surprised or fazed. "But you're here with me."

"He's out of town," she said quickly. That was worse. It sounded as if she was sneaking out on Silvestri. "I mean, he's on assignment at Quantico for six months." She smiled ruefully. "And I like your company."

"And I, yours." He stood there for a moment looking down at her, the fine mist sparkling his gray hair like tiny sequins. Then he cupped her face in his hands and kissed her gently on the lips. She closed her eyes and he did it again, lingering a little longer. He dropped his hands, and when she opened her eyes, he had flagged down a taxi. "I'm not going anywhere, Leslie," he said. He put her in the cab, and before she could protest, gave the driver some bills and she was whisked away.

She stretched out long under the quilt. The wine. The food. The dilemma. She eased her head out from under the quilt. She'd liked his kiss. What was she to do? He was sure of himself, comfortable with himself. Maybe she could keep him as a friend. *Get real, Wetzon.*

Whistling in the dark. What time was it, anyway? The bedside clock said 9:45. It wasn't even late, yet it felt like the middle of the night.

She crawled over to the phone and dialed Smith's number, and when Smith answered, said, "Hi, it's me."

"Weeell, *tell* me."

"There's nothing to tell." Her sigh was unintentionally audible, and of course Smith picked it up.

"He's married, isn't he? I knew it."

"Wrong!" Wetzon buried her face in her pillow.

"I always tell you everything, sweetie. Be fair. Your secret is safe with me."

A muffled "Ha!"

"Who would I tell? Cross my heart. We have a bad connection. You keep fading out."

"And hope to die?" Wetzon gave up. "Swear. And that means Twoey, too." Twoey, too—Twoey Two. God, it was like jabberwocky.

Smith was silent. Wetzon could hear her thinking. Then Smith said slowly, "I swear."

"Alton Pinkus." She rolled over on her back and said it fast, maybe hoping Smith wouldn't hear, then covered her face with the pillow, hugging it.

But she heard. "Alton Pinkus? Alton *Pinkus?* That old commie fart?"

Wetzon threw the pillow aside and sat up. "Excuse me?"

"I really thought it was someone *special.* I don't know, you made such a big deal over it."

"E-ex-excuse—" Sputtering.

"I really hoped you'd written off Dick Tracy once and for all. You can do so much better. But really, sweetie—"

Wetzon was outraged. "Excuse me, did you say *commie?*"

"Among other things. He ran that big union, didn't he?"

"Yes."

"Well, everyone knows these union people are all commies."

"Smith, if you say one more word about this, I'm hanging up." She was snarling into the phone. Why did Smith always make her react like this?

"Oh, for pity sakes. Why do you take everything so personally? I'm only being honest." She sounded so goddam pleased with herself.

"Because it *is* personal. Why do you always use the guise of honesty to hurt me?"

"Hurt you? I *love* you. You're my dearest friend. Why would I want to hurt you? You are entirely too sensitive. I only want what is good for you."

"Did you ever consider that what *you* think is good for me may not be what I think is good for me?"

"Be that as it may, don't you want to hear about Brian's apartment?"

"Please tell me about Brian's apartment." At least it was a change of topic, no matter how perilous.

"Well, partner in crime, I had no trouble getting in. There wasn't even any police tape on the door. The elevator man was obliging enough to open the door for me. I said I was Rona, and there'd been this accident, and the greaseball let me in and left me there because someone was buzzing for service."

Wetzon frowned. That did not sound at all like the way Smith normally talked. Of course. Smith was playing detective, so she'd adjusted her language to hardboiled. "You didn't find Tabitha Ann?"

"No, and furthermore, every scrap of paper was gone, and I mean *every*. Empty desk drawers, calendar pages ripped out."

Wetzon had to smile. Leave it to Smith to search the apartment, probably inventorying and tagging as she went along. "Did you find anything you wanted?"

"What *are* you talking about, sweetie?"

"I mean, where do you suppose she is?"

"I wouldn't be at all surprised if she turned up with Tony Maglia and family, just like her dim-witted mother said. You can call him tomorrow and see—"

"*I* can? What about you?"

"I did Brian's apartment. Now it's your turn. I can't do everything." There was a *click-click* on Smith's line. "Sorry. That's probably Twoey. Hold on, sugarplum."

Call waiting made Wetzon insane. "Smith! Remember your promise." She was talking to air. Damn Smith.

There was another click, and Smith came back. "It's Twoey. Maybe he has money."

"Who, Twoey?"

"No, not Twoey." There was resignation in Smith's voice. "Alton Pinkus. It grieves me, but I rather think Dick Tracy is safe this time around."

"Smith, you're making me angry." Wetzon's voice was tight. "Alton is a friend. That's all." *Liar,* she thought. *Liar, liar, liar.*

"Too boring, sweetie. Anyway, just keep in mind naked old men are not a pretty sight."

"How the hell would you know?" Wetzon slammed the receiver down, fury propelling her off the bed like a rocket. "This is it! I'll kill her! I'll kill her!" Wetzon thumped through the apartment in her bare feet. *Why do I let her do this to me?* Shadowboxing, she KO'd Smith with a mighty right to the jaw and gave her—in the guise of a tufted hassock—a karate kick when she was down. The whirring noise of the phone off the hook in the bedroom stopped Wetzon from totally annihilating the helpless hassock.

Nursing sore toes, she hopped into the bedroom and replaced the receiver. At once the phone began to ring. She was absolutely pissed. She grabbed the phone and shrieked, "Just a minute!" Then got back into bed, pulling the phone with her and the covers over her head. She was angry with Smith, angry with Silvestri, angry with

Brian Middleton, who had had the nerve to get himself killed, angry with Rona and the pea-brained Penny Ann Boyd, angry about her apartment, angry about Alton's self-assurance, and angry with herself. What was happening in her life that she'd suddenly lost control? One thread unraveled—Silvestri—and her world had turned topsy-turvy. Hot tears stung her eyes, and she angrily wiped them away with the quilt.

She put the receiver to her ear and barked, "Who is this?"

"Wetzon? I'm sorry to bother you so late. This is Jerome Gordon." The voice was warm, full-bodied bourbon, laced with a shot of unfiltered cigarette. It rumbled in a friendly way.

"Jerome Gordon?" Who the hell was Jerome Gordon? What firm did he work for? Merrill, maybe. The name was vaguely familiar. How else would he have gotten her home number? "What can I do for you . . . Mr. Gordon?"

"Doctor. Call me Dr. Jerry, please," he said. "I suppose you're wondering who the hell I am and how I got your phone number."

"You suppose right."

"I'm a friend of Rona Middleton's and Penny Ann Boyd's. I was a friend of poor Brian's, too. They are in my group."

"Ah, the therapist."

"In a manner of speaking."

"What manner of speaking? Please get to the point, Dr. Gordon. I'm expecting a call." She saw that this "consulting" job Smith had taken on for them was getting more convoluted.

"Jerry."

"Jerry." She was not about to call him Dr. Jerry.

"The point, Wetzon, is that Rona would appreciate your not talking to the police until you talk to her."

"Fine. Put her on." She didn't understand why Rona needed this Jerry to do a preamble for her.

"I seem not to be making myself clear. Forgive me. I'm calling for Rona, who is *unable* to talk to you now."

"Why?"

"I am here with her at the Central Park Precinct. The police have invited her to come in and talk about Brian's murder."

18

·······

What did the police want with Rona at this time of night? Wetzon yawned, then reached over and turned out the light next to the bed. *And what do they want with me?* she wondered, yawning again. Whatever it was, it would wait till tomorrow, for sure.

She lay on her back under the quilt in the sponge position and meditated, feeling the beginning puffs of sleep creep over her limbs, moving slowly to her brain.

A siren clanged. God, where was she? Clanged again, but now the sound was recognizable. The telephone. It had sounded like a siren next to her head. Carlos. She was at Carlos's apartment, in his bed. She sat up, tight as a wire; the muscles in her back scrunched. Three more rings. She reached over and answered it.

"Detective Ferrante, Central Park Precinct, Ms. Wetzon. Is this a good time?"

"Is this a good time? You have to be kidding. You woke me out of the first sound sleep I've had since Friday night, Brian is dead, I got flooded out of my apartment, and I've had to move into a friend's place in the Village."

"I know," Ferrante said. "Your doorman told me."

"How helpful of him." She didn't even try to keep the sarcasm out. "What do you want?"

"Police business," Ferrante said, not reacting to her tone. "I'd like to come up."

"Now? Tonight? Can't it wait?"

"There's something I want to show you, Ms. Wetzon. It's important."

"Oh, all right." Why not just let all the shit hit her at once? She hung up and got out of bed. She'd have to get back into her clothes.

The downstairs buzzer rang.

What the hell? She shambled into the kitchen and pressed the intercom button. "Yes?"

"Detectives Ferrante and Martens," Ferrante's voice crackled.

"Oh, fuck," Wetzon said, not even bothering to cover the mouthpiece. He must have been downstairs when he called her. The hell with it. She tied her terry robe tighter and pressed the button to open the downstairs door. Almost immediately, she heard the elevator go into action, groaning its ascent.

She poured water into the coffee maker and measured coffee into the filter, then turned it on. Moments later when the doorbell rang, she let them in.

"Sorry to disturb you," Martens said, not looking sorry at all.

Ferrante let his eyes run over her robe down to her bare feet. He grunted and looked around the apartment. He was carrying an envelope.

The coffee maker burbled, filling the kitchen area with aroma. Martens's nostrils flared. He leaned against the wall.

Wetzon took three mugs from the shelf and set them on the table. "Sit down, please. What's so urgent it couldn't wait? And why not on the phone?"

"Are you alone?" Ferrante shifted his eyes toward Martens, who wandered casually into the living room and then on into the bedroom. Ferrante pulled out a chair and sat down, placing the envelope on the table. He studied her openly, and she felt he knew she was naked under the robe. She tightened the belt again.

"You should have asked me that before you came up." She poured coffee into the mugs. "Sure fellas," she said to the ceiling, "go ahead, have a look around."

Martens could be heard opening the bathroom door and the closets. She heard him open the window, checking the fire escape, no doubt, to see if someone was hiding there. "You ought to have a gate put on this window," he called.

"Thanks a lot."

"Do you own a gun, Ms. Wetzon?"

Her eyes skimmed back to Ferrante. "I . . . uh . . ." She thought of Silvestri's gun in the drawer under her panty hose. "No!"

It came out too precipitously, too explosively. He had to know she was hiding something. Well, technically it wasn't *her* gun, was it? "What are you guys up to?" Wetzon planted herself, hands on hips, in front of Ferrante as Martens returned and reclaimed his wall.

The phone on the butcher-block counter rang. She looked at it, at Ferrante, who didn't react, then walked over and answered it.

Rona said breathlessly, "Wetzon. Did Dr. Jerry reach you? They had me in for questioning. Do you believe it?" She sounded frightened. But why?

"He did, and I'd like to talk with you further about this, but I have someone here right now. I'll call you as soon as I can."

"Wetzon—"

Wetzon hung up, but not before Rona's shriek burst from the phone. It settled in the air between her and Ferrante. She shrugged.

"That Mrs. Middleton." Martens grinned. "She's one piece . . . of work."

"Ms. Wetzon—" Ferrante began.

The phone rang again. She smiled a phony apology and answered it. "Grand Central Station."

"Les? What kind of answer is that? Where have you been? I've been trying you all evening."

"Oh, God, Silvestri, what delicious timing." A slightly hysterical laugh burbled up into her throat.

"Are you all right?"

"As can be expected, what with a broker I was working with being murdered and my getting flooded out of the apartment. I'm in Carlos's loft on West Tenth Street."

"Jesus, Les, I don't understand why there's always turmoil." He sounded angry with her, as if it were her fault, and she felt her shaky composure collapse.

She pressed her lips together. "Look, there are two detectives here from New York's Finest, and they're asking me if I own a gun—"

He snapped, "Put one of them on. *Now.*"

She pointed the receiver at Ferrante and, when he got up and took it, dabbed at her eyes with a used tissue she'd dug out of the pocket of her robe. Martens left the wall and pushed a mug of coffee at her, and she slumped into a chair and sipped, elbows on the table.

Her gaze drifted to the material Ferrante had removed from the envelope. Glassine bags. Martens emptied them in front of her. A gold Rolex. A black billfold. A diamond tiepin. A gold pen. A gold chain. Her gaze slid back to the diamond tiepin. Brian had a diamond tiepin.

Ferrante hung up and came back to the table. "He said he'll call you in a half hour."

"Whoopie!" She stuck her index finger up in the air and twirled it. *And who cares,* she thought dully. He wasn't here when she needed him, so who cared anyway. And if he were here, he would yell at her and carry on as if it were something she did on purpose. Alton, she was sure, would never do that.

"You recognize this stuff, Ms. Wetzon?"

"The tiepin looks like one I saw Brian wearing."

"Yes. It's his billfold with his credit cards. The pen is his."

"That was pretty fast, wasn't it? Where'd you find them? In a pawnshop?"

"No. Try a trash basket not far from the murder scene."

"A trash basket?" she said slowly, turning that over in her mind. "Why would the mugger throw away stuff he could sell? Why take it in the first place, why kill for it?" She stared at Ferrante and then at Martens.

"Because it wasn't a mugging," Martens said, packing Brian's possessions back into their bags.

Ferrante looked at her expectantly. What was she supposed to say? She kept silent, waiting.

Finally he said, standing, "The killer was able to get right up close to him. A witness has come forward who saw a man arguing with a woman early that morning in the Conservatory Garden. We think Middleton knew his killer."

19

·······

"Wetzon, I'd like to hire him, but I can't. He writes small tickets. I can give him fifty percent for six months, but once that's done, he'll fall off our grid. It wouldn't be good for him or for us. So we're going to pass."

"Good-bye, Lee." She sighed and put down the phone.

"Now what?" Smith asked, strolling in carrying a slim leather briefcase. It was after ten, and she looked great. Wetzon, having had another almost sleepless night, hated her.

"Ozzie Haber. He has two thousand clients, each of whom buys a hundred shares at a time. His tickets range from seventy-five to a hundred dollars, if we're lucky, and at Rivington Ellis, to make grid the tickets have to be over a hundred. He'll end up working for nothing." She ran her eye down the first page of the client book and then turned it to the next. "Where am I going to send him?"

"To our new client." Smith was actually preening, she was that pleased with herself.

Wetzon sat up. "Music to my ears."

"I told you I was working on something big." Smith pulled out her chair and sat down.

"Oh, *moi* of little faith . . . Tell me."

"Ameribank is opening a freestanding brokerage network. They want to have at least three working branches in Manhattan, one each in White Plains, Garden City, and Huntington, and then national before the end of this decade."

"Ooh la, what a treat. So much for Glass-Steagall."

Smith opened the door to the reception area and called, "Boys, come in here and let's have a little meeting."

"Boys?" Wetzon began to laugh.

Smith waggled a finger at her as Max Orchard waddled into the room, squeaking on his thick gum soles. The waistband of his trousers was pulled up to his chest and hung there on suspenders, the pantlegs stopping at his ankles revealing sagging brown socks. There was a dab of dried shaving cream near his left earlobe.

"Max, *sweetie*," Smith gushed. "You always look so perfect."

Wetzon coughed behind her hand and walked to the windows that looked out on their garden. When she turned back to Smith, B.B. was standing behind Max.

"Max, B.B., we have a new client, Ameribank, and we're going to saturate the field for qualified candidates. With the repeal of the Glass-Steagall Act, banks are now legally able to compete with brokerage firms for retail business. Ideally, they want young bodies, asset gatherers, and brokers will be paid for assets under management with basis points. Clean U4s."

"U4s?" Max looked confused.

"You've heard us talk about this, Max. The broker's registration."

"Oh, right." He nodded. "That's what I thought."

Smith rolled her eyes at Wetzon. "May I continue? Thank you. We're looking for brokers who do business like certified financial planners. In fact, they will train and license every broker to be a CFP."

"And that's a terrific tool for us," Wetzon said. "Highlight it when you prospect. It's an expensive course if you're paying for it yourself."

"They're offering a twenty-five-k salary for the first year against a fifty-percent payout. Then the grid, which doesn't penalize for ticket size. They want to start interviewing next week."

"How do we get paid?" B.B. asked.

"Oh, for pity sakes." Smith threw Wetzon a look that said, *See, we're breeding another monster here.*

"I think it's a fair question, sugarplum," Wetzon said sweetly. "How *do* we get paid?"

"Humpf. Banks are so conservative, they hate to put money on the line before proof of service, so I couldn't get us anything based on trailing twelve months, I'm afraid."

Wetzon groaned. "Not another on-the-come client, please."

"Not quite. I got us a three-k down payment and six percent of months two to thirteen."

"Followed by six to twelve months of the-check-is-in-the-mail," Wetzon added.

B.B. snickered.

"Go on and laugh, B.B." Smith was furious. Her eyebrows came together and stayed that way. "Just remember, if we don't get paid, *you* don't get paid." Turning to Wetzon, she said, "As for you, *sugarplum*, they agreed to pay us within thirty days after first billing or tenpercent late charges are tacked on for each succeeding month that no payment is received."

"I'm impressed. Okay, fellas, let's smile and dial. I want to have at least ten good candidates lined up by the end of the week." Wetzon shooed them out of the office and closed the door. She smiled at Smith. "Partner mine, you're amazing."

"You should tell me that more often, sweetie," Smith said ruefully. "Sometimes I think you take me for granted." She leaned back against her desk. "And I wish you wouldn't involve the help in our finances. It's none of their business."

"Oh, come off it, Smith. They should know how we get paid so they don't think we're shortchanging them."

"That liberal democratic thinking was what lost us Harold, and now he's sitting over there with Tom Keegen stealing food from our children's mouths."

"Ye gads, Smith, let's not get carried away with this. They're not *our* brokers, they're anyone's brokers. The lists are available. It's relationships that count, that and who gets there first. We've been through this a hundred times."

Smith threw her hands up. "They're all whores, but let's not argue." She smiled a sleek feline smile. "I haven't even told you the best part. I've got us an exclusive for a year, and we have a deposit of nine k for good faith."

"I hope we get that in writing," Wetzon said.

Smith opened her briefcase and pulled out two typewritten pages. "Done."

"I think we probably take each other for granted," Wetzon said.

She sighed. "I'm sorry. I'm not in good shape." To her horror, she began sobbing.

Smith was at her in a flash and gathered her in. "What is it, sugar? The apartment? It'll be all right, you'll see. It'll be beautiful."

Wetzon pulled away and reached into her desk for some tissues. "It's not just the apartment. I feel as if I'm dancing on the wrong beat." She sank into her chair, her back to Smith.

"I'm taking you out to lunch, and you're going to tell me all about it."

"Maybe—"

The phone rang.

"Did you call Tony Maglia?" Smith asked.

"Yes. I made an appointment for after the close tomorrow. He thinks we're going to ask to work for him. I could tell. He was so full of himself."

"What a broccoli, a complete and total broccoli. Doesn't he know it's easier to pull people *out* of Bliss Norderman? Their stock is down to two and their capital rank is in the high three-figure zone."

The phone rang again. Stopped. Then the second line rang. Max opened the door. "Mark collect on two for you, Smith, and Joan Boley is on one for you, Wetzon."

"Joan Boley? When is she starting?" Smith snatched up the phone and pressed two. "Hold on for Mother, baby." She looked over at Wetzon.

"She told Fred she'd bring over her books to be copied tomorrow night."

"Good." Back to the phone, Smith trilled, "How's my darling boy?"

"Moving right along," Wetzon murmured. She blew her nose and blotted her face. "Hi, Joan. What's up? I thought you don't like to talk during market hours."

"Wetzon, I just wanted you to know that I've been to see Simpson, Milgram, and Quinn and I was impressed."

Wetzon felt her eyes cross. "SMQ? We work with them. Didn't you tell me you would only move as a sales manager? SMQ doesn't have any management positions open." And even if they did, Wetzon knew, they would never hire a woman to fill them.

"You're right, they don't. It was this other headhunter. He was such a pest. I told him not to call me, but he called and called every hour practically. I couldn't get rid of him, so to make him stop I said I'd go and talk to SMQ."

"I'm so proud of you, baby," Smith said into her phone.

"I guess I must have the wrong approach, Joan. You set up the rules, I followed them, and look what happens. May I ask who the other headhunter is? Maybe I should call him up and have him give me some pointers in recruiting."

"I wouldn't have told you, Wetzon, if I thought you'd take it like this. You're my friend."

Smith was making kissing noises into the phone.

"How do you expect me to take it?" Wetzon asked, brushing off the you-are-my-friend crap. She had no friends in the business. Except for Laura Lee.

"Don't worry, Wetzon. I'm not going. I just thought I should be honest with you. They made me a wonderful offer." Joan was trying to assuage her, but Wetzon wasn't assuageable. "Better than Fred's. They offered me a guaranteed salary for a year of four hundred thou."

"Upfront is better, because the money begins earning out for you right away. Besides, with Fred you'll have the additional four-teen-k salary as sales manager."

"Well, I still think SMQ's is a wonderful offer. . . ."

"But you're not taking it?"

"No. I'm going to go with Fred. I do want to be a sales manager, because sales managers at the major firms always get the privilege of handing out accounts and first choice on which to keep. The only thing is, Wetzon, I'm not sure I want to go this soon. I haven't been able to sell my condo in Brooklyn Heights, and I'm closing on the house in Westchester in two weeks. It's just too much pressure all at once. I'm sort of looking at Thanksgiving week."

"Moving home or business is always difficult, Joan, and I agree with you it would be better not to do both at the same time, but don't delay too long. I hear they're going to revise the deals in November. You want to get in the door before—"

"Fred assured me that even if they do, I'll be grandfathered in on the old deal, so long as I sit before the end of the year."

"Oh, really? Fred said he'd give you till the end of the year?" Wetzon repeated for Smith to hear.

Smith promptly gave Fred the finger in absentia.

"My, isn't Fred wonderful?" Wetzon said, but she was thinking, *Curse Fred, the schmuck.* If a broker doesn't make the move on the first momentum, he probably wouldn't later. It worked on the seize-the-day principle. If not for the broker, at least for the headhunter.

"I'll touch base with you later in the week, Joan. And if you decide you want to look at any other firm, just tell me. Please."

"Don't you want to know who the other headhunter is?" Joan asked.

"No," Wetzon said. She hung up and swiveled around. "You heard?"

"Enough. There's another headhunter involved?"

"Yup. I don't want to know who. I have enough on my plate right now."

"It's that dirtbag Keegen. He's getting in my face," Smith hissed. She was seething. Wetzon could almost see smoke coming out of her ears.

Their doorbell rang, then Max brought in a Federal Express envelope.

"What's this?" Smith took it and opened it, careful not to snag a nail. "Ah, look what we have here." She pulled out a book covered in gaudy purple suede. Across the front in gold script it said, "My Diary."

"Tabby talks," Wetzon said.

20
·······

"This is on me, sugar," Smith said, as if she had a big surprise for Wetzon. "Do you have the diary?"

"Yes. Where are we going?" Wetzon was feeling petulant. Sleeplessness always made her cranky.

"Don't snap my head off. It's not my fault," Smith said very agreeably.

"What's not your fault? Watch that car!" Smith was towing her across Forty-ninth Street against the light.

"Everything. Anything. Did you and Dick Tracy have a squabble? Is that what this is about?"

"I hate when you call him Dick Tracy. He has a name." Wetzon stopped in her tracks.

Smith smiled a syrupy smile. "It must have been some fight." She tugged on Wetzon's arm. "Why are we stopping here?"

"So I can genuflect in front of Steve Sondheim's house." Which Wetzon did, making a sweeping ballet bow to the sightless windows of the imperturbable town house.

A derelict in matted dreadlocks, picking cans out of a city refuse bin, stopped in midmotion. Then he began to applaud. "Way to go, bitchin' lady!" he yelled.

Across the street, a skinny-legged poodle on a leash barked its two cents at them. Its owner, a skinny-legged matron in a short, swingy dress, stopped to watch.

"Oh, for pity sakes. Let's go before he comes out and sees what a fool you are making of us."

"Are you kidding? He'd love it." A few paces farther, Wetzon tipped an imaginary derby and said, "Hi, Kate," to Kate Hepburn's town house. There was something symbolic, Wetzon thought, in the fact that these two admirable icons of show business lived on the same street and only half a block from Wetzon's office. It was, for her, a psychic connection to her past life in the theater. Having completed her obeisance, Wetzon said, "Okay, Smith, I'm all yours."

When they crossed Third Avenue and Smith walked them up Lexington, Wetzon knew where they were going. The Four Seasons was their favorite place in the City. They had put their firm together over drinks in the Bar Room. Smith entertained clients in the Pool Room, and developed new business in the Grill Room. And Wetzon interviewed brokers there.

All the same, Wetzon never saw the brown awning and the downstairs lobby without acutely remembering her discovery of Barry Stark's body in the phone booth almost four years earlier. She shivered and walked a little faster. "Let's go in through the building," she said.

Smith stopped and looked down at her. "You're not still—"

"Humor me."

"Oh, very well."

They went up the stairs and into the splendid lobby of the Seagram's Building, turned right, and walked into the restaurant level of the Four Seasons. On the wall in the corridor connecting the Pool Room and the Grill Room hung the magnificent Picasso stage curtain from the 1919 production of *The Three Cornered Hat.* This work of art never ceased to thrill them, and they stood for a moment feasting their eyes, and their souls.

It was twelve-thirty, power-lunch time in the Grill Room, where every day the room was packed with the movers and the shakers of New York City, from publishing moguls to politicians, heads of artists' agencies, chairmen of corporations, film producers, financial masters of the universe. Fashion designers. Architects. Writers. Labor leaders. The tops in each field. Wall Street to Dream Street.

The setting inside, which changed by the season, was now fall, and the decor was ruddy leaves on oak branches and chrysanthemums. The room had been spruced up; the old tufted brown Naugahyde upholstery was gone, replaced by dark-blue worsted, and the informal brown-and-black plaid carpet was now a patterned dark blue-and-rust. But the atmosphere was the same: the dynamic crackling energy of successful people who were regulars here for lunch.

They were greeted by name and ushered to a small table in the rear near the beaded metal curtains. Smith took the chair facing the room so she could see who was there, and immediately began to recite a who's who in New York to Wetzon.

"Lillet," Smith ordered when the waiter in the pumpkin-colored uniform of the fall season appeared.

"Perrier," Wetzon said.

"She'll have a nice glass of dry white wine, dear," Smith told the waiter. "Forget the Perrier, please."

"Ms. Wetzon?"

She waved her hand. "Oh, sure. Fine." It was not worth arguing about.

"Now let's talk about your love life."

"I have no love life, and I don't want to talk about it. Better we should talk about this business with Brian. If they think he was murdered by someone he knew, we may know that person, too."

"Could be Penny Poop was right about her daughter. That the pussycat had a rendezvous with him at the Conservatory Garden."

"Yes, but where would a sixteen-year-old get a gun? And why would she want to shoot Brian? Do you think they were having an affair and he was going to dump her?"

"Get that diary out and let's see."

Wetzon reached into her handbag and brought out the volume, opening it, just as their drinks were served. "I want the spa meal," Wetzon said.

"Make that two."

The inside cover of the diary was a graffiti of pierced hearts, peace signs, cutouts of photographs pasted every which way, including one of Tom Cruise flexing his muscles. "He doesn't have any hair on his chest," Wetzon said.

Smith sniffed. "Hair is disgusting." She sipped her Lillet.

"What do you know?" Wetzon retorted.

"Now, now." Smith reached for the diary. "Typical adolescent mind." She flipped through it, frowning. "What kind of nonsense is—"

"Let's see." Wetzon pulled the book to her, looked down at the page, and laughed. "Igpay atinlay." She flipped through a few more pages and laughed again. "It's all in pig latin."

"You read it, then. I don't have time for this."

Wetzon sighed and tucked the diary back in her purse. She'd get into it later. She took a sip of the wine and stared at Smith, whose eyes had widened, looking behind Wetzon. "Oh my," Smith said, smiling her phony smile. "Don't look now, but *he's* here."

"What?" Wetzon turned and looked out at the room and into the eyes of Alton Pinkus. Unnerved, she turned back to Smith.

"You looked. You're so gauche. I told you not to look." Smith produced one of her real dazzlers over Wetzon's shoulder, lots of teeth and all.

"Spare me. If you're finished being Miss Charming, can we talk about Tabby Ann?"

Their lunch was served. "That can wait. Tell me again what this Dr. Jerome what's-his-face said."

"That Rona was invited for questioning and that I shouldn't talk to the police before I spoke to her, but of course it was too late." Wetzon moved the Salisbury steak around on her plate listlessly.

"Too late?"

"Two detectives had come up and planted themselves in the apartment. That's when Rona called and I couldn't talk to her or let on she was on the phone. But they knew. Then the detectives showed me Brian's things that had turned up in a trash can near where he was killed and told me someone he knew did it because he was shot at close range and there was no sign of a struggle."

"Why didn't you tell me all that right away? You are really exasperating with your little secrets."

"Damn it all, Smith, you came in with your news about our new client and that was that."

"Well now, he's coming over. And look who he's got with him."

"Who?" She turned and saw Alton was heading toward them, accompanied by a tall, attractive young woman with shoulder-length dark hair.

"It's Sandra Semple," Smith breathed. She stuck out her hand.

"Leslie Wetzon, Xenia Smith," Alton said, shaking hands with each. "My daughter, Sandra Semple."

"Daughter! My dear, you don't look old enough to be Sandra's father," Smith gushed.

Wetzon put the toe of her shoe on Smith's and pressed hard. Smith pulled her foot away.

Alton looked pleased.

"Gotta go, Dad," Sandra said. Her voice had a kind of sexy croak. "Nice to meet you." She was wearing a long black double-breasted jacket over about four inches of mauve silk skirt, hose that matched the skirt, and slouchy black suede boots. She looked Wetzon over thoroughly, kissed her father on the cheek, then took her leave.

"Do have a seat, Alton," Smith said.

And he might have, but to Wetzon's relief, he was hailed by Si Newhouse and he excused himself. "I'll call you, Leslie," he said, taking her hand as Smith beamed at them.

When he was gone, Smith said, "You have my blessing, sweetie. He's a very attractive man. Why did I think he looked like an old frog? He really doesn't."

"Excuse me." The waiter was standing at their table with a telephone. "A call for you, Ms. Smith." He handed the phone to Smith and left.

Wetzon groaned. "Is this something you arranged? God, it's so humiliating."

Smith frowned at her. "Yes? Xenia Smith here. Oh? What time? Uh-huh. Thank you, Max, you're a *dear*." Pause. "Oh, really? That's too bad." She hung up and punched out some numbers. "Rona dear?"

Wetzon's mouth opened.

"Yes. Oh, well, I'm sorry to hear that. Okay. We'll be there." She put the phone down.

"What's going on?" Wetzon paused as the waiter returned and removed the phone. They were so efficient here.

"The market is down fifty. No volume."

"What was it this time?" The market had been edgy for weeks.

"There was a rumor that George Duckworth was going into Chapter 11. It's being denied vigorously."

"Damnation, do you know what that will do to the banks?" Duckworth was a real estate mogul, another regular at the Four Seasons, but it was common knowledge that he was overextended and cash poor, that he had paid top dollar for his properties and the recession had hit him hard. He was having trouble refinancing. The news made Wetzon reach for her wine. "What did Rona want?"

"She wants us to come to the Sussex House tomorrow at six."

"The Sussex House? How tacky."

Smith laughed. "My thought exactly. Dr. Jerome Gordon's suite. He probably looks like Max and smokes a cigar. Who else would stay at the Sussex House?"

"What's it about? Did she say?"

"Um." Smith was eating voraciously.

"Did she say?"

Smith nodded, swallowed, took a sip of her drink. "Penny Poop just confessed to Brian's murder."

21

·······

At four o'clock on Tuesday afternoon
Wetzon stepped off the elevator on the twenty-ninth floor of 1251
Sixth Avenue, where Bliss Norderman had its offices. She was familiar
with the building, because both Morgan Stanley and Oppenheimer
had offices there. She pushed the glass door open and entered a small
but plush reception area where a black leather sofa on metal legs and
two matching chairs sat on pale-cranberry carpeting. A receptionist
was ensconced in the windowless room at a large mahogany desk with
an appointment book laid out in front of her. The air conditioning
was on and the room was uncomfortably cool.

"Leslie Wetzon," Wetzon said. "I have an appointment at four
o'clock with Tony Maglia."

"Have a seat, please, Ms. Wetzon." The young woman picked up
the phone and pressed two digits as if she were playing the piano.
"Ms. Wetzon for Mr. Maglia." She pulled her syllables like Lily
Tomlin's Ernestine. In fact, Wetzon thought, stealing another look at
her, she even wore her hennaed hair rolled back from her face in a
'40s style and was decked out in one of Joan Crawford's old suits with
the huge shoulder pads. It was not unattractive. Wetzon wondered
idly if she was wearing the Joan Crawford backless fuck-me shoes.

"Wetzon." A rugged man in white shirt sleeves, gold cuff links,
his tight curly hair so black it looked dyed, held out his hand. He was
wearing suspenders on which gold coins were needlepointed. He
shook her hand enthusiastically. "Tony Maglia. Welcome to Bliss
Norderman."

He was short, of course, and pompous. Somehow it went together. He led her through what appeared to be an H-shaped layout to his corner office with a spectacular view of downtown Manhattan through a full wall of glass that was never meant to be opened. No wonder the air-conditioning stayed on.

"Very nice," she said, drawn to the panoramic view. But looking out, she felt both claustrophobic and acrophobic and came away dizzy, taking a seat in front of the pseudo-Chippendale desk.

A computer tipped slantwise on the right side of the desk, made little blipping noises.

Hank Cooperman, a broker Wetzon had known for years, stuck his head in the open doorway. "Excuse me, but would you sign these for me, Tony?" He handed a sheaf of papers to Maglia. "Both sets." While Maglia was delivering his lefty scrawl, Hank gave Wetzon a big wink. It wouldn't do to let his manager know he knew her, unless he felt secure enough to torture Maglia and not have it boomerang.

After Cooperman departed, Maglia leaned back in his chair. "I've been wondering when you and that snazzy partner of yours would get smart and want to work with us. We have the best story in town." His smile was militant, brandishing bonded teeth. He gave her smarmy charm; she gave him her card. She leaned forward in her chair; she was going to enjoy this.

"Much as we'd like to work with you, Tony, that's not why I'm here today."

"Really?" A tiny shaft of curiosity glimmered in his eyes and blended with hostility, which was already there. He put his feet on the desk, practically in Wetzon's face. "What's on your . . . mind, Wetzon?"

Snake, she thought. So it was going to be like that, was it? All right. She was game. She locked eyeballs with him and said, "Brian Middleton."

"Poor Brian. We'll miss him." He took a nail clipper out of a drawer and began clipping his nails. *Snap. Snap.* "What about Brian?" He didn't even look up.

Snap.

She wanted to say, *Listen, you dirtbag, you sleaze bucket, I don't have to put up with this from the likes of you*, but she wanted information, and the only way she was going to get it was by not letting him get to her. So she smiled.

Snap. Snap. Snap.

"I'm doing a favor for one of his clients, a Penny Ann Boyd."

Snap. Snap. He didn't look up, but she watched his jaw tighten. "That lying bitch. She made Brian and me crazy, and it cost us money. But we got her. Did she tell you? The whole idea was hers, the strategy, everything. Then she blames it on Brian. She got better than she deserved. And only because we never found the correspondence."

Snap. Snap. Slightly louder.

Wetzon leaned forward again. "What correspondence? I don't know anything about that, Tony."

Snap. Snap. "And you don't know anything about *me*, Wetzon. You cross me and I don't forget. I'm a good friend to my friends. I don't make a good enemy." *Snap. Snap.*

A sliver of nail sailed up over the desk and landed on Wetzon's lap. Smith was a hell of a lot faster in the nasty-retort department. Wetzon's style was slow burn. Smith would have put this scumbag in his place. And fast. "I don't follow you." She rose, and the nail clipping fell on the carpet.

Snap. Snap.

"I know you took Rona out of here, and I know you were working on Brian."

"How do you know that?"

"Brian told me. He told me everything. I was his adviser. We had a real good working relationship."

"Oh, and did he tell you he was going to start at Loeb Dawkins last Friday?"

Maglia laughed and put his clippers away. "Did he tell you that he changed his mind and was staying put?"

"No," she said. Was that true? Shock made her sit down.

He swung his feet to the floor, opened a drawer, and flung a document at her. "Go on, read it."

She ran her eyes over the paper. It was a contract in the form of a letter agreement. It offered a sixty-five-percent payout to Brian Middleton for one year, and it had been signed by both Brian and Maglia. The date was the previous Thursday.

She read it again and handed it back to Maglia.

"Close your mouth, Wetzon. You headhunters think you're so fucking smart, you can't stand it when you're outmaneuvered." He laughed a thin, snaky laugh, like a B-movie villain.

So Brian wasn't going to Loeb Dawkins after all. He'd been using that offer as leverage, screwing Simon Loveman and Smith and Wetzon. "Who's going to get his book, Tony? Surprise me."

"The manager, of course."

"Of course."

"You can fucking tell Rona not to count on getting anything out of this. I'm offering the clients free trades for six months."

"You're a class act, Tony."

"It's a small business, Wetzon. Someday we could be working together." He was laughing at her.

"I certainly look forward to it," she said, hoping her words were filled with venom. "You play a nice dirty game."

"Tsk, tsk," Maglia sneered. "You girls just don't make it in this business. You never will. We can outthink you every time."

Wetzon clenched her fist. She wanted to smash him one in his insolent face, but she hadn't asked the question she'd come to ask, and he was right. As the Street shrank, she really might have to work with him one day, or maybe Smith would, over Wetzon's dead body. "Tabitha Ann Boyd is missing. Do you know where she is?"

Maglia's eyes glinted at her. He suddenly got serious. "Why should I tell you?"

"Her mother is worried about her."

"Her mother!" It was an explosion. "What a joke! The woman is an alcoholic child abuser. My wife and I took Tabby Ann in after her mother threw her out."

"Her mother threw her out? I can't believe that." She couldn't believe the alcoholic and the child abuser labels either.

"Believe it, Wetzon. In the arbitration, Tabby Ann testified for Brian and against her mother."

22

·······

The Sussex House was not really the Sussex House anymore. It had been renamed the Park Royale. Out-of-towners and recent arrivals called it by its new name, but true-blue New Yorkers still called it the Sussex House, much as they stubbornly held on to Sixth Avenue instead of the ostentatious Avenue of the Americas. For years, the Sussex House had stood on Central Park South, its seedy splendor a throwback to more elegant days.

Having been acquired by a Japanese company in the mid-'80s, it was royally renamed, its exterior sandblasted, the interior refurbished. A three-star restaurant serving haute cuisine in the French manner replaced a spotty, vaguely continental kitchen.

Many of the longtime residents on the three upper floors, which were condos, who had bought their suites years earlier, took attractive offers from the new management and sold. The suites had then been renovated and resold.

It was in one of these suites that Dr. Jerry Gordon had an office.

Wetzon walked briskly into the rear lobby from the Fifty-eighth Street entrance, passing a series of leather chairs and coffee tables. Not seeing Smith, she settled herself on the last available leather chair, partially hidden by a column. She was early, which was good, because she needed time to think. And for thinking she needed brain food. Out came the remnants of a dark-chocolate Lindt bar. She bit off a chunk and wrapped the rest in its cover, replacing it in her briefcase.

She let it melt in her mouth. Chewing destroyed the wonder of it. Now she could try to pick her way through the confusion of events since Brian's murder.

Even if what Tony Maglia had told her about Penny Ann Boyd and her daughter was true, Wetzon still had trouble understanding why they had come to Smith and Wetzon for help, and furthermore, why Smith and Wetzon were helping. This was between mother and daughter and had nothing whatever to do with the expertise Smith and Wetzon had in the brokerage business. So what was it? Smith's greed had once again gotten them involved. But why them?

Now, a tragic, but simple, case of murder during a mugging had turned into first-degree murder and by someone Brian knew, and mousy Penny Ann Boyd ups and confesses she done it. Just like that. When they'd met her, hadn't Penny Ann said she was worried that her daughter was involved? Or could it be she had been more worried about herself?

There was a missing piece here somewhere.

Wetzon looked at her watch. Twenty of six. She took the diary out of her bag. She'd fallen asleep over it when she'd tried to read it the night before. Now she tried again, starting at the beginning, mentally translating as she went along. It began, it seemed, just after the father's death and was not a daily record. Wetzon read about ten pages of tiny scrunched-up script that was so full of raw pain and confusion, she felt like a voyeur. The first reference to Penny Ann's drinking problem popped up on page twelve. On page thirteen, Tabby mentioned talking to the family therapist, referred to as Octorday Erryjay, about it.

"Octorday Erryjay," she said out loud.

"Ah, there you are." Smith had burst through the revolving door and was bearing down on her. Wetzon checked the time. Ten after six. Late as usual.

Tucking the diary away again, she rose to meet Smith, who, flushed and beautiful, was turning heads in her wake. Ah, to be tall, Wetzon thought enviously. To have just two or three more inches in the leg. "What floor are we going to?"

"I don't know. We'll ask at the desk."

The desk clerk looked like Mick Jagger, but his accent was a vowelly Aussie. "Nineteen E," he said.

"How did it go?" Smith asked as they headed for the private

elevators reserved for the condo owners. Hotel guests had separate, public elevators.

"He's a pig."

"They're all pigs."

"No, Maglia gives pigs a bad name. I wouldn't tar them all with the same brush. I hope we never have to work with him. He clipped his nails the whole time I was there."

"He what?"

Wetzon mimed the act, making snapping motions with her fingers.

"Disgusting. Does he have her?"

"I think so. He claims Penny Ann is a drunk and a child abuser. What do you think?"

"Nothing would surprise me. Passive aggressive." Smith pursed her lips, thinking. "Definitely."

"He also told me that Tabby Ann testified against her mother in the arbitration."

"Oh ho!" Smith ran the tip of her tongue between her teeth. "I love it!"

"And he says the only reason she got anything out of the settlement is that the correspondence file that would have proved Brian innocent is missing. He claims that all the bad strategies and choices were Penny Ann's."

"I find that pretty hard to believe."

They got out of the elevator and walked down a hall carpeted in gold fleur-de-lis on a navy field. Walls were in muted gold-on-gold striped paper.

"Tasteful," Smith said, wrinkling her nose.

"Let's not get carried away. Here it is. Ready?"

Smith fluffed her hair and opened the top button of her silk shirt. A bit of lace camisole peaked through the opening. "Go."

"Is that really necessary?"

"You get information your way, I'll get it my way. They never expect us to be very smart, so they spill everything. My way is more efficient, because if you get 'em by the balls, they don't know what hit 'em."

"I'll try to remember those sage words. I'm sure they would make Gloria Steinem proud." Wetzon rang the bell.

A huge, blue-eyed, blond-haired teddy bear in a brown blazer and tan trousers opened the door. "Welcome. Wetzon, right?" He said it to Smith, instantly captivated.

"No," Wetzon said. Smith was running true to form.

"Xenia Smith, Dr. Gordon," Smith said, giving him her hand.

"Oh, please call me Dr. Jerry. Everyone does."

He was taller than Smith by three or four inches, which put him over six feet, and broad and hulking as a bear. His hair was crinkly curly with just the right white streaks at the temples, and his face was round and jovial, his smile framed by deep dimples. He exuded warmth and kindness and modest charm, all of which somehow went with the suede patches on the elbows of his jacket.

"I'm sure Brian must have told you all about me," Jerome Gordon said to Wetzon.

"Absolutely everything," Smith answered with a flirtatious wink before Wetzon had a chance to.

The living room was a waiting room, done in hotel Louis XV. An exhausted-looking Rona, her shoulders high and tense, was standing near the windows sipping a glass of red wine. She wore a black knit dress, a black-and-pink plaid jacket, and a sullen look on her drawn face.

Barbara Gordon came through the swinging door from the kitchen carrying a cheese board containing a wedge of brie and a roll of water biscuits. She was in black again, a short pleated skirt, opaque hose, and a long sweater with sequined collar and cuffs. She looked like an adorable French maid, or the star of a porno film. She sat down on the couch and crossed her legs.

"I hope we haven't kept you waiting," Wetzon said, and received a glare from Smith, whose motto was Never Apologize.

Rona said angrily, "That shit Maglia gave my clients—Brian's clients—six months free commissions to stay at Bliss Norderman."

"I heard."

"You heard? Who told you?"

"He did. He was thrilled with himself. I thought you and Brian and Tony and his wife were still friends."

Rona snorted. "There's no friendship in this business. You see money in front of your face, you grab it. You'd have to be crazy not to."

"Absolutely," Smith agreed.

God, Wetzon thought, ten years ago that sentiment would come from the men, never from the women. Affirmative action had taken hold in the wrong places. Women could be just as disgusting about money as men, sometimes more. And she had a partner who was not an exception. Wetzon sat down on the blue damask sofa and propped her briefcase under a round table next to it. On the table were a porcelain urn-lamp and half a dozen photographs of children in silver frames and at different ages. A boy and a girl, both with tousled red curls, and Barbie, looking not much older than the children. The boy had the deep dimples of his father, as well as his bulk.

Smith sauntered over and picked up one of the photographs. "A beautiful family," she gushed.

Barbie smiled, but it wasn't warm. She seemed not to like Smith, which was refreshing. Most people were completely bewitched by Smith, at least from the first meeting.

"Thank you. I think so, too," Dr. Jerry said, pride in his voice. "Our son Aaron will be bar mitzvahed in a few weeks."

"Where's Penny Ann?" Wetzon moved to head off Smith, who had a peculiar look on her face.

"We're arranging bail. She should be here any minute." He picked up a bottle of red wine from the coffee table. "I'll get some glasses."

"Not for me, thanks," Wetzon said.

"I'll have a glass, darling," Barbie said sweetly.

Jerry gave her a sharp look. He poured a glass for Smith and handed it to her. "I feel terrible about this. I've let Penny Ann down."

"Oh, Jerry, good heavens." Rona rushed over and put her hand on his face, stroking it. "You've been absolutely wonderful to her, to all of us." To Smith and Wetzon, she said, "He took a second mortgage on his house to pay her lawyer in the arbitration."

Barbie got up and went into the kitchen. The door whooshed back and forth. She returned with a glass of what looked like Coke.

Jerry watched his wife uneasily out of the corner of his eye. "Shh, Rona—"

"Don't shush me, Jerry. He's done everything for her since Wilson died, and now look how she repays him." She poured herself more wine and sat down next to Wetzon on the sofa.

"Aw, Rona, come on. You've all been my friends, not just my clients. And I know for certain she didn't kill Brian."

"Really? How would you know that, Jerry?" Smith asked.

"I know, trust me." The sincerity in his voice was real. It was the phrase that niggled at Wetzon. "Trust me" was code for "fuck you" in brokerese. Okay, so what? Hadn't she just told Smith not to tar everyone?

"Penny Ann confessed because she thinks Tabby Ann did it. Did the diary come?" Rona's mascara had left a dark ring under her eyes.

"Yes, today." Wetzon patted her briefcase. "I've only glanced through it."

"What diary?" Dr. Jerry asked. He was uncorking another bottle of wine. "Are you sure I can't get you something, Wetzon?"

"No, thank you."

"Tabby had a diary, Jerry. Didn't Penny Ann tell you?"

"No. But she's had so much on her mind. . . ." He frowned. He was having trouble getting the cork out. His thick, stubby fingers were working too hard. "So what did you think, Wetzon?"

"I need more time. It's written in pig latin."

Dr. Jerry laughed. "Children have wonderful imaginations."

"As do adults." Barbie waggled her finger at her husband.

"She's sixteen," Rona said.

"Still a child." The cork came out crumbled, but he smiled. "You'll forgive a little cork?"

"Of course," Smith said, graciously, giving Wetzon a withering look that said, *No class.*

"Tabby Ann couldn't have killed Brian. I know her too well," Dr. Jerry said. "The child's like another daughter to me and Barbie, isn't she, dear? She's not capable of taking a life, even Brian's."

"What do you mean, 'even Brian's'?" Rona said sharply. "Tabby told me that Brian had seduced her."

"Brian was my oldest, closest friend, Rona. You know that. If not for Brian, you and I would never have met, right?" He had a soothing voice. The dimples flashed.

Rona nodded and did a slow melt, as if he'd embraced her, but then he had, with his voice. It was more paternal than sexual, like daughter and Big Daddy, though they were probably the same age.

Barbie sipped her drink. Her eyes were closed and she seemed to nod off, then came awake and sat up as if she'd remembered something important. "Oh, gee." She looked at her watch. "I'm late. I have to go." She didn't sound too unhappy about it. She picked up her leather jacket from the closet doorknob and fled without saying good-bye.

They all stared at the door. Jerry shrugged. "The baby-sitter has to go home." He shifted his attention back to Smith and Wetzon. "Now I'm going to tell these nice ladies what I know, and they're going to help us get Penny Ann's name cleared. Okay?"

"Why don't you tell us why Tabitha testified against her mother at the arbitration?" Wetzon suggested.

Smith sat down in a club chair and watched the reactions.

Rona gasped.

"Oh, you know? Well, that's what I mean. Brian used that poor child. He claimed that the choices of stock-index futures and strategies were Penny Ann's, but of course, there was no real evidence except his word against hers until the child came forward." He lowered himself into one of the fragile Louis bergieres. Wetzon held her breath, waiting for it to collapse, but it didn't. "She worked for Brian over the summer, running errands, doing mailings to his clients."

"She was taking acting lessons," Rona said.

"She's quite a little actress." Dr. Jerry winked at Smith and Wetzon.

"I'll bet." Smith crossed her legs, showing an expanse of attractive thigh.

Dr. Jerry was enthralled by Smith's thighs. "She's been depressed since her father died. You know how adolescents are. She imagined everything, and it became real. There was nothing between Tabitha and Brian. She had trouble recognizing what was true and what wasn't."

"I don't believe it, Jerry. She was pretty convincing."

"Rona, you and I both know she was obsessed with him. She wouldn't leave him alone. She followed him around. She was driving him crazy."

"Are you saying Tabitha Ann is pathological?" Smith crossed her legs in the opposite direction.

"I had them both up here Thursday night. I thought I could help her cut through to reality."

"The poor kid," Rona said. "What happened?"

"Nothing."

"Come on, something must have happened," Smith said. "What

did she say?" She narrowed her eyes, finger to her nose. "Did you tape the session?"

Dr. Jerry blanched. "How would you know about that?"

"Good thinking, partner," Wetzon said.

"I know a lot of therapists who do," Smith said placidly. "Where is the tape?"

"I destroyed it."

"You—tape—our—sessions, Jerry?" Rona was weighing each word carefully. She didn't sound happy.

"It's standard procedure, dear," Smith said.

"I'm not talking to you, Smith. Stay out of this. Jerry?"

Jerry dimpled and looked embarrassed. "Rona, she's right. It is standard procedure—"

Rona cut him off. "We'll talk about this in private, if you don't mind."

"Let's stick with Tabitha's tape, please," Wetzon interceded. "What did she say on it that made you destroy it? Or was it something Brian said?"

The doctor sighed. "What I'm going to tell you is confidential. Can I trust that you will not repeat it to anyone?"

"Of course," Smith vowed. Somehow she managed to look like Joan of Arc, palms together piously under her chin.

"Agreed." Wetzon wondered if detectives worked the way lawyers and the confessional did. What a client told you could never be repeated. One thing for sure, Smith had no such compunctions.

Jerry looked unhappy. He rose, and the chair rose with him; he peeled it off and set it back on the floor. "Brian told Tabby Ann there was nothing between them. She took it very badly."

"What did she say?" Smith insisted.

Reluctantly, he said, "She didn't mean it." His kindly eyes were miserable.

"Oh, for pity sakes!" Smith threw up her hands.

"She said, 'I'll kill you for this.' "

23

·······

"Nonsense!" Rona exclaimed. "She didn't mean it."

"I understand," Wetzon said, without reservation, "that Penny Ann has a drinking problem."

Rona's eyes flew to Dr. Jerry.

"I've been counseling her," Dr. Jerry admitted.

"Did she abuse her daughter?"

"Wetzon, what is this?" Rona demanded.

Jerry held up his hand. "Have you seen Tabitha? Did *she* tell you that?"

Wetzon shook her head. "No. Tony Maglia told me. I think she's with the Maglias."

"Jerry—" Rona hesitated. "We should tell them."

"Keeping secrets from us?" Smith said, a sharp sting in her voice. "We're only working extremely hard on your behalf—"

The doorbell rang.

Surprisingly graceful for so big a man, Dr. Jerry Gordon moved with swift giant steps. He opened the door and held out his arms to Penny Ann, who fell into them. Behind Penny Ann was someone Wetzon recognized instantly from television interviews, magazine profiles, and newspaper coverage of his trials. Richard Hartmann was a criminal lawyer of the blame-the-victim school and the media's darling because his clients were usually notorious drug dealers, mafia dons, and uncommon murderers. A consummate performer, he was rumored to have a major PR firm on his payroll.

"Richard, come in. You know Rona Middleton. This is Xenia

Smith and Leslie Wetzon." Jerry was petting Penny Ann's head, gradually moving her into the room. Big Daddy again, Wetzon thought.

"I'm Xenia Smith." Simple words, but coming from Smith it oozed seduction.

"Dick Hartmann." Hartmann shook Smith's hand, then Wetzon's. "Ms. Wetzon." He was looking over her shoulder, but she saw it was not intentional. There was something wrong with one of his eyes. "Jerry, she's in your hands. I promised the judge she wouldn't leave the city."

"She can stay here. The sofa opens up. How about it, my dear? Hotel service and everything."

"Dr. Jerry, you're so good to me," Penny Ann sniffled. "What would I do without you?" Her eyeglasses were askew, and her hair hung in straggles. She wore sensible pumps, a camel sweater set, brown plaid skirt, and pearls. She swayed, and Dr. Jerry caught her.

Her glasses tumbled to the floor near Wetzon, who picked them up, held them, then looked through them. Major blur.

Dr. Jerry carried her out of the room, down a short hall and into another room. Wetzon followed with the eyeglasses. His consulting room was still more hotel French Louis, a desk, a brown leather chair, and analyst's couch. On the wall behind the desk was an acre of framed diplomas and certificates. Jerry settled Penny Ann carefully on the chaise, straightened her clothes, and took off her shoes. She moaned. "Poor thing," he said.

"Her glasses." Wetzon handed them to him.

He set them on a side table where a Chinese porcelain lamp gave off a faint rosy light. "Thank you, Wetzon. Would you stay with her for a few minutes? I'll get her a cup of tea." He patted Wetzon's shoulder and left without waiting for a reply.

Oh, well, Wetzon thought. She walked to the windows and looked out at a clutter of office buildings. Night was falling rapidly. It was after seven. At eight, she was meeting Laura Lee at her wrecked apartment. This Louie friend of Carlos's was going to talk to Wetzon about the renovation.

She closed the blinds and shivered. There was a chill in the air. The figure on the chaise didn't move. Had Penny Ann murdered Brian? She had a motive, a double, if one could accept that Tabby Ann was having an affair with him. But then, Tabitha also had a motive, and so did Rona, who also had more than one reason to wish to see her husband dead.

Could Tabitha Ann get a gun somehow, point it at someone, and shoot him? Although she didn't know the girl, Wetzon found it hard to believe.

Penny Ann's face was dead white against the brown leather of the chaise. Some people led such tragic lives, Wetzon thought. She had no right to complain about her apartment or her love life.

In the living room Wetzon could hear Hartmann holding forth. She stood in the doorway listening. He was telling war stories, trying to impress Smith no doubt, and she could hear Smith's phony tinkling laugh. What the hell, she and Smith had been good together just now—real teamwork. She smiled.

Rona came down the hall and passed her. "Do you believe that shit heap of testosterone? God, I hate men."

"Will you be all right, Rona? I mean about what Maglia is doing with the accounts."

Rona's smile was derisive. "Wetzon, I'm a survivor. Don't you know that?" She continued down the hall and closed the bathroom door behind her.

Wetzon slipped back into the consulting room. What was keeping Jerry? She could hear his rich rumble from the living room and Smith's responding laugh.

A strange sound came from the chaise. Penny Ann was trembling violently. Wetzon looked around quickly. She threw open a door. A closet full of bulging garment bags. On a shelf was a folded-up blue blanket. She stood on tiptoe and pulled the blue blanket down. A large round hatbox thudded to the floor, upside down.

Dropping the blanket, she righted the hatbox, and as she did so, the cover came off. There was no hat. It was chock full of papers and letters. The shivering sound came again, and she hurriedly replaced the lid and shoved the box back on its shelf in the closet. She leaned over Penny Ann and covered her with the blanket from neck to foot, tucking her in.

Penny Ann's eyes popped open suddenly and darted back and forth around the room, coming to rest on Wetzon. "Wetzon," she whispered. Her voice was so soft that Wetzon bent closer to hear. "I begged him to leave Tabby alone." She clutched Wetzon's hand through the blanket. "I said I'd kill him, and he laughed at me. He said I'd already gotten away with murder. He wanted the papers—"

Wetzon bent closer, her eyes straying to the closet. "What papers?" Penny Ann let go of Wetzon's hand.

"How is she?" Dr. Jerry was standing in the doorway holding a teacup and saucer. A geyser of steam swirled up from the cup.

Wetzon looked back at Penny Ann. Her eyes were closed.

24

·······

The only person in the lobby of Wetzon's building on West Eighty-sixth Street besides Harry, the doorman, was a real estate broker named Nancy Strohl. Nancy had owned the apartment across the hall from Wetzon, but had sold it two years earlier. Because she was so well liked, she managed to get listings in the building.

"Hi, Leslie. I hear you had a flood." Nancy was sitting, legs crossed, on the brown club chair that had appeared, with three mates, after the lobby was redecorated last month. Wetzon had never seen Nancy in other than tailored pants and a silk shirt, or a bulky hand-knit sweater. Today she was wearing the bulky hand-knit sweater in an oatmeal color.

"Bad news travels fast. How've you been, Nancy? Who's selling?"

"Three B and ten D. Business could be better, though. I have plenty of buyers, but the sellers don't realize they have to lower their prices. How's your business?"

"Recruiting is slow. Consulting is active." Wetzon looked at Harry. "Has anyone been here tonight looking for me?"

"A lady. She said she'd be back."

"Must be Laura Lee. I'm going up." She said to Nancy, "I'm expecting a contractor who's going to give me the bad news."

"Hello, Louie." Nancy spoke to someone behind Wetzon.

Wetzon turned. Louie was a woman, older than Wetzon, but not by much. Taller. Wasn't everyone? Louie wore jeans and a red sweater and combat boots; a big canvas bag hung solidly on her shoulder. She was ruddy-complected, her hair brick-red and cut to just below her chin. Freckles decorated her face, in the nicest way.

"Don't tell me you're going to work with Leslie? That's wonderful. Leslie, Louie is just terrific. She gets things done."

"I'm glad to hear that."

"You're Birdie?" Louie asked, shaking her hand firmly.

"Only to Carlos, who's got nicknames for everyone, in case you haven't noticed. Please call me Leslie, or Wetzon." She shoved her rubber-banded package of mail into her briefcase. To Harry, she said, "I'm expecting Ms. Day. Send her right up."

In the elevator, Louie asked, "Carlos says you're going to want the works?"

"I guess. It's pretty awful," Wetzon said. "I don't know if Carlos gave you the details—"

"Just flooding, right?" Louie took a flat leather portfolio from the canvas bag, balancing everything easily, and opened it to a yellow legal pad.

"Just?" They got off on twelve.

She grinned at Wetzon. "What I meant was, no fire. Fire *and* water, that's the worst."

"Right, no fire." Wetzon unlocked her door and pushed it open. Mildew mixed with something more. Mold? Rot? "Yuk." And it was freezing cold. Carlos's Hazels had left all the windows open to air out the place, so the stench could have been worse. She left the door ajar for Laura Lee, and turned the lights on in the foyer and the kitchen. "I don't know about the other lights because of the water damage."

"S'okay. I can get an overall picture." Louie pulled a wide-mouthed flashlight from the huge canvas shoulder bag and bent to examine the buckled floor in the dining room, then sent the torchlight about the room, past the barre, focusing on the remains of her ceiling. "Dancer, huh?"

"Used to be. Now I'm a headhunter."

Louie's eyes flicked over Wetzon's pinstripe uniform. "Let's see the rest."

Wetzon followed Louie down the hall and waited. "Pretty bad, huh?" She couldn't look at her bedroom.

Louie grunted and made some notes on her pad, seemingly able to see in the dark.

"The bathroom, too." The light danced across the caved-in ceiling and around the small room. If possible, it looked worse than it had on Sunday, in daylight.

"Hi, y'all," Laura Lee called.

"Wait there, Laura Lee. It's an obstacle course." Wetzon looked at Louie, trying to see her expression. "Pretty bad, don't you think?"

"I've seen worse." Louie stepped out of the bathroom and made some notes on her legal pad, surefooted as a mountain goat in her combat boots. Wetzon in her dressed-for-business pumps tottered along behind her.

"Oh, Lordy," Laura Lee said, her voice closer.

"Don't come further, Laura Lee. It's too depressing."

"I'll get a written estimate and proposal to you in a few days." Louie was giving the living room a tour with her big flashlight.

"Laura Lee Day, Louie . . . ?"

"Armstrong. Where do you want me to send it?"

"Louie Armstrong?" Laura Lee giggled.

Louie smiled. "Thanks. No one ever mentions it anymore. Makes me feel old."

"Behave yourself, Laura Lee." Wetzon and Louie exchanged cards. They stepped out of the apartment and waited while Wetzon made sure the lights were out. The door locked, Wetzon handed the keys to Louie. "You might as well have them. I have another set in the office." She glanced at the card in her hand: LOUISE ARMSTRONG, CONTRACTOR, INTERIORS. She had the same address as Carlos—West Tenth Street.

"Oh, you're in Carlos's building. I'm staying in his apartment."

"I'm just below you, then. Good. I can call you and hand-deliver my proposal. If we agree, we can move a little faster." They shook hands on it.

"Give me as much detail as you can, because I have to get board approval for renovations."

In the lobby Wetzon asked Harry to keep collecting her mail. "I'll come up for it a couple of times a week."

"Poor darlin', you look so put-upon," Laura Lee said. She was looking especially chic in kicky black silk pleats, a red silk T, and a longish black and red paisley jacket. "Let's go get a blue plate special at EJ's and I'll tell you what happened to me today." She tucked Wetzon's arm into hers and they walked out on the street. The air was cold, with a raw bite to it. October.

"Where did you say we're going?"

"A great place right here on Amsterdam. EJ's. It's diner-type food, good and cheap."

"And what happened to you today?"

"I was walkin' home on Broadway, mindin' my own business, I might add, and this wino with a shoppin' cart pulled over to me while I was waitin' for the light to change, and would you believe he starts screamin', 'Everybody, look here, it's Kim Novak. It's a *real* movie star.' "

Wetzon started laughing. "Kim Novak?"

"You haven't heard the rest, darlin'. A crowd started formin', and this lunatic starts interviewin' the crowd about what they think, do I or don't I look like Kim Novak. I couldn't believe it was happenin', and I almost walked right out in front of a bus to get away from him. Finally, this nice man in an Armani suit, carryin' an attaché, took pity on me and he said, 'I don't think she's Kim Novak, but she's really cute.' And I kept duckin' my head and thinkin', 'God, I've been really good. Please get me out of this.' "

"You should have said, 'Actually, I'm Tippi Hedren.' "

Laura Lee stopped in her tracks, looked at Wetzon, and they both howled. The Dominican domino players who hung out on the street, talking and drinking, saluted them with beer cans. A radio played salsa loud. Children who should have been in bed played tag while the mothers sat on the stoops gossiping. They were a raucous bunch, but not threatening. They were all that remained of a much larger Hispanic community that had been nudged out by the new buildings and gentrification.

A kosher pizzeria and falafel restaurant had opened on the corner of Eighty-fourth Street, and now klezmer mingled with salsa.

"There now, darlin'," Laura Lee said after the steaming bowls of onion soup were set in front of them. "Spill the beans. Tell me everythin', and I mean *everythin'.*"

"I can't. I'll just be whining, and I hate that." Wetzon filled her spoon with soup and lifted it to her mouth, blowing on it gently.

"You want to talk whinin'? I'm an expert. You should hear these men on the Street whine about the market. I mean, what *are* they doin'? Just today John Applegate called me from Charleston and went on and on. You remember him—he's with Shearson now. May I tell you his picture appears next to 'whine' in the dictionary. I wanted to say to him, 'Take me off your speed dial, sweetheart.' So you go on, Wetzon, and whine to your friend. What else are friends for?" She swallowed a spoonful of soup and her face lit up. "Is your guy still away?"

Wetzon nodded. "That's part of it, I guess. I can't even get him on the phone. We play telephone tag for days, and then we have these terse, awful conversations." She stared into her soup and poked at the gobs of melted cheese with her spoon, had a taste, set her spoon down. "This is heavenly."

"Didn't I tell you?" Laura Lee had a glow about her, an incandescence, a spontaneity. Physically, she was Wetzon's size, but with slightly rounder edges, short dark hair in a big fluff around her face. She still played the violin seriously with a chamber group two nights a week and managed a number of very sophisticated portfolios at Oppenheimer. Life, for Laura Lee, was a continuous adventure. She threw herself into it with an energy and a joie that Wetzon envied.

"About Silvestri . . . I guess I got attached."

"Well, of course you did." Laura Lee broke off a chunk of bread and wiped up the remnants of the soup from her bowl. "What would you have said if he'd asked you to marry him before he left?"

"Oh, Laura Lee, he wasn't going to the Middle East, he was only going to Virginia." She wrinkled her forehead. "I don't know what I would have said. Maybe, yes. But I don't know. I'm confused about everything." Watching Laura Lee, she said, "And now I've met someone else."

"Uh-oh." Laura Lee grinned at her.

"He's older. Established."

"How old?"

"Don't look so thrilled. It's making me sick. He's in his fifties. A widower. Grown children. High profile in the City." Her voice caught in her throat. "What am I going to do, Laura Lee? I want to be honest. Do I tell Silvestri?"

"You absolutely do not, darlin'. Are you mad? He's not around anyway, so what's he goin' to be able to do? Let it work itself through. Things happen because they're supposed to happen. If it's goin' to be Silvestri, believe me, it will be Silvestri. Now are you goin' to tell me who this other man is?"

"Alton Pinkus." Wetzon concentrated on the huge blue plate of meatless chili in front of her.

"Ah. Interestin' man."

"Do you know him?"

"I know his daughter. She's a client."

"I'm in such a muddle."

"Go with it, darlin'. What else have you got?"

"Besides that? My apartment is a mess. God knows when I'll be able to move back. It's going to take time for the insurance to come through, so I'm going to have to lay out a ton of money. Business isn't great. And Smith has us involved in investigating Brian Middleton's death."

"For money?"

"Well, of course, Laura Lee. We are talking about Smith, aren't we?"

"How could I ask? She's a real winner, your partner is."

"It now seems that his murder was not a mugging. They found his wallet and jewelry in a park trash can. And he was shot at close range. They think it may have been someone he knew. Revenge or something having to do with the arbitration."

"Really, now? I was wonderin' when clients would start killin' off their brokers. Not a minute too soon for some of them. Wetzon, you can't believe the slime that some of these firms hire from each other. They're givin' my profession a bad name. And Brian—well, I told you my feelin' about him."

"Yes, but he won the arbitration except for the two small annuities that the client was awarded. Brian claimed that the stock-index options and highly speculative OTC stocks he put her in were all her idea. And that couldn't be verified. All they were able to come up with at Bliss Norderman was the paper the client signed allowing Brian discretion. Supposedly, correspondence was missing from Bliss Norderman's files." A little bell suddenly went off in the back of Wetzon's head.

"I'll bet you anythin' that Bliss was makin' Brian pick up the tab for the annuities and would have held up his license so he couldn't move until he paid up."

"Tabitha," Wetzon said.

"Tabitha?" Laura Lee snapped her fingers at Wetzon. "Where are you, darlin'? Who is Tabitha?"

"She's sixteen years old and the daughter of the client who sued. She worked for Brian in the summer. She was feuding with her mother, and Brian even got her to testify against her mother in the arbitration."

"What did I tell you about that Brian? And considerin' how laxly brokerage offices are run—"

"Laura Lee, wait a minute. Tabitha had access. *She* could have removed the papers."

25

•••••••

It was almost ten o'clock when Wetzon got out of the cab on West Tenth Street, and she was beat. She was putting the key into the outside lock when she heard a car door slam behind her. Sneaking a look over her shoulder, she saw Detectives Ferrante and Martens crossing the street toward her. Martens was wearing a suit and a tie and a snappy gray fedora.

"Oh, come on, guys. What's going on? I feel as if you're hounding me." She shouldered the door open, and the men followed her to the elevator. "Sure, old pals," she said. "Why not come up and have a cup of coffee."

"Don't mind if we do," Ferrante said.

The loft was warm and getting less and less alien. Wetzon put up the coffee. "Make yourselves comfortable," she said, dropping her handbag and briefcase on the kitchen counter. "I want to check my messages."

In the bedroom, drained, she sat on the edge of the bed for a few minutes, took off her shoes, and flexed her toes. There were four messages on the machine.

Carlos: *I'm off to La-La-Land, pet, for a few days of sitting around the pool at the Beverly Hills Hotel and looking famous. Hope everything went well with Louie.*

Silvestri: *Call me, please.* Cold, gruff. Not a happy camper. She wrote the number down again, could never remember it. Freudian, she thought.

Smith: *Don't call me, please. I'm going to sleep. Talk tomorrow.*

Twoey: Twoey? Now what was that about? "I'll be right with you, fellas," she called, punching out Twoey's number.

"Hello."

"Twoey? Wetzon. You called?"

"Yeah, Wetzon. I need your help."

Uh-oh. Trouble between Twoey and Smith. "Is anything wrong? Is Smith okay?"

"Sure. Why wouldn't she be? Are you girls up to something I should know about?"

Why did she feel that Twoey didn't take them any more seriously than other men on the Street? "We girls," she stressed, "we girls are always up to something, Twoey. Don't you know that?"

He laughed. "Yes, I do. I called because Xenia's birthday is coming up."

"The thirty-first, Halloween. Yes."

"It's the big one. The big four-o."

"It is indeed."

"Well, I'm making her a surprise party."

Wetzon choked and held the phone away from her. "Excuse me. You are?"

"At the Odeon. I want to go over a list of people with you."

"Are you sure you should, Twoey? Not the party, I mean the surprise part."

"Oh, she'll love it. I know her."

Oh, no you don't, buddy, Wetzon thought. "Famous last words, Twoey."

"Oh, come on, Wetzon. I can just see her face when all her friends yell, 'Surprise.' "

"Yeah, so can I." Smith would hate it, for sure. And to have the world know how old she was, bad news. "If you're really determined, you can count on me, Twoey."

She hung up. What a mistake. This would not be pretty. In fact, it could sound the death knell to a fine romance.

"Whenever you're ready, Ms. Wetzon."

She looked up. Martens was standing in the doorway. She had quite forgotten about the two detectives in the kitchen. Weary, she rose and followed him. One of them had poured coffee into the mugs.

"I see you found everything." She felt wrinkled and grungy. A strand of hair slid from its knot, slowly down her nape; a hairpin fell to the floor, and she picked it up. Her back ached. She came up slowly. "What do you want? I'm tired to the point of collapse."

"We could use your help." Ferrante took a sloshy sip of coffee. "The Chief says you're all right." He took a handkerchief out of his pocket with his free hand and blew a clarion blast on his nose.

"Oh, have you decided I'm not a suspect?"

"No," Ferrante said. "According to Anthony Maglia, Middleton had no intention of moving from Bliss Norderman. That could have made you awfully unhappy."

"Unhappy, yes. Enough to kill him? Come on. Only someone crazy would do that."

"Or scared. Or angry."

"Or angry. You don't think Penny Ann Boyd did it?"

"The vic was shot in the right ear and the slug came out the left eye. The angle of the bullet leads the M.E. to suspect that the shooter may have been left-handed."

"Gee, the things science comes up with these days." She brushed the hair out of her face. "Is Penny Ann left-handed?"

"No," Martens said. "Are you, Ms. Wetzon?"

She said, "Sorry to disappoint you, boys," in her best Bogart imitation. "Drink up. I want to catch some shut-eye."

Martens's mouth twitched, but Ferrante didn't find her funny. These Italian cops were all alike. No sense of humor. She couldn't squelch a bubble of laughter.

Ferrante said, "Just because you think you're connected to the department, Ms. Wetzon, doesn't mean you didn't commit murder."

That did it. She stood up. "Listen, I've tried to be friendly. I'm cooperating, but you're making me mad. Out, please." She pointed to the door, then marched to it and opened it. The men exchanged glances, shuffled to their feet, and tramped out.

"The Chief sends you his best regards." Ferrante was not even covering up his laughter.

"Do give him my love," Wetzon snapped, furious, and slammed the door. The nerve.

She sleepwalked herself through a shower and stood in front of the medicine cabinet mirror blow-drying her hair. Her eyelids were swollen, with black smudges beneath. She braided her hair and crawled into bed. Lights out. Sweet sleep. She rolled over on her stomach and reached for Silvestri.

Silvestri. Blast. She sat up and put on the light, blinking to adjust, found the number, and tapped it out on the phone. Then she turned out the light and lay back, listening to the call go through, ringing, one, two, three, four. Odd.

"Hello?" A woman's voice.

"I must have the wrong number." She was about to hang up.

"Who do you want?"

"Silvestri."

"Hold on. Silvestri, it's for you."

Wetzon hung up. She was wide awake and she was in a fury. With a thump she was out of the bed, on her knees unplugging the phone. Then into the kitchen, doing the same. The fucking nerve of him. How could he do it to her? And he was flaunting it, too.

She poured herself a cup of cold coffee and sat at the kitchen table, head in her hands. Was he wrong? Wasn't she playing around with Alton? But he didn't know that, she thought resentfully. For all he knew, she was sitting around waiting for him to come home. Oh, hell. There was no clear fault here. They were both wrong, because neither of them wanted to make the final commitment.

Get on with it, she commanded. Enough self-pity. She rinsed the coffeepot and mugs and put them in the dishwasher. Her bag and briefcase were still on the counter where she'd left them when she came in.

The diary. She'd read the diary until she fell asleep. It was work, translating. She would certainly get drowsy. She looked in the briefcase. It wasn't there. Shook everything out on the counter. No diary. Her purse. She'd put it in her purse when Smith had met her in the lobby of the Sussex House. Where was her head?

She looked in her purse. The diary was gone.

26

....

"Hi, Frank, this is—" Wetzon balanced the phone in the crook of her neck as she slit open her mail. Three announcements from brokers she'd placed.

"Hey!" Which was a warm greeting in Brooklynese. "I'd recognize that voice anywhere, Wetzon."

"Thanks, I think. How's it going?" One announcement from a broker she hadn't placed and didn't even know was contemplating a move. Damnation. How to be everywhere at once?

"Not bad, I guess. I'm sitting here humping and pumping the numbers out, and if we can keep the market from tanking, I might just have my best year yet. Then you can go shop me a great deal."

"I'd love to. Anything happening in your office?"

"Actually, I do have a lead for you, but not here." Wetzon listened carefully, making notes, asking questions, then hung up and waited for Smith to finish her conversation. Then she said, "Do we want to work with Stan Lavell?"

"Stan Lavell?" Smith wrinkled her brow. "The manager?"

"Yes. Burlington Kramer in Red Bank. He was just removed for sexual harassment—and dipping into the till. The latter being the worse offense, of course."

"Of course."

"He's sitting in the office as a broker right now."

"Why bother? We have no management jobs, and he'll have to build a book. Why would we want to work with that kind of creep?"

Wetzon rolled her eyes to the ceiling and pursed her lips. "He produces half a mil."

They looked at each other. Smith smirked. "Well, of course we'll work with him. Tsk, tsk, poor man. These are only charges, aren't they? And this is the real world. Women want equality, they have to make their own way."

Wetzon laughed. Smith would always be Smith. "Right. And isn't it part of his job as manager to reach out to his employees? Besides, dipping into the till is much worse than copping a little feel, isn't it?"

"We'll have B.B. handle it. He's been here long enough." Smith got serious. "Business is so bad we can't afford to pass it up." She opened the door and hollered, "B.B., would you step in here, please."

Wetzon sighed and wrote Stan Lavell's name on a fresh suspect sheet, along with the name and address of his firm and branch. On the left, under "Notes," she wrote, "was producing manager, removed October 1st for sexual harassment and till-dipping." Under "Production," she wrote "five hundred range." She handed B.B. the sheet. "Be sympathetic, but don't let on you know much about it. Ask if you can be of help."

"Will other firms talk to him?" B.B. looked doubtful.

"Is the Pope Catholic?" Smith said.

"He's a five-hundred-thou producer. Most of the firms, including our dear clients, would work around it. I'm sorry to say, ethics—"

"We're not in the ethics business," Smith said tartly, pulling her chair out and sitting down.

"Go for it, B.B." After he left, Wetzon said, "I've sold out."

"If you felt that way," Smith said, "you should never have even mentioned it."

Wetzon frowned. "You're right." Why had she mentioned it? She could have just let the information die. Perhaps because she'd wanted Smith to make the dirty, money-grubbing decision. She rubbed her eyes, then stared at her pink message slips, not seeing. God, she was tired. She could hardly keep her eyes—

"Wetzon!"

"Huh? What?" Wetzon's eyes popped open. Her head was on her desk.

Smith grinned at her. "Where were *you* last night? You look as if you could use some sleep. How is he, anyway? In the sack, I mean."

"Who is *he?*"

"Alton Pinkus, babykins. Don't pretend."

"Smith, I was up at my apartment with a contractor last night. And for your information, I have had dinner with Alton only once. I have not heard from him since. I am not, repeat, not, having an affair with him."

"Why not, sweetie?" Smith opened her eyes wide and put on her most ingenuous air.

"Can we not talk about this now, please?" Wetzon said, feeling more annoyance than she was willing to show. "Those two detectives were waiting for me when I got home last night."

"Oh?"

"They said that Forensics thinks Brian was shot by a lefty."

"Why would a Communist shoot Brian?"

Wetzon snapped her fingers. "Smith, wake up, the Cold War is over. I meant a left-handed person."

"Humpf."

"Penny Ann, it seems, is right-handed." She thought for a minute, pictured Rona at the Carnegie attacking her Reuben, and said, "Rona's left."

Smith clappèd her hands over her ears. *"Don't* tell me any more. I don't want to hear. Rona's just got to stay her year at Rosenkind or we'll never see a penny more on her."

"But what if she did it? She certainly had the best motive."

"No jury in its right mind would convict her, but she would lose her job, her license, and we would be out a bundle." Smith groaned.

In her mind's eye, Wetzon saw Tony Maglia scrawling his signature on the papers. "Then again, Maglia is also left-handed."

A knock on the door interrupted them. "Yes?" Smith sounded combative. She crossed one long leg over the other and picked at a nick in the heel of her new black patents. "It never fails. These crummy city streets."

Max put his head in. He was wearing a white-on-white shirt and a large yellow paisley bow tie. He never showed any fear of Smith, treating her more like a wayward daughter. The surprising thing was that Smith seemed to like it. "The Park Royale for Wetzon."

"Oh?" Smith said.

"Nothing." Wetzon picked up the phone. "Leslie Wetzon."

"Rogers here, Ms. Wetzon. I'm afraid nothing of that description has been turned in."

"Thank you for checking." She hung up and looked at Smith.

"You didn't lift Tabby Ann's diary from my bag for some light read-ing, did you?"

"Why would I do that?"

"Then I'm sorry to tell you, Tabitha's diary has been purloined."

"Speak English, please. No jokes and games. Are you trying to tell me you *lost* it?"

Wetzon gnashed her teeth. She couldn't help it. Smith was al-ways placing blame. "I had it when I went to see Maglia, when I met you, when we were with Jerry Gordon and Rona, not to mention Richard Hartmann. And I left my briefcase and purse on the kitchen counter with Ferrante and Martens while I checked the answering machine. Anyone could have taken it. And I'd only read about four-teen pages or so."

"Rona wouldn't have taken it. She was the one who said we should have it."

"She didn't know it was written in code until I told her. It's pretty farfetched, but Rona might have found that unsettling for some reason. Even so, it's just very strange that someone would want to take it."

Smith shrugged. "What real difference does it make in the long run?"

"Maybe none. Maybe a lot. I feel terrible about it. It was my responsibility. How are we going to tell Penny Ann?"

"Why would we tell her anything? Forget it."

"Smith, you were in the room with Jerry, Rona, and that egomaniac Hartmann. Are you sure you didn't see anything?"

"Positive. Look, if it comes up, we'll just say the cops confiscated it."

"Penny Ann said something about papers to me last night, then Dr. Jerry came in with the tea and she clammed up."

"She's dim-witted."

"If she's so dim-witted, why did Brian and Maglia claim she made the investment decisions?"

"Puh-*lease*. Consider the source. If she had won the arbitration, Tony might have lost the office. Bliss Norderman wouldn't keep a manager who brings in losses. And who says you have to be smart to make investment decisions? Do you want to talk about the chimpan-zee who is a better stock picker than any of your financial consul-tants?"

"No, thank you. I won't touch that one." Nor would she touch the dart-board comparison that someone had made a couple of years back during the bear market of 1990. The random dart had picked better than most of the financial consultants and money managers. "Listen to this, will you, Smith? When I was looking for a blanket to cover Penny Ann, a hatbox full of papers fell off the shelf of the closet."

"What were they? Did you sneak a peek?"

"I didn't have a chance to. Dr. Jerry could have come back at any time."

Smith threw up her hands in disgust. "You are such a wuss."

Max knocked again. Wetzon growled at Smith, got up, and opened the door. "Fred Benitos for you, Wetzon, on two."

Wetzon stabbed two, doing a slow burn about Smith calling her a wuss. "Yes, Fred? Was Joan Boley in last night?"

"Yeah. She had all her books copied, but she didn't leave them with me to do the broker-to-brokers."

"She didn't? I don't get it. You mean she took them all away with her?"

"You got it. I don't like it, Wetzon."

"Let's not jump to any conclusions, Fred. I'll find out what's going on." She hung up and stared at the phone, thinking.

"More trouble?" Smith was studying her reflection in her folding mirror. "They're beginning to show."

"I have to call Joan Boley. She had Fred copy her books last night and then took off with the copies." Smith wasn't listening. "What's beginning to show?"

"The lines, sweetie pie. I think maybe I should get my eyes done. What do you think?"

"I think I'm going to grow old gracefully. The thought of anyone taking a knife to my face—ugh! Besides," she couldn't resist a needle, "you have great character lines." Smith looked stricken, held the mirror closer to her face, again touching the lines around her eyes and mouth. Wetzon, with a guilty inward grin, punched out Joan's number and was told by her sales assistant that Joan was with a client and would get back to her. Replacing the receiver, she said, "Shall we check in with Rona and see what's going on? We *are* getting paid until the end of the week."

Lines three and four rang simultaneously. She could see that

Max and B.B. were on one and two. "Grab four, will you, Smith?"
Then line one began blinking and Max knocked. "Alton Pinkus for
Wetzon on three and Dr. Jerome Gordon for Smith on four."

"Hmmm," Smith said. "Your call is infinitely more interesting."
She picked up the phone, yawning. "Xenia Smith here."

Wetzon hit three and found a lump had formed in her throat.
Nerves. "Hello."

"Leslie." There was pure pleasure in his voice. Why didn't
Silvestri ever let her hear that? She almost missed Alton telling her
that he had a late board meeting at Mt. Sinai on Thursday afternoon.
Would she have dinner with him afterward?

She gave him a breathy "Yes," and agreed to meet him at Mt.
Sinai at the end of her day. She hung up, cheeks tingling, and looked
at Smith.

"Seven hundred a day plus expenses. Of course, Jerry. We'll keep
you informed." Smith cradled the phone with a flourish.

Wetzon raised an eyebrow at her partner. "Did we just take him
on as a client?"

"Yes. He's going to pay us to investigate Brian's murder and
clear Penny Ann. I agreed we'd apply what was left of what Rona gave
us to it. He says Tabitha will turn up. And he's going to take me to
hear Richard's summation today in the Bostwick murder case."

"What a convoluted mess. Doesn't he know? Penny Ann has
been cleared."

Smith grimaced. "But we're not going to tell him, are we,
sweetie?"

"He'll find out soon enough." She paused. "You're going to take
the afternoon off to hear that repulsive Hartmann on an ego trip?"

Smith nodded emphatically, annoyed. "And I don't find him at
all repulsive. I think he's rather attractive. Enter, B.B." His knock was
lighter than Max's.

B.B. was holding Stan Lavell's suspect sheet. "I've talked to
Lavell and he says he's very happy, wouldn't think of leaving . . .
but he's willing to talk to Rivington Ellis and Rosenkind, Luwisher.
Shall I set it up?"

"No, I'll take it from here." Smith plucked the suspect sheet
from his hand.

"Simon Loveman returning your call, Wetzon," Max said
through the open door.

"Wetzon here."

"What do you have for me?"

"No one right now, Simon. I just want to check out something I heard yesterday from Tony Maglia."

"Yeah?"

"He told me that Brian made a deal to stay on at Bliss Thursday night. He showed me a signed contract."

Simon's laugh was abrupt and nasty. "Wetzon, don't be naive. Brian was playing us. He was here Thursday late, told me he'd re-signed, and signed a contract with us. I can show it to you. We even advanced him money to see that his debit at Bliss was paid. What does that tell you?"

She hung up the phone and said aloud, "That you're an idiot, that Brian was a con man, and that Tony Maglia is a liar."

27

....

Who was telling the truth, Wetzon wondered, as she walked up Fifth Avenue. Maglia or Loveman? Or maybe they both were. Maybe Brian hadn't made up his mind . . . but no, he had brought his personal stuff over to Simon's office, hadn't he? So it had to be Maglia who was lying. Unless Maglia was blackmailing Brian into staying put. Could Maglia himself have lifted those incriminating papers? And what had happened to the money Brian had gotten from Simon Loveman?

All of which meant that neither, or both, had a motive to kill Brian. Back to square one.

Strolling tourists mingled with rushing, impatient New Yorkers. Snaky lines of commuters were fleshy obstructions as they waited for their express buses to take them out of the City. It was still light at five-thirty. Soon enough now the clocks would be set back an hour for Eastern Standard Time and Thanksgiving would be around the corner. The City would become a cornucopia of lights and Christmas decorations, all of which seemed to appear earlier and earlier each year.

The Channel Gardens in Rockefeller Center was a field of fall foliage and mums, lavender and white, and deep purple. Foreigners abounded. A group of Japanese, every single one with a camera, was snapping Atlas carrying the world on his shoulders in front of 630 Fifth Avenue.

Booksellers with their folding tables had laid claim to every corner, because you didn't need a license to peddle books. It was a First Amendment prerogative.

Wetzon turned west on Fifty-seventh Street, past the pretzel vendor, ignoring the enveloping lure of the honey-roasted peanuts, one dollar please. Charivari's window was a Halloween parade of designer clothes, the mannequins all fixed with grotesque masks.

Turning away, she caught a momentary glimpse of her solemn and solitary self, and felt such a stab of anguish, she was staggered. Her extreme sense of loss took her breath away. It was as if someone had died. Silvestri, she thought. He could be uncommunicative, gruff at times, wrapped up in the job, but oh how she missed him, and the ache seemed all-encompassing. Was it over between them? Was this what she was feeling—a sense of mourning?

She chose a ballet class rather than jazz tonight, because the ballet movement demanded total control and pure concentration. The figure in the mirror in the faded pink leotard, ragged tights, and sagging legwarmers was still young and fit. Though in January she'd be thirty-eight, she had changed little from the eager young dancer who had come to New York seventeen years before. Her back was straight and long; her head, with its topknot, balanced regally on a slim, unlined neck. The squeak and brush of the ballet shoes was sweet to her as the dancers completed their leaps, bowed, and applauded their teacher.

After tying her hair up in a ponytail and drying herself, Wetzon got back in uniform and folded her damp gear into her briefcase. On Fifty-seventh Street, she stopped in front of Carnegie Hall. She was ravenous. She'd call Carlos. They always told each other everything. Her feet had taken her all the way to Central Park South before she realized she was heading in the wrong direction. The Upper West Side was no longer her home. And Carlos was in La-La-Land.

A gray stretch limousine pulled over to the curb, its headlights cutting the deepening dusk, and Michael Jackson, white jacket and black trousers, got out. She wondered if he thought wearing sunglasses would make him incognito. Because it didn't, although New Yorkers routinely took celebrities in stride and left them alone. Jackson and his huge entourage all paraded into the Sussex, or rather, the Park Royale.

Wetzon ambled behind the army of luggage bearers, who were unloading a second stretch limo full of the Jackson party's belongings. Maybe Dr. Jerry was still out. She stopped at the house phones and asked to be connected to his apartment, then listened to the phone ring. There was no answer. If no one was there and she could figure out how to get in, she might be able to get a look at the papers in that hatbox.

No one was around on the nineteenth floor as she walked purposefully down the hall and stopped in front of Dr. Jerry's door, 19E. Tried the knob. Locked, of course. What had she expected? She thought for a minute. Took a tour of the hall, down and up. The western end had a door marked HOUSEKEEPING and another marked STAIRWAY, with in-case-of-fire instructions prominently posted.

After listening and hearing nothing, she tried the knob of HOUSE-KEEPING. The door opened to shelves of towels, soap, cleaning tools, a small desk. A black knit dress in a large size and a stained, tan raincoat hung from hangers on a coatrack. Spike-heeled pumps with worn-down tips were tucked under the desk. A spicy scent musked the air. Pachouli.

Get a move on, she prodded herself, and began opening one drawer after another. Hotel stationery, envelopes, postcards. She lifted them and probed underneath. Her fingers found a key ring with a single key. The master, she hoped. Should she or shouldn't she? She should. She snatched up the key and headed down the hall. At the Gordon apartment she rang the bell sharply. Dum da dum dum. If someone was there, she'd play dumb, *Oh, isn't Smith here? I could swear she told me to meet her here.* She was hyper, shifting from one leg to the other, jiggling, antsy. No answer. She looked up and down the hall and, seeing no one, fit the key into the lock. *Come on, baby*, she prayed, and, turning the key, felt it smoothly unlock. Pushed the door open. She slipped the key into her pocket, stepped in, and closed the door.

She went right to the office and threw open the closet door. There were all those fat garment bags. The hatbox was still on the shelf. Standing on tiptoe, she pulled it down, setting it on the floor at her feet, then kneeled and lifted the cover. Bundles of letters, broker-age statements—photocopies. Handwritten notes from Penny Ann to Brian. Brian and Tony may have been right. This sure looked as if Penny Ann was running her own account. But wait, there were letters here from other people also, to Brian. She sifted through them looking for familiar names.

So absorbed was she that the click of the outside lock came as a shock and she froze, clutching a handful of papers, heart suddenly in her throat. She slid the lid back in place hastily and shoved the hatbox up on the shelf. Damn, she was still holding a bundle of papers—

Voices cut the silence, then Dr. Jerry's booming timbre. She didn't wait to hear more. Grabbing her briefcase and her purse with her free hand, she dived into the closet, pushing aside the cloth garment bags. She reached back and pulled the door closed behind her. Groped her way as far back from the door as possible. Stopped. Thrust the papers into her briefcase. Listened.

Her nose tickled, and she pinched her nostrils to keep from sneezing. There was more than one person in the living room. Someone spoke, others joined in. Someone came into the consulting room and closed the door.

Without warning, the closet door opened and Wetzon clamped her hand over her mouth to keep from screaming. A shaft of light cut through almost to where she huddled. She closed her eyes, tried to disappear behind the bags, which kept getting in her face.

Darkness again. She opened her eyes. Couldn't see anything. The door was closed. She crept forward and listened.

Jerry's voice murmuring, ". . . all there was . . ."

Another man—Richard Hartmann. "You're a fool. Get rid of it."

Jerry now: "But you told me—"

"Not like this."

A woman's voice called from the other room. Penny Ann. A second woman. Smith's phony tinkling laugh floated disembodied.

"Not now—" Hartmann again, very irritated.

"All right, I'll come back for it later."

A door closed. Silence.

Wetzon opened the door slightly. They were gone. She got to her feet, separated the bags, and stepped out of the closet, but the clothing bags entangled her briefcase. Damn. She gave it a tug, heard a ripping sound, lost her grip, and dropped the briefcase upside down near the door to the closet. Since she never kept the top zipped except when it rained, everything spilled out onto the floor. Cursing, she scrambled to the desk and found the light. God, her stuff was all over the floor.

She scooped up her Filofax, dance clothes, suspect sheets, pens, legal pad, the bunch of papers from the hatbox, and shoved all but the papers back inside the case, set the case down, turned back to the closet for the hatbox.

She blinked and closed her eyes. Opened them. The only thing on the shelf was the folded blue blanket.

28

....

Wetzon stared at the shelf, her mouth hanging open. She closed her mouth, stood tall, and felt around the empty space as if to make the hatbox reappear. The distinct click of a key making contact with the tumblers broke the spell. *Oh, shit.* No time to turn out the light. She plunged back into the closet, caught her heel on something, heard another ripping sound, and belly flopped, making such a racket she had no doubt she'd be discovered.

Easing herself up on her haunches, she settled among snares of loose shoes and oblong shoe boxes, mashing the tops. Her heart was thudding in her ears. How had she gotten herself into such a fix? She heard Silvestri's voice in her head: *You need a keeper, Les.*

I do not, she thought. *I can get out of this.*

Someone was moving around the apartment quietly. A burglar? Had Jerry come back for whatever it was Hartmann said he had to get rid of? It had to be the hatbox. Was Hartmann acting as a lawyer, or was he involved? She didn't dare open the door, but could see a tiny slit of light from the lamp under it.

Something cold and sharp swatted her cheek. She flinched, and her hand grasped the object. An ornate buckle. She could feel the carving. She traced the metallic material of its strap to the garment bag. The bag was torn. That accounted for the ripping sound. Her groping hands felt the burst bag's contents: chiffons, velvets, fancy dresses. She fingered sequins and beads. A slight tug brought a fur wrap down on her knees. Barbara must store her fancy clothes here.

The hair rose on the back of her neck. Someone was in the consulting room. Suddenly the closet door opened, and Wetzon, clasping her knees to her chest, ducked her head to make herself a tiny ball. Perfume. A woodsy scent. Was it Barbara? She was looking through the dresses and finally picked out what she wanted and closed the door. Wetzon breathed a silent sigh and huddled in the fur wrap. A sense memory arrived with the soft warmth. Some event from her childhood. She had been frightened and her mother had wrapped her in a cashmere shawl . . .

Music. Voices murmuring. Were there two people? Sinatra singing: *Send in the Clowns.* You're telling me, Frankie baby? She hugged her knees. The closet was warm. She was so tired, her eyelids kept closing. She had to stay awake.

Music filled her ears. The orchestra played the Merry Widow Waltz. Everybody was in costume, but the masks were grotesque, Freddy Kreuger, Norman Bates, the Phantom of the Opera. Jewels glittered. She was Fred Astaire, dancing solo, sleek in a black cutaway, crisp white shirt, sequined bow tie, just like the one Carlos had. *Puttin' on my top hat . . .* A giant skeleton caught her up, arm around her waist, swirling her, stumbling over her feet.

"Oh, I'm so sorry," the skeleton said, swirling her once more, stumbling again, crushing Wetzon's toes.

After the third time, Wetzon said irritably, "Listen to the music."

"You listen. You're the one who's out of step." Another voice, and unmistakably Smith's, but the costume was regal and Elizabethan.

Overhead a ball of little squares of mirrors revolved, casting eerie reflections on the revelers. When the music stopped in midmeasure, everyone scrambled for the red velvet and gold-leaf chairs, which were set back-to-back in a long line across the floor of the Exchange.

"Here, here, move it," Elizabeth the Queen ordered. Up close, she looked a lot like Smith. She was occupying two chairs with her voluminous skirts, and she cleared the way for Wetzon to sit on one. "I shouldn't be doing this for you." Queen Bess pointed to the huge banner in purple suede overhead: APPYHAY ORTIETHFAY IRTHBAY, ITHSMAY. "You betrayed me."

"*Moi?*" Wetzon said. She loved being Fred Astaire and couldn't care less what Queen Xenia had to say about it.

"Off with her head," Elizabeth the Queen commanded, pointing to Wetzon. A chorus picked up on it. "Off with her head . . . Off with her head . . ."

The executioner was gray-shrouded; he bent and peered at Wetzon. "You took my seat," croaked from decaying lips. Brian's dead face. It whipped off its shroud, making a great wind, and threw it over her, covering her with its cold clammy ether. Her limbs were so heavy. She was being lifted, helpless, thrown over someone's shoulder, carried to her grave. To her grave. The closing bell tolled. She sank into the shroud, unable to save herself. She was laid into a coffin and the lid slammed shut with the dead sound of the door of Smith's Jag.

Someone jerked the shroud from her, and she lifted her head, shaking, frantic. Where was she? Oh God, she was still on the floor of Jerry Gordon's closet. She'd fallen asleep. Barbara must have just pulled the fur from her without even realizing it covered an intruder.

Limbs locked, Wetzon gave her brain the signal to loosen up. No sound came from the bedroom or elsewhere. Had the woman gone out? Was the closing of the door what had awakened her? Wetzon crawled to the closet door and listened. Pushed it open a crack. No sound. The light hurt her eyes. She shaded them and waited for them to adjust. The office door was closed. The lamp cast a greenish glow on the brown chaise. She had to get out of here before Jerry and his wife got back and caught her. What the hell time was it, anyway?

She crept from the closet and found she couldn't straighten up. Half tilted, she leaned on the desk, tried again, breathing into her lower back. *Curses for you, Wetzon. Falling asleep on the job and then throwing your back out.* Her watch said ten minutes after ten. *Move it, kiddo.* Worse still, she had to pee.

Her briefcase and purse were still in the closet. How was she going to do this? She grit her teeth to cover the pain and slipped to her knees, crawling back into the closet, found her things, backed out. Somehow she got to her feet, teeth rammed permanently into her lower lip. The effort was excruciating. *Serves you right. Sticking your nose in—*

The phone on the desk rang, ending the deeply personal silence between Wetzon and the empty apartment. Rang again. And again. Tempting. She rubbed her eyes. Her head was cotton wool. Leaning against the desk for support, she reached her hand out and picked up the phone, put her fingers over the mouthpiece, and mumbled, "Um?"

What was she doing? She was about to replace the receiver when she heard an infinitesimal click, as if the line were tapped, then, "Penny Ann, good. I'm glad I caught you—"

"Um," Wetzon mumbled. She sat down in the chair.

"Don't talk. Just listen," Rona snapped. "No one else should know about this."

"Um." What was Rona up to, anyway? Wetzon picked up her cardcase from the desk and slipped it into her pocket.

"Listen carefully. Tabitha just called me. You were right. She knows something about Brian. I'm meeting her at Lincoln Center, at the fountain. I want you there."

"When?" Wetzon, imitating Penny Ann's plaintive whine, came close enough for Rona to accept—or was Rona just too single-minded to hear the difference?

Whatever it was, Rona said, "Now."

29

■ ■ ■ ■ ■ ■ ■

In the blue-black sky a waning moon hung over Central Park. A big woman in evening clothes was just getting into a cab in front of the hotel, and two people were waiting for the next one.

She was jumpy as hell, hearing things. She'd used the bathroom in the apartment and thought she'd heard a door close. Almost gave herself heart failure. Then the elevator had taken forever to come. And the lobby was crowded with people who wouldn't move or get out of her way. And now cabs were whizzing by, occupied.

Perhaps she should walk it. Seven or eight blocks. She could do it faster than waiting for a cab. She crossed to the park side and walked swiftly toward Columbus Circle. The park seemed to be in another dimension, expelling danger, redolent with horse dung and dense moisture. *The woods are lovely, dark, and deep, but I have promises to keep.* Robert Frost's lines floated up, and she shivered.

It was cold, and she had no coat. She should have been home toasting her toes, not to mention a bagel. She was almost giddy with hunger. On her left, Christopher Columbus stood on top of his obelisk, hand on hip, lit to beat the band, gazing over the domain he had not discovered. In front of the equally well-lit Remember the Maine monument at the entrance to Central Park, five or six dealers were hawking crack, among other highs. Buyers and the curious clustered around them. Not a cop in sight.

Wetzon crossed over to Broadway, stopped in front of the Gulf and Western Building. She parked her briefcase between her ankles, pulled one of her legwarmers out, and wrapped it around her bare neck, tucking the ends in; she felt better immediately. Before moving on, she dug out the remains of the chocolate bar and finished it off.

Traffic was backed up on Broadway around Lincoln Center. Philharmonic Hall, the Metropolitan Opera, the State Theatre, and the Vivian Beaumont and Mitzi Newhouse must all have let out at once. A deafening cacophony of horns came from the gridlocked cars, most of which were cabs and limousines.

Lincoln Center's plaza was light as day, a dazzling spectacle of lights and people, many in evening clothes. Limousines were parked and double-parked on the surrounding streets and the driveway bordering the plaza. How would she ever find Tabitha Ann, or for that matter, Rona, in this chaos?

There was a throng of people around the fountain, and jazz music bubbled up from somewhere within. She heard laughter and moved among the brightly dressed people, found a pocket of space— she didn't need much—and insinuated herself.

Two young men, possibly Middle European from their clothing and slouchy caps, were manipulating two string puppets to jazz music. One puppet with long scraggly hair and dark glasses was playing a saxophone, down and dirty. The equally hip second puppet was half bent, beating the keyboards. Wetzon saw a third young man keeping his eyes on the recorder, hovering over a third puppet, the drummer. They were wonderfully talented, and their audience reacted appreciatively by dropping bills into a woolen cap that lay on the ground.

Wetzon scanned the faces around her. Across the way, a teen-aged girl with a dark mass of attack hair laughed at the puppets. Tabitha Ann? Wetzon raised her hand. But no, the girl was with her parents. The father gave her a dollar bill, and the girl dropped it into the hat while the puppet played his sax and caressed her leg with his backside. Everyone laughed.

Stragglers were still coming from the theaters. Rona should have been here by now. And where was Tabitha? Wetzon drifted toward the State Theatre, looking for anyone who even vaguely resembled either Penny Ann or the apparition she and Smith had met at the door of Brian's apartment.

The City Opera was doing Sondheim's *A Little Night Music*, and Wetzon saw with a start that Daisy Robera was playing Desiree Armfeldt. She hadn't seen Daisy in years, and here she was coming toward her now. Daisy had already been a lead dancer when Wetzon was a rookie. They'd gotten to be friends in *Chicago*, Daisy, she, and Carlos. It had been Daisy who'd helped Wetzon make the decision to leave the business.

"Go now, while you're still young," Daisy had said. "Look at me. Fewer and fewer parts, more and more injuries. More and more one-night stands."

"Sing out, Louise!" Wetzon yelled the famous line from *Gypsy* and held out her arms.

"Leslie, my love," Daisy cried, sailing right into her arms, a tiny bundle of bleached-blond fluff. "Did you see the show tonight?" Daisy looked the gypsy in a long wrap skirt and a huge woven shawl. Her hair hung loose down her back. "Wonderful to see you, darling." She blew Wetzon a kiss and moved on. "Come on, Mort, I'm starving."

"Hello, Mort," Wetzon said. Mort Hornberg, director of concept musicals, had come up behind Daisy. He'd been a protégé of Hal Prince when Wetzon first met him and had gone on to outconcept the master. Carlos was working on a new show with Mort—top secret, too. Wetzon and Mort had always had a moderately adversarial relationship, because, as he was fond of saying, "I can read what you're thinking on your face."

She hoped that wasn't true, because she was thinking that Mort had acquired a little potbelly, and while the cap covered his head, she knew from Carlos that he was bald as a Spaldeen underneath.

"Leslie." Mort gave her a peck on the cheek, and she smelled mouthwash and Misha. He was wearing a tight tuxedo with a red silk ascot. He didn't stop.

"Good-bye, Mort." Wetzon watched them disappear in the direction of Broadway. Turning, she saw that the two-sheet in front of the State Theatre billed Mort Hornberg as director of the production.

She sighed, shivering. When she ran into people from her old life, she always felt as if someone were walking over her grave. It was creepy.

The crowd was thinning out considerably. In front of the Metropolitan she looked up at the Chagalls and the glimmering crystal chandelier, then back around at the people. Tabby was not here. A grinding pang of hunger brought her up short. She should get into a cab and go home. Maybe pick up something to eat if it wasn't too late. She was still groggy from her doze in the closet; maybe she'd dreamed the whole phone call. Or could this be some sort of setup?

The main plaza stopped in front of the Metropolitan Opera House, then spread right to the Beaumont and Newhouse Theatres and left to Damrosch Park. She went right. They were turning out the lights at the Beaumont. A neon sign blinked a revival of John Guare's *Six Degrees of Separation*, which she had seen two years earlier. As she stood watching, it went dark.

The moon cast a cool shadow on the reflecting pool, with its Henry Moore sculpture, in front of the Beaumont. Trees dipped almost imperceptibly in the light breeze. The night was hushed, and the hush was palpable. At the far side of the reflecting pool was the staircase down to Sixty-fifth Street. Voices floated up from the street below. It was one of Manhattan's beautiful, pristine fall nights.

The Henry Moore sculpture, lit by a spotlight on a tall stem in the plaza, seemed to float on the surface of the reflecting pool. A huge flying fish and a smaller piece that looked like a giant molar. In the bottom of the shallow pool, coins that people threw in shimmered, melting and distorting, along with candy and gum wrappings, plastic containers, programs, pieces of newspaper. People were such pigs.

Oh, well. Once around the pool and then home, James, she thought. A clean-cut young man, a white silk scarf debonair around his neck, was sitting on a marble bench passing money to a black teenager, while a nervous young woman in leggings and sagging socks stood on the fringes. What made her think they were dancers?

Wetzon walked a little faster and took the turn near the entrance to the Beaumont. *Don't look back*, she told herself tersely. She looked, instead, out at the pool. A piece of the sculpture seemed to be moving. She squinted at it. God, it had broken off and was floating toward her.

This is what happens when you skip meals and wander around thinking you're a goddam detective. She stepped up to the edge of the pool. No, she wasn't seeing things. It was definitely floating toward her. She wasn't crazy.

She bent over to get a better look, and that's when she started screaming.

30

....

The rectangular plate windows of the Vivian Beaumont looked dull-eyed at a scene more dramatic than anything that had inhabited her stage. Wetzon's shrill scream scattered the entrepreneur and his clients into the shadows with or without the buy. No quick rush tonight, kids.

Almost as if he were beamed down from the *Starship Enterprise*, a Hispanic security guard with a bandito mustache materialized and pulled the sodden heap from the bloody pool. He sputtered into a walkie-talkie, asking for an EMS wagon and the cops. Then he tried CPR while Wetzon held the enormous flashlight. People—where had they come from?—stood by, mesmerized by the tragedy. A very young white woman had drowned in a pool no more than a foot deep and in full view of everyone leaving the theaters. How could it have happened?

Sirens stained the night. Blue-and-white squad cars began rolling up, tires crunching on the low, flat steps and across the plaza; lights beamed onto the reflecting pool. A few minutes later, a white EMS van arrived. The security guard, his uniform stained with blood and water, scrambled to his feet, relinquishing his place to one of the medics.

The medics rolled the girl over on her back. Bluish skin, glazed eyes wide open, surprised. Tabitha Ann Boyd in black leggings and a bulky, patterned sweater too waterlogged to show its colors, long dark hair matted, wet and entangled with refuse from the reflecting pool, her fists clenched. Her neck had ballooned grotesquely, almost hiding the small red hole in her throat.

Strangling, Wetzon clawed at the legwarmer imprisoning her own throat and tore it away. Saliva choked her. *Don't throw up, don't* . . . She pressed the legwarmer to her mouth, but wrenching dry heaves racked her. She staggered over to a marble bench and crashed.

Another squad car added its harsh shaft to the rest, making the plaza a bizarre night shoot on a movie set. Dispatcher voices free-floated incomprehensibly, crackling static. More cars, brakes screeching, doors opening, slamming shut. The plaza was dense with uniforms and detectives. The medics stopped working on Tabitha. They waited a few minutes, as if there might be some mistake, then packed everything up and took off into the night. The police took over.

Wetzon sat huddled on the marble bench, shivering. She drew an uneven breath, filling her lungs with air as cool and crisp as an ice-cold beer. Around her, the ethereal October night; above her in the velvety sky, stars, the Big Dipper. A tiny airplane, lights blinking, silently crawled across the heavens. She was alive. So alive she could hear her blood coursing through her veins and arteries, follow the amazing brain mechanism, the winding serpentine of her spine. She was breathing with her heart.

The Crime Scene Unit arrived and began the tedious work of going over the area, inch by inch. They would most certainly have to dredge the reflecting pool.

How long had she sat here? Long enough for the marble to turn her to ice, until she was numb. She'd never get up again. On the other hand, if she could get herself up, she could walk away. . . . No! What was she thinking? She was a good citizen. She— Someone blocked out the lights.

"You're the witness, miss?" The man who spoke was big and black, his belly spilled over his belt and, with each word, a wheezing whistle. He rubbed his nose and straightened his tie, giving her a puzzled look. "Hey, don't I know you?"

Wetzon squinted up at him. She recognized him, too. The detective from the Twentieth Precinct, was it four years ago? When she was drawn into the mess after Barry Stark was murdered. What was his name?

"Walters." He answered her unspoken question. "I do know you. You're Silvestri's lady, right?"

She stared at him for a moment. Was she? Then she nodded. "Leslie Wetzon."

"Yeah. I never forget a face," Walters said, congratulating himself. He took a handkerchief from his pocket in time to catch a mighty "Cachew!" He blew his nose. "Goddam allergies hang around all year now." He stuck his hand up in the air and yelled, "Over here, Conley," without looking around. Despite the chill in the air, sweat beaded his crown and upper lip.

The worker ants from the Crime Scene Unit toiled on, and Tabitha Ann Boyd lay a wet lifeless lump on the cold stone. Wetzon shivered violently. Behind her, she saw the curious and the thrill-seekers clustered along a barricade of wooden horses, distance set by some of the uniforms. How, she wondered, do they find out? Was it some underground signal through a modem, or a designated listener to police transmissions? "Your turn to tune in tonight, and if it's a real juicy murder, call me and I'll get the chain going"? Is that how it was?

Conley detached himself from the men and women of New York's Finest around the reflecting pool and came toward them, a tall pale stalk of a man with very fine baby hair in a pinkish-blond color. Small features, gangly in clothes too big for his build. He stopped to greet a smart-looking woman in a slouch hat and black leather coat, carrying a doctor's case. The medical examiner was a woman. *Hooray for our side*, Wetzon thought.

Walters waved to her. "ASAP, Riccardi."

"Tell me something new, Al," Riccardi said.

"Excuse me a minute." Walters left Wetzon and spoke to Riccardi and Conley briefly. They looked over at Wetzon. Riccardi left them, and Conley and Walters came back to Wetzon.

"Yeah." Walters nodded. "I remember you now."

"You look cold," Conley said.

"I am." She hugged herself, but couldn't stop shaking.

Walters took off his tweed sports jacket and put it around her shoulders. He wore a shoulder holster just like Silvestri's. Wetzon felt the warmth from the jacket. It was as if Silvestri were here. Did detectives all smell the same, of summer and smoke?

Walters signaled up a uniform who looked as if he were still in high school and wearing a costume. "Cohen, let's see if we can get some coffee over here. There's an all-nighter over on Broadway." He looked down at Wetzon. "Shove over, Miss . . ."

"Wetzon. Decaf for me, please," she said to Cohen.

"Yeah." Walters sat down next to her, radiating heat. "You saw it happen? Right?"

"No. Wrong. I found her."

"Security guard says you knew her name."

"I think she's Tabitha Ann Boyd."

Conley pulled a glassine bag from his pocket. Inside was a very shiny, fat wallet. "On the nose," he said.

"I was meeting her there . . . at the fountain." Wetzon pointed to the main plaza. What about Rona? What had happened to her? "But she never showed up. I thought I'd just walk around the pool once and go home—"

"You knew where to look, didn't you." Walters frowned. It wasn't a question.

"Don't do that. I didn't kill her."

"Okay. Go on."

"At first I thought she was part of the sculpture."

"Do you own a gun, Miss Wetzon?" This from Conley.

"No, I do not." She was firm. It was not her gun.

"How do you know her?"

"I didn't really. I never met her. I saw a photograph of her. Her mother— They had a fight and Tabitha ran away from home."

Conley dangled the bag with the wallet at her. "Redding . . . Connecticut."

"Yes. But she wasn't on the streets. She was staying with a man named Tony Maglia and his wife. I think so, anyway."

"Spell it." Walters nodded at Conley, who dropped the bag containing the wallet into his coat pocket and took out a notepad.

"M–a–g–l–i–a. He's the manager of the Bliss Norderman office in midtown."

"How come you were meeting her?"

"It's a long story."

"We have all night." Walters looked up. "Good. Here we go." Cohen carried an open cardboard box full of coffee containers.

"This here's the decaf." He handed it to Wetzon. Conley and Walters each took a cup and Cohen brought the rest to the gang around the pool, some of whom were methodically stringing glossy yellow crime-scene tape, blocking the steps to Sixty-fifth Street.

Wooden horses were put up between the Philharmonic and the pool. More tape was strung.

The M.E. in black leather came toward them carrying her bag. She signaled to a couple of aides with a gurney.

"So whadja find, Doc?" Walters asked, getting up and moving away slightly.

"One gunshot wound in the throat. Hit an artery."

"Did it kill her outright?"

"Might have, but don't think so. I'm guessing by the look of her, it was contained in the neck and she probably died of compression. I won't know for sure till I open her up. It was quick either way."

Wetzon warmed her hands on the cup. The steam rose and mingled with the night. A dog barked. Reporters queried the cops on the barricade; the rubberneckers kept up a steady stream of comments. The entire scene was underscored by the staccato blare of the police dispatcher.

"Anything else?"

"Found this in her hands." The M.E. held out a glassine bag.

"What's this?" Walters shook it, and what was inside danced. He popped it open and poured its contents into his hand. "What the hell is this?"

"Sequins," Wetzon said.

31

·······

Harlequins of sequins discoed in Wetzon's head. Sequins on costumes. Sequins on evening dresses. Sequined scarves. She herself had once owned a sequined cloche, and somewhere in some box with her winter hats was a sexy red sequined beret. And there was Carlos's sequined bow tie. Smith had just bought a smashing little white sequined sheath, a stretchy bit of business that came to midthigh.

"Which side, miss?" Officer Cohen broke into her meditation on sequins.

"Over on the left, please." When she leaned forward in her seat, her back sent up such a strong protest she was left gasping.

In the loft, she went around closing the blinds, then turned up the heat. The pantry closet yielded a can of gourmet cream of mushroom soup—whatever that was—which she opened, poured into a saucepan, and set on a low heat while she got out of her clothes and into her terry robe. Chilled to the bone, hands shaking, knees quivering, she lowered herself slowly to the floor and lay on her back, hugging her knees. Breathing deeply, she began counting. At twenty, she opened her arms and, knees still to her chest, rolled from side to side keeping her back flat on the floor. Better. Finally she came up on her knees, sat back, and lowered her torso into a flat position on the floor, reaching out with her arms, stretching, breathing into the tightness in her lower back.

Although almost rigid with exhaustion, she knew if she didn't deal with it now, she'd never be able to get out of bed in the morning.

The soup began to make sissing noises. She came out of her crawl and cautiously tried to stand. And did. Turning off the flame under the soup, she went into the bathroom and scrubbed her face. She ran hot water into Carlos's deep marble tub and poured a capful of raspberry-scented bubble bath, which was stationed with the shampoo on a Lucite table nearby.

A bowl of hot soup, Carr's water biscuits with butter, and her gnawing hunger was eased. It was too late to call anyone. There were messages, she'd seen the machine blinking, but she didn't want to know about them. Not tonight. She wanted to think everything through: Brian's murder, Rona—the phone call—Wetzon hadn't been able to hide that Rona's call had brought her to Lincoln Center, but she'd glossed over where she'd taken the call, so for now, no one knew she'd broken into Dr. Jerry's office. She sighed. Penny Ann, poor Tabitha, Dr. Jerry Gordon, Tony Maglia. Richard Hartmann, Alton Pinkus. Smith. Twoey. Silvestri. Her whole life. It was so complicated.

She poured herself a glass of orange juice on the rocks and rinsed the empty soup bowl, stacking it in the dishwasher. The biscuits went back on the shelf but in an airtight Ziploc bag. A plastic bag, like the sequins.

And it was the sequins she was thinking about again when she lowered herself into the steaming, raspberry-scented foam with an "Aaaah." She took a sip of the orange juice, set the glass on the floor, and lay back in the suds, resting her head on the rim, closing her eyes. Floating. Everything was such a mess. Relationships were so messy. Look at Penny Ann and Tabitha. Rona and Brian. Smith and Twoey. But weren't those extremes?

Why couldn't things have just gone on the way they were? She shook her head emphatically and was rewarded by a swatch of hair sliding from her topknot. Reaching up with both hands, she took all the pins out of her hair and dropped them on the black-and-white marble tiled floor. Her ash-blond hair tumbled from the knot and fanned out in the water like a wet curtain.

I am a mermaid, she thought. *Doesn't anyone understand that?*

The phone bleated from the wall just above her head, and she started, splashing water on the floor. Good God! It was after one o'clock. Who would be calling this late? She lay back in the tub listening to the bleat, watching the phone upside down. Reaching back and up with her hand, more suds and flow, she picked the receiver from its wall hanging and put it to her ear. "Yes?"

"Did I wake you?" Silvestri's voice was scratchy and gruff, as if he had a cold or was emotional, or something. *Forget that.*

"No." The water had gotten cool. She turned on the hot spigot.

"Are you in a water bed?"

"I'm in the tub. Carlos has a phone in his bathroom."

He cleared his throat. "I'm not going to try to explain—"

"Good." He knew her well enough to know it was highly unusual for her to be up this late, and she wasn't going to make it any easier for him.

"Les." He cleared his throat again. "I'm not good at this." He left her an opening wide enough to dance a chorus line through, but she said nothing. She wanted him to keep talking. People always talked to fill a vacuum. And there certainly was a vacuum between them. "Are you listening?" he said.

"Yes." She turned off the hot water and lay back again.

"I hate this crap. Look, I want us to be together." Again he left her an opening. When she didn't fill it, he said, hotly, "I'd like to kick your butt for—"

"Oh, I see. You want us to be together and you want to kick my butt." If she weren't so miserable, she would laugh.

"You *want* to misunderstand, don't you?" She could hear him coming to a boil.

"No. Being together means just that."

"This is my *job.*"

"I know that. I have a job I love also. But there's no give with you. You went down there and suddenly I no longer exist. Do you honestly think I'm going to sit around waiting for you?"

"That's not true." But she heard defensive in his voice, and he was ignoring what she said about waiting around for him.

"I don't know who you are anymore, Silvestri," she said, and then couldn't help herself. She started to cry.

"Aw, Les, don't do that." His words were all bunched up with emotion. "Come on. We'll work it out. Come down this weekend—"

"I don't want to come down there. I don't belong. It's a cop world."

"A cop world? That's my world, Les."

"This is not a one-way street, Silvestri. I don't want to talk any more tonight. I'm too tired." She hung up and lifted herself carefully out of the tub, releasing the plug. She rolled her hair into a hand towel and wrapped herself up in a bath towel.

"Beddie-bye," she murmured. No more thinking.

She turned out the lights and crawled into bed. All this emotion was tearing her up.

A clang—metal against metal. The sound of her iron garden chairs, if one hit the other. Had it come from inside the apartment? Had she fallen asleep and dreamed it? She didn't want to get up, went fetal and pulled the covers over her head. It would go away.

It came again. Along with a scream. Then thumping, clanging. The gun. She threw off the covers, left the tangle of towels, and pulled the black leather box from under her lingerie. The gun emerged, a cold ebony carving, and she held it in her hand. With her other hand she calmly punched out 911, gave her name and address, and asked for help.

A woman screamed. More clanging. A thud outside her window. The squeal of metal tearing. Footsteps.

Someone was on the fire escape outside her bedroom window.

32

. . . .

The pounding on her window came again. Someone was shouting. A familiar voice. More pounding.

Grabbing up the terry robe, Wetzon put it on, shifting the gun from one hand to the other.

"Leslie! Let me in! It's me, Louie."

Wetzon flung the window open. The screen had been torn away. A fire alarm bit the fragile silence of night in Greenwich Village. "God, Louie, you scared me. What happened?"

"Are you all right?" Louie, barefoot, in cut-down jeans and a worn paint-stained sweatshirt, slipped through the open window. "Would you point that somewhere else, please?"

Wetzon looked down at her hand. She was still holding the gun. "It's not loaded. At least, I don't think it is."

"Here, let me." Louie held out her hand and Wetzon gave her the gun, handle first. "What you have here is a revolver, double action." Expertly, Louie flipped the cylinder sideways and held it up to Wetzon. "See." The six slots were empty. She snapped it closed and handed it back to Wetzon, saying, "Nice piece."

"You do that very well." Wetzon slipped the gun back in the leather box and returned the box to its place in the chest of drawers. "How do you know all this?"

"I come from a long line of cops. Broke tradition."

Wetzon turned on the bedside light. "Do you want to tell me what this is about?"

"There was someone on the fire escape. I was putting together my proposal for you when I saw a shadow pass my window, and then he knocked over one of my flowerpots. That's when I started making a ton of noise. To scare him off."

"I guess you did. Thank you. I can't believe he climbed up in full view of the street." Suddenly weak-kneed, Wetzon sat down on the rumpled bed.

"It's these druggies. Dark apartment. A fire escape. They take chances."

Wetzon shuddered. "I've always hated fire escapes."

Louie patted Wetzon's head. Her face was pale under her freckles, and she had a smudge of blue paint on her chin. "Listen, kiddo, I've lived in the Village twenty-five years. Eight years here. Never had a problem—ask Carlos. But things are changing down here. Too many strangers, kids, gay bashers, dopers. The homeless . . . and God knows what." She ran her fingers through her red hair, pulling it away from her face.

Wetzon stretched and rotated her head from side to side. "Well, I can forget about a good night's sleep. Would you like some coffee?"

The buzzer sounded downstairs, startling both women.

"Omigod," Wetzon said, hand to her mouth. "I forgot. I called 911." She checked the small video screen near the door and saw two uniforms. She buzzed them in. They'd come pretty quickly. So much for the statistics on poor response time on the part of the NYPD. She retied the belt on the robe firmly and unlocked her door.

The first officer off the elevator was a man with a bulbous nose, black pores, and deep-set tired eyes. He was accompanied by a young, powerfully built man with skin the color of cordovan.

"Officers Drucker and Heminway," the man with the big nose said. "I'm Drucker." His dyspeptic eyes examined them, two women, barefeet. "You reported a prowler?"

"I did. Louie saw him." The cops exchanged a look. What the hell was that supposed to mean, Wetzon thought.

Louie stepped forward. "I live downstairs. I heard him because he knocked over one of my pots."

"She screamed and made a lot of noise and scared him off."

"I'll give a look-see," Heminway said. "Which window?"

Wetzon led all of them back through the bedroom to the window, which was still open from Louie's entrance. Heminway pulled his flashlight and lit up the fire escape, sending the light above, around, and below. "You better get a gate on this window." He slipped through the window and walked the fire escape, his heavy footsteps clanging on the iron steps.

"Did you get a good look at him, Miss—er?" Drucker's voice was a bored monotone.

"Armstrong. I'm afraid not."

Heminway slipped back through the window. "Nothing there."

"Thanks for coming," Wetzon said. She let them out.

"You better keep that window bolted till you get the gate." Drucker flicked his eyes over Louie.

Wetzon closed the door. "What was that all about? I felt as if I was missing the subtext."

Louie sighed. "He thought we were lovers."

"Really?"

"I'm gay."

"So? I'm not. Do you want some coffee? I'm wide awake."

Louie smiled at Wetzon, and the reserve Wetzon had noticed about her dissolved. The sharp blue eyes softened. "I have a better idea. I have a pint of Häagen-Daz's chocolate chocolate chip in my freezer, and I have the proposal for your apartment ready. Why not come down to my place?"

"You're on." Wetzon closed and locked the window, then slipped on her Keds, grabbed her purse, and followed Louie.

The loft directly below Carlos's, although the same size, was radically different. Such was the advantage of loft space. The entranceway was four feet of rust quarry tile, then one step down to wood floors the color of unbleached muslin. A wide, open kitchen on the right, and straight ahead, a huge living room with a comfortable arrangement of tan leather sofas and chairs. In a far corner, near the windows, was a drafting table and a wall of bookshelves. Large, vivid paintings covered every bit of bare wall space with extraordinary splashes of color. Wetzon found herself staring openmouthed at the one closest to her, a turbulent mixture of red and black slashes on a stark white background. She found it so disturbing, so enthralling, she backed away from it, and caught Louie watching her.

"Complicated, isn't it?" Louie looked embarrassed, almost shy.

Then it dawned on Wetzon. "They're yours. They're beautiful."

"You don't have to say that."

"I know, but I mean it. They make me feel—I don't know—as if I were—this is crazy—falling, losing control."

Louie smiled. "Thank you." She touched Wetzon's arm and steered her into the kitchen area.

Here were a wide relative of a parsons table in bleached wood with white Formica squares inlaying the surface and six sturdy chairs with red tie-dyed cushions attached. Louie marched right over to the big white refrigerator, opened the freezer, and took out the pint of ice cream, which she set on the table. From a drawer under one of the glass-doored cabinets, she lifted two long-handled spoons—iced-tea spoons—and from another drawer, a package of paper napkins.

"Dig in," she said, lifting off the cover. "I'll get the proposal."

Wetzon sat down and reached for the container. "Oh, boy." She scooped up a spoonful of the dark-chocolate ice cream. "What a good idea."

"Hey, leave some for me," Louie called.

"You'd better move fast, then."

She brought the proposal in a manila file folder and handed it to Wetzon, taking the pint of ice cream from her and spooning some into her mouth.

All the estimates were neatly printed out for plastering and painting, as well as new floors. The price for replacing parquet was outrageous, but Wetzon consoled herself that the insurance should cover most of it. Automatically, she reached for the container of ice cream.

"Don't mind me." Louie got up, padded across the floor, and opened her window on the fire escape. "I want to see how much damage he did to my poor aloe plant." She was back in a minute, hugging a big earthenware pot. "Only chipped, but I'm going to need more earth. All these roots are exposed. . . ." Her voice drifted off. "That's funny."

"Everything here looks fine, Louie. I love your apartment, so I think you'll take good care of mine. When do we talk about colors?" When Louie didn't answer, Wetzon looked up. Louie had set the pot with the plant in the sink. "What's funny?"

Louie's hands were crusty with damp dirt. "Look at this. How do you suppose this got here?"

Wetzon got up and came over to the sink. In Louie's hand, glinting in the dirt, were three gold sequins.

33

·······

"My Lord, you look ghastly" was Smith's greeting the next morning. She had the phone to her ear. "Rose, please."

"Thanks awfully. I needed that." Wetzon hung her Burberry in the closet and slammed the door. "Listen, Tabitha—"

"Oh, sugar, is it supposed to rain?" Smith was in disgustingly good spirits.

"How would I know? Smith, Tabitha—"

"Hi, Rose sweetie, is my dress ready? Oh, good. I'll be by later." She disconnected and stared at Wetzon.

Wetzon flopped into her chair, took the folders, suspect sheets, legal pad, and *New York Times* from her briefcase and stacked everything to the right of her telephone. Then she called Rona. When the machine answered, she hung up.

"Oh, my, aren't we in a foul humor. Do you want to tell me about it?"

Wetzon punched out another number. Rona's sales assistant answered and told Wetzon that Rona was in a meeting.

"Are you sure?"

"Excuse me?"

"Never mind, I'll call back." *Oh, Wetzon, why pick on the sales assistant?* she asked herself. *Have you sunk that low?* She looked down at the pile of pink phone messages on her desk and put her head on top of them. "I'm so tired."

"I left a message on your stupid machine last night. Tsk, tsk, when the cat's away . . ."

Raising her head, Wetzon mumbled testily, "And where were you last night, if I may ask?"

"Well, let's see." Smith looked so pleased with herself, Wetzon's fingers itched to strangle her. "Would that be before dinner or after dinner?"

Wetzon fanned her messages out on the desk. Dr. Jerome Gordon had called. *Oh, God.* "How was Hallelujah Hartmann's performance?" She went down her list of calls to be made.

"Brilliant. All around."

Something in Smith's voice made Wetzon put down her pen and look at her partner. "What am I missing?"

"I did hear you ask me how he performed, didn't I?"

"You didn't . . ."

"Didn't what?" Smith gave Wetzon a slow, guileless smile.

"With Richard Hartmann. He's such a slug."

"Well, now, sweetie pie, I wouldn't say that." There was a prickly note in Smith's voice.

Wetzon threw up her hands. "What about Twoey, for god-sakes?"

"Twoey's a sweet boy, of course, but—"

"Don't say another word." *I can't take it,* she thought distractedly. *Not today. Not ever.*

B.B. knocked on their door and opened it to Smith's honeyed "Yes, B.B. dear?"

"Mr. Hartmann for you, Smith."

"I've got to talk to you," Wetzon said, spinning her finger in the air impatiently. "So make it fast."

Smith gave her a smug smile and reached for the phone.

Wetzon looked again at her list of calls. She had to touch base with some of these brokers whose suspect sheets she'd been carrying around with her to call at night, but her nights had been . . . well . . . She picked up the stack of material she'd removed from her briefcase and dumped the newspaper under her desk. Fumbling through the folders and suspect sheets, she pulled out a wad of strange papers wrapped in a rubber band. "Oh, no!" she exclaimed. But Smith didn't even look up.

Turning her back to Smith, Wetzon slipped off the rubber band and unfolded the handful of papers she'd grabbed from the hatbox in Dr. Jerry's closet. What she saw in front of her were statements—

someone's brokerage statements from Bliss Norderman. Someone named Mrs. Leonora Foley, Alcott Arms, 510 West Seventy-second Street, New York, New York 10023. The broker of record was Brian Middleton. Well, all right now. The statements covered January, February, March, April, May, June, July, and August.

"All right, sweet thing, call me back—"

Blast. Smith was about to hang up the phone. Wetzon quickly folded her *Times* business section around the statements and withdrew to the privacy of the bathroom. She sat down on the lid and inspected the statements with more care.

Brokerage statements were the hardest thing in the world to read, probably on purpose. It didn't seem to matter which firm; not one was clear and to the point, and the abbreviations were impossible to decipher.

Either this Mrs. Foley was a trader or Brian had been churning her account. That was obvious. In and out. In and out. Some stocks were sold only a few days after purchase. Small amounts of money invested every month. $7,500 in January, $8,750 in February, $8,000 in March—

"Wetzon!" Smith rapped on the door. "You've been in there forever."

"I'll be right out." Wetzon folded the statements back inside the newspaper, flushed the toilet, washed her hands, and opened the door, newspaper under her arm.

Smith eyed her suspiciously. "You were reading the newspaper in there. You never do that."

"'A foolish consistency is the hobgoblin of little minds.'" Wetzon sallied forth and sat down at her desk.

"Humpf," Smith said. "You're really not as funny as you think you are." She went into the bathroom and slammed the door, came out a minute later, and flounced to her desk, just as B.B. announced that Mr. Hartmann was on the phone again. She picked up the receiver and purred, "Where were we?"

Wetzon put the newspaper stuffed with Mrs. Leonora Foley's brokerage statements into her briefcase. This required some concentrated thought . . . later.

All things considered, she was feeling pretty good. This new puzzle energized her. Where was she? She scrutinized the suspect sheets in front of her and started with the top one, a broker at Smith Barney she'd been trying to get to for the past two weeks.

She picked up the phone and punched out his number. Gary Friedman was a nice guy with a good business. Wetzon had been talking to him for three-plus years. He was intelligent and fairly well read. And he took brokering very seriously. For him it was a profession.

"Hi, Wetzon. What's happening?"

"Same old stuff, Gary. What's happening with you? How's business?"

"Um, ummmm," Smith was purring into the phone. She sounded as if she was having an orgasm.

"Business is steady. I'm up about thirty percent over last year."

"Hey, that's great! You're one of the few, you know."

"Ummmm, *hummmm*," Smith said.

"Read any good books lately?" Wetzon asked loudly, trying to drown out Smith.

Gary proceeded to tell her he had just finished Martin Gottfried's book about Bob Fosse, *All His Jazz*, and then they chatted on about the state of the musical theater and the good old days when Wetzon had been one of Bob Fosse's dancers. Finally they got down to business.

"Listen, Wetzon, I know I told you to call me toward the end of October, but I'm just not motivated to do anything right now. I'm in line for Chairman's Club and I'll get my V.P. title if I hit half a mil, and I will. And I'm getting married in January."

"Mmmmmmm, ummmm." Would Smith never quit?

"That's super. Congratulations." Cross Gary off for at least six months. It was too traumatic for most people to make two huge changes in their lives at the same time.

"But listen," he said, "stay in touch. And send me another card. You're the only headhunter who calls me who has a brain."

Wetzon hung up and shot Smith a menacing look.

Smith moaned one last "ummmm," bestowed a Mona Lisa smile on Wetzon, and replaced the receiver tenderly. She opened her mouth to say something, and Wetzon exploded.

"I don't want to know. Twoey—"

Smith brushed her off. "You said yourself Twoey's too hung up on his mother."

"I love how you rearrange what I say to rationalize your behavior." Wetzon took a deep breath. "Can we talk about our case?"

"Of course." Smith looked disappointed. She'd obviously wanted Wetzon to coax more about Richard Hartmann out of her.

"Have you seen the papers this morning or heard the news?"

Smith frowned. "No."

"Well, Tabitha turned up last night—"

"Oh, good." She didn't sound very enthusiastic.

"Dead."

"Dead?"

"Dead. She was murdered—shot—in front of the Vivian Beaumont."

"My, my. So what does it all mean?" She picked at a stray thread in the hem of her skirt.

"It means that probably whoever killed Brian also killed Tabitha and that maybe they both knew something they shouldn't have known. Was Dr. Jerry with you and Hartmann last night?"

"Babycakes, a ménage à trois? How quaint."

"That's not what I meant, and you know it."

"Actually, Dr. Jerry's not my type. Besides, Barbie's family is some sort of Jewish royalty."

"Jewish royalty? What's that?"

"Dickie keeps calling her the Princess Orlafsky." Smith was perfectly serious.

Wetzon broke up, laughing so hard she almost fell off her chair. "I may never recover from this," she gasped.

Smith was offended. "I really don't understand you, Wetzon. Can we get on with this? I do have some important business calls to make."

"Okay, okay. Here goes." She squelched a giggle. "Quickly, after my dance class I was near the Park Royale, so I wandered over, thinking I might run into you." *Liar*, she thought. She went on to tell Smith about stealing the key and getting caught in the closet for hours. "By the princess, I assume."

Eyes sparkling, Smith cried, "I love it!"

"You would."

"And there I was in the living room and you were hiding in the closet." She clapped her hands, gleefully.

"Yup." Now she had Smith's undivided attention. "Barbara, incidentally, has bimbo taste in clothes. Feather boas, bugle beads, and—" She stopped dead.

"And what?"

"Sequins."

"Sequins? Everyone is wearing sequins these days."

"Then Dr. Jerry wasn't with you and Hartmann last night?"

"I thought I told you he wasn't," Smith said, annoyed. "Why do I have to repeat myself? He went off to talk to the caterer about the bar missa."

"Bar mitzvah."

"Whatever. It's at the Palace. He's inviting us. I told him we would be delighted."

"Oh, shit, I *hate* affairs like that."

"There you go again. Wetzon, listen to me when I tell you it's important for us to meet these people. They have Power. The cards are telling me—"

"Fuck the cards!"

"I'm ignoring that, because you're obviously upset about your personal life. Dr. Jerry is a very nice, almost simple man, considering what a celebrity he is."

Wetzon curled her lip at Smith. A jury would definitely acquit her if she murdered Smith right now. "Celebrity?"

"Well, aside from the talk show, he's written some sort of philosophical book called *The Loving Logs of Life.*"

"Give me a break."

"No, I'm not kidding. He got a huge advance from the people that published that kindergarten book."

"I'm not finished with my story, Smith, if you don't mind."

"Oh, for pity sakes. Go on." She groaned and fluffed her curls. "It's taking you forever."

"Because you keep interrupting me." Wetzon slammed her pencil down and it bounced up and flew across the room.

"Temper, temper," Smith chided. She fluttered her lashes at Wetzon.

I'll kill her, Wetzon thought. *Slowly.* "May I finish, please?"

"Be my guest."

"I got caught in the closet while the princess was dressing, and I fell asleep."

Smith rolled her eyes heavenward.

"Then when I woke up and crawled out of the closet, I was so foggy, I answered the phone when it rang. But I disguised my voice."

"I'll bet."

"Shut up, Smith. Listen to this, because it's important. It was Rona, and she thought I was Penny Ann. She said Tabitha had called her, terrified, and asked her to meet at the Lincoln Center fountain."

"Oh, no!" Smith yowled. "Not Rona. We'll lose our entire investment in her."

"She's left-handed, too."

"Excuse me," B.B. said, knocking.

Wetzon pointed her finger at Smith. "Don't start."

"Yes, B.B., dear," Smith said sweetly.

"Neil Munchen on the phone for either of you."

"I'll take it." Smith grabbed the phone. "Hello, Xenia Smith here."

Wetzon drifted into the reception room and poured herself a cup of coffee, wondering what the head of retail at Rosenkind, Luwisher wanted. B.B. was on the telephone in his cubbyhole coaxing a broker to "explore another situation." She smiled and looked down at Max's orderly desk. He'd be in later. She wandered back to the open doorway.

"Well, really." Smith looked at Wetzon and arched her brow. "How should I know, Neil?" Pause. "Of course that's ridiculous. Thank you for telling us." She replaced the receiver. "Damn, I just chipped a nail." The face she turned to Wetzon was mottled burgundy with anger.

"Spill it."

"You'd better sit down."

"No, I'll take it standing up, thank you very much."

"The police came up to the office and arrested Rona an hour ago."

34

$\blacksquare\blacksquare\blacksquare\blacksquare\blacksquare\blacksquare\blacksquare$

Wetzon was nonplussed. Nothing was going right. "I should never have told them about her phone call."

"You *told* them?" Smith turned on her in a fury. "How could you have done that? You know what it means to us."

"I'm sorry. I did what I thought was right." What she still thought was right.

"Sorry, humpf. Now we've got to drop everything and really involve ourselves in this investigation. We've got to clear her."

"But wait a minute, Smith, the police don't just arrest someone like Rona out of the clear blue sky without some real hard evidence. What if she did it?"

"Who cares? Read my lips, babycakes—we *will* get her off or we *won't* see another dollar on her."

"I can see Rona murdering Brian, possibly, but not Tabitha. Never Tabitha. Not even if Tabitha and Brian were making it."

"That's gross. Of course, we *could* give them another suspect."

"Oh, yeah?" Wetzon looked at Smith suspiciously. "Like who . . . whom?"

Smith didn't say anything, just stared at her hard.

"If you're thinking what I think you're thinking, Smith, you can forget about it."

"You were there. You have no alibi for Brian's death. It would be so easy, sweetie pie. And it would buy us some time."

"No!"

"Oh, very well, then. Trust you not to be cooperative when times get tough."

"Come off it, Smith. You wouldn't do it if the roles were re-versed." See Smith backpedal herself out of that.

"I was joking. Where's your sense of humor, sugar? I'm going to call Dickie right now. He's got to defend Rona."

"Dickie? You mean Dick Hartmann?"

"Of course." Smith picked up the phone and tapped out the numbers with the eraser end of her pencil.

"I see you've committed that to memory."

"Carved on my heart, sweetie pie," Smith said flippantly.

"What about Twoey, if I may ask?"

"You may, sugar." She smiled one of her hot sultry smiles. "One can be in love with two men at the same time, you know."

Wetzon groaned loudly. For all that, Smith's last words were disquieting. Was their association rubbing off on her? Was Wetzon becoming more like Smith? Oh, God, no, she thought, shuddering inwardly. "Well, if you don't mind, I'm going to get back to work. We are trying to run a business here." On her desk was a long list of people on her TBC list, starting with Joan Boley, who had never called her back. She pulled Joan's suspect sheet and called her private number.

"Marley Straus."

That was odd. She'd dialed the private number and had gotten the switchboard. "Joan Boley, please."

"Do you have an account with us?"

Wetzon's hand froze on the receiver. She moved her lips, but nothing came out. Finally, she managed to squeeze out a "No, why?"

"Because Ms. Boley is no longer employed by—"

"Do you know where I can reach her?"

"You're not a client?"

"No. I went to . . ." She quickly checked the suspect sheet. ". . . Simmons with Joan and I'm in town on a buying trip."

"I'm sorry, I can't help you."

Damn. Usually that fabrication worked. Wetzon hung up and called Fred. She held the receiver in place with her shoulder and tried to get Smith's attention, but Smith was wearing her client voice, talking in crisp tones into her telephone.

"Fred Benitos's office."

"Hi, Elaine. It's Wetzon. Is Joan Boley there, by any chance?"

"No, but she was in the other night and we made a copy of her books. Did Fred tell you, she took all the copies with her?" Elaine sounded pissed because she'd stayed extra hours to make those copies to facilitate Joan's move, and then Joan had not left the copies with her so Elaine could get the broker-to-broker transfer of accounts set up and ready to go to clients the minute Joan came on board.

"Ask Fred to call me when he gets back."

Behind her, she could feel Smith all pumped up and ready to burst, which she did the minute Wetzon replaced the receiver.

"Wait till you hear this. Rona already called him. He's on his way to handle the bail hearing."

"Good for Rona, but you know they'll never let her back at Rosenkind, Luwisher unless she's cleared."

"True."

"And that could take a long time if there's a trial."

"Unless we clear her, and we will."

"Oh, Smith, pie in the sky." Wetzon was resigned to losing the fee.

"Why are you being so negative all of a sudden? That's not like you. Do I have to remind you it's not over till it's over? And even when—"

"It's over, it's not over," Wetzon finished with her, halfheartedly. "I know, but I think we're about to take another hit here. Joan Boley is missing." She waved the suspect sheet at Smith, giving her coffee mug a swat with her elbow. The mug spit a shower of coffee on her papers.

Smith stamped her foot. "No!"

Coffee stains soaked into suspect sheets. *Very nice, Wetzon,* she told herself as she blotted up the mess with a tissue. "If it's true, I'll see that there's blood on the Street, personally. My God." She tapped her forehead with her index finger and looked at Smith.

Smith had gotten out of her chair and was half sitting on her desk, one long leg on the floor, the other swinging back and forth. "What *are* you talking about?"

"That's what the psychic said." Wetzon laughed nastily. "If it meant that I'd commit murder, she was right." But the psychic had also talked about separation and changes. Had she foreseen the problems with Silvestri and the appearance of Alton Pinkus?

"Didn't I tell you she was good? You never take this seriously. Now where do you think Joan Boley is?"

"She might have gone to SMQ."

"With us?"

"I'm afraid not."

"Why would she go to SMQ? I thought she wanted to get into management. Wasn't Fred offering her that?"

"Yes." Wetzon gave her a sardonic grin.

"I'm sorry I asked. I should know if you look for logic on Wall Street, you'll never find it. And brokers never know what they want anyway."

"I have a funny feeling this is a Harold Alpert special via Tom Keegen."

Smith splayed her hand on her left breast. "I am not a violent person, but I will do violence if I get my hands on either of them."

"You'll have to stand behind me." Wetzon flipped through her Rolodex for the number of SMQ and dialed it. "Joan Boley, please. Oh, thank you very much," she murmured, covering the mouthpiece. To Smith, she said, "They're ringing through. Would you believe—"

"Joan Boley."

"Well, Joan—"

"Wetzon—oh, dear—let me call you back—"

"Do, please." Wetzon hung up. "Fred's going to be wild."

"When she calls back, beat the shit out of her. Tell her she's made a terrible mistake, but don't say anything bad about GTQ."

"You should know by now that I'm not going to bad-mouth a client. And I'm not going to beat her up. You know damn well that's not my style. She's there already, for godsakes."

"At the moment your style, sweetie pie, is not lining our pockets." Back and forth her silken leg swung.

"Okay, *sweetie pie*, would you like to take over my interview with Stuart Beck for me at four-fifteen today?"

"I would not." Smith wrinkled her nose. "Just be aware." She stopped when she saw Wetzon's face, and changed the subject. "Do you have anything on for tonight?"

"I have an appointment."

"Oh, really?" Smith rolled her eyes to the ceiling.

"A *dinner* appointment. Why?"

"Well, I think we have to set up a brainstorming session about Rona as soon as she's out on bail. The sooner we get her cleared, the sooner we'll see our money. I'm going to see if I can arrange with Neil that the clock doesn't start ticking on our year until she's back."

As if by mutual agreement, they picked up their weapons and went back into the fray, Smith trying to buy time on their deal with Rosenkind, Luwisher and Wetzon to get back in the saddle with candidates. She knew full well that too many tumbles and you lost your nerve. She had to get right back on the horse again.

When Fred Benitos returned her call, she broke the bad news about Joan Boley to him.

"I don't understand, Wetzon, I gave her everything she wanted —the upfront, the higher payout, the sales assistant, cold callers—and I was making her a sales manager. She told me, 'Fred, you can count on me. I'll be there on November twenty-seventh.' I really have to question her ethics. Not even to call me and give me another shot at her. . . . What do you think they offered her?"

"I don't know, but I'll find out. I'm really sorry about this, Fred." These days she found she was spending more and more time apologizing for bad behavior, for downright rudeness, for thoughtlessness. This was a business where you never burn your bridges. There was no telling, with mergers, acquisitions, and insolvencies, where people you've stepped on will end up. After she hung up, Wetzon sat and stared at her papers without really seeing them.

When Smith finished her conversation with Neil Munchen, she was triumphant. "All right! Now we're talking! Neil's agreed to give us three months. If Rona's not back by then, it's a loss." She rose and looked at her watch. "I've got to run over to Saks to get a few odds and ends. How about lunch?"

"I'll order in. I have my meeting to confirm and people to talk to. Seymour Wells, for example." She picked out his number. Wells was the producing manager at White, Mooney, and Wetzon had known him when he was a wild rookie. It was hard to believe he was a manager now.

"You mean Sleazemore Wells, don't you?" Smith shrugged into the jacket of her suit.

"Good morning, thank you for calling White, Mooney," an operator announced in a lilting voice.

"Slea—I mean *Seymour* Wells, please." She put her fingers over the mouthpiece to cover Smith's naughty laughter and hissed, "Get out of here, will you, before I throw this at you." She gestured with the phone.

"You might call one of your police contacts and find out what they have on Rona."

Wetzon made hissing noises at Smith.

"Seymour Wells."

Wetzon threw Smith her best hard-eyed look, then smiled into the phone and said, "Seymour, how are you? This is Wetzon. I'm just calling to see where we stand with—"

"Wetzon, talk fast. I haven't got time. I have someone who's a real recruiter on the other line."

"Excuse me?"

"I'm going to talk to a real recruiter. You know, one who doesn't look like a Donna Mills doll."

"Donna Mills? Seymour, what are you talking about?" She was almost sputtering with rage.

"Lighten up, doll," Seymour said. "Talk to you later."

Left with a dial tone, Wetzon slammed the receiver down. "Lighten up!"

Smith, the door half open—one step out—stopped. "Now what?"

"Men! They will never take us seriously on the Street. I don't know why we bother. I was talking to him as a professional and he gives me this crap about how I'm a doll recruiter—Donna Mills, to be exact—and he had a *real* recruiter on the other line, and when I protest he says to *lighten up*."

Smith's eyes flared. "Donna Mills looks like a—"

"Exactly. A sex object."

"It's what I always say, and you never listen. The male rats crossed the electrified grid for sex more than food." Smith closed the door behind her. Which was a good thing, because Wetzon threw her Filofax and hit the door with a loud thud.

Wetzon was frazzled. Loose ends were all around her. Her work, her life, this case. And nothing got settled. Everything just kept getting more and more complicated. And she needed things to be settled.

Smith was right. If they could find out what the police had on Rona—but wouldn't *Dickie* be able to fill that in for them? She picked up the phone. Ferrante wouldn't tell her, that was for sure. Walters?

No. She tapped at the numbers for the Seventeenth Precinct and asked to speak to Artie Metzger, Silvestri's partner.

"Metzger." Metzger's voice was funereal and suited his basset-hound face.

"Hi, Artie, this is Leslie."

"Leslie! How are you?" She could hear phones ringing and the familiar general precinct clamor.

"I don't really know, Artie. Can we get together and talk? Do you have any time for me?"

"Always. You tell me."

"I need some information. A broker was murdered in the Conservatory Garden and then a girl who worked as his assistant was killed at Lincoln Center yesterday. Do you know what I'm talking about?"

"Yeah. Some."

"Well, another broker—the ex-wife—has been arrested for the murders. I need to know as much about it as you can tell me, legally."

"Uh, you know . . ."

"I don't want to put you on the spot, Artie, but if you can . . ." She let it hang there.

"I'll see what I can dig up, but I'm not promising."

They fixed a meeting at Rusty Staub's for lunch the next day, and neither of them mentioned Silvestri, although Silvestri, or rather, Silvestri's absence, was very much there between them.

She opened the back door and stepped out into their garden. Dry leaves, plants getting ready for winter. The sky was muffled by gray clouds. Wetzon sighed and went back to her desk. She ordered her soul food—a tuna on pita and decaf coffee—from What's Cooking. That was infinitely better. At least she was doing something constructive. The only really important thing left she had to do was confirm today's interview. Stu Beck's office number was in her appointment book next to his name at four-fifteen. Her mind was full to overflowing of so much garbage, she hadn't considered where he worked.

Stu Beck worked at Bliss Norderman. He was one of Tony Maglia's brokers.

35

....

Wetzon looked at herself critically in the full-length mirror. Her skirt ended about two inches above her knees, but they were good knees. "Smith, do you think my skirt's too short?"

Smith had just come through the door carrying a fat shopping bag from Saks. She tilted her head and studied Wetzon. "No, but I think it's time to stop wearing black."

"Black? Oh, am I wearing black?" Wetzon turned back to the mirror. She was wearing a black suit with a long jacket, black hose, little black heels. "If I stop wearing black, I will decimate my entire wardrobe."

"Women of a certain age and all that."

"Oh, come *on*, Smith!"

"Look at you, it's absolutely too severe. Black suit, white blouse. No color. You're as pale as a ghost. And you've got to do something about those black rings under your eyes."

"Couldn't you just pretend I look wonderful? All I need is one uninterrupted night's sleep."

"Well, then you shouldn't have made a dinner date." The way Smith said it made it sound as if Wetzon was in the middle of a triple-X-rated love affair.

"Oh, shut up, Smith."

"On the other hand," Smith continued in the same tone, "if it's with who I think it is, you'll probably sleep well. These old men . . ."

Wetzon showed Smith the palm of her hand. "That's enough. I'm leaving now. If you need me for any reason, I'll be interviewing Stu Beck at the Four Seasons."

"And where will you be later, sugar?" Smith was laughing at her.

"At home," she said firmly. She began packing suspect sheets into her briefcase.

"Wait! I have something for you. It will jazz up your Vampira costume." Smith was pulling tissue-wrapped items from the shopping bag, peeking into them, and setting them aside. "A little giftie-poo. Ah, here it is." She pulled a long silk scarf in a brilliant blue, black, and crimson paisley from one of the bags and clipped off the tag with her cuticle scissors. "Stand still." She tucked it under the collar of Wetzon's silk blouse and knotted it loosely in front. "There now, look. It gives you some color. . . . And don't go out of here without lipstick, please."

Smith was right, Wetzon thought. The scarf made a big difference, pulled the whole outfit together. "Thank you." She added the lipstick. "Where were you so long? I thought we'd miss each other."

"There was a sale on shoes . . . and I wanted to talk to Dickie. His office is in Rockefeller Center."

"Oh? Did you find anything out?"

"They're arranging bail for Rona. A hundred thou." She was repacking the shopping bag.

"God!" Wetzon opened the door to their reception area. Max was in the middle of a very thorough interview with a broker.

Smith shrugged. "Well, she killed two people."

Wetzon pulled her Burberry from the closet and returned to their office, closing the door.

"Watch what you say, Smith."

Flapping her hand, Smith said, "Oh, for pity sakes. Now don't make plans for tomorrow night, please. We're holding a meeting. I don't know where yet, probably in Dickie's office."

"Okay. See you tomorrow." Wetzon closed the door on Smith and stood for a moment in front of Max's desk.

"Would you be willing to take a call from one of our principals, Leslie Wetzon?" Pause. "What time of day is good for you?" Pause. "Okay. Expect a call . . ." He looked up at Wetzon and she mouthed *tomorrow.* "Tomorrow," Max said. "It was a pleasure talking with you." He hung up and nodded to Wetzon, placing the suspect sheet in a growing stack for Wetzon to call.

"Good work, Max." She gave him a thumbs-up sign. "I'm off to interview Stu Beck at the Four Seasons, in case he should forget where he's supposed to be at a quarter after four."

Stepping out on the brick landing, Wetzon narrowly missed bumping the woman coming down the steps to their door. "Oh, I'm sorry. Can I help you?"

The woman had shoulder-length brown hair and was about Wetzon's age, give or take two years. She wore a business suit under an open gray raincoat. "I'm Marissa Peiser, from the D.A.'s office. You are?" She dug a bent card out of her coat pocket, among a collection of crumpled tissues.

"Leslie Wetzon."

"Good." Peiser handed Wetzon the card and stuffed the tissues back in her pocket. "I have some questions to ask you. About Rona Middleton."

"I'm just heading out to an appointment. If you'd like, you can walk with me to the Four Seasons, and I'll answer your questions, but I have to tell you I don't think Rona murdered Tabitha."

Without further preamble, both began walking.

"Why not?" Marissa Peiser had a nice, forthright face, the kind of face that didn't judge. People probably opened up to her.

"Because Rona cared for the girl. She was her goddaughter." They walked across Second Avenue and west on Forty-ninth Street. The air was damp and chilly, the sky overcast. It would rain later.

"What about her husband, Brian Middleton?"

"Brian was a shit—to everyone. I'm sure you know from Ferrante about how Rona reacted at the M.E.'s office the day Brian's body was found. You don't need to hear it from me. Brian was screwing his old manager, Tony Maglia, his clients, like Penny Ann Boyd, and his new manager, Simon Loveman. Not to mention me and my partner. He was a real—pardon the expression—dirtbag."

"They were both killed with the same gun."

"Then Rona certainly isn't guilty. Do you have the gun?"

Peiser shrugged. Wetzon squinted at her. That probably meant they didn't have the murder weapon.

The women turned north on Lexington and walked up to Fifty-second Street, where the assistant D.A. stopped and confirmed the spelling of Tony Maglia and Simon Loveman, which she wrote on a ragged notepad she took from her shoulder bag.

"I'm leaving you here, if you don't mind," Wetzon said when Marissa finished writing.

"Fine. I'd like to continue our talk later."

"Can't."

"Tomorrow?"

"How about around this time? Call me in the office." Wetzon looked for her cardcase in her briefcase, then searched her handbag, found it, and handed Peiser her card. "My schedule is pretty jammed over the next two days." This was no lie, but Wetzon felt she should call Arthur Margolies to get some legal advice before she talked further with anyone. She—Wetzon—was what linked Rona to Lincoln Center and Tabitha's death, and she had fudged with Walters, had not told the detective that she had broken into Dr. Jerry's apartment. She hadn't told anyone but Smith.

"Your partner, Xenia Smith, is she still in the office? I'd like to talk to her."

Wetzon grinned. She couldn't help it. "Go right back. I'm sure you'll catch her. And I'm sure she'll be helpful. She *loves* lawyers."

Her cardcase still in her hand, Wetzon stopped under the awning of the Four Seasons. She didn't believe in the supernatural or tarot cards or psychics, but she . . . something . . . a message . . . no, an idea was coming through and wanted space in her thoughts. The cardcase seemed to burn in her hand. She held it out in front of her, looked at it carefully.

Then the scene in Dr. Jerry's consulting room played back in her head, *ratta-tat-tat*. Dr. J., Hartmann, Smith, and Penny Ann finally leaving. There she was, coming out of the closet and spilling the contents of her briefcase, stuffing everything back, someone at the door, hiding in the closet again. She saw herself crawl out of the closet, heard the phone ring. Saw herself answering it. She was sitting at the desk talking to Rona on the phone, pretending to be Penny Ann. In her mind's eye, she saw herself pick up the cardcase and slip it into her handbag. She hadn't questioned what it was doing on the desk. She'd thought she'd gathered everything up, but she must have missed the case. And she'd been too stupidly groggy to realize it.

Could someone have known, then, that she was there? Chagrined, she remembered now that the swinging doors to the kitchen had been open when she came in and closed when she left.

Someone had been in the apartment and overheard Rona's call.

36

•••••••

Because it was only four-thirty and the bar at the Four Seasons was not yet teaming with the usual end-of-the-day crowd, Wetzon chose one of the banquettes along the west wall and ordered a club soda with lime from the bartender. After five, waiters began servicing the area around the bar.

Stu Beck had been a confidential referral from another broker, and Wetzon had been talking to him every other month for the past seven or eight months. Her first call had been a cold call and she'd told him she'd heard that he was dynamite and had always wanted to talk to him. Flattering, but also true.

The bartender slapped the glass of club soda on the bar for Wetzon and went on to serve a tall man with silvery hair wearing a beautifully tailored dark blue suit. Something told her he was not a solitary drinker but was waiting for someone.

She got up and collected her club soda and sat down again on the banquette. The Four Seasons at this time of day was quiet, conducive to thought. She unleashed her mind and let it wander. Whoever had been in Dr. Jerry's office had rushed up to Lincoln Center and killed Tabitha. It couldn't have been Rona.

Picking at the dish of salted nuts, Wetzon found an elegant Brazil nut and placed it in her mouth.

Stu Beck was easy enough to spot when he came up the stairs. Short and chubby, his suit was not quite conservative, the knot of his tie not quite pristine, the collar of his white shirt a bit too wide. His hair was also a bit too long and too curly. He was just a little off all around. And he was round. When he looked in her direction, she waved to him and he wove his way through three women and two men, who were standing at the bar drinking beer, talking loudly enough for Wetzon to discern that the firm they were with was First B-O.

Stu set his overstuffed briefcase on the end of the banquette and grinned at her. His thick slash of brown mustache jiggled, didn't look real. She wondered, was it pasted on with spirit gum? He beckoned to a tall man with sandy hair in a charcoal pinstripe on the stairs.

"So, Wetzon, we finally meet." He caught the bartender's eye and raised his voice. "Gimme two Becks." Grinned at her again. "Have to keep the money in the family."

"Very funny, Stu." She knew there was no connection.

The man in the charcoal pinstripe was suddenly seating himself in the chair opposite the banquette. He was younger close up, perhaps late twenties, early thirties, with boy-next-door looks. Younger than Stu. "I'm Larry Sellica," he said, shaking Wetzon's hand. "You look surprised. Didn't Stu tell you I was coming?"

"No, but it's okay. Are you two partners?" Two! She tasted a very nice fee here.

"We're keeping our own numbers and sharing a number on some accounts when we bring them in together. We're going after the big pension funds," Larry said, taking one of the beers, which Stu had set on the small cocktail table.

"Yeah, Larry is a great asset gatherer and not a bad stock jockey, and I'm the expert in fixed income."

"So you'd like to move together?" Larry was the exact opposite of Stu in appearance. He was almost a mannequin, with a perfect haircut, perfect shave, buffed and square-cut nails on beautiful hands with long tapered fingers. Just the right amount of white French cuff visible with the classic gold cuff links from Tiffany's. "If I take both of you, Maglia will put out a contract on me."

Stu snorted. "We want the biggest deal on the Street. Together we do well over a mil—"

"More." Larry overrode him, as New Yorkers tend to override one another when they talk in tandem. "I just picked up two accounts from Dov Berkowitz."

Wetzon knew Berkowitz was a young rookie, a great account opener. A bundle of energy, he was itching to get into a cold-calling situation. She'd advised him to sit tight until he had a full year in production under his belt. Had he jumped somewhere without her?

She asked, "What happened to Dov? Did he jump ship?"

"Yeah, right out of the business." Stu scratched his mustache and dispelled the foam from the beer that had settled there. "He couldn't hack it."

"That's right," Larry agreed. He had that clear, steady gaze that spelled honesty, and he looked you right in the eye when he spoke to you. "Look, I'm in for the long haul, and if you burn a client, you burn him. You lose him. You find another client. That's the way the business is. The trouble with Dov was that he couldn't burn a client. He got all those accounts open with good clients, and then he couldn't take the risks you have to take to make it in this business."

The callous words were incongruous, coming from someone so clean-cut. *So what else is new, Wetzon,* she asked herself. "Okay, guys, why do you want out of Bliss Norderman? You'll be asked that. Do you have a good answer? No manager likes to think you're coming to his firm just for the money, even when they know in their hearts you are."

"They're schmucks, then. If you don't go for the big bucks on a move in this business, you gotta have your head examined," Stu said. "Besides, it's a distinct possibility that Bliss is heading south."

Of course, she'd heard those rumors, rumors about the insurance-company parent of Bliss Norderman being disgusted with the losses of the brokerage firm. "I can't believe Jefferson Mutual will allow that to happen."

"Think again, Wetzon," Larry said. "Shit, everyone knows we're on the block. The losses in real estate keep piling up. Any buyer is going to have to write in a fat slush fund."

"So, Wetzon," Stu said impatiently, "tell us what the deals are out there." He ordered two more beers with no thought to what Wetzon was drinking.

"For you guys, they're great. Thirty to thirty-five percent up-front from one of the big wire houses."

"How does it work? Is it a loan or what?"

"You get a check for the whole thing when you walk in the door, and it's called a loan, with a third forgiven each year. You'll have to sign a contract for the three years."

"What's the bogie?"

"You keep your gross production at least at seventy percent of what it was when you walk in the door. That should be easy. If you come in the door doing five hundred thousand, you have to come in the next year at a minimum of three fifty to meet the bogie and not lose the deal. You can do that."

They looked at each other and nodded. "But what if there's another crash, or one of us gets in an accident and is laid up?" Larry asked.

"There are two of you. If there should be a crash, no firm is going to hold anyone to the bogie. They didn't in 1987."

Grabbing a fistful of salted nuts, Stu devoured them without closing his mouth, so that pieces of nuts spilled over his lips and stuck to his mustache.

Larry looked at his watch. The ubiquitous timekeeper of Wall Street, the gold Rolex. "What about Rosenkind, Luwisher? We heard they do deals."

"Not really. A decent guarantee and a high payout for a year."

"Well," Stu said, "they gave Rona Middleton a deal and she didn't even have a book. Now they got nothing." He looked at Larry, and they both laughed.

So word had spread over the Street only hours after Rona's arrest. The Street was a maze of networks, all attuned to spreading gossip. "You heard about Rona?"

"Yeah." Stu looked gleeful. "I just spent the last two hours calling her and Brian's accounts."

God, Wetzon thought. "You're not even waiting until the body is cold, Stu?"

"Aw, come on, Wetzon, I deserve those accounts. Rona got them the easy way—on her back." He gave a lewd guffaw, and Larry joined him.

"What's that supposed to mean?" Why did the men of Wall Street always assume a successful woman made it to the top on her back? Was it too threatening to think she made it because she was smart? Maybe smarter than they were?

"Wake up, Wetzon. Rona and Tony have been taking each other's temperature since she got into the business."

"You have to be kidding." She felt her mouth drop open and

gave herself a silent order: *Close your mouth, Wetzon.* "Silly me, I thought they loathed each other."

"Word of honor," Stu said, hand on his heart. "They think it's top secret, but you'd have to be blind *and* dead not to know."

Larry said, "They're getting it on, all right. Everyone knows about it."

"Oh, come on, fellas." The idea was preposterous. They must be setting her up. Tony was half Rona's size. They loathed one another. "This is a joke, isn't it?"

They exchanged smirks, and Stu nodded knowingly. "They got this place, whadayacallit, a shtup nest?" He hooted. "In that Jap hotel. You know, the Park Royale."

37
·······

Afen Stu and Larry left, Wetzon ordered an Amstel Light and sat on the banquette making notes about each broker, his production, business mix, choice of firms, and availability for appointments. But she couldn't keep what they'd told her about Rona and Tony Maglia from intruding. Had Brian known? Was that why he'd refused to acknowledge Megan as his child?

What strange alliances resulted. Brian and Tony against Rona after she moved to Rosenkind, Luwisher. Brian and Tony against Penny Ann Boyd, Brian's client. And Tabitha Ann Boyd, Tony, and Brian against Penny Ann. Were Rona and Tony still involved? And what about Tony's wife? How did she figure in all of this?

She played with the beer glass, turning it around and around, doodling in the frost, sipping it, and watched the group clustered around the bar. The silver-haired man had been joined by a young woman who was not his daughter. Daughters don't stroke their father's lapels and fathers don't fondle their daughter's necks. At least not that way. *But oh, well, yes, do lighten up, Wetzon.*

She remembered once, when she was still in college, spending the day with a date in Manhattan. She'd known Alan at Rutgers and then he went to law school at Cornell. They'd gone to a bar in the Village and met another couple: Howard, a law-school chum of Alan's, and another man, who was Howard's friend, a teacher, and his fiancée, a social worker. It was easy to see that everyone but Wetzon and the fiancée thought Howard was terrific. He dominated the conversation, made it circle around him. The fiancée and Howard argued about everything. It was a clash of wills, and everyone seemed to enjoy it except Wetzon.

On the ride home Alan had asked, didn't Wetzon think Howard was wonderful. Wetzon replied that Howard was loud, coarse, egocentric, and rude. All the things, she now thought, that probably made a good criminal lawyer.

"The women love him," Alan had countered, as if that made him a deity.

"Not *this* woman. And certainly not his friend's fiancée."

"That's how much you know. Howard's making it with her."

All these years later, she was having the same reaction about Rona and Tony, and she wondered, with slow amazement, did she live her life in another dimension from everyone else? Smith wouldn't have been shocked, nor would Carlos. And certainly not Silvestri.

Carlos always kidded her with "You can take the girl out of the farm, but you can't take the farm out of the girl." It must be true, for growing up on the farm had isolated her from the world, had colored her approach to life, and she still found herself shocked by deceit, greed, and gratuitous evil.

She paid the bill and went downstairs to collect her coat from the checkroom. Coat on, tip in tray, she was ready to go up to Mt. Sinai to meet Alton Pinkus. The phone booths—two of them—were in a private cubbyhole, each in its own private mahogany casing. The right thing to do first was to call Smith and report the latest news about Rona and Tony Maglia, but the almost four-year-old image of Barry Stark, sliding out of one of the booths very dead, gave her pause.

Come on, you're a big girl now, she told herself, and marched into the cubbyhole. Barry's booth was occupied; relieved, she slipped into the other and called Smith. The phone rang fifteen times and she hung up, thinking Smith's not having an answering machine was a manipulation. You had to keep calling her, and that meant your time and concentration were always revolving around her.

She got up and left the booth, standing a moment and feeling a chill as if someone had walked over her grave again. Brushing it away, she hurried out of the Four Seasons onto Fifty-second Street. She caught a cab that was dropping an English couple, who greeted the doorman by his first name, as if they were frequent visitors.

In the cab she thought of Silvestri. She'd met him that same day Barry was murdered.

The cabdriver, a youngish man with a heavy Russian accent, was not a talker. His radio was playing a WNEW tribute to Sinatra. Wetzon leaned back in her seat and closed her eyes.

"Hey!"

She woke with a start. The cabdriver was knocking on the glass partition. "Sorry." She fumbled in her bag and gave him a ten. "Give me two dollars back, please."

It had turned warm again, and pleasant. The sun, having made a first brief appearance while she was in the cab, was beginning to sink westward. She was truly exhausted, had no business keeping this appointment. Date. It was a date. *Face it, Wetzon.* Why hadn't she just canceled and gone home to bed? She could still do it, make a call, get out of it. But she got out of the cab and walked past the pay phone.

There were several entrances on Madison Avenue between Ninety-eighth and 100th Street to the huge hospital complex, but Alton had been very specific. He had even left her name with security. The elevators jammed with visitors and medical personnel crept slowly, and the smells and activity of the hospital were oppressive.

She found the administrative offices eventually after straying down the wrong corridor and receiving directions from an orderly wheeling an empty gurney.

A small woman, blond streaks on gray hair, wearing earphones, was clicking away on a word processor, working from a dictaphone. She stopped when she saw Wetzon and tilted the earphones away from one ear. The sign on her desk said "June," and since it was October, June must be her name.

"I'm supposed to meet Mr. Pinkus here."

"Oh yes, Ms. Wetzon, right? His meeting is running late, and he'll be another half hour. You can wait here."

Wetzon looked around the room. It was windowless, spare, somewhat scruffy, and much too hot. Medicine intruded, seeped through everything here. "I think I'll take a walk. It's gotten nice out."

"I wouldn't go too far. This area can be dangerous, particularly after the sun goes down."

"What about Fifth Avenue? There are museums there." *Wait a minute*, she thought. She knew just how to entertain herself for the next half hour.

"Well," the woman said doubtfully, "I suppose—"

"I'll be back." She was on the move then, with quick steps, knowing her destination. Like a bird dog with one thought on her mind, Wetzon made her way through doctors and hospital personnel and visitors.

Once on the street she walked over to Fifth Avenue, crossed to the park. The day suddenly seemed elastic for her, stretching out its last hour of light.

She quickened her steps till she came to a tall Victorian Gate. The Conservatory Garden.

38
·······

The Conservatory Garden was a scooped-out, defined part of Central Park, an oversized and serious garden with plantings created in two distinct styles. North of Vanderbilt Gate it was French, parterres of gray-leafed santolina and thousands of chrysanthemums around a working fountain sculpture of gamboling maidens. South was an English garden of flower beds and yew hedges and topiary. Flagstone paths looped their way through both sections, surrounded by ivy-layered yew trees that sprung from ivy carpets. Asters, snapdragons, and ornamental grasses grew in clusters; clumps of tiny yellow daisies on tall, narrow stalks fought for space among stiff-stemmed, fragile blues, like baby's breath. She'd been invited to a wedding here once, years ago, but she'd had a Sunday matinee performance and had to send regrets. Regrets. Rosemary was for remembrance. What was for regrets?

Although it wasn't raining, a lone woman strolled on the path that skimmed the circumference of the gardens, holding an open umbrella, and Wetzon followed her. In the hills beyond the garden, Central Park looked like an uninhabited wilderness. If one listened carefully, she wondered, would one hear a wolf howl?

But here in this peaceful place, where the silence was only broken by the extravagance of songbirds, there was no sign that a murder had been committed.

Passing through the French garden, Wetzon came upon a broad walkway flanked by antique-style iron and wood slat benches. Somewhere she remembered reading that these benches had been designed for the 1939 World's Fair. Old crabapple trees sent their limbs reaching across the flagstones to each other, the ruddy foliage serving as a tent above.

Two women in white pants sat talking quietly, drinking coffee from cardboard containers. One was knitting something red and bulky while her coffee cooled on the flagstone at her feet. Three teenagers, their jeans frayed in just the right places, knees showing, were staring at one of the benches, and Wetzon joined them. It was conspicuously marked with yellow crime-scene tape.

"That's where the dude bought it," one said. As ragged as they looked, it was a contrived poverty. Two were white, one black, and all three were not street by any stretch of the imagination.

Checking Wetzon out, one skinny kid elbowed the others. "Shut up, dork." They became hyper, punching and jabbing one another, bouncing and wriggling until they passed out of Wetzon's sight, leaving Wetzon alone at the scene of Brian's death.

She sat down across the paved path and contemplated the offending bench. Obviously, it was an assignation, a planned meeting. It was too far out of Brian's way to be anything else. The bench was only big enough for two people. . . . Could he have been sitting and talking to someone he trusted, as the two women were? She turned and saw they'd gone. So who was it? There were motives aplenty when it came to Brian. If it was Penny Ann, how about revenge? For funds lost, for a daughter lost? If it was Tabitha, a soured love affair? But then, who killed Tabitha? There had to be a connection. Brian had gotten an advance from Simon Loveman, for the twenty thou to cover the settlement with Penny Ann. What had happened to that money? And Maglia? Whatever Maglia had said, she was certain Brian was making the move to Loeb Dawkins. He was a dirtbag, but he never would have taken the money from Loveman if he wasn't making the move. He was going to screw Maglia. Which brought everything right back to Rona.

A small, blond woman, a tan raincoat over her maid's uniform, walked two schnauzers past. The dogs sniffed at Wetzon's feet, wagging stumpy tails. She held out her palm to them and scratched each solemnly on the head, smiling at their walker, who tugged on the leashes and said, "Come, Milli, Vanilli."

Either Milli or Vanilli looked up at Wetzon with something like irony; both allowed the woman to lead them off.

The atmosphere was suddenly heavy with humidity. Dusk fell

rapidly. Wetzon looked at her watch and rose. A half hour had passed. The garden would close soon, and it was time to get back to Mt. Sinai. She stood for a moment in front of the taped bench, hoping for an epiphany, then, on a whim, lifted the tape and wiggled into the spot on the bench where Brian had died, willing him to send her a message. She sat suspended, meditating a minute or two, but nothing came except the thought out of left field of Barbara Gordon and all that finery in the closet. So much for signs. She'd be better off with Smith's tarot cards. A parks employee was waiting at the entrance gate, and Wetzon passed through and out to Fifth Avenue. Streetlights glowed, cars had their headlights on. She hurried past the Museum of the City of New York. The hospital was lit up like a giant ocean liner.

When the traffic signal turned green, Wetzon crossed Fifth. The thought struck her halfway across, and she stopped. *Rona must have a key to Dr. Jerry's office.* The signal changed again, a car blew its horn, and she jumped, hastening to the opposite sidewalk. She'd better snap out of it, or she'd be in Mt. Sinai as a patient, or worse, a client of Dr. Jennie Vose at the morgue.

If Rona and Tony were trysting at the Park Royale, as Stu Beck and Larry Sellica had said, you could bet they weren't springing for a room, not when they could get one for nothing. Could Rona have been in Dr. Jerry's office, found Wetzon's cardcase, and guessed Wetzon was still there? Could she have pretended to leave and then made the phone call from a phone in the kitchen? No. *Come on, Wetzon, how convoluted can you get?* There would have to have been a separate line. And how could Rona have gotten up to Lincoln Center that fast? Still, it was true, that old rhyme about the tangled web we weave when first we practice to deceive.

She squeezed onto an overloaded elevator, because she knew if she didn't she'd have to wait at least ten minutes for another. Why were elevators in hospitals and municipal buildings always slower and more crowded than those in commercial buildings? It confounded her.

Did the police know yet about the affair? It would strengthen the motives of both Tony and Rona. And both were left-handed.

When she got back to the office at Mt. Sinai, June was packing away her earphones and tidying up her desk. The meeting had just adjourned. A group of well-dressed men and women, all in their forties and upward, were shaking hands and taking their leave. Almost before she realized, Alton was drawing her in and introducing her around, and soon she was shaking hands with the head of a major cosmetics company, a legendary fashion designer, and several star surgeons whose names had a familiar ring.

Alton's obvious delight with her was unsettling. Wetzon felt like some sort of trophy. What had been so flattering, and still was, seemed in a vague way threatening. Not seemed—was. Threatening to her way of life, her relationship with Silvestri. *What relationship?* she asked herself angrily, fighting what she didn't understand.

It was raining when they got to the street, and Alton, disdaining her offer to share her umbrella, bolted to a nearby parking garage, handed his ticket to the clerk, and waited for her to join him. He moved like a much younger man.

Would he drive, she wondered, a Mercedes? A Jag? Something Japanese, like Silvestri's Toyota? Wrong in all respects. He drove American. A Mercury Cougar, to be exact. And when she wondered aloud, he said, "I always buy union."

She adjusted herself under the seat belt and realized it was the same movement as adjusting oneself under crime-scene tape on a park bench. "How could I think otherwise?"

Alton looked over at her and laughed.

They drove down Fifth in sheets of rain so torrential that the windshield wipers were useless and the windows fogged up. At Eighty-fifth Street, they drove slowly through the transverse from the East Side to the West Side. Traffic crawled and great pools, minireservoirs, sprang up everywhere. They didn't talk. The windshield wipers went *chung-chung, chung-chung.*

"I thought I'd play chef tonight," he said. "And besides, it's such a lousy night to be out." He glanced over at her. "What's the matter?"

What was the matter? Everything. She felt a flutter of panic in her chest. He wanted her to have dinner with him, but in his apartment. She remembered what had happened last year when Chris Gorham had asked her to wait in his apartment. . . . She was not handling this well.

When they got through the Park, he pulled into a bus stop on Central Park West and stopped the car and looked at her.

She said, "I'm sorry. I had an unpleasant experience last

year, and when you said we'd be eating in your apartment, I panicked."

"Leslie," Alton said, softly. He took her fisted hands and gently
pried them open. "You don't have to be afraid of me. I'm not saying
I'm a saint. I'm a man, and I want to make love to you. But that's
something that has to be mutual. Let's take it one step at a time,
okay?"

"Okay." *Grow up, Wetzon. It had happened once. It isn't going to
happen a second time. Still . . .*

"And I'll get you home at a decent hour, for me as well as you.
I'm sitting on an arbitration panel tomorrow morning."

39

· · · · · · · ·

Wetzon was perched on a high stool, her stockinged feet curled around the legs, watching Alton—sleeves rolled to his elbows and tieless—finish the salad dressing. He turned back to the stove, gave the risotto another spin with his fork, and took a sip of wine. Her shoes had gotten a soaking from the short distance between the car and the awning of Alton's building, and she'd packed them with towel paper and set them down with her purse on the red vinyl tile floor at her feet.

Alton was sure of himself in the kitchen, too. His collar was open and his face was flushed with the heat of the stove. Deft of hand, purposeful, his movements were calm and smooth, and she wondered if he made love like that.

Wetzon played with the stem of her glass, disconcerted by her thoughts.

"How are you at tossing?" he asked.

"What?" What had he said? Tossing? She felt her face get hot. "The salad."

"Oh, sure." *Why are you behaving like such a dork?* she asked herself. She stirred the dressing vigorously and poured it over the salad, a colorful mix of greens and purples, then tossed it between two giant plastic forks. She felt weary.

Alton turned, skillet in hand, ready to serve the risotto, and caught her. "Tired?"

"Yes. I've had only one decent night's sleep since my apartment was flooded last Friday. . . . God, that was almost a week ago." In six days her whole life had done a complete turnaround. It was amazing. She grinned at Alton. "But I'm famished, too, so don't just stand there, feed me."

He divided the risotto with porcini mushrooms between each plate. "We can sit here or at the table."

"Let's sit here. I like kitchens."

"So do I." He got up on the stool next to her, and they rubbed elbows.

The risotto was just the right half-custardy consistency. "This is wonderful," she said, but she was thinking how nice it was that he and Silvestri both loved to cook. The wine was tart and acidy on her tongue, and she sighed.

"What are you thinking?" he asked, helping himself to more salad.

"Boring things." She finished everything on her plate.

"Try me." He emptied the bottle of wine, a bit in each glass.

"The mess in my apartment, business—which is not so good right now because one of my brokers didn't make a planned move—and a complicated, convoluted consulting problem." There was no reason to bring murder into it.

"Do you know this fellow Middleton who was murdered last week?" He got off the stool and took a package of coffee from his freezer, holding it up. "Decaf espresso?"

"Fine. Yes, I know him—knew him. Don't look so surprised. There are very few brokers in New York I don't know. Brian, however, was the broker who didn't make the move I'd planned for him." Her smile was rueful.

He began measuring coffee into an electric Krups, and he didn't respond at first. She thought he hadn't heard her. She picked up the plates and silver and put them in the sink, then watched him cut strips of rind from a lemon and put them on a small plate. The coffee maker pshshed and pshshed. Smiling down at her, Alton touched her face, and she caught the lemon scent from his hands.

"Does your hair ever come down?" He took her in his arms.

"Never," she said. It felt good to be held, like being snug under a blanket, but she wasn't ready for this. The coffee maker sputtered and spit, finished, and she eased away. "Where's your bathroom?"

His bathroom was at the end of a short hallway past his bedroom. She took a quick surreptitious peek. Tan wall-to-wall carpet, terra-cotta walls, two wing chairs in front of a fireplace, bookshelves, big bed. *Keep moving, Wetzon.*

In the bathroom she took her hair down and rolled it up again tightly, reapplied her lipstick, smiled at herself to make sure there was no food in her teeth. Her eyelids were heavy and dark, darker than the shadow she normally used.

It felt good to be wanted, to have someone like Alton Pinkus desire her, but she was starting to feel like a zombie.

When she came back down the hall, he called to her, "In here," and she followed his voice into the living room. He had a fire going in the fireplace, that seducer Mozart on the stereo; on the coffee table, coffee cups sat on a silver tray with a carafe of coffee next to a bottle of liqueur and two small glasses.

The furniture was traditional, leaning toward the modern, the floor covered with a huge Oriental in lush rusts and earth colors. She sat on the sand-colored sofa and curled her feet up under her, watching Alton pour the coffee and twist the lemon peel into each cup.

"Sambuca?"

"*Un poco.*" She indicated with her thumb and forefinger, then took the glass after he filled it. She thought in Smith's voice: *You are going to hell, sweetie pie.* The sambuca coated her tongue licorice.

Handing her a cup of coffee, Alton sat down opposite her on a club chair.

"What's the arbitration process like?" she asked, sipping her coffee. "I mean, when it's client v. broker and brokerage firm?"

He leaned forward and set his cup down on the table. "The client files a complaint against his or her broker and the firm."

She was having trouble keeping her eyes open. They kept sliding shut and daring her to open them.

"It works for quarrels between firms, between employees and firms and clients. You know, of course, clients sign a mandatory arbitration clause when they open an account with any firm."

She nodded, covering her mouth over a yawn.

"In June of '87, probably because of heavy lobbying by Shearson, the Supreme Court ruled that clients must arbitrate even claims of violations of securities law, rather than go to court. The arbitrators are chosen from a list of candidates recruited by the brokerage firms."

"Sounds a bit biased to me. How many arbitrators make up a panel?"

"Three. One from the securities industry, two from the public."

"Where do you fit in?" Her hand trembled, and she set the coffee cup down.

"I'm no longer on the board of Luwisher Brothers—not since Luwisher Brothers merged with L.L. Rosenkind—and I have no real connection with the industry."

"And you have a reputation for being fair-minded and . . ." she searched for the right word. Her brain wasn't working. "Clean."

"Clean?" He smiled at her. "I suppose so. Arbitrators are chosen by the New York Stock Exchange and the National Association of Securities Dealers, so the process might be called biased, but speaking for myself, it's not. And now that our awards are no longer secret and how the process works is not a mystery, I think we're on the right track." He paused. "And then I went out and robbed a bank."

What had he said? "Robbed a bank?" She was having trouble opening her eyes.

He shook his head, laughing at her. "Just checking. I once sat on an arbitration between Middleton and a client."

Her eyes snapped open. He'd moved. He was sitting next to her on the sofa. Had she slept? What had he said about Middleton?

"You weren't listening," he accused.

"I was," she protested weakly. She was so tired, and the fire made the room cozy. "You said . . ." She blinked.

He put his arm around her and she rested her head on his shoulder to keep from sagging forward. "I said I once sat on an arbitration between Middleton and Bliss Norderman and a client, and it was a beaut."

"Um." She lifted her head and separated herself from him. "I heard the client's daughter testified against her mother—"

"Where did you hear that?" His voice was cool. "Come on, I'd better get you home." But he was looking at her with stern eyes, waiting for an answer to his question.

"Oh, around." She rose and got her shoes, throwing the towel-paper stuffing in the garbage and slipping her feet into the damp leather. Ugh.

"Around where?"

Stop pushing, she thought, angry with herself, with him. "Tony

Maglia told me. Remember him? He was Brian's manager. It is true, isn't it?"

Alton stared at her from some remote place, and she saw his jaw tighten. It felt longer, but it was probably only a few seconds before he said, "I'm not going to comment on that, Leslie."

40

●●●●●●●

The rain had slackened to a light drizzle. Alton pulled up in front of a fire hydrant across the street from Wetzon's temporary home on Tenth Street and left the motor running. There were no legal parking places on the street, for which she was thankful. They had spoken very little since leaving his apartment. Now she said, "Alton, I'm sorry if you think I was pumping you for information—"

"The process is supposed to be confidential." He turned off the gas, put his arm on the back of the seat, and studied her.

"You told me you were on the arbitration. You opened the door. It's my nature to go through open doors." *That's who I am*, she thought. *You'd better get it straight.*

"I did, and I was wrong." He was almost, but not quite, smiling.

"And I *was* pumping you for information."

The almost-smile disappeared. "Why?"

"Because I'm trying to keep Brian's ex-wife out of jail for his murder."

He frowned. "What does that have to do with you?"

"I have a sideline, my dear Alton," she said in an upper-class English accent, "that of consulting detective."

He laughed then, and cupped her cheek. "Leslie, I—" But she slid away from him and opened the door.

"I did not see you tonight because I knew about your role in the arbitration." She got out of the car and closed the door. When she came around to his side of the car, he was on his feet on the street.

He said, "I know that."

A car, driving too fast, shot past them, trapping them in headlights, backing them into each other against his door. Although the
danger was over, he did not release her, and she stood for a moment
in his arms, feeling her body begin to respond. She wrenched herself
away with more force than necessary, and gave him her hand, formally. "Good night. Thanks for dinner."

For the first time she saw confusion in his eyes, and she felt an
inane pleasure. He took her hand. "I'll see you to your door."

She shook her head, then pointed to the loft building with her
free hand. "See those dark windows on the top floor? That's me. If
you could just stick around until you see the light go on . . ."

He nodded. "I'll call you." He lifted her hand to his lips and
kissed her fingers, then got back in his car and lowered the window.
"Who's the woman's lawyer?" he called.

"Richard Hartmann."

Alton whistled. "I know Dick Hartmann. He's good."

"Two people connected to your precious arbitration are dead,
Alton. Who knows who'll be next, old chum." She started across the
street.

He called out something to her, but she didn't hear, didn't
look back. Upstairs, she turned on all the lights and looked down
at the wet, light glancing street and waved. The headlights went
on, then off, then on again. The car pulled out into the street and
drove off.

Alton had sounded like Silvestri there for a minute, and she'd
slipped right into the kind of spikiness she fell into with Silvestri.
God, relationships with men were difficult. Why bother? The closer
they got, the messier it became. She stuffed her shoes with towel
paper again, hung up her clothes, washed up, brushed her hair into a
soft braid, and climbed into bed.

She dragged the phone to her, called Arthur Margolies, and let
him ask her all kinds of tedious questions about her insurance, the
building's liability, the shareholder's responsibility. He went on and
on until she almost nodded off.

"I'll get you a copy of my shareholder's agreement. Is Carlos
back yet?"

"He'll be back this weekend. Is everything all right downtown?"

"Yes. I guess it's a little late to ask you since I've already talked to
her, but I need some advice, Arthur, if you have another minute or

two." She told him about the visit from the assistant D.A. "Is it okay to talk to her?"

"Do you have anything to hide?"

"Arthur! For heaven's sake!"

"Leslie, this is Arthur talking."

"I'm sorry, Arthur, I guess I'm a bit edgy. Someone tried to break in here from the fire escape last night."

"I thought you said everything was all right?"

"Arthur! Don't give me a hard time. You sound like Silvestri." Come to think of it, all men sounded like men when it got to basics. You could almost program their responses to given situations.

"Do you want me to be there when you talk to the D.A.? We could do it in my office tomorrow afternoon."

"No, thanks. I'm not a suspect. I'll just tell her whatever I know." Wetzon hung up feeling that she was very much on her own.

She played back her messages. The first was for Carlos's previous tenant, a man from a local boutique about an unpaid bill. Then there were two hang-ups. The third was Twoey, calling from Boston about Smith's surprise birthday party. So that's why Smith was freer than usual. He gave her the new buffet menu, the third one in as many days. It was a good thing he didn't have all this indecision when he traded stocks.

Beep. Smith's dulcet tones: *Tomorrow, five-thirty in Dickie's office in Rockefeller Center. Rona's out on bail. Hope you're having an exquisite night.* This last was said lasciviously.

She punched out Smith's number, and when Smith said, "Hello," in her sexiest voice, Wetzon said, in her sexiest voice, "I just want you to know that I'm at home and in bed—alone."

"Well," Smith murmured, "I am, too, but I'm not."

"It might help if you'd get an answering machine."

Smith ignored her. "Call Joan Boley at home. Here's her number."

"Wait a minute," Wetzon grumbled, bobbling the pencil. "Okay, go." She wrote down the number. "She's just returning my call. Guilty conscience."

"Wrong church, wrong pew."

"Forgive me, she is a broker. How could I forget? Sorry about the interruption. I did have something interesting to tell you, but it can wait." She started to hang up.

Smith howled, "Wait! Tell me!"

Wetzon smiled. "I found out that Rona's had a long-standing—oops, long-*lying-down* affair with Tony Maglia."

"How disgusting!" Smith paused. "He's a head shorter than she is." She laughed. Wetzon heard another, deeper voice, and Smith's whisper.

"My thought exactly." Now Smith would say it didn't matter if they were lying down.

"Of course, it really doesn't matter when you're lying down." Smith never failed her.

"How did I know you'd say that? That's it for tonight. Over and out." She hung up and tried Joan Boley's number. "Hi, Joan."

"Wetzon! I'm so glad you called. I can't really talk now, though. Can we have breakfast tomorrow—early?"

"Like what time? Where?" Wetzon suppressed a groan. Couldn't the woman just say she was sorry over the phone?

They agreed to meet at the Hyatt at seven-thirty. Why did she have to pay for Joan's breakfast, too, while she was apologizing? Damn. *Because,* she told herself, *you never know.*

This time when she hung up, the phone rang. Probably Smith calling back with some lawyer questions. "Hello!"

"Wetzon, this is Louie. I heard you come in. I took a delivery for you this afternoon."

"A delivery?"

"Yes. Go stand at the elevator and I'll send it up."

"It?" But Louie was gone.

She put on her robe and opened her door. The door to the elevator opened noisily on the floor below, then it closed and started upward. When the door opened again, there was a padded book mailer on the floor. She grabbed it as the door started to close. "Got it, thanks," she called down the shaft.

Inside, she looked at the package. She didn't recognize the handwriting—printing, rather. Who was sending her a book? She squeezed it. It felt like a book, not a bomb. *Well, dummy, what does a bomb feel like?* There was no return address. She pried the staples up with a kitchen knife and opened the flap.

"Good God!" She almost dropped the package. She opened it, looked again, then reached in and pulled out Tabitha's missing diary.

41

·······

Joan Boley: stockbroker, heavy smoker, fading suntan, leathery skin, thick blond hair with shoulder ends flipped up, teased and sprayed, looked like an aging Sandra Dee. She was average height, ten pounds overweight, divorced and remarried, with a son at the U. of Colorado studying to be a vet.

She turned to Wetzon. "I promised Morty I'd stop smoking, and I can't." She put a cigarette between her lips; her nails were long, oval, and French manicured.

"We're in nonsmoking," Wetzon said. She blended the yogurt, fruit, and granola.

Joan looked cornered. "Shit!" She put the cigarette back in the pack, the pack in her purse.

"Have some coffee." The Crystal Fountain at the Hyatt offered a nice, calm breakfast, but Joan wasn't buying into it. She'd broken up her toasted—"burn it"—bagel in small chunks and lathered on the cream cheese.

"Wetzon, I think I've made a terrible mistake."

Wetzon put down her spoon. This required her undivided attention. "Tell me about it." *Make my day,* she thought.

"Well, you know there are very few women at SMQ. I noticed that right away; they assured me it's not a chauvinistic place."

"That's like saying women have equality in Saudi Arabia."

"Wetzon, we both know that Wall Street is a male enclave, but you wouldn't believe these guys. I was invited to a priority luncheon yesterday; senior management, the top people in the firm were all there. I was introduced as their most recent acquisition, and then they proceeded to tell jokes and stories that demean women. Worse, they didn't even know they were doing it."

"I believe it. What would you like to do?" *That's cool, Wetzon,* she congratulated herself.

"Do you think Fred would put his offer back on the table?" Joan chewed nervously on a piece of her bagel. A smudge of cream cheese clung to her lower lip.

"If you're serious. I wouldn't want to get his hopes up and have you knock them down again."

"My clients are going to think I'm crazy. The accounts are just starting to come over, and now they'll be getting more transfer forms—"

"Talk to them, explain. But first you have to think it over carefully." Wetzon signaled for the check. "Meantime, I'll talk to Fred, but only to feel him out. I'll let you know, and we can go forward or not." She dropped her Gold Card on the bill that had just been presented.

"Can you give me something to put this in?" Joan asked the waiter. She pointed to the remains of her bagel.

When the waiter returned with a square of foil, Joan neatly wrapped up the pieces and put the package into her briefcase.

Forty-second Street and Lexington Avenue was a gridlock of early-morning traffic. Cars and trucks cheated across the walk lines when the lights were a mere yellow. Pedestrians snaked around halted traffic where bumper didn't touch bumper. Commuter buses, cabs, and city buses all vied for a piece of the street.

"It's not over till it's over," Wetzon commented to the Greybar Building. "And even when it's over, it's not over." She breezed up Lexington and east on Forty-ninth Street toward her office, feeling light of foot. And what was particularly delicious was the knowledge that Tom Keegen, who had certainly placed Joan at SMQ, would lose a juicy commission, just when he could taste it.

In front of Sondheim's town house a determined young man in a tight, white T-shirt was horizontal-parking—jockeying back and forth a maroon Rolls-Royce convertible, its top down. He negotiated it into a space that left only inches back and front. How the hell was he going to get it out without scratching one of those magnificent fenders?

She crossed Second Avenue breathing the redolence of the best leather seat covers in the world and sympathized with the Rolls being in such a tight place.

By the time Smith arrived at the office, Wetzon had spoken with Fred Benitos and Joan Boley. "The Boley train is back on its tracks," she announced to Smith.

"Well, isn't that a treat. And isn't Keegen going to be wild!" Smith dumped a load of newspapers on her desk. "I'd say we deserve that." She grabbed one of the newspapers and held it up. "Look at this!" The *Post*'s headline:

DOUBLE MURDER
STUNS STREETERS

It was accompanied by a blurred head shot of Rona, or maybe an ax murderess, and a snapshot of Brian with a nubile Tabitha on his lap.

"God, Smith, Rona looks like Ma Barker. Where'd they get that picture?"

"Probably her driver's license." They both laughed.

"Do you believe Brian? That's really sick."

"Babycakes, this goes on all the time. You just dance through life wearing blinders." She threw the paper down and gave Wetzon a searching look. "What's the matter? Don't tell me you didn't sleep last night."

"Fitfully, at best. I got Tabitha's diary back in the mail yesterday, so I stayed up and read most of it. The last two pages have been torn out." She took the mailer out of her briefcase to show Smith, but Smith had her head buried in another newspaper.

Smith lowered the newspaper. "You did say *Tabitha's* diary?"

"I did."

"Where did it come from?"

"No return address, alas."

"Did you find anything out you didn't know?"

"Yeah. Tabitha had an abortion." Bortion-ay?

"Humpf." She lowered the paper. "Whose? Brian's?"

"Supposedly. Dr. Jerry made the arrangements. What do you think he gets out of all of this?"

"There are people who get off on being all things to their patients, their friends, family. He's probably one of them. I rather like him. He's harmless."

Wetzon suddenly thought, then said out loud, "Barbara wears sequins. . . ."

"Now what is that supposed to mean?"

"Someone in sequins tried to break into my apartment, and Tabitha had a fistful of sequins in her hand when she died."

"I think we've been through all this before. The world wears sequins." She grinned suddenly. "And we've only seen Barbie in black leather."

"Are they going to be at this meeting today?"

"I suppose so."

"What about Penny Ann?"

"I hardly think so. Is that the package the diary came in?"

"I was wondering when you'd ask." She handed the padded envelope to Smith.

The phone rang, stopped. B.B. had gotten it.

"This doesn't tell us anything."

"It was an overnight mailing, courtesy of the postal system. No return address. And as I said, the last two pages gone." She rose and stood over Smith. "Do you recognize the writing?" The women stared at the block letters of Wetzon's name and Carlos's address. Eerily, it dawned on Wetzon that this person knew she was staying in another place.

Smith shook her head. "It's the police. They're trying to trick you. Do you know a really frumpy assistant D.A. was here yesterday asking all kinds of questions about Brian and Rona?"

"I know. They got me, too, but I couldn't talk because I had to meet Stu Beck. They're going to try again today."

"Well, don't tell her anything."

"Why not?" Wetzon sat down at her desk.

"Let them do their own work. And you might incriminate Rona."

"Rona's already incriminated."

"Oh, for pity sakes."

"Stu Beck brought a partner, by the way. Very nice production figures. They think Bliss Norderman is going under."

"Good. We'll pull a lot of people out. I might even give Maglia a break and try to place *him*." She gave a nasty laugh. "If we don't sub him for Rona. Don't you think he's our new best bet?"

"I'd like to hear what Rona has to say about the affair."

"Yum, so would I."

B.B. knocked on their door, and Wetzon rose and opened it. She needed some coffee.

"Twoey on one, Smith. And a Dr. Gordon for you, Wetzon."

"Sweetie! I miss you so much," Smith simpered into the phone. "When are you coming home?"

Give me a break, Wetzon thought. She picked up Max's phone. "I'll take it here, B.B. Hello?"

"Wetzon, this is Jerry Gordon. Are you free to talk?"

"Yes."

"I have a confession to make."

42

....

"To me?" Wetzon stuck her head in the doorway to their office, waving to get Smith's attention. "To me?" *Pick up*, she mouthed to Smith, miming the motion.

Smith cut her conversation with Twoey short with a lot of kissing noises into the phone.

"To you and your partner, that is. You are coming to the meeting this afternoon at Richard's office?"

"Wouldn't miss it." She rolled her eyes at Smith, who had managed to get on the line without a sound.

"Well, it will come up, so I thought I'd better confess and clear the air. Are you there?"

"Yes." She made sweeping *get on with it* motions with her free hand.

"Barbie and I'd heard about you and your partner from both Brian and Rona, and of course, we read all about you last year when Goldman Barnes died. So when Tabitha ran away and Brian was murdered, I thought it would be best to keep the police out of it, under the circumstances. Tabitha couldn't have gone far, and the group felt Penny Ann needed to think someone was looking for Tabitha, so—"

Instantly, Wetzon was angry. "So it was all meaningless. And perhaps if the police had been involved earlier, Tabitha might still be alive."

"We can't blame ourselves, my dear, or each other. Blame creates a negative force field—"

"Excuse me, Jerry—"

Smith stuck her finger in her mouth, indicating she was throwing up. Wetzon turned her back on Smith.

"Look, Jerry, I have two calls waiting, and I'm late for an appointment. Can we talk about this later?" She didn't give him a chance to reply. When she hung up, she looked at Smith, who exploded with laughter. "Do you *believe* him? What do you think he is, an ESTie group leader or something?"

"Sounds more like the Forum or Life Spring."

"I don't know," Wetzon said solemnly. "Maybe he's an advanced reader of tarot cards."

"Dissss-believer," Smith hissed. She held up a stack of suspect sheets. "I'm going to set this first group up with Ameribank."

"I have to schedule Stu Beck and his friend Larry, then I have a lunch appointment . . ." But Smith was no longer listening. Wetzon walked back to her desk and looked at her calendar. One of B.B's brokers was starting today. Small fee, but it went toward his salary, so every little bit helped. She went to the door. "B.B.?"

"Yes."

"Did Steve Weissman start?"

"Not yet. He can't find anyone to resign to. His manager is away till Monday, and the assistant manager is out sick. He may not be able to do it today."

"That's ridiculous. Tell him to resign immediately to the ops manager, or leave a letter of resignation, dated today, on his manager's desk. He'll find it on Monday when he gets back. If Steve sits now, he'll probably have clearance before the end of the day. Then he can spend the weekend getting the transfers signed. Never let them delay, B.B. It stops the momentum of the move, stalls it. The broker has a chance to think—and get cold feet. You could lose him."

"But it's such a good move for him. . . ."

"Oh, B.B., spare me." He still thought like the preppie he was.

The phone rang, and B.B. scrambled to answer it. "Smith and Wetzon, good morning. Hold on."

"Who?"

"Mr. Pinkus."

She sat down at Max's neat desk and moved his folders. A flutter appeared in her chest and she ordered it to subside, but it didn't obey. "Hi."

"Leslie, I'm sorry about last night."

"So am I."

"Can we try again?"

"I don't know." Her hand was shaking, and the phone clunked her ear. Damn it all.

"Monday?"

"No more weekdays. I don't function well without sleep. . . . I mean . . ." She felt her face flush.

"I know what you mean."

"Twoey is throwing a surprise birthday party for my partner a week from tonight. Do you want to come?"

"I'd like that. I'm going to be in Chicago over the weekend. I'll call you when I get back."

After telling B.B. she had a lunch appointment, she put on her raincoat, belted it, and went out on the street. It was raw today, another hint of approaching winter. She shivered and turned up her collar.

Would she be in her own home by Christmas? Louie hadn't promised, but Wetzon's board had given their approval to the renovations and Louie and her crew were starting work on Monday. She hoped Louie would remember to pick up her mail.

Metzger, tall, lanky, with mournful basset-hound eyes, was standing in front of Rusty Staub's watching the passing parade. She hadn't seen him in months. She'd grown very fond of him in the time she'd been with Silvestri.

"Artie," she called, waving. He turned to look, spotted her, and his smile dispelled the solemnity. She gave him a great hug and he kissed her cheek.

It was obvious immediately that Metzger was known here, because they were shown to a somewhat private table without waiting. After they ordered their burgers and beer, Artie gave her the eye. "What are you up to?"

"You sound like Silvestri."

"I'm standing in for him." The way he said it told her that he was *au courant* with their situation.

"Oh, shit, Artie, things aren't good with us." Her voice cracked, failed her.

"Listen, kid." He looked down at his plate and said quickly, as if the words embarrassed him, "It'll be okay. You love each other. There are just these bumps along the way. Carol and I've been married eight years. I ought to know. And being separated doesn't help. You ought to get yourself down there."

She shook her head. "I tried that. He can damn well get himself up here one weekend or two a month." She felt angry tears, took out a tissue and dried her face, blew her nose. "Let's not talk about this now, okay?"

The beers and the hamburgers materialized.

"So you wanna tell me what you've gotten involved in?" Metzger put a bunch of fries between the burger and the bun and added enough ketchup to blanket them.

Wetzon discarded the roll and cut into the burger with a knife and fork. She told him about Brian, how they were hired to find Tabitha—he groaned—and she left nothing out, not even hiding in Jerry Gordon's closet. Metzger kept shaking his head, but he didn't scold her, as she knew Silvestri would have.

Finally, he took a swig of beer and said, "What are we going to do with you?"

She grinned at him. "Humor me."

"What do you want to know?"

"What did the autopsy find?"

"The girl was dead before she hit the water. She was killed at close range with the same gun, a .32, that was used on Middleton."

"Did they find the gun?"

"Nope. You're not eating those?" When she shook her head, he helped himself to her fries.

"Any surprises in the autopsy?"

"A couple. She was three months pregnant."

"God! What's the other?"

"There were too many broken and healed bones, burns, scars. Looks like she was one of those poor abused kids from upper-class homes that slip through the cracks. It's amazing that she made it through alive."

Wetzon stared at him. "But she didn't, did she?"

43

·······

"Be a good girl," Metzger said. "Cut him some slack."

"Be a good girl?" Wetzon was outraged.

"Now don't get pissed at me."

"Ha!"

"Do you want a ride?" He had his hand on the car door.

"No, thanks. Okay, Artie, he wants slack. I'll give him slack, but it's going to be quid pro quo from now on."

She was pissed at Metzger, pissed at Silvestri, generally pissed. On Fifth Avenue between Forty-seventh and Forty-ninth, three different sets of Senegalese peddlers were selling "replica" watches, mainly Rolex and Cartier, from attaché cases. Five dollars will get you nice faces and empty cases. Tourists were inspecting the merchandise. These unlicensed entrepreneurs made more in one day than most stockbrokers, paid no taxes, and were always one step ahead of the police. They had lookouts posted and seemed to know when to snap the lid shut and hightail it out of there before their junk could be confiscated.

Metzger's information about Tabitha as a battered child fit what that scumbag Maglia had told her. Rona was Tabitha's godmother. Why hadn't she done something about it? Then again, maybe she had. Maybe that's how Tabitha had ended up staying with the Maglias.

Wetzon walked into Saks and toured the ground floor, looking at the handbags on the countertops, trying on the leather gloves. A smoky-blue silk shawl woven with tiny red flowers lay on a counter.

She held it up to her throat. The effect was startling, making her gray eyes vivid. On an impulse she bought it, then took the escalator up to the lingerie department. *Cut him some slack, sure.*

At this hour there were few shoppers. She pawed through the racks and pulled out a sexy black teddy with a lacy bosom. Her size. Holding it up to herself in a side mirror, she thought, *Racy, Wetzon.* She tucked it under her arm and went back to the rack. The teddy also came in pale peach.

"May I be of help?" A slim black woman, her hair beaded in cornrows tight to her scalp, was standing at her elbow.

"Yes, I'll take both of these." She thrust the two teddies at the woman before she got cold feet.

"Do you want to try them on? They can't be returned."

"That's all right." She gave the woman her charge plate and then wandered over to a circular rack of nightgowns.

A woman on the other side of the circle was furiously flipping through the nighties, making grunting noises and carrying on a whispered conversation, with hostile overtones. When she worked her way around to where Wetzon could see her, it turned out to be Barbara Gordon, or someone who looked a lot like her. And there was no one with her.

"Barbara?"

Barbara pulled her eyes from the rack and dropped them on Wetzon. Her face was floridly psychotic, and she'd cut her red curls off close to the scalp in a punky crew cut. "Wetzon." Her hands continued to fumble through the flimsy garments. She was wearing a matte gold raincoat over tight black leather pants and black leather riding boots. All she needed was a whip. . . . Her strange eyes flitted from here to there. She leaned close to Wetzon. "I love the way you do your hair. Will you show me how?"

"Of course," Wetzon said cautiously. "After yours grows in."

Barbara's clawing hands flew to the short bristles on her head. "Oh—I—uh—" Her eyes took on a lunatic glaze, which immediately vanished, replaced in quick succession by suspicion, then fear. "I've cut my hair off," she said, as if she'd just discovered it. "Jerry will kill me."

"Oh, come on, Barbara. Jerry may be upset with you, but killing is a whole other thing. And it'll grow back."

"Your package, Ms. Wetzon, and your card. Will you sign here, please?"

Wetzon took the bag and signed the charge slip, then slipped her card into her purse. When she turned back to Barbara, Barbara was gone.

Loony tunes, she thought. Right in the doctor's own home. Sad. Could Barbara have murdered Brian and Tabitha? Did she have psychotic lapses during which she did things she couldn't remember? Like cut her hair off? Or kill?

The sun had not been able to break through the overcast and had obviously given up. She walked back to the office slowly, thinking, feeling vaguely depressed. It was a little after three when she hung her coat in the closet. She might be able to get some calls sandwiched in between the meeting with the assistant district attorney and the one in Richard Hartmann's office. She took the stack of pink message slips that B.B. handed her into their inner sanctum.

"Oh, really? How very kind of you, but we don't do freebies." Smith's voice was ice on cold steel. "There's nothing to think over." She hung up and looked at Wetzon. "Can you believe that veggie Cafferty? He says we can get back in his good graces if we give him a freebie—someone who produces one-fifty or more."

"Fuck him," Wetzon-the-ruthless said. "The minute he pays us what he owes us for Evan, let's scorch his earth."

"Now you're talking!" Smith looked delighted with Wetzon's bloodthirsty reaction. Spotting the Saks bag, she pounced. "What did you buy?"

"Um, just a few odds and ends." Wetzon felt herself flush clear up to her cheekbones.

Smith was eyeing her critically with her X-ray vision. "Show me."

Wetzon pulled the shawl out of its bag. "See, just a shawl, which I'll probably never wear."

"Very nice." Smith dismissed the shawl. "What's in the other bag?" When she saw Wetzon's hesitation, she wheedled, "Come on now, sweetie pie."

Reluctantly, Wetzon pulled the black teddy from the bag and held it up. "Don't make a big deal, please." She was not about to show Smith the peach teddy. She'd never hear the end of it.

"Well, now." Smith put her finger to her cheek and smirked. She raised her coffee mug. "I salute the King of Cups."

"Will you stop that." Wetzon crumpled the teddy and stuffed it back in the bag.

"He appears in every reading I do for you. And last night he was the resolution. This is serious."

"What the hell does that mean?"

"It means that he is the focus in your life right now."

"Oh, God, Smith, let it be." Then, because she couldn't help herself, she asked, "Where was Silvestri?"

"The King of Swords is in your past," Smith intoned ominously.

The words were like slashes. Her lips trembled and tears flowed. "What a jerk I am." She gulped back more tears. And in a flash, Smith gathered her in, soothing Wetzon's sniffles, hugging her.

"Sweetie pie, you know what your problem is? You don't keep control of the affair. You must let them love you more than you love them. It always works out better that way. And Alton is the perfect subject. You gave your all to Dick Tracy, and see where it got you. Believe me, you will have a wonderful affair with Alton—"

B.B. knocked, interrupting Smith's monologue. Frowning, she patted Wetzon's shoulder and opened the door. "Mr. Bahash from Ameribank for you, Smith."

Wetzon went into the bathroom and washed her face, then touched up her eye makeup. She looked at herself in the mirror. Time was marching on. The tiny laugh lines around her eyes were more pronounced, but her neck was smooth and her back was straight. She wondered if she would take reaching forty as badly as Smith was. Aging had only mattered to her when she was a dancer and knew that time was running out on her joints and sinews.

She smiled at herself and tucked a flying strand back into her topknot. "You can still pass for thirty," she told her reflection.

Smith had certainly had more experience with men than Wetzon. Maybe she was right. Carlos would go out of his mind if he heard that. He could never understand why Wetzon put up with Smith. She'd explained over and over, and perhaps it was a particularly female thing, but there were people in your life who'd entered it at a particular time, when there'd been some mutual need. And they remain because they're part of your history, and you are always having to explain them to your friends. So it was with Smith. And their business partnership worked, better than either of them had dreamed.

Smith was hanging up when Wetzon came out of the bathroom. Where was that assistant D.A.? she wondered.

"Are you feeling better?"

Wetzon nodded. "I ran into Barbara Gordon in Saks. She'd hacked off all her hair, and I mean all. She looked like a pink-haired marine."

"That's crazy."

"Precisely. She looked and sounded psychotic—red-faced, talking to herself."

Smith's expression was openly doubtful. "She's probably just upset about Tabitha and Rona."

"I don't know, Smith. It occurred to me that she might be crazy enough to kill someone."

The phone rang once, twice, three times. Wetzon could see B.B. was talking on the other line. She sighed and picked up the phone. "Smith and Wetzon."

"Ms. Wetzon, please." The voice was familiar.

"This is she."

"This is Marissa Peiser, of the district attorney's office. Can we switch our meeting to tonight? Something rather urgent has come up."

44

· · · · · · ·

The Promenade, called the Channel Gardens because on one side was the British bookshop and on the other, the French, was a meadow of mums. Wetzon and Smith had arrived in Rockefeller Center early, and without talking, they walked down the sloping walk to the skating rink and joined the sprinkling of watchers as the ice skaters waltzed around the rink to piped-in organ strains of *The Merry Widow.*

Where were her skates? What shelf had she put them on? Had they been ruined in the flood? It had been years since she'd been on skates. Wetzon closed her eyes and conjured up the memory of a much younger self and Carlos, spinning around the Wollman Rink, dancers on ice.

She turned to Smith, eyes wide, excited. "Let's rent skates and do a quick twirl around the ice."

Smith looked at her as if she'd proposed walking through the New York Stock Exchange stark naked. "You can't be serious. We're going to an important consultation. We're in our business clothes."

"Oh, well, it was only an idle thought."

"Banish such thoughts from your mind."

Wetzon shrugged. The air was tangy with evergreens and roasting chestnuts. Her feet in their black pumps itched to dance her off, and she lagged behind a determined Smith as they walked back past the Channel Gardens to Fifth Avenue. The vendor with the roasting chestnuts was on the corner, and choking smoke spewed from his roaster. So much for quaint; the chestnut roasters were polluters.

They crossed over to 630 Fifth, Atlas's building. At a quarter past five, workers, particularly the bridge-and-tunnel crowd, were rushing from offices to get their trains and buses home. This was Friday, so even executives were eager to start their weekends.

Wetzon trailed after Smith through the revolving door, past the escalator leading to the subterranean world of shops and restaurants and intricate passageways beneath that connected all of Rockefeller Center's buildings to one another.

"Well, hello, look who's here," Smith said in a husky voice, saturated with curiosity.

Wetzon peered around her partner and saw Neil Munchen coming toward them from one of the elevator banks.

"Smith, Wetzon, how nice to run into you." His stilted tone belied his words. The head of retail for Rosenkind, Luwisher looked exceedingly uncomfortable.

They shook hands all around, then he quickly made excuses and left.

"What do you suppose Neil is up to? He was acting as if we caught him at something." Smith pursed her lips and frowned.

"Why does he have to be up to anything? He's Rona's manager. Maybe he was talking to Hartmann. . . ."

"Didn't you see how guilty he looked?" She was staring after Neil thoughtfully. "And he wasn't seeing Dickie either, because he got off the wrong elevator bank."

Smith could very well be right. Bernard Freres, the international investment bank, had offices in this building. Was Neil thinking of making a move?

At that moment, Barbara and Jerry Gordon came through the revolving doors; Barbie caught sight of them and waved. She was wearing the same black leather costume and gold raincoat, but her ragged hair was covered by a gigantic black sequined beret. Her eyes were hidden behind small, round-lensed dark glasses. In the artificial light her face was a skull of tight pink skin.

Smith and Barbara greeted each other by barely touching cheeks and kissing the air. "You look so smart, sweetie," Smith gushed.

Spare me, Wetzon thought, looking for Dr. Jerry. He had disappeared. She strolled over to the newsstand and caught a glimpse of him in the well near a bank of telephones. He was talking to Neil Munchen, as if they were old friends.

Wetzon turned her back and bought a copy of *Business Week*, then returned to the women. Jerry Gordon appeared from the other side of the elevator bank.

"I thought you were right behind me." Barbara was whiny but did not appear unbalanced as she had earlier in the day when Wetzon ran into her at Saks.

"I was right behind you, dear." Dr. Jerry was carrying a distended briefcase. He took a package of chewing gum from his pocket. "I stopped to buy you some gum." His gray suit was tight across the shoulders and arms, wrinkled across his belly and upper legs, and needed a pressing badly. There was an oily stain on his tie.

"You're so lucky to have such a sweet husband," Smith burbled. Smith and Wetzon got on an empty express elevator car and the Gordons followed. Jerry pressed 41.

"You can have him if you want him."

Jerry gave an embarrassed laugh. "You're such a tease, Barbie."

Smith rolled her eyes at Wetzon. Wetzon brushed Smith's elbow, trying to steer Smith's eyes to Barbie's head. As close as she was, with that huge beret, Wetzon could not tell Barbie had a crew cut.

The entrance to Hartmann, Veeder and Kalin, P.C., was on the left of the elevators. Two secretaries in dress-for-success suits were leaving and the one behind the glass-enclosed area was setting up the phone system for night calls. In the small waiting room, a large man-eating plant took up all the space on a side table to which a Naugahyde banquette was attached on either side. The same arrangement, sans plant, appeared against the opposite wall. This table had the latest issues of *Fortune*, *Forbes*, and *The American Lawyer*—Hartmann featured, story on page four—and of all things, *Spy*, laid out neatly.

Dr. Jerry tapped on the glass, and they were buzzed in through a door of bleached walnut, set into glass bricks. The secretary put them in a conference room that, although the ashtrays were empty, reeked of cigarettes. Sections of the *Wall Street Journal* lay in flagrante delicto with the *Post*, which featured Rona Middleton as Ma Barker. The *Journal* reference to Rona's case was:

BROKER DENIES
DOUBLE MURDER

Wetzon threw her coat on a chair and sat down. She could think of a hell of a lot of places she'd rather be right now than here. She closed her eyes and listened to Dr. Jerry tell Smith things about his group-therapy clients, which seemed entirely inappropriate to Wetzon. Smith asked about his training and Jerry launched into a lengthy, pompous oration about his undergraduate and graduate years at Columbia with a two-year intermission for army service. Intelligence, of course. Wasn't everybody? Wetzon opened her eyes. They were sitting directly across from her, Smith's hand resting on Jerry's arm.

On the conference table were a stack of yellow legal pads and freshly sharpened pencils. A sideboard featured a phone system and a television set. The surrounding walls held bookshelves crammed with law books.

Barbie, who had gone off to the ladies' room, returned carrying a can of Diet Pepsi. "There's more if anyone wants any." When no one responded, she said, loudly, "I'm talking to you, fat boy."

Smith looked up, genuinely startled.

Jerry Gordon rose and put his arm around his wife, leading her to a chair next to Wetzon. "Have you taken your pill?" he whispered. "Take it now."

Barbie sank into the chair, a look of terror on her face, but she reached into a leather pouch around her waist and took out a small bottle of pills, shook one into her palm, and popped it into her mouth. She put the bottle back into the pouch before Wetzon could see the label. Dr. Jerry patted the sequined beret and returned to his seat next to Smith, picking up the threads of their conversation, while Barbie simmered next to Wetzon. The whole scene gave Wetzon the creeps.

A door across the room opened, and Rona appeared with Dick Hartmann. Rona was wan and nervous. Dark roots streaked her blond hair. She was wearing a black wool crepe suit and a green sweater that contrived to make her skin look even more washed out than usual.

"How are you doing?" Wetzon asked, because no one else spoke.

"My brain is fried." Rona took a seat on the other side of Wetzon and gave her hand a squeeze.

A young Asian woman in a gray suit came into the room and closed the door. Her black hair was clipped back at the nape.

"My associate, Robin Huang," Dick Hartmann said. He introduced everyone by name.

Hartmann sat down at the head of the table and placed Robin to his immediate right. He wore an obviously expensive made-to-order suit and was clearly in his element.

"For the record," Rona said, looking slowly at each of them, "I did not kill Brian or Tabitha."

"Of course, sugar," Smith said.

"We know," Wetzon said.

"No question in our minds," Dr. Jerry said.

"Fat boy," Barbie Gordon said.

Hartmann gave Barbie an inscrutable look. "The evidence they have is all circumstantial." He took a legal pad from the pile on the table and a Mont Blanc pen from his inside pocket. "Rona has an alibi, so we may be able to get the indictment thrown out."

Good, Wetzon thought. *Can I go home now?*

"But he's refused to come forward," Hartmann continued.

It came to Wetzon in a flash. Maglia.

"Tony Maglia," Rona said, looking at Wetzon defiantly. "We've been lovers for years, since before Brian. I was with Tony when Brian was murdered."

"That gives him an alibi, too," Wetzon said.

"I suppose so."

"And what about Tabitha?" Smith asked.

"I waited at that fountain for over half an hour, and then I figured she wasn't coming. I've never even held a gun in my life. This is all ridiculous."

Wetzon reached over and patted Rona's hand. "Was Tabitha staying with the Maglias?"

Rona nodded.

"If we have to, I'll hit Maglia with a subpoena," Hartmann said.

"What can *we* do?" Smith asked.

"You two can fill in the blanks for us. I want to go over everyone who might have had something against Brian."

"Get on line," Rona said.

"That's enough, Rona." Hartmann's tone was sharp and final.

"Then there's Penny Ann Boyd," Smith said.

Almost as one, Rona, Hartmann, and the Gordons all said, "Leave her out of this."

"Well, okay," Wetzon said, exchanging glances with Smith. But it wasn't okay. "Simon Loveman, the Loeb Dawkins manager, gave Brian twenty thousand dollars to cover Brian's debt at Bliss

Norderman. I'm sure Brian resigned, although that slimebag Maglia denies it." She looked at Rona. "I'm sorry." Rona shrugged, and Wetzon went on. "Brian must have repaid the twenty thousand. Can you check on whether he did, because if he did, he had definitely resigned." Robin Huang was writing copious notes. "If he didn't, Simon might have a motive. If Simon doesn't replace the twenty thou, he may lose his job."

"What about Penny Ann?" Smith persisted.

Yes, what about Penny Ann, Wetzon thought. Penny Ann was hardly innocent, especially when it came to Tabitha. Either she had abused her daughter or she'd stood by in silence while her late husband had.

"What about the missing correspondence file? Brian's." Wetzon checked Barbie's reaction. There was none. "Would those papers give us a motive for Brian's murder, and Tabitha's?"

Barbara turned her head slowly and stared at Wetzon with her shaded eyes. Did Barbie know Wetzon had seen the papers in the hatbox? The woman was downright scary.

"Oh, I'm sure they'll turn up," Rona said. "The filing system in Tony's office is a disaster."

Wetzon said emphatically, "The fact that they were missing cost Penny Ann the case. Although it made Brian crazy, the twenty thousand for the annuities was nothing but a pity fuck."

Everyone in the room stared at Wetzon, and Barbie began laughing, hiccuping, choking, and couldn't stop. Jerry turned worried eyes on his wife, and she gasped, "God, I'm sorry. It's so funny." She started laughing again. Tears rolled down her cheeks. He handed her a handkerchief across the table and she dried her eyes without removing her glasses. "God, it's hot in here," she said. She tore the sequined beret from her head, and it was Wetzon's turn to gasp.

Red curls cascaded from under Barbie's beret to her shoulders.

45

·······

"Well, at least she had the sense to get herself a wig," Smith said. "Or maybe we've just met her evil identical twin."

"Penny Ann," Wetzon said thoughtfully. She and Smith were alone on the elevator, shooting down to the lobby of the building.

"My thought exactly. This is what we'll do. You'll drive up to the country with me tonight and we'll go talk to Penny Ann tomorrow."

Wetzon shook her head. They got out of the elevator and walked slowly back to the skating rink. She had this little pulsing pain over her right eye and a burning sensation behind her eyeballs. "I want to go home, get into bed and sleep ten or twelve lovely, uninterrupted hours. If I go up with you tonight, it'll be pajama-party time. We'll talk ourselves to death, and I won't be good for anything. Why not drive up tomorrow morning?" They leaned, elbows on the low marble wall, and watched the skaters. A father was adjusting a red cap on a child of about four; both seemed perfectly balanced on their skates until the child tottered and went down smack on his snowsuited bottom, pulling his father after him.

Smith hugged herself. It was getting too cold to run around without a coat. "Mark is coming in for the night with a friend. They're going up to Killington with a group tomorrow morning. He'll be sorry not to see you." Her eyes got shiny. "My baby's growing up so fast. . . ."

Wetzon put her arm around her partner. "He's sixteen, going on seventeen, Smith. Not a baby anymore."

"I know." Smith sniffed and fumbled in her pocket for a Kleenex. "But I hate to see it. It means I'm getting older, too. That's why I'm just going to ignore my birthday." She looked at Wetzon suspiciously. "You haven't told anyone, have you?"

Wetzon felt a pang of guilt. "Who, me? No, of course not, but I'm sure Twoey must know."

"Why do you say that?"

"Oh, come on. You've been seeing him for over a year. You know when his is, don't you?"

"Humpf. If you take the nine-oh-seven, you'll get in at ten-ish and I'll pick you up."

"When's the next one?"

"Ten-oh-seven."

"That's the one I'll take."

Smith shivered. "It's too cold to stand here. I'm going to get a cab."

"I just want to watch a little longer." Wetzon fluttered her hand at Smith. "See you tomorrow. Give Mark a kiss for me." They clasped hands for a minute, then impulsively hugged each other. Wetzon pulled the collar of her trench coat high around her neck and watched Smith make her way up the stairs to Fiftieth Street until she was out of sight.

A girl in a fuzzy white bunny suit was doing spins on the ice to "Putting on the Ritz." Judy Garland's tremulous voice on the recording touched off some emotional trigger in Wetzon, made her sad, nostalgic for the gypsy life she'd led before she became a headhunter, which as she well knew was unreal and unrealistic.

Enough of this maudlin, self-indulgent crap. She'd let her mind stray from the case in hand.

Penny Ann, in some way, was the key to this. Was she in danger, then? Would she be next? Or had she committed both murders? It was a terrible fact that parents abuse and kill their children. But with a gun?

Her hands were freezing. She put her briefcase under her arm and thrust her hands in her pockets. The flags of the United Nations that surrounded the skating rink snapped crisply in the wind. Prometheus, washed in gold, observed all under the soaring towers of Rockefeller Center. When Perry Como began singing "You're the

Only One I'll Ever Love," Wetzon felt herself turn to mush. She left the skaters and started walking west, toward the subway. *How silly and sentimental of you, Wetzon,* she scolded.

A D train was just coming into the Rockefeller Center station; it was seven o'clock, and the platform was no longer solid with people. She found a seat and took out *Business Week.* But her mind wasn't on her reading. She kept seeing Tabitha's turgid neck and bloated face on the page. Finally, she put the magazine away. She was tired. Her fellow passengers looked tired. Most were going home, but there were a few young people, bursting with energy, in hand-torn jeans, undoubtedly heading for the Village. And sure enough, they pushed off in front of Wetzon on Eighth Street, making a joyful noise.

She stopped at Balducci's, the Village's amazing answer to Zabar's, and bought a container of minestrone and half a pound of pasta salad, with vegetables and sun-dried tomatoes, a long sour-dough baguette, a small piece of Roquefort, and a container of nicoise olives. Her last selection was a big buttery brownie. This was the kind of food that made her feel safe.

At Schapira coffee shop, sacks of coffee lay about and a huge roaster was the objet d'art; it was a heavenly place, totally dedicated to multiblends of coffee and tea. She bought a pound of water-washed decaf, and then was homeward bound on Tenth Street with other Villagers, all carrying groceries. She walked right past Three Lives Bookshop, stopped, and retraced her footsteps. The door was open, beckoning to her, and there were friendly faces behind the counter. She stepped into the small, cozy space, packed with books on wooden bookshelves. It was just the kind of place she would have if she owned a bookshop.

She bought John le Carré's *The Secret Pilgrim,* which had just gone into paperback, to read on the train the next day, and was on her way again.

The Village was bustling. Restaurants were filling; the narrow streets and sidewalks were crowded, but it was all alien to Wetzon. She missed her Upper West Side. As she walked west, it grew quieter: a few people out walking their dogs, some attorneys and investment bankers just getting home, and Leslie Wetzon.

There was a note Scotch-taped above Carlos's bell: "Leslie, I have your mail. Buzz me. Louie." She pressed Louie's buzzer.

"Yes?"

"Hi, it's Leslie. I'm downstairs."

"I've got a shopping bag full of stuff for you."

Impulsively, Wetzon said, "Come on up and share my dinner."

"I'm a vegetarian. I just made a big fruit salad."

"That'll be your contribution. Unless there's meat in the minestrone, I know the rest is okay."

Her spirits lifted. She suddenly realized she hadn't wanted to be alone. She changed into leggings and an old white cotton dress shirt she'd appropriated from Silvestri, and put the soup in a pan to heat. When Louie arrived, they spread their smorgasbord out on the trestle table and worked their way right through it.

"Did you do anything on the apartment today?" Wetzon measured coffee into the filter, poured in the water, and turned on the machine.

"No. I just took my crew up to see it." Louie was wearing jeans cut off at the knee and a blue V-neck sweater, sleeves rolled up. "Aren't you going to check your mail?"

"Oh, I guess so." She pulled the Bloomingdale's bag to her. "Probably bills and junk." Pushing the plates and cartons aside, she took everything out of the shopping bag and set the mail on the table. All that was left of their dinner was some of Louie's fruit salad, the Roquefort, and the brownie, which Wetzon had cut in two equal pieces.

While Louie poured the coffee, Wetzon began opening envelopes and throwing things away in the shopping bag. "See what I mean?" There were bills from New York Telephone, Con Edison, and American Express, and her monthly brokerage statement from Oppenheimer. Her maintenance bill on the apartment she wasn't living in. *New York* magazine, *Forbes*, and under everything, a thick, stiff envelope postmarked Washington, D.C., and addressed in Silvestri's crabby handwriting. She took it into the bedroom and dropped it on the bed. Not now, she thought.

Slowly, they drank their coffee, not talking very much, and ate their way through what remained on the table. Then they looked at one another over the debris and laughed.

"I guess we were hungry," Louie said.

"Sort of. I had a pain right here." Wetzon put her hand under her breast. "Funny how certain food can make you feel better." She smiled at Louie.

"You seem sad tonight."

"I am, a little. I'm glad you were here."

"So am I." Louie stood and began cleaning up.

Wetzon watched her for a few moments. "Louie, may I ask you something personal?"

Louis stopped scraping a plate. "Fire away."

"Is it easier to love women than men?" She paused. "God, I hope I'm not offending you."

Louie smiled. "I wouldn't give you an unbiased answer. And no, you haven't offended me." She tied up the plastic garbage bag. "I'll take this down with me. It has to go out tonight for a pickup tomorrow morning."

After Louie left, Wetzon showered and put on the white shirt again while she blow-dried her hair. The package from Silvestri was waiting for her on the bed. She sighed and sat cross-legged and opened it. It was a compact disk. Harry Connick, Jr. They had heard him sing "I've Got You Under My Skin," and it had given her goose pimples. This young man who sounded like Sinatra had a voice so full of tenderness, it made you cry.

No note was enclosed. Damn him. He was manipulating her. She threw it down on the bed. She wouldn't play it. But Carlos had a really nice stereo unit that included a CD player.

She slipped the disk into the slot and fiddled with the buttons. "Let there be music," she murmured. And there was. Closing the blinds, she danced dreamily around the room. He was singing to her, and that's what Silvestri had wanted. A stand-in. When Connick got to "I've Got You Under My Skin," she came apart, dropping to the floor. Damn him. She smacked the carpet with a fist. No, this wouldn't do. This was some kind of psychological brainwashing that Silvestri was learning at Quantico.

The downstairs buzzer sounded. Who could that be? Louie?

She got up and walked over to the monitor. There were two people crowding the tiny entranceway downstairs.

The buzzer shrilled again.

Wetzon sighed, and pressed them in.

It was the assistant D.A., Marissa Peiser, and she was accompanied by Detective Ferrante.

46

·······

Marissa Peiser was wearing a gray suit with a red turtleneck sweater under the same grubby gray trench coat. Little puffy bags under her eyes made her look older than she probably was, but her straight brown hair had a nice sheen and she was wearing lipstick. There was blusher on her cheeks. The hand she offered Wetzon was cold and tight as a coiled spring. "Sorry it's so late," she said, giving only lip service to the words. "You know Detective Ferrante?"

Ferrante came right in behind her and closed the door.

"So nice to see you again, Detective Ferrante." Ferrante's mustache twitched. He gave her a sharp was-she-being-snide look, but Wetzon kept her face expressionless. "You might as well sit down. Do you want coffee?"

They did.

"Nice apartment," Peiser said. She ranged around the living room, stopped, peered into the bedroom. There was a run in her black panty hose.

"It's what you might call a loaner. What can I do for you?"

Ferrante ran his hands through his curly hair, jiggled from one foot to the other, and finally sat down at the trestle table, an intimidating bulk in a brown tweed sports jacket and tan slacks. He pushed out a chair for Peiser with his foot, and she took the hint.

"We want to walk you through both murders to see if there's something you've forgotten," Peiser said, slipping out of her coat and dropping it over back of the chair. She sat, crossed her legs, then uncrossed them, and leaned against her coat. No wonder it looked like that.

"Has something new come up?"

"Why would you ask?" Peiser fished around in her raincoat pocket and took out a small notebook.

"Because the two of you seemed wired, and you told me that's why you were canceling our previous—Oh, hell, let's stop fencing. I don't know anything about Brian's murder. He had my card. Right, Ferrante? That's how you got to me." She poured the coffee into three mugs. "It'll have to be black. There isn't any milk. Where's Detective Martens tonight?"

Ferrante ignored her question. He nodded at Peiser, and Peiser said, "According to your partner, Ms. Xenia Smith, you met the Boyds and the Gordons socially through Rona Middleton."

"Socially?" Wetzon smiled. Smith certainly had a way with words. "I don't really think it was social. Although we had a drink with Penny Ann Boyd, Barbara Gordon, and Rona the Sunday after Brian died, it was to introduce us to Barbara and Penny Ann. Rona set it up. They wanted us to help them find Tabitha, who'd run away— and not for the first time."

"Christalmighty," Ferrante swore under his breath.

"What made them think you'd be able to do that?" Peiser frowned at Ferrante and lifted the mug to her lips.

"Frankly, I don't know." Wetzon joined them at the table. "They seemed to think Tabitha was staying with someone who'd worked with Brian, perhaps his manager, Tony Maglia." She stopped and said, almost to herself, "Wait a minute. Wouldn't Rona have known Tabitha was with Maglia if she was having an affair with him?" Then to Peiser she said, "The affair, do you know about it?"

Peiser nodded. "Go on." She was making notes in her pad, and Wetzon recognized the graceful loops of Gregg-style shorthand. In her mind's eye she saw Peiser as a secretary-drone working her way through law school, and was drawn to her.

"Well, they wanted us to see if we could ask some discreet questions."

Ferrante shot up, knocking the chair on its back. His face turned beet red. "We ought to haul you in as an accessory—"

Peiser raised the palm of her hand. "You said 'they.' Who?"

Ferrante righted the chair, but he was fuming. He sat down again, noisily.

"Rona, Penny Ann, and Barbara Gordon. I suppose the husband, Dr. Jerry Gordon, too, although he wasn't there the first time. It was all subterfuge. I found out later that Dr. Jerry—he's some sort of therapist—just got us involved to keep Penny Ann from going to the police. Penny Ann was afraid Tabitha had killed Brian, because she was supposed to be meeting him in the Conservatory Garden that morning."

"Withholding evidence," Ferrante growled.

"Listen, Ferrante, you didn't ask me about Tabitha and Brian, and at the time I wouldn't have known anyway." He was making her angry. He always made her angry.

"How do you know that Tabitha was meeting Brian Middleton at the Conservatory Garden?" Peiser asked.

Wetzon sighed. With Tabitha dead, there was no point in keeping the diary. "It was in Tabitha's diary. Wait a minute and I'll get it for you." She walked into the bedroom and took it from the table next to her bed and brought it back, handing it to Peiser, who pushed it to Ferrante. "You'll notice there are pages missing from the back."

A vein pulsed in Ferrante's forehead. "How'd you get this?" He pulled a plastic bag out of his inside pocket and, using his handkerchief, slipped the diary inside and sealed it.

"I think that's a waste of time," Wetzon said.

Ferrante shook the bag at her. "I suppose you're going to tell us that a lot of people have handled this?"

Wetzon sighed and reached for her mug. "Penny Ann gave it to us, then someone lifted it from my bag before I had a chance to read it—you, for example—and then mailed it back to me sans those end pages. Actually, Penny Ann seemed more interested in finding some missing papers dealing with the arbitration in her lawsuit against Brian and Bliss Norderman than she was in finding her daughter." That was it, wasn't it? Penny knew where Tabitha was. Penny wanted those papers. But why was Rona covering for Penny, and what was in it for the Gordons?

"This is the first we hear about missing papers. What else are you keeping from us, lady?"

"Ferrante, would you get the hell out of my face? I don't have to talk to you. I'm being a good citizen."

"Good citizen!"

"Cool it, Bobby, will you?" Peiser was sitting on the edge of her chair, leaning across the table. "This Jerry Gordon, he's an M.D.?"

Bobby? Wetzon thought, shifting her eyes from Peiser to Ferrante and back. "I don't think so. I never asked to see his CV. That's a résumé, Detective. He has a call-in program on a Connecticut radio station, 'Ask Dr. Jerry.' What he really is, I think, is some kind of guru, or group therapist. They all went to him."

"All?"

"Rona, Brian, Tabitha, Penny Ann, her late husband Wilson, and God knows who else."

Ferrante stood up again and started prowling, into the living room, back to the kitchen, back to the living room.

Peiser nodded. Her hand shook over her notebook. Well, Ferrante would make anyone crazy. "What did you do about finding Tabitha?"

"We thought we knew where she was. Brian's apartment. We'd gone up there that Friday to find out why he hadn't started at Loeb Dawkins—we didn't know he was dead—and we ran into someone we thought at the time was the maid. After we talked to Rona et al., we realized it must have been Tabitha, but when Smith went back to the apartment, there was no sign of her."

From the middle of the living room, Ferrante yelled, "You're talking about that place on West Seventy-ninth Street?" Then, without waiting for an answer, he plowed right on. "You cleaned it out, didn't you? What did you take? Is that where you got the diary? Christ, no wonder there was nothing there. These bimbos have their hands all over everything."

"We didn't take anything."

"I'll bet."

"Then what?" Peiser interrupted, throwing Ferrante a beseeching look.

"Then Penny Ann made her fake confession, probably to cover for her daughter."

Peiser and Ferrante made eye contact for a fraction of a second.

"It wasn't real, was it?"

"Go on," Ferrante said.

"I just want to mention the twenty thousand dollars."

"See what I mean?" Ferrante gestured to Peiser.

"Simon Loveman, Brian's manager-to-be, advanced Brian twenty thousand to pay off his debt at Bliss Norderman."

"Okay," Peiser said, making a note. "Let's stick with what you were telling us about—"

"Their conspiracy to obstruct justice." Ferrante was roaming the living room again.

Wetzon turned her back on him. "Jerry Gordon called a meeting at his office in the Park Royale, and Richard Hartmann came in with Penny Ann, who immediately collapsed. Jerry put her on the chaise in his consulting room and went to get her some tea, while I stayed with her. I opened the closet looking for a blanket, found one on an overhead shelf, but I knocked down a hatbox by mistake. When I picked it up to put it back, the lid came off, and I saw all these letters and financial statements. I thought they might be the missing papers, but then I heard Jerry coming back, so I put the box on the shelf."

"Did you mention it to anyone?" Peiser bit her lip and moved restlessly in her chair, taking quick glances at Ferrante.

"Only to Smith."

"I'm not clear on how you got the phone call about meeting Tabitha at Lincoln Center," Peiser said. "You told Detective Walters . . ."

"I didn't tell him everything," Wetzon said. Ferrante made a rude noise. "I couldn't get the papers out of my mind. I knew that Smith and the Gordons, at least Jerry, were going to watch Hartmann do his summation. I decided to drop by and see if I could get into the apartment."

"You *broke* in?" Ferrante looked as if he were ready to clap her in irons. "Or did Dr. Gordon give you a key?"

"I borrowed a key from housekeeping." She looked at Peiser.

"Bull!" burst from Ferrante. "She's in it up to her—"

"Am I in trouble for this, Ms. Peiser?"

"For B and E, no. For obstruction of justice, maybe."

"And maybe more." Ferrante was standing at the table.

"Wait a minute, Ferrante. Why are you always trying to make me look worse than I am?" Wetzon rose. "I'll be right back." She went into the bedroom. The suit she'd worn that night was on the chair. She hadn't had a chance to take it to the cleaners. In the pocket was the housekeeping master key. She returned with it and handed it to Ferrante. "Maybe you'd like to return it for me."

Ferrante growled.

"Forget it, Bobby," Peiser said. There she went again with Bobby. Why didn't she just call off her dog? Was this the good cop–bad cop routine? "Did you see the papers?"

That stopped her. What was she to do? She still had Mrs. Leonora Foley's statements. But what did they have to do with the murders? Probably nothing, she decided, so she fudged. "Yes and no. I saw them, but they all came back to the apartment after court, and I had to replace the hatbox and hide in the closet. When they left and I looked for the hatbox, it was gone."

"Maybe it was never really there," Ferrante taunted. "Her and her connections. I heard all about you."

"Ferrante, I've had it. I'd like you to leave. Now."

"Hold it," Peiser said, briskly. "Back off, Bobby."

Wetzon belatedly realized there was something else going on here, apart from Ferrante's reaction to her. "No maybe. It had been there. Someone else came into the apartment then, Barbara Gordon, I think, and I jumped back into the closet. The problem was I'd dropped my briefcase earlier and everything'd spilled out. I thought I'd got it all, but I didn't know it at the time, I was missing my cardcase."

"You saw her?" Ferrante asked in a normal voice.

Wetzon shook her head.

"How do you know it was Barbara Gordon?"

"Her perfume. And she was getting dressed in evening clothes. The closet was full of evening dresses." Wetzon refilled the coffee mugs with what was left of the coffee, turned the machine off, and sat down. "Look, Ms. Peiser, I blew it. It was hot in there—the closet I mean—and I fell asleep. I heard the outside door close, and I woke up. I thought I was alone, but someone could have been in the kitchen. It has these swinging doors. I never checked. I was really dopey from the nap, so when the phone rang, I answered it. It was Rona. She thought I was Penny Ann, because Penny Ann was supposed to stay in the city and Jerry had offered her his office."

"Was there a phone in the kitchen?" Ferrante asked.

"How would I know?" Wetzon said irritably. "Isn't that your job?"

"It's all my job, and you stuck your face in it."

"We're almost finished," Peiser said, giving Ferrante a sharp look. "What did Rona say?"

"She said Tabitha wanted to meet at the fountain at Lincoln Center. She had something to tell." Wetzon looked down at her hands on the mug of coffee. "Listen, I used the bathroom before I left. Someone could have heard everything on a kitchen extension and rushed up to Lincoln Center and gotten there ahead of me and Rona, barely, but—"

"Did you see Rona Middleton there?" Peiser asked.

"I think, and I'm guessing, that Rona saw the whole thing come down, but I didn't see her, and I didn't see Tabitha either. I was there for about a half hour. I walked around and was really ready to leave—when I found her. It was horrible." She got up and made herself busy, washing the coffeepot. With her back to them she said, "Rona didn't do it."

"Come off it, the kid was sleeping with her husband," Ferrante said. "Broke up the marriage."

Wetzon burned. "Ms. Peiser—"

"Just a couple of more questions, Ms. Wetzon."

Wetzon turned to Ferrante. "What marriage? Rona's been carrying on an affair with Maglia since before Brian." She looked at Peiser. "Rona has an alibi for when Brian was killed. You have no case."

Peiser put down her pen and rubbed her eyes, smearing her eye shadow. "Bobby?"

Ferrante shrugged. "She doesn't have one for the girl."

"Coincidence, Ferrante. Neither do I. And you haven't found the gun, either. . . ."

There was a long silence during which they all glared at one another.

Finally, Peiser said, "The gun's been found."

"The murder weapon?"

"Yes."

"Where?"

"At Rona Middleton's house."

"Oh, I don't believe it. Is this a trick? Rona says she's never fired a gun in her life. I bet Rona's prints aren't on it."

"It's no trick," Peiser said. She got to her feet and grabbed her coat.

"There were no prints." Ferrante held Peiser's coat so she could slip into it, then lifted her hair over the collar. Too intimate a gesture for a cop and an assistant D.A. "It was wiped clean."

"Then it could have been planted there, couldn't it?"

Peiser headed for the door, and Ferrante followed.

Wetzon persisted. "Couldn't it?"

Peiser said, "It's registered in the name of Wilson Boyd."

47

·······

Wetzon was riding a handsome white horse as the carousel spun around and around on the ice of the Wollman Rink; her hair streamed behind her like a curtain in the wind. Smith in crimson riding britches and a crimson helmet rode the palomino just ahead. She flicked her crop at the wooden flanks and called back at Wetzon, "Hurry, look behind you."

Wetzon looked through the scrim of her hair and saw a posse of stockbrokers gaining on them: Joan Boley on a giraffe, Stu Beck and Larry Sellica on elephants, Rona in a safari hat. All were carrying guns, all shouting and waving tickets. All wore sweatshirts saying, "Go For Broke."

"Birdie, darling, come back to the theater, where you belong," Carlos shouted. He was skating alongside the carousel, pleading with her, until the wooden horses outpaced him.

Wetzon threw herself on the carved mane of the pony and heard a *ping*, felt the pony shudder.

Circling the carousel on skates were the branch managers: Neil Munchen, Simon Loveman, Tony Maglia, Fred Benitos, Jim Cafferty. They had teamed up for the privilege of taking potshots at Smith and Wetzon.

"You sold us damaged goods," Cafferty yelled. "Spin your wheels somewhere else. We can do it without you."

"No, you can't, dirtball!" Smith shouted. "You'll die without us. Tell them, Wetzon. Tell them they need us."

Bullets were whizzing all around, *ping, ping, thump*. Keeping her head down, Wetzon clung to the pony.

"You can't close to save your life!" Smith screamed at the gang of managers. That did it. There was a barrage of gunshots, and Maglia held up a big sign that said "40, Count Them."

"Now see what you've done," Smith shrieked at Wetzon. "You've told everyone about my birthday."

The organ was playing "I'm Looking Over a Four-Leaf Clover."

Warm maple syrup oozed onto Wetzon's hands, red as blood. She stared at her hands, shocked. "My God, my pony is bleeding. Is there a doctor in the house?"

"Look no further. I'm a doctor." Jerry Gordon in a teddy-bear costume appeared carrying a hatbox. The lid flew off and brokerage statements took to the air. Wetzon caught one and looked at it. It was Mrs. Leonora Foley's.

"You're not a doctor," Barbara Gordon said. "You're nothing but a fat boy." She was a Valkyrie, her sequined robes flowing in the wind created by the spinning carousel. She staggered right up to Ferrante, who was sitting on a park bench cooing and necking with assistant D.A. Marissa Peiser, grabbed his .38 service revolver from his leather waist clip, and shot her husband in the face.

The carousel hurtled to a stop, and the music ceased. Wetzon slid off her pony onto something soft and warm, and lay there with her eyes closed catching her breath. The cooing got louder.

Wetzon opened her eyes. A pigeon was cooing lovingly to its mate as they paused on the fire escape outside her bedroom window. Carlos's loft. She didn't move. The dream vividly replayed itself. If one believed in omens, Jerry Gordon's life was in danger.

But Wetzon didn't believe in omens. Not at all. No, sir. No, ma'am. No way. That sensible refrain accompanied her to the kitchen as she shook the container of orange juice and poured herself a glass. It ran through her head as she filled the coffee maker. She took a swallow of juice and dribbled orange spots on Silvestri's white shirt. She'd slept in it. That's probably what had given her bad dreams. She sighed and pulled on her leggings, then with Harry Connick, Jr., on the stereo, she allowed herself a slow, thorough workout on the barre.

Hot water dissolved what remained of the bad dream, and by the time she stepped out of the shower, she was feeling great. She used the blow dryer until her hair was just damp, then braided it into one long braid and let it hang down her back.

After reviving a slightly stale half a bagel in the toaster oven, she gave it a skimpy topping of cream cheese and sat down with a mug of coffee and listened to the pigeons. Her fingers were restless; she missed the home delivery of *The New York Times*. After the flood she'd canceled it instead of having it delivered here, because there was no doorman in Carlos's building. Except for those stupid pigeons who wouldn't quit, Tenth Street below her window was quiet. Just before nine on a Saturday morning, the Village was barely stirring.

The dream came back to haunt her. Her worries about the business, the murders, the crazy cast of characters. Then there were Leonora Foley's statements from January through August, which Wetzon had back-burnered, but which were obviously troubling her since they'd turned up in the dream. What the hell were they doing in a hatbox in Dr. Jerry's consulting-room closet?

She poured the rest of the coffee into the mug, then went into the bedroom, took the statements from her briefcase, and laid them out on the kitchen table. Maybe, just maybe, somewhere in all of this was the answer to why Brian Middleton was murdered. But she saw nothing more than she'd seen before.

Perplexed, Wetzon dug about in the mail Louie had dropped off and found her most recent statement—September's—from Oppenheimer. She placed it next to Leonora Foley's August statement and compared them.

On her own statement she saw the notation of the check she'd sent to Laura Lee. Its entry was followed by the abbreviation "CHK." That would mean check, of course. Her eyes ran over Leonora Foley's statement, and there it was. The entry after the $8,500 was "CSH." The thrill of recognition was like a shot of caffeine. She raced through the rest of Leonora Foley's statements. The monies received were all marked "CSH." Cash.

"My, my," she said aloud, "this Mrs. Leonora Foley is laundering money." So long as cash amounts received were under $10,000, they did not have to be reported to the Exchange or the Feds. She clucked her tongue on the roof of her mouth and took a sip of coffee. How was she going to deal with this? She had the statements illegally. That was fair. Dr. Jerry had had the statements illegally, too. Hadn't he?

Was Mrs. Foley another of Dr. Jerry's patients? Was he more

than Mr. Nice Guy? Her mind was going click, click, click. Why not call her and ask her? Wetzon knew this was her forte. She could coax information from people. . . . The Nynex white pages. She'd seen them on the floor of the bedroom closet. She brought the fat phone book to the bed and tore though it, running her finger down the F's.

Her watch said 9:00. She was going to have to move it to get the train. Leonora Foley. She was listed! Wonderful. Wetzon picked out the numbers carefully and heard the call go through.

"Mrs. Foley's residence." The voice was a woman's, with a Jamaican lilt.

"Hello. I know it's early, but this is Mary in Dr. Gordon's office. May I speak to Mrs. Foley about her appointment?"

"You must have the wrong Mrs. Foley."

"Mrs. Leonora Foley on West Seventy-second Street?"

"Yes, but Mrs. Foley can't talk."

"It'll only take a minute for me to verify—"

"No, you don't understand. Mrs. Foley had a stroke. . . ."

"Oh, I'm so sorry." She'd hit a brick wall. "Was it sudden?"

"Mrs. Foley, she been paralyzed for four years. Hasn't moved or said a word since I been here, three years now. You got the wrong party for sure."

"I don't know how that could have happened. . . . I'm really sorry." How could Mrs. Foley have been making regular cash deposits in her brokerage account if she was non compos? "Well, thank you. . . . Is there anyone else there I can talk to? Mrs. Foley's daughter, perhaps?"

"Maybe you want to talk to Mrs. Foley's grandson. He usually comes on Sunday afternoon. He handles all her business."

"Okay. I'll call back on Sunday and talk to Mr. Foley."

"Not Foley, Hartmann."

Good God! "Hartmann? With two *n*'s?"

"Yes. Richard Hartmann."

Twenty minutes later, in heavy black leggings, boots, a long red sweater over one of Silvestri's sleeveless undershirts, she was out on Sixth Avenue looking for a cab uptown. Her carryall was stuffed with a change of underwear, John le Carré, and the *Times* from the corner newsstand. Brittle fall sunlight warmed glancingly but not well.

Westport was always a touch cooler than Manhattan, so she'd worn her lined black leather jacket with a long leopard silk scarf she could wrap twice around her neck. She was worried. She was going to have to warn Smith not to get more involved with Hartmann. But would Smith listen? Unlikely.

A cab pulled up beside her, and she got in. "Grand Central." The driver looked familiar, but he wore his brown hair long and shaggy. She leaned over to see his name. "Perry Carlino," she said out loud. The name tickled her memory.

Carlino cocked his head and looked at her in his rearview mirror. "Hey! Did you ever work for Shearson?"

Bingo! She remembered. "No, but you do know me. I'm Wetzon. A headhunter. We met a long time ago, before the Crash."

"Hey, yeah, I sort of remember you. The Four Seasons, right?" He drove with his right arm on the back of the seat, turning to talk to her now and then when he came to a stop.

"Right. I moved you to Marley Straus. Are you moonlighting?"

He was an aggressive driver, tooling up Sixth Avenue, weaving around trucks and cabs, then east on Twenty-third Street to Third. "Naa," he said. "I left the business about a year after the Crash, or rather, it left me. My clients were wiped out and scared shitless to come back in."

"I'm sorry."

He drove up Third Avenue to Forty-second Street and waited for the light to change. "Don't be. I do okay with the cab, and I don't have to listen to complaints from my clients on one side that I wasted their assets, and my manager on the other, pushing me to do more business, get my clients out of cash and T-bills. It was a no-win situation. Listen, the Street invited the small investor into the shower years ago, dropped the soap, and has been—excuse me—fucking him ever since." He made a left and pulled up in front of Grand Central Station, magnificent and glowing in the sunlight. Weekend travelers were streaming in and out. Carlino turned to her. "But that isn't to say I wouldn't go back in when things get better. I'm just waiting for the right time."

She gave him ten dollars and told him to keep the change. A four-dollar tip. Was she crazy? No, just guilty. She walked into Grand Central and over to Zaro's, where she bought half a dozen sticky buns to take up to Smith. If she hadn't moved Carlino out of Shearson when she did, she wondered, would he still be in the business?

She said so to Smith an hour and a half later in Westport as she strapped herself into the passenger seat of the Jag.

"We didn't twist his arm to move." Smith backed the Jag up and turned around. "He's responsible for himself. And he wasn't about to turn down that nice upfront check."

"Yeah, I guess—"

"Guess, nothing. How was the train?"

"Uneventful. But last night, now *that* was interesting. Tell me first, how is Mark?"

Smith's face softened. "They were so cute. You should have seen them. They left at seven this morning carrying so much equipment they could hardly get on the bus. He's gotten so tall. And grown up. His friend is such a nice, clean-cut boy. His mother is married to George Herzinger."

"Gee, Smith, not the newspaper tycoon?" Wetzon fluttered her eyelids, teasing.

But Smith nodded seriously. "Uh-huh. Such good connections for my boy."

And for his mother, Wetzon thought, but she didn't comment. Instead, she told Smith about the visit from Peiser and Ferrante. "They found the gun."

Smith's mood turned dark. "That Rona is a bigger fool than I gave her credit, to have kept the gun—" She made a sharp turn.

"Smith, for godsakes, Rona isn't that stupid. I'll bet someone planted it. And there were no prints on it at all." She looked out the window. The terrain did not look familiar. "Where are we going?"

"Humpf. She's doing everything to see that we don't get paid."

"You're acting as if she's doing it on purpose to spite us. I think she'd rather be cleared and go back to work. It has nothing to do with our getting paid or not. But I haven't told you the rest about the gun." They were passing a reservoir, a beautiful preserve of trees and undergrowth.

"What haven't you told me?"

"The gun was registered in the name of Wilson Boyd."

"Well! Good!"

"Good?"

"Yes." They were passing through a quaint little village called Weston, if you could believe the signs on the few stores.

"Ah, the village of my ancestors," Wetzon quipped.

"What? Oh, I see, one of your little jokes." She looked over at Wetzon. "I'm glad you're wearing black."

"Clue me in, please, Smith. Where are we going?"

"We, my dear Wetzon, are about to make a condolence call."

48

·······

The country road was winding and hilly, the trees rich with fall foliage. Forced to drive at a crawling pace because they followed a nursery truck packed with young spruce trees, Smith leaned on her horn. "Move it," she yelled with all the appropriate gestures.

The object of her fury paid no attention, and Wetzon leaned back and took in the scenery. Large homes, set back, well-maintained grounds, renovated farmhouses. There was something crisp and Protestant about Connecticut, and it wasn't just the climate. Its people moved around with clear Yankee purpose and energy; the work ethic was alive and well here.

A lot of theater and film people, writers, and artists lived all over Fairfield County, particularly Lower Fairfield, which encompassed villages like Greenwich, Westport, Wilton, Weston, Redding, and various other small connecting towns.

Smith was concentrating on the right side of the road. "Ah, here we are." She put her brakes on, then made a quick right into what looked to Wetzon like shrubbery but was another narrow, winding road that cut through a small, dense wood of evergreens for about a hundred yards and came out beside an expanse of lawn and a broad, single-story house with a huge porch chock full of green wicker furniture.

"Do you see what I see?" Wetzon put her hand on Smith's arm.

Not responding, Smith drove up to the side entrance, slowly passing a maroon police car with rooftop lights. She pulled up in front of a double garage next to a white Ford station wagon. Turning to Wetzon, who was craning her neck to look at the unoccupied police car, she asked, "What's in that box?"

"Sticky buns for tomorrow's breakfast."

"Not anymore." Smith appropriated the box and got out of the car. "Come on."

They had just reached the steps to the door when two men in dark-gray uniforms stepped out, still holding the open door, talking to someone inside. The wrinkled, menacing face of a brindled English bulldog pushed its head between the men and began barking.

"Rambo, get back in here this minute. Don't let him out." Penny Ann's disembodied voice.

The first officer, beefy-faced under his hat, squat, his belly resting over his belt buckle, firmly pushed Rambo back with the tip of his cowboy boot. The other cop was much younger, perhaps mid-twenties, and thin to the point of frail. There was enough room in his uniform for another cop his size. He caught sight of Smith and Wetzon and gave his partner an exaggerated poke.

"We'll be back later, y'hear?" the older one said to the closing door. He looked down at Smith, who was smiling up at him with her most dazzling smile. "Well, now, what do we have here?" He looked ready to jump her bones.

"We're paying a condolence call, Officer," Smith said, making a big thing of the cake box. "Is everything okay with poor Penny Ann?" She nodded to the police car.

The older cop's eyes rested on Wetzon, then slid back to Smith. She was really giving him the treatment. "If you're friends of Miz Boyd, you tell her to work with us. Everything will be hunky-dory."

Hunky-dory? What year is this, Wetzon thought. "What's the problem, Officer?" She directed her question to the older man.

"Police business." He put on his mirrored sunglasses and got into the car on the driver's side. When the younger man was settled, they drove off.

"Knock on the door," Wetzon said impatiently. But the door opened at once, and Rambo thrust himself in their way, breathing stentoriously, slobbering, showing a fearful arrangement of teeth. Penny Ann was just behind him, tugging at his chain collar. She was having no effect on him whatsoever till she began thumping him on the nose with a rolled-up copy of *Money*. Rambo immediately drew back with a clatter of toenails on linoleum, and ungraciously allowed them entry.

"Penny Ann, sweetie pie!" Smith thrust the cake box into Penny Ann's hands. Penny Ann wore jeans overalls over a leotard on her pudgy body, sneakers, and a shell-shocked expression. Her face was blotchy. Her hair was pulled back with a faded blue bandanna. She peered at them from behind her glasses. "Don't you remember? I have a home in Westport." Smith walked around the kitchen, conspicuously trying not to let anything touch her. "We're so sorry about your personal tragedy."

"Oh, yes." Penny Ann's voice was expressionless. "Thank you." She stood helplessly holding the box, not seeming to know what to do or say.

They were standing in a spacious country kitchen with built-in closets and all the best appliances. A long work island was centered in the room. It was on this counter that Penny Ann finally placed the box.

An open loaf of Wonder bread stood on another counter near a toaster oven, along with an unappetizing bowl of tuna fish steeped in mayonnaise. On the floor near the overflowing garbage pail was an empty bottle of Booth's gin.

Wetzon was hungry, but not that hungry. There was something about Penny Ann that made her queasy. "Have we disturbed your lunch?" Wetzon asked. The woman looked dazed. "Why don't you finish. Come on. We've already eaten," she added hastily, just in case food was to be offered. "You have to eat to keep your strength up." There was also something about Penny Ann that made Wetzon talk in clichés.

Rambo placed himself in the doorway to the dining room and snorted and snarled. Then he farted loudly.

"Lord," Smith murmured. She was trying not to breathe.

With a bit more animation, Penny Ann picked up a glass of milk and made a move for the rolled-up magazine. Before Penny Ann even picked it up, however, Rambo backed off, scampering noisily into the next room, and Wetzon and Smith followed her into a carpeted, wood-paneled room with high beamed ceilings; the room held a round dining room table surrounded by chairs. The single place mat next to a paper napkin contained a plate with a sandwich. On a tall oak sideboard a basket of fruit, still in its yellow cellophane, had just begun to rot, raising steam under its wrapping.

Framed hunting prints decorated the walls, and a moose head complete with antlers stared down at them from the mantelpiece over a working fireplace.

"My life is shit," Penny Ann said suddenly. "First Wilson, then losing the arbitration, now Tabitha." She bit into the sandwich.

Smith wandered through an archway, was gone a moment or two, and returned in time for Rambo's second pungent fart. "Charming home, dear." She made tracks for the other side of the room and studied the hounds-at-bay print on the far wall.

"I've put it on the market. I can't stay here—"

"Penny Ann." Wetzon pulled out a chair and sat down. It had a pink oilcloth cushion tied by strings to the back rails. Penny Ann's upper lip wore the remnants of a milk mustache. The odors from the fruit coupled with the noxious dog made Wetzon's eyes tear. The house had a musty smell, as if it had been closed up for some time. "What did the police want?"

Smith came over and leaned on the back of a chair.

"Wilson's gun. They said Wilson's gun killed Brian and Tabitha. It couldn't have. Wilson has been dead for over a year."

"Did you give the gun to someone?" Wetzon asked.

Penny Ann shook her head emphatically, too emphatically. Could this wreck of a woman have beaten and abused her child? Had this woman speculated in the stock market with her husband's insurance money?

"Who abused Tabitha, Penny Ann?" Smith said suddenly, staring at Penny Ann with loathing. "You or your husband? Or did you take turns?"

Penny Ann burst into tears, which mingled with the tuna salad left on her face. She put her head on the place mat.

"Jesus, Smith." Awkwardly, Wetzon patted Penny Ann on the back.

"*Who*, Penny Ann?" Smith's voice was chilling.

"Wilson. Wilson did it," she blubbered. "He had such a terrible temper, and then the brain tumor must have been growing—"

"And you didn't do anything about it?"

"I tried in the beginning, but he could be . . . cruel, vicious when he was crossed. I couldn't . . ." Tears were gushing out of her eyes.

"Oh, Lord, I'll never understand women like you," Smith said.

"What about Brian, Penny Ann?"

Wetzon's question just increased the blubbering. "Brian . . . made my baby pregnant." Gasping for breath, wiping her face with her hands, Penny Ann said, "We had a terrible fight. I wanted her . . . to have an abortion, but she said . . . Brian would marry her. Oh, God, I wanted to kill him—"

"What about the gun?" Wetzon prompted.

Penny Ann rose. She motioned them through a living room of faded chintz, past another fireplace, more animal heads and hunting prints, into another room, which was a study in leather, an office, with a desk and bookshelves on a long wall. Penny Ann walked right up to the bookcase and pressed a button on one of the shelves, then stood aside. With a click, three of the shelves swung open. On the wall behind the shelves hung an arsenal. Handguns, rifles, each in its allotted place.

"My God," Wetzon gasped. But there were—Wetzon looked at the wall carefully—three empty spaces.

"Who knows about this?" Smith demanded. "Do the police know?"

Penny Ann shook her head. "They're coming back with a search warrant and some detective from New York."

Wetzon couldn't take her eyes from the array of weapons. "Penny Ann, how many guns are missing?"

Penny Ann shrugged. "A rifle, I think. The other two were handguns."

"Three? Who took them? You've got to tell us."

"I don't . . . know."

"When did you notice they were gone?"

Penny Ann started crying again, sobbing horribly. They could barely hear her choked-up words. "After . . . Tabitha . . . ran away."

49

·······

"Being a detective makes me ravenous." Smith's eyes sparkled. She rubbed her hands together gleefully and fastened her seat belt.

"You're hungry because it's after one o'clock and we haven't eaten lunch." Wetzon felt irritable. She set the box of sticky buns down at her feet, Smith having snatched it back with a "She'll never even notice it's gone," on their way through Penny Ann's kitchen.

"Is that not the dimmest woman you've ever met? Can you believe a child running around with three *guns?*"

The motor purred, and Smith drove back on the narrow driveway. Burnished leaves floated off the trees into their path. Wetzon wondered idly how often cars had to back out because there was no way for two cars to fit.

"That child was three months pregnant."

"How do *you* know that?" Smith was obviously annoyed.

Wetzon's smile was cheerless. "Trust me," she said.

"Humpf." Smith put her foot on the gas, and they spurted forward.

When they came out onto Lonetown Road, Smith pulled over to the side and stopped. "See what's inside the mailbox."

Wetzon looked across the road at a red mailbox that said "BOYD" in big white letters. She hesitated. "I think that's against the law." A car drove by just fast enough to make the dry leaves spin.

Smith gave her a withering look. "Just look. We aren't going to take anything."

Wetzon rolled her eyes and slipped out of the seat belt. She

waited for a station wagon and a truck to drive past, then crossed the
street and opened the mailbox. It was stuffed with magazines, bills—
lots of them—a bank statement, financial reports, a statement from
Bliss Norderman, several of what appeared to be sympathy cards. A
smudged envelope without a return address. She fingered the envelope for a moment, ducking her head when a car drove by. *No*, she
thought, and shoved everything back into the mailbox, closed the box,
just as quickly opened the box, found the envelope again and took it
out, weighing it in her hand. The address was handwritten, the ink
smeared. The handwriting was a tentative, almost childish scrawl, and
the envelope was calling out to her loudly, *Open me.*

"What are you doing?" Smith fretted. "Snap to it."

Oh, shut up, Wetzon thought. She stuck her nail under the flap,
which was slightly detached, and eased it open the rest of the way.
She pulled out a sheet of yellow lined paper and read:

> Ma,
>   I didn't kill Brian. I was going to meet him, but I was to
> scarred. I want my baby. Rona said she'd help. Please don't
> be mad any more. I left everything with Dr. J.
>
> > Love,
> > *Tabby.*

A Mercedes tore past, kicking up gravel. Wetzon slipped the
letter back in the envelope and checked the postmark. The morning
after Tabitha was murdered. She must have slipped it into a mailbox
on her way to Lincoln Center. Wetzon shivered. She licked her finger
and reglued the flap with what was left of the stickum. After slipping
the letter back in the box, she waited for another car to pass and
crossed the road.

"Well?" Smith asked eagerly, starting the motor. "What took
you so long? I saw you reading something."

"Magazines, bills. And a letter from Tabitha. Judging by the
postmark, probably mailed just before she died."

"What did it say?" Smith waited for an entry space in the line of
slow-moving cars on Lonetown Road, and was rewarded by a woman
in a black BMW, who stopped and waved them in. She pulled out
onto the road just as a maroon police car came into view, coming
toward them. As it passed them, Wetzon saw Ferrante sitting in the

back. She watched the police car pause at the mailbox while the skinny deputy reached in and pulled out the mail. A curve in the road took them out of sight.

"That she wants to keep her baby, that she's scarred—but I think she meant scared—that Rona's going to help her, and that Jerry has the papers. Whatever all that means."

In Weston, Smith parked the car in the lot near a grocery store. "I'm just going to run into Peter's Market for some chicken salad and stuff. Twoey's driving down from Boston with lobsters for dinner. I'll get some baking potatoes. . . . Do you want to come in with me?"

Wetzon shook her head. "No, thanks. Supermarkets don't turn me on. Just bring back something to eat, and fast." She wanted to think about the letter and the missing guns. After Smith left, she got out of the car. The sun was warm on her face. She shaded her eyes from the glare and looked around. The local market was busy with a steady traffic of shoppers, those departing carrying an assortment of brown bags, all heading for Mercedes, Jaguars, BMWs.

Why would Tabitha have taken three guns? All she needed, if she was going to scare or even shoot someone, was one. What had she given to Jerry? All three guns? The papers in the hatbox?

Maglia was the pivot. He was Rona's alibi, Tabitha's safe house, not to mention Brian's friend and mentor, if you were to believe him. He knew more than he was telling. She had to think of a way to approach him. A brisk gust of wind swirled dead leaves and dirt, whipped trees, and jostled the brown fedora off an elderly man's head. Several people scrambled to recover it, and when the fedora was once more in its place, Wetzon smiled. If you were unlucky enough to lose your hat in New York, it would be instantly run down by a city bus or trampled to death by people rushing to their destinations.

She got into the car and punched up the radio, settled back wearily, and closed her eyes. Catch a quick catnap, all the while letting the right side of her brain do its work.

". . . consider that your behavior may be setting him off. What happens just before he . . . ? Familiar voice. She listened for another minute. Dr. Jerry.

"Like goes ballistic?" The other speaker was young.

"All right, Evie. That's a good word. What sets him off? Think about it. What did it the last time?"

"Like when I say we're going to my mother's for Thanksgiving, but he takes it okay. Then when I put the meat loaf on the table, he jumps up and like punches me in the face, and I start screaming and he punches me around and like someone calls the cops. It's always like that."

"Where are you living now?"

"Here. Like where else would I go?" Evie sounded astonished he was asking.

"Stay with me, Evie. We have to break for a commercial here. This is Dr. Jerry. When we come back, we'll talk to Evie again, and then I'll take more calls. I see we have three people waiting to talk to us. Wayne, Didi, and Mona. Stay tuned to 'Ask Dr. Jerry' until three o'clock, and don't forget we're back again this evening to help you with your problems from ten to midnight. And let me remind you that we switch to Eastern Standard Time in the wee hours of the morning, so turn your clocks back one hour before you go to sleep tonight."

Wetzon turned it off. She hated call-in shows, on any topic. It titillated voyeurs and nurtured crazies, and she questioned if they did any good at all except get people all heated up. Still, they were enormously popular and sold plenty of advertising. She looked over at the entrance to the market. What was taking Smith so long? Some chicken salad and baking potatoes? She willed Smith to leave the market. And there she was, just coming through the door with a grocery bag, accompanied by a slim, long-legged woman in black tights, boots, and a long green suede shirt, pushing a cart laden with brown bags.

Barbara Gordon was talking animatedly. Wetzon got out of the car, and Smith waved at her, calling her over. The two women were heading for a black Mercedes with New York plates. Wetzon followed.

She came in on Smith saying, "My place is in Campo Beach—on Blue Water Hill."

Barbara unlocked the car and popped the trunk. "We're renting in Wilton, on Clover Drive, to see if we like it. Of course, Jerry's practice is mostly in the city, but we're up here every Saturday because he does two shows, and in the winter, well, it's just, oh, I guess I'm chattering." She was wearing a green suede beret pulled down over her ears, revealing not a strand of red hair, and chunky Chanel-style gold earrings with gigantic pearls.

"Wetzon, there you are! Barbie and Jerry live right around here. Isn't it amazing?"

"Amazing," Wetzon agreed. "Where does Jerry do his show from?"

Barbie's weird white-lined irises lighted on Wetzon, who was standing on the driver's side of the car. She frowned and pursed her lips. "A station in Norwalk." She began hurriedly loading the groceries into the trunk.

"And do you know what else?" Smith was talking loudly, as if they were all deaf. "Rona is there for the weekend with Megan. Dickie got special permission for her to spend the weekend out of state."

"How nice," Wetzon said. "And, I suppose, Tony Maglia's joining you for dinner?"

Those creepy eyes, now tinted with suspicion, bore down on Wetzon.

"Now that's an interesting thought," Smith said, pouncing. "Is he, Barbie?"

Barbie's hands froze on the open trunk, and her eyes turned wary. "You followed me here, didn't you?"

"Oh, for pity sakes," Smith groaned.

Wetzon came around to where Barbie and Smith were standing. Seven grocery bags were stacked in the trunk along with two suitcases, coats, and . . . She looked away.

"Oh, shit, I forgot the peanut butter." The woman's face grimaced in a violent tick. "He's a freak for it."

"Barbie," Wetzon said, "if you want to run back and get the peanut butter, we'll watch the car for you."

"You will?" The white-rimmed eyes were uncertain. She started to close the trunk, stopped, looked at them. The trunk slid closed by itself, but didn't connect.

Smith patted Barbie's shoulder. "Of course, sweetie pie. Now you run right along."

Barbie hesitated only a split second, then rushed back inside. When she was out of sight, Wetzon moved in on the trunk of the car and lifted it. "Do you see what I see?"

"What?" Smith's eyes followed Wetzon's pointing finger.

In the rear of the trunk was the missing hatbox.

50

·······

They made their escape howling.

"Nancy Drew lives!" Wetzon shrieked.

"That was very clever of us." Smith smirked. She was driving like a maniac, way over the speed limit.

Wetzon had appropriated the hatbox, passed it to Smith, who did an end run around a red Chevrolet and shoved it in the trunk of the Jag. They'd waited for Barbie to return with the peanut butter and waved good-bye to her as she drove off.

"Let's pull over and see what's inside."

"No, we're almost home. It's too conspicuous here. I might see someone I know."

"We'll be lucky if we don't see a cop. Will you slow down?"

When they turned onto Blue Water Hill, Wetzon's excitement tempered. Soon they'd find out what the missing papers were all about—and then what?

Smith's house was a supermodern split on three levels. The ground level had garage space, a laundry room, and a large family area that Smith had divided into a darkroom and studio when Mark got interested in photography two years before. In the open second level, four steps up, were a kitchen, dining area, and living room, with a cathedral ceiling and a huge skylight. From a large deck off the living room there was a wonderful view of Long Island Sound. The bedrooms were on the third level, each with its own skylight.

Smith balanced the groceries on top of the hatbox, leaving the sticky buns to Wetzon. "You'll be in Mark's room," she called over her shoulder, tilting the hatbox so that the bag of groceries slid to the kitchen counter.

Smith's kitchen was white-on-white. The only spot of color came from the green frog magnets holding phone numbers on the fridge. Even the tea towels were white, but with green embroidery along the borders.

"Okay, are you ready?" Smith set the hatbox on the oblong glass-topped coffee table in the living room. Her face was infused with excitement.

Wetzon dropped her jacket and scarf on the sofa. "Go."

Smith lifted the lid of the hatbox. "Damn!" She flung the lid like a Frisbee at the doors to the deck.

Wetzon stared into the round box. It was packed with tissue paper and contained a Stryofoam head on which was pinned a curly, long-haired red wig. She began laughing. "I don't believe it! Serves us right." She felt around the tissue paper supporting the head. Nothing. No papers. Disappointment took the wind out of both of them, and they sank onto the sofa.

"Oh, dear," Smith murmured. "What's she going to do without her hair?"

Wetzon giggled. "This is awful. We have to find a way of getting it back to her."

"We can't do that. She'll know. I'll get rid of it. I'll put it out with the garbage."

"Oh, Smith, that's cruel. Better that I take it back with me and drop it at the hotel. It's important to her."

"Spare me." Smith held up her palms to the ceiling.

"We must be crazy, anyway. Reading people's mail. Stealing things from the trunks of their cars. Those papers were probably destroyed." She rose. "Can we eat something now, before I pass out?"

They made themselves sandwiches and ate them on the deck.

"This is fabulous chicken salad."

"The best-kept secret in Connecticut."

A skywriter wrote "Happy Birthday, Linda Silverman" across the lapis sky.

"Who is Linda Silverman?" Wetzon asked. She'd scarfed down her sandwich and was working on her second beer. She was feeling mellow.

"I have no idea," Smith said. "But anyone who would have her name written across the sky like that has to be Jewish."

"Excuse me. Silverman? I would say that's a Puerto Rican name. Damn it, Smith, what, may I ask, has that to do with anything?" Smith's bigotry drove Wetzon up a wall. She stared daggers at Smith. "On second thought, don't answer that, because you're going to say things that will make me crazy."

Smith shrugged. "Whatever." She stretched her legs out on the chaise. Pots of yellow and purple mums dotted the deck. "Let's not argue. I'm feeling so good. Dickie Hartmann is such a love."

Wetzon got to her feet and began pacing nervously. Trust Smith to shatter her peace one way or the other. And she was about to shatter Smith's right back.

"Look, Smith, I don't quite know how to say it, but you really should cool it with Hartmann."

"What are you talking about, sugar? He's the best thing that ever happened to me."

"Mark is."

"Oh, for pity sakes, I know that. I mean, after Mark."

"I would think Twoey is—"

"Twoey, Twoey—that's all I keep hearing from you. If you think he's such a prize, you can have him."

"You are an absolutely impossible person. I don't know why I bother, but I want you to promise me you won't tell anyone what I'm about to tell you. Do you promise?"

Smith groaned. "You are so melodramatic."

"Promise."

Another groan. Then, "All right!"

"This is important, Smith. It has to do with two murders. I don't want to be the third."

"All right! I said I promise."

"I think Hartmann and Brian were involved in a money-laundering scam."

Smith sat up and put her feet on the deck with a thump. "I don't believe it. Not Dickie. He's a lawyer—"

"Do I have to remind you that not all lawyers are honest?"

"That's not what I mean." She smiled. "Dickie is too smart to be involved in a scam that's obvious to you." She lay back in the chaise.

"I give up!" Wetzon went back to her nervous pacing.

"If you're going to go on like that, why don't you get the watering can and water my plants? It's downstairs next to the washer." Smith began to shuffle her tarot cards.

Wetzon watered the plants and set the can on the deck. Smith had spread her tarot cards out in a Celtic cross, and was murmuring, "Woman. Powerful woman." She looked up. "Someone's going to get hurt."

"Someone's already been hurt."

"The murderer is a powerful woman."

"Like you, perchance?"

"Spare me." Smith gathered up her cards and placed them back in their silk bag. She watched Wetzon through slitted eyes. "What's going on between you and Alton?"

"Nothing." Wetzon walked over to the rail and looked out at the Sound. Sailboats dotted the water, their sails fat with wind. She sighed.

"You haven't slept with him." It was an accusation rather than a question.

"No. Do we have to talk about it?"

"Yes. You're not still carrying a torch for—"

Wetzon turned on her, snapping, "What if I am?"

Smith smiled at her warmly, undeterred. "My advice is, do it with Alton. If it's good, it'll erase the residue of Dick Tracy and you'll get attached. Trust me."

She sat there looking so smug, Wetzon wanted to kill her. "I'll take it under advisement." She drained the dregs of her beer.

"Humpf."

"I heard some of 'Ask Dr. Jerry' on the radio while you were in the market. He's pretty good for what it is."

"He's more than that. I hear they have to turn advertisers away, and he'll probably be syndicated once his book comes out."

"That's impressive. And sad."

"Sad?"

"His wife's bananas, maybe worse."

"Anyone home?" Twoey had arrived.

They gathered up their empty plates, bottles, and cans and found Twoey in the kitchen shaking live lobsters from a sack into the sink.

"Sugar! I've missed you." Smith and Twoey exchanged a lingering kiss, then Twoey winked at Wetzon. "What are you girls plotting now?" He rummaged in the fridge. "I need a brew."

Smith arranged the potatoes on a piece of foil and lit the oven. "How do you know we're plotting anything? Wetzon drank the last beer."

He straightened. "No problem. I picked up a case on the way in. I'll get it."

Each time Twoey opened a beer for himself, he opened one for Wetzon, too. Wetzon knew she was sloshed; she'd stopped counting after the fourth. She was dozing on the sofa while Twoey boiled the lobsters and Smith made the lemon butter sauce.

Twoey had brought a bottle of Stag's Leap white for dinner, and Wetzon switched from beer to wine.

"So tell me what mischief you've been up to," Twoey said. "Have you cleared Rona yet? We're losing money every day she's not in the office."

"No one's working her book?" Smith asked.

"Not yet. And she's got the upfront we gave her sitting some-where working for her."

"We are investigating thoroughly." Smith collected the plates and dumped the shells in a plastic garbage bag.

"Would you like anything, Wetzon?" Twoey was grinning at her, his face a mass of red freckles. Why was he grinning at her? "How about another beer?"

"Okay." Wetzon was sitting on the long bench that Smith used for chairs on one side of the table. She swayed.

"Twoey, leave her alone. She's had too much already." Smith scowled at him.

"I think she's cute. Alton thinks she's cute."

"You're bad, Twoey." Wetzon shook her finger at him, felt a burp start, and clamped her hand over her mouth. She could hear Smith banging dishes into the dishwasher, slamming cupboard doors.

"Come on, Wetzon," Twoey said. She was leaning slightly. She could feel it. He took her hand. "Wetzon's going to show me how to do a soft-shoe, aren't you, Wetzon?" He helped her up.

She swayed unsteadily on her feet. He gave her his arm. "Okay, Twoey, watch me." She dum-ta-di-dummed "Singing in the Rain." "Come on, sing it with me. First you have to learn the brush step. See

—front brush, back brush, side brush, Fuller brush." She giggled, but she found her way. She always found her way.

Twoey, all six feet of gangly arms and legs, tried, couldn't follow, took off his shoes, began to follow, all the while propping Wetzon up and bracing himself with a bottle of beer. He collapsed on the couch, laughing.

Wetzon put herself down very carefully on the bench and lay supine, one leg on the floor on either side, her arm over her eyes.

"You are both disgustingly drunk," Smith fumed. "I hate this. I'm going to bed." She stamped off.

"Oops," Wetzon said. Her head lolled on the bench. The skylight was spinning over her head. She laughed.

"I'm in the doghouse, I guess," Twoey said. He grinned again and opened two more beers and handed one to her. Then he toasted her with his bottle.

"We both are." The hard plank of the bench felt solid on her back. She stuck her arm up and toasted him with her bottle.

"I'm not that far gone," he said. "I wanted to talk about Xenie's birthday party."

She rolled her head in the direction of his voice. He was back on the couch. "Twoey—" She heard him say something about grilled salmon and, sometime later, chocolate truffles. "Twoey—" Did he say *thirty* people? "Twoey, listen." He didn't interrupt this time, and her words tumbled out. "Don't say forty, whatever you do. She's not taking to it well."

"Xenie? You're wrong, Wetzon, but okay."

Through a blue haze Wetzon saw him tilt his head back and finish the beer. He rose, stumbling a little, and looked for his jacket. Wetzon lost track of him until he was a big shadow standing over her. The light glinted on his gold-rimmed glasses. She couldn't see his eyes. "Look," he said. What was he showing her?

"I can't move," she said. "What's that?" She commanded her eyes to focus. God, he was dangling diamond grapes in front of her face. "Gosh, Twoey, they're gorgeous."

"They are, aren't they?" She thought he looked pleased, but wouldn't swear to it. "You're a nice girl, Wetzon."

"You're a nice boy, Twoey."

He bent and kissed her forehead. "Alton's a good man." He

stood there looking down at her as if she was supposed to say something.

She said, "I know. He's coming to the party with me."

"He told me."

"Uh-huh."

"Okay, then. Do you need help getting up the stairs?"

"No. I'm going to stay here for a while."

He said good night and she lay there until the spinning stopped, then got up slowly and staggered to the bathroom to pee. When she came out, she looked at her watch. It took a while to come into view. Eleven o'clock. Tomorrow night at this time it would be only ten o'clock. She'd have to remember to set it back before she went to bed.

She put her jacket on and rolled the scarf around her neck, opened the door to the deck, and stepped out.

The proximity of the Sound gave the night a special grace and a particular loneliness that was not lonely. She stood watching the moonlight glinting on the water, listening to the night sounds. Rock music. Laughter. A child crying. A dog with the shrill bark of a poodle, answered by a yapper. The eleven-o'clock news on TV. Wetzon sighed. Her ears tingled, and the tip of her nose was cold.

Below her in the wooded brush between the houses, she heard the little night animals, the scavengers, raccoons, chipmunks, squirrels. She looked into the darkness and saw lights on the water, glimmers from surrounding houses.

She hated the country. The dense darkness had always frightened her, made her feel vulnerable. She remembered the isolation on the farm when she was growing up, the chores, the chicken shit on her sneakers, the dust in her nostrils, the lack of water pressure, the cesspool, the hurricanes that turned electricity off for days. The bugs took over in the summer, moths and mosquitoes, ants, Japanese beetles. Green lawns reminded her of blisters. If she ever had a country house, which was highly unlikely, she would cement the lawn and paint it green.

Stop. Tears were running down her cheeks. The stars were so low she could almost touch them. She wanted Silvestri and their life together back.

She dropped down on the chaise and heard a car backfire. Something warm flew past her head and landed with a *wuhump* in the wood shingle behind her.

51

·······

Wuhump. *Wuhump. Wuhump wuhump wuhump wuhump.* She sat immobile on the chaise, listening to the sound ricochet through her consciousness. The silence of the night lay like a moist blanket over her. Finally, she rolled off onto the deck and crawled to the sliding door.

She tugged at it. It wouldn't open. It was locked. No, how could it be locked? She just couldn't get the leverage she needed from down here. Now she was caught in a to-the-death struggle with the goddam door, which wouldn't let her in.

God, Wetzon. Paranoia and personification over a door. She gritted her teeth, jumped up, and tugged the door open, throwing herself on the floor of Smith's living room. Rising, she slid the door closed and dropped back on the floor, limp and giddy. She didn't dare put on a light and make herself a real target, if that's what she was.

Wuhump made her head spin. Cold sweat laced her forehead, her upper lip, rolled down her underarms. Someone was trying to kill her. The undigested lobster, the wine, all those beers, began churning in her stomach like a washing machine on the spin cycle. She scrambled to her feet and raced for the bathroom just outside Mark's room, losing everything in one long, wrenching convulsion. On her knees on the tile floor, she hugged the toilet bowl, shivering violently, tears pouring from her eyes.

Miserable, she wished herself dead. No. No, she didn't. She got to her feet, weak-kneed, flushed the toilet, wiped up, rinsed her mouth and washed her face. She'd drunk too much. Where was her common sense? Drowned in beer.

Wuhump wuhump wuhump . . . again and again. Get out of my head, get out of my head.

Too frightened to turn on the light in Mark's room, she groped her way to the bed, dropped her clothes on the floor, and tried to make herself disappear.

Eastern Standard Time blew in during the night, and Wetzon should have been rested, having picked up an extra hour of sleep when the clocks were set back. But instead she fell into a pattern of dozing, waking with a jerk, checking Mark's digital clock radio, and seeing only fifteen or twenty minutes had elapsed since she'd last looked. She listened to the creaking, settling noises of the house, straining to pick out sounds that didn't belong. The blankets strangled her. She was freezing cold, then hot, throwing off the blanket. And all the time, the *wuhump*ing sound reverberated through her, chilling her to the bone.

She was a country girl, but never was easy with it. All kinds of horrible insects flew through the air under cover of darkness. She told herself, reasonably, it was probably a flying beetle . . . or a big, fat moth.

At five-thirty, she called it quits and pulled on her leggings and sweater and went down to the kitchen. She needed coffee. Little men were laying carpet across her face, hammering their sharp little tacks around and behind her eyes. Her empty stomach sent up queasy signals. God, she was wasted. Oh boy, was she wasted. It had been years since she'd let go like that, and she fervently vowed that it would be years before she did it again.

The coffee was probably loaded with caffeine, but at this point she didn't care. In Smith's cupboard she found a white porcelain mug and filled it with liquid darkness. Liquid darkness was what she'd felt she was in last night on the deck.

Now at dawn, it all seemed foolish, the product of a drunken imagination. Feeling steadier with each sip, Wetzon slid open the door she'd warred with and stepped out on the deck. The temperature had dipped during the night, and it was still quite cold, but dawn was tinting the sky over the Sound a pastelly pink and yellow, and a flight of birds in a V formation swooped down into the water cawing and jabbering.

She was avoiding what she had to do. Forcing herself, she turned and looked at the chaise, where she'd been seated the night before. A fine, sheer layer of cold dew made the rubberized cloth shiny, but it was otherwise intact. What she was hoping not to see was very much in evidence behind the chaise. A splintered shingle with a hole. She touched it, then pulled her hand away.

It could have been an accident, of course. Hunters. Kids drunk on a Saturday night. Who was she kidding? In her uneasy gut, she knew otherwise. For some reason Brian's murderer, Tabitha's murderer, was coming after her. He—or she—no longer had the handgun. Still, there was another handgun missing, and the rifle. She got back in the house fast and topped off her mug of coffee, found the le Carré book, and got into bed. Somewhere between five-thirty and nine, she slept deeply, waking only when she heard the sound of the shower and voices. She rolled over on her back.

Mark's room was awash in trophies, tennis and track. A Groton banner was pinned to the wall over the bed. Over the desk was a large black-and-white grainy photograph of Smith in an Aran turtleneck on the brink of some sort of prank—from the look in her eye, which Mark had caught brilliantly. There were snapshots of Mark and his friends on the walls. Mark had become a tall, slim, attractive young man. Tennis rackets and cans of balls were piled in a corner of the room, and the bookshelves contained schoolbooks and, surprisingly, plays and theater books.

Wetzon knew Mark was applying to colleges now. She found it hard to believe he was the same soft, sensitive little boy who'd made breakfast daily for his mother five years ago. It had been Jake Donahue, one of the sleaziest of Smith's old boyfriends, who'd insisted that Mark be sent away to school, and it may have been the only decent thing Donahue had ever done. And it was certainly not intentional. Jake had just wanted to get rid of Mark so that he could have Smith's undivided attention. And he'd succeeded until last year, when Smith had met Twoey.

Twoey was a sweetheart, Wetzon thought. Too bad. His days were probably numbered. She took a shower in Mark's bathroom and packed yesterday's underwear in her carryall with the book. The kitchen below was giving off waves of fried eggs and butter; feeling better, she followed her nose.

Smith was putting sticky buns in the microwave when she looked up and saw Wetzon crooking her finger at her. Wetzon put her finger to her lips and then crooked it again.

Smith closed the oven door and followed Wetzon to the deck. "What's—"

"Don't talk, just look." Wetzon pointed to the damaged shingle. Her heart was beating so fast it threatened to smother her.

"Did you and Twoey do that in your drunken state last night?" Smith bristled malevolently.

"No, we did not. Will you kindly shut up and look at it closely." Smith gave her an exasperated look and bent closer, rubbing the splintered opening with her fingers. "I was out here last night around eleven, and somebody took a potshot at me. At least, I think—"

"There's a bullet in there?" Smith was incredulous.

"A ballistics expert could tell, I suppose. It'll have to be dug out."

"Dug out? What about my house?" Wetzon could see Smith calculating the cost of replacing the shingle. "I think whatever it is is now a permanent part of the house."

"Smith, *I* think you'd better alert your local police or state trooper. This is serious. Someone is trying to kill me. I'm going to call Marissa Peiser when I get back to the city."

"Nonsense. You're overdramatizing everything, as usual. Even if it was a bullet, it could have been a stray. Hunters."

"Hunting what? Fish? I'd love to believe that, but Penny Ann and Barbie both knew we were here. That means Rona and Dr. Jerry also knew. For all we know, Maglia could have been up here last night to see Rona. You never got an answer from Barbie, if you recall." And Richard Hartmann must surely have known.

Smith groaned. "You should never have gotten us into this mess."

"I didn't get us into this, you did. I was the one who suggested they go to the police about Tabitha."

"Oh, for pity sakes!"

"Breakfast!"

Twoey's cheerful shout cut off Wetzon's retort, but Smith managed to snap, "Not a *word* to Twoey about this."

They settled at the table over onion, bacon, potato omelets, and the sticky buns Wetzon had brought from the city. Smith put a carafe of fresh coffee and another of orange juice on the table and sat down. Wetzon saw with satisfaction that Smith was rattled. Twoey looked from one stony face to the other and shrugged. "Come on, girls. Get over it. Dig in. Breakfast's getting cold."

"I'd like to take an early train back," Wetzon said.

"What?" Smith looked up, startled.

"I said I want to take an early train."

Smith smiled lazily. "Take the Jag. I'll come back with Twoey."

"Good idea." Twoey, blooming with good health, could have posed for a milk ad; he never looked dissipated. There was no sign of the amount of liquor he'd put away yesterday.

Wetzon, on the other hand, knew she wore her boozing on her face, especially around her eyes. Women of a certain age should not drink, she thought regretfully. She looked from one to the other. They'd probably get back into bed the minute she left.

So it was that an hour later Wetzon was flying down I-95, the temporary mistress of her universe in outrageously expensive, imported wheels.

Why did she know that Smith would do nothing at all about the bullet in the shingle? Because it was not the kind of local notoriety she wanted, for one.

Traffic was spotty heading into the City; there was much more headed out to see the fall foliage or to spend one of the last nice autumn days in the country, visiting friends with fireplaces and trees. And guns.

She turned on the radio and found a classical music station near where WQXR hung out on the dial and listened to Glenn Gould play one of Bach's *Brandenberg* Concertos.

It could have been anyone last night, even Maglia. It could even have been an accident. Well, couldn't it? Barbie was a nut case; Penny Ann wasn't glued together really well. Rona? Dr. Jerry? He was just too perfect to be true. But what would be his motive? She was thinking that the same person had to have killed both. Was Hartmann left-handed? Why hadn't she thought to ask Smith?

Traffic merged at the Cross Bronx Expressway where the repair work was perpetual, and she slowed down to a crawl. That's when she realized that it couldn't have been Dr. Jerry. He'd been doing his second show from ten to midnight.

52

....

She left the Jag in Smith's garage and walked down Third Avenue carrying Barbie Gordon's hatbox. At Ecce Panis, a small Italian bakeshop owned by the Sign of the Dove restaurateurs, she stopped and bought an olive focaccio and a chocolate bread, and one slice of cherry focaccio because she was hungry. She'd only nibbled halfheartedly on the omelet, and Twoey had finished both hers and Smith's.

It was warm and sunny in the City, and everyone was out promenading. At noon on Sunday, restaurants were doing their big brunch business and a lot of people were heading for Bloomingdale's.

But not I, Wetzon thought. She took a big bite out of the focaccio; the cherries had a slightly tart taste that heightened the flavor of the yeasty dough.

At Fifty-ninth Street, she began walking westward toward Central Park and the Park Royale. A horse and carriage was parked in front of the hotel all decked out in wedding regalia—white ribbons, festoons, and flowers. A bride in a long satin dress, the train flowing, was held aloft by her groom in black cutaway. She threw her bridal bouquet into the air just as Wetzon broke through the crowd. The bouquet hovered for a moment as if looking for a spot to land, then tumbled, pink streamers flying onto Wetzon, momentarily blinding her. Applause filled the air.

"Oh, no," she cried, embarrassed, "it's a mistake." She tried to hand the forget-me-not bouquet back to the bride, but the bride and groom were climbing into the carriage. "Oh, dear."

"It's yours, honey. Fair and square," a woman in a pink suit said. "Enjoy it."

This is the silliest thing, she thought, holding the bouquet gingerly. She trotted into the hotel, right up to the desk, and handed over the hatbox to the clerk. "This belongs to Dr. Jerry Gordon. Can you see that he gets it?"

The clerk stared intently at her. Was he trying to memorize what she looked like so he could tell Dr. Jerry? She ducked her head. "Caught the bridal bouquet, did we?" the clerk said, with a good dose of jaded cynicism. "Well, congratulations." He'd been looking at the bouquet. Good. That's what he'd remember.

Still holding the ridiculous bouquet, Wetzon took the Sixth Avenue subway down to West Fourth and got out at the Eighth Street exit. If the City was alive on the Upper East Side, it was frenzied in the Village. Vendors clogged the sidewalks as the bridge-and-tunnel crowd gawked. A Sikh artist in a white turban was doing portraits in charcoal, and there was a waiting line. She didn't stop anywhere except at the newsstand on Seventh Avenue for the Sunday *Times*. She just wanted to be home.

It was almost two o'clock when she was back in the loft. Saying, "Go away, world," she double-locked the door. Dumping her loot from Ecce Panis on the table, she stuck the bridal bouquet in a glass of water and made a big pot of coffee. Then she played back her messages.

Marissa Peiser.

One, two, three, four hang-ups. Thanks a lot.

Ferrante.

Marissa Peiser.

Louie.

Alton Pincus. Calling from Chicago? He didn't leave a number.

Marissa Peiser one more time.

The last message. Carlos. Carlos! He was back. She stopped the machine. Thank God he was back. Her brain needed a good airing. She desperately needed a heart-to-heart with Carlos. She pressed the play button and Carlos's voice came on; he was yelling at her.

Where are you, Birdie? Don't you know people worry about you? I heard from Arthur someone tried to break in, and I can't believe you'd be thoughtless enough not to let us know where you are.

WUHUMP. The echo in her memory stirred the turmoil.

She was dismayed. Had she been thoughtless? She had only been gone twenty-four hours. Oh, hell, what did everyone want of her? She was a grown-up. And someone was trying to kill her.

She kicked off her boots and put on the radio, more classical music, to drown out the sound in her head of the bullet making contact with the shingle. In a sponge position flat on the bed, she took deep breaths until the tension left her body, then settled the phone on her stomach, receiver next to her ear. She called Carlos's number.

"Hello."

"This is your wayward ward, sir, checking in."

"Gawd, Arthur, it's her. Do you believe it? Just as if nothing's happened. Birdie, I swear, you gave us a turn. Where are you?"

"Where do you think I am? At your place." The familiar strains of the Papageno-Papagena duet surrounded her. *The Magic Flute*, her favorite opera. A soothing dressing for tangled nerves.

"Birdie, don't start with me. This is Carlos you're talking to. Remember? Carlos. After trying you all night and getting no answer, we were down there at the crack of dawn. I was afraid I'd find you dead on the floor, but you hadn't even slept in your bed."

"Darling Carlos." She said it lovingly, not wanting to fight with her best friend. And who else in the world really cared that much about her? "Darling Carlos, I have a life of my own, you know. And this may come as a shock, but I don't always sleep in my own bed."

"Arthur! I want you to hear this. She said she doesn't always sleep in her own bed. Dear heart, for me, I don't give a hoot who you do it with, so long as you take precautions. But let a person know—"

"Lord, I have a mother."

"You better believe you have a mother. We are each other's family. I thought you knew we are responsible to and for one another. Birdie? Are you listening? This is serious."

"I'm listening. You're depressing me."

"Arthur, do you believe her? Now she's telling me I'm depressing her."

She heard the rumble of Arthur's voice in the background. "I'm sure Arthur agrees with me."

"Arthur says you're a grown-up adult person. But you and I know no gypsy ever grows up."

"Thank you very much."

"You don't have to tell me where you were."

"Good."

"Where were you?"

"I thought I didn't have to tell you?"

"I lied."

"Oh, all right, then. I went up to Westport and spent the night."

"You are really desperate. You spent the night with the Barracuda?"

"Carlos—" It was their usual routine, Carlos attacking Smith and Wetzon defending her.

"You're all right, Birdie?" His voice became sober. "I mean, the prowler—"

"Louie scared him off. He was on the fire escape." He? Why not she? "Louie's great, incidentally."

"That damn fire escape. I'll get a gate put in. I'm glad you like Louie."

"Good. Are we finished?"

"No, we're not, darling. Carlos wants you to tell him something deeply personal."

Wetzon groaned. "Like what?"

"Like what's going on with you and the cop?"

"Nothing. Nothing is going on. It's off, that's what." Her anger and hurt spewed out.

"Hey, easy—" Carlos sounded shocked.

"He's down there in D.C. and he thinks he can keep a girl in both ports. I've had it, Carlos."

"Birdie, I'm sorry."

"I've met someone else who thinks I'm terrific. Someone successful in the real world—"

"Dear heart, when you say that, why do I think you mean the Barracuda's world? The question is, who do you love, Birdie? I mean, besides me."

She felt her throat contract and her eyes fill. Who would care if someone killed her? Laura Lee, yes. Smith, possibly, but she'd get over it fast. Alton? They didn't know one another well enough for him to care. Certainly not Silvestri. He'd already forgotten her. Only Carlos would really care. She knew that. "I love you, Carlos. I'm having a tough time with this. I feel as if someone I loved died."

"Birdie, I—" He seemed suddenly at a loss for words. "I—uh—I don't know how to say this. I wasn't alone when I was there this morning."

"What do you mean? You and Arthur?"

"No. Silvestri called me last night. He couldn't find you. He'd been up to your apartment looking for something he'd left there and saw that mess. . . . He was pretty upset."

"Yeah, I'll bet."

"Listen to me, Birdie. He was really blitzed by the apartment, and he was worried about you."

"I told him."

"Seeing it was worse."

"That's too bad. So let me get this straight. He was here with you this morning and saw I hadn't slept in the—"

"You got it."

"Well, good. Was he upset?"

"He was."

"Tsk, tsk."

"I see how it is. Who's the new man—if there really is one."

"There is, Mother. Maybe we can double-date some time."

"That does it." He got serious again. "You're okay?"

"Fuhgeddaboudit." She hung up and rushed over to the dresser, opened the drawer. Felt under her underwear. The black box was gone.

Damn him! How dare he go through her drawers. She stamped back to the bed and reached over to turn off the radio. It had just gone from glorious Mozart to some dreary German fugue. An announcer was saying, "This program was recorded earlier in the day . . ."

53

·······

Wetzon was thoroughly confused. She'd been doing barre work to the score of *Pippin* for the twenty minutes, but her concentration was ragged. She kept stopping and starting, unable to break out into a good, drenching sweat.

Conceding, she stopped. She was spooked. Maybe as you get older you lose your nerve, you hang on tighter to every minute you have. The best thing would be to call Marissa Peiser and dump it all on her. Let *her* check Dr. Jerry's call-in show, let *her* deal with the bullet in Smith's shingle. Now she was sweating.

She reached Peiser's answering machine—it must be her home—and left a message that she was in her apartment. Maybe Peiscr was in her office. Where was that card? She searched through every suit pocket and finally found it in her trench coat.

Peiser was not in her office, but someone took a message.

She was being thwarted every which way. Muttering, back at the barre she conducted a ferocious, high-speed run-through of all the positions, left the barre, and did some Fosse combinations her body still remembered. Well, her head remembered, but she was tight, and worse, getting no joy from it.

Where had Barbie said that station was located? What was wrong with her mind that she couldn't remember? Stamford? No. Not Westport, no Wetzon, not Weston. *Very funny, brain,* she thought. Norwalk! The brain had to make a joke before it gave her what she was looking for. Okay. She called Connecticut information.

"What city?"

"Norwalk. I'm looking for the number of the radio station."

"I don't have a listing by subject. Do you have the name?" Wonder of wonders, the operator spoke like a real person.

"I don't know it."

"I'll put in 'radio' and see what we come up with." And accommodating, too.

"Okay, there's a listing in Norwalk for radio—AM 1260, but it's a Westport address."

She wrote the numbers down and then punched them into the phone.

"WMMM."

"WMMM?" She put on an ingenuous voice. "Hi, I'm looking for the local station that 'Ask Dr. Jerry' is on. Would that be you, by any chance?"

"Huh?" The voice belonged to an adolescent boy—or maybe an adolescent girl.

" 'Ask Dr. Jerry,' the radio show." She spoke slowly, forced a smile to keep the impatience away.

"Huh?"

"Listen, do you know what I'm talking about? A local radio show called 'Ask Dr. Jerry.' "

The voice got huffy. "I'm the only one here right now. Can you call back later?"

"Can't you just answer my question?"

"Call back later." He hung up.

Wetzon held the receiver for a moment, then cradled it. Sundays. Someone's kid probably manned the phones on weekends and pretended to know what he was doing. Oh, well, everyone pretended to be something else. She and Smith even pretended to be detectives. She'd be lucky if . . . The tiny tip of an idea began to nudge its way from her subconscious.

Pretended . . .

The woman who owned the apartment next door to Wetzon on West Eighty-sixth Street was a computer something-or-other at Columbia. Sheila Reitman, a wacky Australian woman who'd come to the U.S. with her husband, Pappy Reitman, the travel writer, in the '50s and stayed in New York after he moved on to L.A. They'd never bothered divorcing, and once in a while he'd turn up, a puffed-up, beefy little man, with his battered Hunter's World shoulder bag, cameras, and laptop. The cigarette smoke would seep cartoonlike from the door seams into the shared hallway. This was how Wetzon would know he was there. The screaming and yelling would commence, and then several days later, absolute quiet. He'd be gone. A very peculiar relationship. Sheila had this huge white Persian cat named Sean who sneaked out and sat outside her door on the doormat in protest whenever the Smokestack was in residence.

Wetzon flipped open her Filofax to the R's and called Sheila's number. Sheila answered immediately in her breathy voice.

"Is this a bad time?"

"I'm on my way to a rehearsal." Sheila was an amateur flutist and belonged to a music group. "I saw the mess. My heart goes out to you, Leslie."

"Thanks, Sheila. I just wanted to tell you that my contractor is a woman named Louise Armstrong, and she and her crew will be starting tomorrow. I hope it won't disturb you."

"Me? I'm sure it'll be fine, but thanks for letting me know."

"Ah, Sheila. There's one other thing. I know you're in a hurry, so I'll talk fast."

"I have a few minutes. What is it?"

Wetzon took a quick breath and forgave herself. She was about to lie. "Well, you know I'm a recruiter. . . ." Sheila didn't interrupt. ". . . And I want to check someone's credentials at Columbia, but I don't want to go through normal channels."

"And you'd like me to find out grades and ranking information?"

"No, nothing that involved. All I want to know is are his degrees legitimate. I've been told they might not be. But I don't want to alert him—"

"I can do that. I just have to get into the file. If I get home early enough, I'll use the modem; otherwise, I'll do it tomorrow and get back to you."

"If you know anything tonight, just call me at my regular number." She gave it to Sheila. "The call will get transferred down here— I'm staying in the Village in a friend's loft. Tomorrow you can reach me in my office." She gave her that number.

"Okay. What's the name and what am I looking for?"

"The name is Jerome Gordon or Jerry Gordon, or it might be J. Gordon. He's a psych Ph.D., and it would be in the '70s or early '80s I think."

After she hung up, she thought, *Now that was a wild-goose chase.*

Wouldn't it be stupid of him to have phony credentials when he was getting famous?

The telephone broke into her thoughts with a shrill ring, rattling her. "Hello?" She spoke cautiously, in a low voice.

"Ms. Wetzon? This is Marissa Peiser. I've been trying to reach you for two days." There was no accusation in her voice, just the fact.

"Yes, I know. I was at my partner's home in Connecticut."

"There are a few things I'd like to go over with you."

"There are a few things I'd like to go over with you, too."

"Good. I'm in my office. I can be up there in about three-quarters of an hour, maybe less."

"I was going to go out and get some dinner."

"If you wouldn't mind waiting for me, we can go together."

"Just you and me, right?"

"Right."

"Don't surprise me with Ferrante, okay?"

Pause. Then, "Okay."

Wetzon opened all the windows. A summerlike breeze jiggled the blinds. Friendly Sunday voices floated up from Tenth Street. She put her laundry in the washing machine and pulled on a clean pair of white leggings, floppy white socks, a black and white cotton sweater that came to midthigh, and her pink Reeboks. Dressed for success, all right. She'd just switched everything to the dryer when the downstairs intercom sounded.

Buzzing Marissa Peiser in, she opened her door, heard the elevator begin its climb, and waited.

Peiser looked tired. She was wearing stone-washed jeans and a striped cotton shirt. Her mustard suede jacket was the wrong color for her skin tone and fought with the red hair band, for she wore no makeup. At least she'd dumped the grubby trench coat. She was listing under the weight of a black shoulder bag as big as a horse feeder, with a frayed strap.

"You look tired." Wetzon threw her leather jacket over her shoulder and grabbed her purse. "Do you have to work on weekends?"

"Frequently. Never getting enough sleep goes with the territory."

"Burger okay with you?"

Peiser nodded.

They walked up Eighth Avenue to West Fourth and Jane to the Corner Bistro. "It doesn't look like much," Wetzon said, "but the burgers and BLTs are great and the price is right."

If anything, the Corner Bistro was grungier than usual. It was like walking into a cave. A cave where the odors of beer and whiskey and cigars had become embedded in the old wooden bar with its brass rail, in the scarred wood tables and benches. In spite of this, almost every booth and table was filled. They walked past the bar where the regulars—locals all over the age of sixty—were planted, to the room in the back, took the last available booth, and ordered burgers medium rare and fries, club soda for Wetzon and Diet Coke for Peiser.

"How long have you been with the D.A.'s office?"

"Ten years."

"I guess you like it."

"I love it."

"You like hanging out with cops?"

Peiser stared at Wetzon for a long minute. "Yes."

"I would, too."

They looked at one another candidly, each knowing something about the other that connected them. Peiser nodded slowly, and the moment passed.

Their order arrived on paper plates with paper napkins, ketchup and mustard in their own-brand bottles.

"You were in Connecticut yesterday, you said?"

"Smith and I paid a condolence call on Penny Ann Boyd." She waited for Peiser to say something, but Peiser seemed to be engrossed in drowning her burger and fries in ketchup. "Are you aware that Wilson Boyd had a gun collection?"

"We are now."

"And that three are missing?"

"Two. A rifle and an antique silver Derringer."

"I forgot. You've got the one that killed Brian and Tabitha." She set her burger down on the plate. "Look, Marissa, Ms. Peiser—"

"Marissa's fine."

"This is going to sound crazy, but I think someone took a shot at me last night with one of them—the rifle, I guess." She took a bite out of her burger, amazed at her cool. The truth was, here in the Village, today, it all seemed unreal.

Peiser took her seriously. "You have the bullet?"

"No. Whatever it was smashed into the shingle behind me." She walked Peiser through the events from their arrival at Penny Ann's home to meeting Barbie Gordon, the gunshot, while Peiser took notes. "There was a splintered hole in the shingle. I'm not sure Smith will have notified the local police, because she thought I was over-reacting."

"Let's not jump to any conclusions till we know it's a bullet. I'll take care of it." Her notebook was smeared with what looked like blood but was only ketchup. She licked her fingers.

"Incidentally, Rona and Megan were supposed to be spending the night with the Gordons, so anyone could have done it, except possibly Jerry Gordon, who does his call-in show in the afternoons and from ten to midnight on Saturday . . . unless it was recorded together with his afternoon show. I haven't been able to find out how that works. And what if Maglia drove up to see Rona—I know that may be farfetched—but he could have done it." *Slow down*, she thought, *you're babbling like an hysteric*. She took a bite of her burger. "I still don't think Rona did it."

Peiser picked up a fry with her fingers and munched it thoughtfully. "We don't either."

54

·······

"I've done everything I can to shake him out, Seth." Seth Doolittle was the New York manager for A.J. Wickers, a regional firm out of Chicago and a client of Smith and Wetzon's. Wetzon and Seth had been working on a Shearson broker for the past six months. "The kid is dying. Five years in the business and instead of going up the last two years, he's been sinking. He's got a lock on failure. By resisting this move, he's boarding up his breakout. One more year and he'll be out of the business. I told him that. I don't know why you want him."

Seth grunted. "He works his tail off, but he doesn't work smart. There's something we used to call a clangbird in the air force. It's a plane that flies in concentric circles, smaller and smaller until it disappears up its own anus. I guess I think I can turn him around. Let me try him again."

"He's all yours." Wetzon hung up. It was a waste of time. The kid was a loser and shouldn't be in the business. Even she could see that. He had no wife, no kids holding him back from taking a chance. He ought to take the ball and run with it, but he couldn't get himself out of his failure track. She sighed. She was getting as tough-minded as Smith.

The phone rang, and she could see B.B. was on the other line. She answered, "Smith and Wetzon."

"Leslie?" She loved the way he said her name, giving each syllable emphasis.

"Hi, Alton. Are you back?"

"I'm at O'Hare waiting to board. How about an early dinner tonight?"

"Alton—I—"

"I know you said no late weekdays, but I'll get you home before eight."

Why not, she thought. *Why the hell not?* "Okay."

"That's great." He sounded jubilant. It was so weird. What did he see in her? "How about six at the Union Square Café?"

The door opened and Smith blew in, smashing in a red-and-white checkerboard blazer and a short red stretch skirt.

"That's fine. I'll see you there at six." She put down the phone and waited. Smith would want to know whom she was making an appointment with.

Smith flipped casually through her messages. "Who are you meeting at six?"

"Alton. Tonight for dinner."

"Is this the night?" The question came with a mocking raise of eyebrow.

Amused, Wetzon said succinctly, "Just dinner."

"You are a major—"

"Rona's off the hook. Isn't that great?"

"Really?" Smith's attention refocused.

"She is. Marissa Peiser, the A.D.A., told me last night. It seems that Maglia confirmed her alibi, and they think someone planted the gun."

"Now that's more like it. Did the legal frump say who they think did it?"

"No."

She wrinkled her forehead and dropped her messages in her wastebasket. "I would have said Maglia. Maybe they're just alibi-ing each other. Of course, the tarot says it's a strong woman . . . and the tarot never lies. Do you think she's back at work?" Sitting, Smith tapped out some numbers with the eraser of her pencil and waited. "Rona Middleton, please." She lowered one eyelid at Wetzon. "Is she there, sweetie?" Pause. "Well, be sure to tell her to call Xenia Smith. Right." She hung up. "She's expected."

To B.B.'s knock, Wetzon called, "Come in, B.B."

B.B. opened the door. "Fred Benitos for Wetzon. On two."

Wetzon picked up the phone and released the button. "Fred, how are you?"

"Wetzon, you'll be happy to hear that Joan Boley joined us this morning."

Wetzon motioned to Smith, thumb up. "Well now, Fred, congratulations. You did a great job."

"So did you, Wetzon."

She hung up and jumped to her feet. "Send Joan Boley a gold pen. She's at Marley Straus."

"Mmmm, love that fee." Smith stood, and they gave each other a high five in the middle of the room. "Didn't I tell you it's not over till it's over?"

"And, point of reference here, even when it's over, it's not over."

"Now it is. Things are definitely looking up. With Rona back at work—"

Another knock, and B.B. said, "Phone for Wetzon. Rona Middleton."

"Oh, *I* want to talk to her." Smith picked up the phone. "Rona, sweetie pie, we're just so pleased for you." She motioned to Wetzon. "Sugar, pick up. It's Rona."

Wetzon growled. She hated three-way phone conversations, particularly when Smith was the third party. "When you hang up."

Hand over the mouthpiece, Smith said, "Oh, for pity sakes." Lifted her hand. "The phones are just ringing off the hook, sweetie, so here's Wetzon." She made a face at Wetzon and hung up.

"Rona? I'm so happy you're in the clear."

"Thank you, Wetzon. I'd like to talk something over with you— Oh hi, Neil—" Rona lowered her voice. "This is not a good time. I'll talk to you later."

Wetzon stared at the receiver, then hung up.

"That was fast. What did she want?"

"I never found out. She sure got off fast when Neil came in."

"Well, I wouldn't worry about it. So long as she's back, she's working for us."

"B.B. had a start on Friday."

"How big?"

"Not big. One seventy-five. Covers his draw, though."

"He doesn't bang them out the way Harold did."

"He's also not as devious as Harold."

Smith opened their door. "B.B.!" She left the door open and went back to her desk.

"Yes?" B.B. stood in the doorway with a suspect sheet in hand, always a little uncertain around Smith.

"I hear you had a start on Friday. Well done. Keep it up."

He was beaming. "Thank you."

"What do you have there?"

He looked down at his hand. "Oh. I wanted to talk to Wetzon about him. He does two million and I can't get past his sales assistant, who's his wife."

Wetzon took the sheet. "Paul Schlessinger. I think I've heard about him. He was written up in *Registered Rep* last year. Okay, let me try." She sat down and called his direct number.

"Can I listen?"

She nodded.

"Paul Schlessinger's office."

"Hi, this is Leslie Wetzon. My firm is Smith and Wetzon. Is Paul available?"

"This is Donna Schlessinger." A very tony phony voice. "What is this in reference to?"

"Well, Donna, I'm a recruiter, and Paul was recommended to me."

"A recruiter? You mean a headhunter?"

"Yes."

"Do you have any idea how much he does?" The voice dripped scorn.

"I do."

"We'll only be interested in one million upfront."

Wetzon responded in her own tony voice. "Mrs. Schlessinger, Donna, my clients are all top-tiered firms. They don't *buy* brokers. They want quality. They are not interested in brokers with price tags. Why don't you take my number, and if Paul fits our criteria, he can call me." She left her number, replaced the phone, and shrugged. "Let's see what happens."

The phone rang. He couldn't be calling back this fast.

"Smith and Wetzon." B.B. answered it at Max's desk. Max's hours started Monday afternoon. "Wetzon, Sheila Reitman."

"Who's Sheila Reitmen?" Smith was dialing out. "I'm going to see how our candidates are doing at Ameribank."

"It's about the apartment." Wetzon knew that would turn Smith off immediately. It did. "Sheila, hello. Any luck?"

"Not much. Our computers are all down. This is what I've been able to get, but I couldn't narrow it down to school or degree or even year. Do you want what I have so far? I can call you with the rest when they're back on line."

"Why not."

"I started with Gordon. I found three Gerald Gordons, one Gerard Gordon, one Gordon Jerome—I love people with two first names—six Jerry Gordons, and four Jerome Gordons."

A plethora of Gordons, Wetzon thought. She'd taken a wrong turn, gone off in the wrong direction.

"Just remember." Sheila's voice broke through Wetzon's fog. "We may be able to narrow it down to five or six once I'm back on line."

55

·······

"Sweeeetie?"

Wetzon looked up from her date book, where she was shuffling suspect sheets and writing up her schedule for the next day. It was the wheedling tone Smith had taken that alerted her. Smith was half sitting, leaning against her desk, holding a hand mirror and powdering her nose efficiently with a brush-and-powder contraption.

"Sweeeetie?" Smith said again in that same wheedling tone.

Wetzon set her marble peach paperweight on top of her schedule and checked her watch. They'd promised to meet Rona for a drink. "If we're going to meet Rona, we'd better get going."

Smith snapped the brush back in its case. "I don't want to sit around in a bar and listen to Rona masturbate. She's so self-centered."

Oh, fine, Wetzon thought. "All of us in sales are, don't you think?"

Smith's eyes opened wide. "Well, speak for yourself. I certainly am not."

What was the use? Wetzon shrugged. "Okay, you win, I'll go myself." Probably it was just as well. Rona had called Wetzon for the drink and made no mention of Smith.

"I don't want these scum to think I'm at their beck and call. The way they walk all over you—"

"Shut up while you're ahead, Smith." She was into a medium boil. She went out to the coat closet in the reception area and collected her Burberry.

"What's bothering you? I can always tell when something's bothering you."

"I don't suppose you did anything about the shingle."

"Not again." Smith groaned loudly. "Is that all?"

"You certainly take someone trying to kill me lightly. Should I worry? Have you bought an insurance policy on my life that I don't know about?"

Smith threw up her hands. "Now, there you go again. Paranoia does not become you. If I felt someone really was trying to kill you, I'd certainly treat it seriously, but sugar, be realistic. Why—"

"Forget it!" Wetzon turned her back and started out.

"Since you feel so strongly about it, I'll call the police in Westport and ask them to send someone out to look at it."

"Thank you." Wetzon's hand idled on the front doorknob.

"Then maybe you'll stop overdramatizing—"

"Good-bye, Smith." She was close to stomping out in a fury. And stomping certainly did not become her.

"Sweetie, one more itty-bitty thing."

Wetzon turned to see Smith crooking her finger at her, calling her back. Wetzon ambled to their doorway. "What?"

"I'm canceling dinner with Twoey on Friday. I'm going to tell him you and I are going away for the weekend."

"Wait a minute. Friday's your birthday."

"I know that. I want to spend it with Dickie. We're going to drive up to an inn—"

"You can't."

"What do you mean, I can't?" Smith's eyes became slits.

"It would hurt Twoey terribly."

"Oh, puh-lease. He'll get over it."

"Smith—" Damn, she was going to have to tell her. She braced herself for an explosion. "He's been planning a big surprise party for you for weeks."

Dangerous was the only way to describe the look in Smith's eyes. "And you weren't going to tell me? What kind of friend are you? You know I hate surprises."

"You must never tell him I told you. Try to be gracious—for once—and just let it happen. If you tell . . . Dickie . . . he might actually think you're a nice person."

"I'm sure you think you're very funny." Then suddenly Smith smiled her cat smile. "I won't tell Twoey you told if you get him to invite Dickie."

"Oh, God, Smith—"

"Don't oh-God-Smith me. Just do it." She was absolutely thrilled with her solution and would have licked her paws if she could. You could almost hear her purring.

Wetzon left the office without another word, closed the outside door and leaned against it, breathing calm back into her bloodstream. Sometimes she thought there was more pollution inside than outside, and this was one of those times.

She began walking uptown to the Drake to meet Rona, but her mind was elsewhere. How to find a murderer before he found her. Maybe she should marry Alton and get away from Smith and all this. The warring factions in her head took over. Marry? Marry? Who had even asked her? And the biggest question: Did she want it?

The Drake's bar area was part of the lobby, and Rona, haggard and hollow-eyed, her face framed by a black velvet headband, was sitting at a small table staring into a glass of deep-red wine. Her black suit looked a size too big and was too stark. A widow who'd hated her husband, she still looked like one bereaved.

"Hi." Wetzon slipped into a chair and shrugged out of her raincoat. "Club soda, please," she told the waiter, who was just leaving the next table.

Rona fingered her blond curls, nervous about something. "Thanks for coming. I know you said you have to be downtown at six." Now her fingers played with the neck of the glass; she'd had a manicure, and her nails were blood red.

"I'm okay on time. Actually, I'm glad you wanted to get together. There are a couple of things I'm curious about." Rona nodded, but didn't say anything, so Wetzon rushed onward. "What's wrong with Barbara Gordon?"

Rona watched her for a moment, almost wary. "She's got a chemical imbalance that responds to medication. Lithium, I think. Most of the time she's fine, but if she forgets to take her pills, she's a handful."

Her club soda arrived, and Wetzon set it aside. "Is she dangerous?"

Sighing, Rona stared down at her fingernails as if she'd just noticed their color. "You mean, could she have killed Brian and Tabitha?" She shrugged and took a sip of wine. "I don't know. She's had a few episodes, mostly directed at Jerry."

"Episodes? What kind of episodes?"

"She can get abusive, physically, but as I said, it's Jerry who bears the brunt, poor baby."

"How long have you known Jerry?" Wetzon kept her voice neutral.

"I don't know. A few years. Brian and Jerry go back a long way." She thought for a minute. "They met at one of those private sanitoriums for the wealthy. Peaceful Farms or something like that."

"Who? Brian and Jerry?"

Rona smiled for the first time. "No, Wetzon. Jerry and Barbara."

Doctor marries patient. Wealthy patient. Wetzon poked at the sliver of lime with her swizzle stick. "Jerry's degree is in psychology?"

"It would have to be. That or psychiatric social work."

"Who could have planted the gun in your house?"

"You sound like the police."

"Humor me."

"Almost anyone. The nanny, Dickie, Penny Ann, Barbara, even Jerry. Tony. Graziella, my housekeeper. I know she was working weekends for Brian. Really, Wetzon—"

Wetzon held up her hands. "Okay. I give up."

Rona finished her wine and propped her sagging body up. "Look, Wetzon, I don't want you to take this personally. There's just Megan and me now. The fighting is over, and I'm not bitter anymore. I've got to do what's right for us."

Wetzon sat listening to the long preamble, waiting for the other shoe to drop. "But" or "so" would come next. It did.

"So," Rona said, "when Tony made me an incredible offer last night to come back to Bliss Norderman, I accepted."

56
·······

The BMT station near Carnegie Hall was the closest place to get a train to the west side of Union Square. Wetzon had made a valiant try, but failed to talk Rona out of going back to Maglia's office. Aside from the sexual bond, which was strong, Maglia was offering her a heaping platter of all of Brian's business without a catch. Oh, sorry—one catch. A minor thing for Rona, perhaps. She had to come back to Bliss Norderman. And immediately.

Smith and Wetzon would never see a penny more on Rona's placement, and there wasn't a damn thing they could do. Wetzon could hardly wait to tell Smith. Oh, hell, why spoil the evening? Smith might be vindictive, and Rona might be disloyal, but after all, it was partly a business decision, and Wetzon couldn't argue with that part of it, although she'd tried, reminding Rona of how despicable Tony had been. And Rona had replied that business was business, and that she would have done the same thing in his place. How do you argue with that?

On the emotional decision, the other part, Rona had been equally unbending. Maglia's wife was in a wheelchair, paralyzed from the chest down from a skiing accident eight years ago. Rona had married Brian to try to end the relationship, but it had only intensified.

The clock said six-thirty, which gave her a momentary jolt until she remembered that the Transit Authority was notoriously negligent about adjusting station clocks to the twice-a-year time change. A train was just pulling out, leaving a fairly empty platform that began to fill up almost immediately. The pure, almost ethereal, strains of a Bach saraband rose live from the midst of a small crowd semicircled around a violinist. The acoustics in the New York subway system were better than in most concert halls. On the uptown platform across four or more tracks, people stood listening as if time had stopped and this were not a filthy, airless subway platform at rush hour in the heart of New York. After the young musician played the final notes with a dramatic flourish, the audience on both platforms applauded. Everyone smiled at one another.

Wetzon found four quarters in her change purse and dropped them into his violin case just as the N train pulled in.

At once the accumulated crowd reverted to type and pushed ahead of Wetzon onto the train, scrambling for the few remaining seats. A huge man wearing a red knit hat pulled down over his forehead was holding a racing bike against the side of four empty seats. People milled around, but no one dared to suggest he move his bike. He gave off dangerous vibes, and everyone was giving him space.

Threading her way to the rear of the car, Wetzon found a spot on the standing pole where she could put her hand.

Dangerous vibes. She was musing on that as she climbed out of the subway at Union Square and crossed the street to the Union Square Café on Sixteenth Street. It was still light and the air was mellow, even a bit balmy, for late October.

Dangerous. Barbie Gordon reeked dangerous. Rona did not. Maglia did, Dr. Jerry did not. Smith did, Wetzon did not. Richard Hartmann did, Twoey did not. Look at Penny Ann and her late husband. He probably did, she certainly did not.

Silvestri did, Alton did not.

Did a successful relationship between two people require one of them to be dangerous? And could a pussy become dangerous if pushed far enough? What if Brian had been having an affair with Barbara, and Jerry'd found out about it? Possibly. Then what about Tabitha? Did the girl know something that she shouldn't have known? What if she'd testified against her mother at the arbitration for revenge or to please Brian, then wanted to take it back? That would put Maglia's ass on the line. She smiled. She'd like to see Maglia's ass on the line.

Wetzon opened the door and went in past the smoky tables near the bar, the only place in the restaurant smoking was allowed. She gave her name and Alton's to the man with the reservation book, abandoned her coat and briefcase, then was ushered down the steps to her left to a table for four. The two extra place settings were immediately removed.

She sat with her back to the wall. This was her favorite room in any restaurant in New York. Bright with a warm light, it had no bitty candles in bitty glasses. The floors were wood, tablecloths white, and although it was early, about half of the tables were occupied.

Hungry, she dug into the dish of olives the waiter had left when he asked what she was drinking. After Saturday night, she was off beer, off booze entirely till the memory of how rotten she'd felt disappeared.

She was picking up on the intriguing conversation among the foursome at the next table about what was politically correct when Alton, distinguished in a dark-blue suit, his gray hair trimmed, arrived. He turned heads, because he was a minor celebrity in the City and people recognized him. A man in a business suit stopped him and shook his hand; a red-haired woman blew a kiss.

When he got to Wetzon, she found she was having an unanticipated buzz. She was really glad to see him. He bent and unexpectedly kissed her on her forehead, and she thought, *My forehead's probably a grease pit*, and why hadn't she fussed with her makeup, dusted her face with powder, like Smith?

"You make me very happy," he said, seating himself opposite her. "Now what's the matter? What did I say?"

He was picking up every nuance. She felt naked. "Alton, *you* make me very nervous. I keep thinking, what does he want, what am I doing?"

"Float, Leslie," he said. He caught her flying hand and held it. "Don't ask questions. We're going to have dinner. And we'll talk."

"What will we talk about?" She was insecure, like a freshman dating a senior BMOC. It wasn't going to work.

He smiled at her. "I think we'll find something."

They ordered risotto and the tuna.

"Wine?" He was looking at the wine list.

She shook her head. "I'm not drinking."

He ordered a glass of a California chardonnay and turned his attention to her, asking about her day. She brushed this aside with a word. "Boring. Tell me about the conference."

She heard about the University of Chicago, the panels, the issues discussed, the people he'd met. When he finished, they were working on the tuna. He looked at her for a moment and said, "Your turn."

Her appetite had quit on her. She would take the rest home. She listened to her heart thumping. How could he not hear? Haltingly, she began to tell him about Brian's death and Tabitha's, how everyone's lives were entwined around the Gordons. "It's all about the aftermath of the arbitration decision."

Puzzlement disturbed his assurance. "What if it has nothing to do with the arbitration?"

Wetzon shrugged. "Then we have to look for other motives."

"We?"

"We," she repeated firmly. "I want you to know what I do beyond recruiting. And if it bothers you, we should break it off here— before both of us get too involved."

He put his fork down and grinned at her. "I like where this is leading."

"I'm serious. I like the process of detecting. It's puzzle solving."

"You could get hurt."

"Yes. I try to be careful, but I tend to work by instinct. Someone once said I fly by the seat of my pants." *Get out of here, Silvestri,* she thought. "I guess I would have liked to have been something in law enforcement. They tell me I have an overdeveloped sense of injustice." She stopped to let him say something. When he didn't, she asked, "Does my getting involved in murder bother you?"

"Leslie, I'd be lying if I said it didn't. Let me try to handle it. I'm not going to tell you what to do."

Amazing, she thought. She had a prize. A man who wouldn't tell her what to do.

"Alton, I work with people who are engined by power and greed, passions that make people kill."

"Passions don't always lead to murder."

"Oh, Alton." She pushed her plate away.

"Finished?" the waiter asked.

"Pack this up. We'll take it with us. Do you want dessert?" He didn't seem the least bit troubled, and he made decisions quickly.

She shook her head. Was she sick? No dessert? No chocolate? What kind of lover would he be, this lovely man?

"I don't have the car tonight," he said, tucking her hand into the crook of his arm.

"Good." It was a beautiful evening. An almost-full moon was surrounded by haze. They walked down Fifth Avenue to Tenth Street, then turned west. He carried her briefcase. The siren of an ambulance wailed close by, then stopped with a burp as it reached St. Vincent's on Twelfth Street. A jogger passed them, breathing hard. Tenth Street was quiet.

"This is not the night, is it?"

"Close, but no cigar."

"I'll take close."

In the small vestibule, he set down her briefcase and put his arms around her, holding her for a few moments. Then he was kissing her, tasting of wine, and she was responding. His lips touched her throat. She was losing it. All her reserve. Her control. She was clinging to him. "Oh God, Alton—"

He stopped. "I'd better get out of here."

"Friday," she said. She'd made up her mind.

Touching her cheek, he said, "Okay."

She watched him walk out on Tenth Street and get a cab. Then she got on the elevator and went upstairs.

Dangerous. Alton was dangerous. Or maybe Wetzon was. She put the tuna in the fridge, hung up her coat, and checked the answering machine, pressing the playback button.

Beep. *Birdie, you are never home anymore. Ever. Arthur and I are going to the parade on Friday, so no excuses, you're going with us and then we're going out to dinner.* Carlos was talking about the annual Greenwich Village Halloween parade of bizarre costumes. She'd go with them, but not to dinner. That was the night of Smith's birthday party.

Beep. *Les, it's me.* God, Silvestri. Gruff. Emotional. *We've got to talk. I'll be up this weekend, and I want to see you. Don't run away. I'm sorry about—I'll see you.*

Oh, God, she thought. What was happening to her? How could she feel this way about two totally different men?

Beep. *Leslie, this is Sheila. I think I've found what you were looking for.*

57

·······

Sheila was not at home, or at the very least,
was not answering her telephone. Wetzon hoped fervently that the
Smokestack hadn't dropped from the skies on one of his trips, because Sheila would be incommunicado for the extent of his stay.

It probably wasn't going to make much difference anyway. It had
seemed an ingenious thought, because Dr. Jerry made such a thing of
it. Her experience told her that people don't normally drop their alma
mater into conversation heavy-handed, particularly if it was Ivy or
close to it. Of course, once in a while she'd met someone insecure
enough to drop a non sequitur about the Harvard Club or Yale Club
into a conversation.

Having left word for Sheila to call her, Wetzon went to bed. She
had an important seven-thirty breakfast meeting in midtown, and she
knew she damn well better be alert.

Schiff, McConnell, a classy boutique with a century-old history
on the Street, was opening a second office—their headquarters was
on Wall Street—in midtown, just for million-dollar producers. Brokers whose gross commissions annually came to over a million dollars
were a vanishing breed on the Street. Wetzon—no grass grew under
her feet—had been compiling such a list, with input from B. B. and
Max, of brokers from all firms. The genius behind the idea was Eliot
McConnell, and it was Eliot whom Wetzon was meeting for breakfast. He would do his dog-and-pony show and give her the grand
tour. It was his baby, and he was going to run it.

Her alarm went off at six, and she went on automatic, downed
her vitamins with orange juice, showered, did her morning stretches,

blow-dried her hair, and rolled it into its knot. She needed a trim; the ends were splitting. She'd do it tonight when she got home. Dressed in her most conservative pinstripe, a light gray, she was on the still-lamplit street at six forty-five and heading for the Seventh Avenue subway at Sheridan Square. The sky was overhung with rain clouds, and a misty fog had settled over the city, which had gone overnight from balmy to chill. She parked her briefcase between her feet, buttoned and belted her Burberry, pulled her slouchy fedora down over her topknot.

The dogwalkers were just appearing, owners sleepy-eyed and shivering, dogs hyper after a night indoors.

Sheila hadn't called her back. Wetzon would have to try her again after she got to the office. Right now she had to psych herself to be on her toes—*Easy for you, Wetzonova*—because this assignment could mean a windfall for Smith and Wetzon. Although Schiff, McConnell was already a client, Wetzon wanted to cement the relationship so that Eliot O'Connell would be more comfortable working with them than with any other headhunter.

Schiff, McConnell had chosen for the elite branch, worse luck, the same building on Sixth Avenue as Bliss Norderman. She found herself praying she wouldn't run into that scuz Maglia, or Rona, for that matter.

Face it, Wetzon, it is one of midtown's most outstanding buildings. It had a beautiful, sweeping plaza, benches, and a waterfall. Yet as she approached it, she saw a bag lady in a tattered fur coat, gray hair grizzling out from under a black velour stovepipe hat with a stiff brim, ensconced on one of the benches surrounded by a half-dozen crammed black plastic garbage bags, a lifetime of belongings. On her feet were cracked and worn black patent-leather tap shoes, the taps still in place. Her face was made up for the stage, down to the false eyelashes. An open tissue on her scrawny lap showed a half-eaten almond horn. She lifted it daintily and took a bite, eyes fixed on Wetzon as if she knew her.

The intensity of the gaze gave Wetzon a start, but it was no one she knew. She'd been afraid it might be an aging Broadway gypsy. Was it every dancer's nightmare or just her own, the fear of ending up alone and broke on the street, a bag lady? Controlling a shiver, Wetzon had to choose whether to pass right by the woman or take a detour and come in on the other side of the building. The woman eyed her with, it seemed to Wetzon, a challenge. That did it. No way was Wetzon going to be intimidated into choosing another entrance. The woman's eyes found hers. God, she was going to say something. Wetzon moved forward.

"You look stunning," the woman said.

Wetzon passed the bag lady, giving her an uncertain smile. How do you handle something like that? She'd never been able to figure it. Maybe you had to have been born in New York to be that blasé.

On the fifty-fifth floor a slim, dark-haired woman with a slight French accent was arranging lilies in a tall glass vase and stopped to greet her. This was a big plus. Make a note: receptionist in office at seven-thirty. Impressive.

As for the office itself, it was equally impressive. Everything was wood paneled, including the reception desk, in warm walnut, smacking of wealth and luxury. Rich black leather sofas and chairs sat on a low-pile taupe carpet. Plants were discreet.

Eliot McConnell, a short, wiry bundle of enthusiasm in a blue pinstripe, had a machine-gun speech pattern that forced concentration. Wetzon always had to replay in her head the rat-tat-tat of words coming at her at top speed for translation.

But the office was beautiful, subtly lit, dripping wealth in a laid-back way. There were thirty-six enormous private offices. "I have eighteen offices not spoken for, Wetzon, and another six I'm holding for a group coming over from First B-O." He threw open a door to a private dining room, all windows, round tables, white linen, china, crystal, and a dazzling view of the city. Some of the tables were occupied by thousand-dollar suits. Everyone looked to be in his—because Wetzon was the only woman present—forties or fifties, more like corporate executives than stockbrokers. And indeed, most million-dollar producers ran their business as if they were running a corporation. Truly a private men's club.

"We want to do this on a fee basis." Eliot signaled to a tall, distinguished black man in a black suit. He motioned Wetzon to a table away from those occupied. "I'll have my usual, John, thank you. What'll you have, Wetzon?"

"A toasted English and decaf." John moved on without a word, without writing anything down. Wetzon turned to Eliot. "What do you mean, fee based?" *On guard, Wetzon,* she told herself. *You're about to get screwed.*

"We're capping you at fifty-thousand a hire."

"Fifty? Eliot, let's be serious here." John came by and poured coffee into their cups, then left. "Fifty is five percent for a million in production, and we're expecting to show you people who do a good deal more than a million. Our other clients pay us more than that. Where's the incentive to send these guys to you?"

"Wetzon, look around." He waved his hand, sweeping the room. "Does one of your other clients have anything like this? We have a great story to tell. We have every service in the book all built in, health club included, memberships, everything. I guarantee, you send me the right people, I'll close them." He kept right on talking as they were being served.

Linen napkins. Superb coffee. Perfectly toasted English muffin. "I'll have to discuss it with Smith. I feel fifty is inappropriate if we bring you a two-million-or-more producer."

Eliot's breakfast was a soft-boiled egg served in a white porcelain egg cup, whole wheat toast, mixed fruit, and coffee. He wore his light-brown hair close to his head, combed flat and to the side in a failed effort to hide a widow's peak. Did he think it made him look like a wuss? He paused, spoon perched over his egg, then gestured with the spoon. "Two mil, sixty k. Three or more, seventy-five, and that's it." He dug his spoon into the egg.

"I'll let you know."

"Don't wait too long. I'd like to give you and Smith first crack at this, for old times' sake."

"For old time's sake, Eliot, you should pay us our fee." She thought, *Old times' sake? Give me a gigantic break. What old times?* They were being chiseled to death.

"Wetzon, I know you girls do a good job, so I'm willing to work with you. And incidentally, we can use a woman or two, so we can keep affirmative-action wackos out of our faces. Our fee structure is a business decision. If you don't want to participate, we'll get someone else. I'm having lunch with a couple of your competitors today, Tom Keegen and his associate, and they've made it quite clear that they're amenable."

Wetzon shook hands with him and took her leave without telling him he had egg yolk running down his chin. *Yeah, that'll show him, Wetzon.*

It was only eight-thirty, and she'd already been bamboozled.

They'd say yes, tell themselves it was a spec sit—special situation—
and do it. Eliot was right. Fifty was better than no fee, and what
Schiff, McConnell had to offer was prime. Most firms took their
million-dollar producers for granted, especially if they were women,
figuring they wouldn't want to disrupt their business by moving.
Having become entrenched in the system, with deferred comp, stock
and stock options, huge books, they'd be the body-at-rest principle.
But Wetzon, hazarding a guess, thought these guys, and the few
women who fit the criterion, might respond to the elegance and the
pampering.

She stopped in the lobby at the newsstand to buy the *Times* and
the *Journal*, digging in her purse for change.

"Aren't you going to congratulate me, Ms. Sleazy, Low-life
Headhunter?" Maglia was standing beside her, holding a pack of
Marlboros he'd just paid for.

"Come on, Tony." Rona was behind him, and she looked uneasy.

"What for?" Wetzon didn't even try to keep the anger out of her
words. He was a dirtbag opportunist, but maybe they all were. She'd
just been had by the top of the line at Schiff, McConnell.

"Let's go, Tony," Rona said, unable to meet Wetzon's gaze. She
began walking toward the elevators.

"Not before I tell Wetzon that she can't play with the big boys
and expect to win. Forget it, it's over." He leered at her. "Rona got
what she wanted. And I got what I wanted."

"Tony, sweetheart, you have a lot of class. Did anyone ever tell
you that?" Wetzon turned her back on him and handed the clerk a
dollar, dropping her change in her pocket.

A hand on her shoulder spun her around roughly. She shook it
off and made tracks out of there. Maglia's voice followed her, fairly
spitting venom. "You stay out of my face and away from my brokers,
girlie, if you know what's good for you."

58

·······

She was still fulminating about Maglia when she got to the office. He had threatened her—and in public, at that. Was he all mouth?

Max, wearing a red polka-dot bow tie, was at his desk in their reception room methodically preparing his suspect sheets for the day. A thumbed-through and folded *Wall Street Journal* lay at his elbow. The coffee maker had a full carafe of fresh coffee, and she could hear B. B. on the phone getting someone's availability. The wonder of the whole scene assuaged her. A smoothly working machine, that was Smith and Wetzon.

Max looked up. "Good morning, Wetzon. Is there anything new in the industry that I should be aware of?"

"Let's see, Max." She hung her coat in the closet. "We're still looking for people for Ameribank. That'll be one hundred fifty to two hundred thousand in gross, whistle clean, no compliance problems, five years or less in the business. And if you come up with someone doing over a mil, please give me his suspect sheet, whether he expresses interest in talking or not." She poured herself a mug of coffee and retired to her office.

Their garden in the back of the brownstone was a riot of dried leaves. In the murky mist it looked bleak. It looked the way she felt.

"You dope," she said out loud, toasting her reflection in the window. "You have your health, two men who care for you—in their own peculiar way—good friends, and no money troubles. What is there to be bleak about?" But just the same, she felt it. It seemed, now that she thought about it, since her visit to the psychic, everything had gone wrong.

She sat down at her desk and called Sheila. She'd probably already gone off to work. Right. The answering machine again. How annoying. She left a message with her office number and hung up as Smith came through the door followed by a bearded young man in jeans. He carried a burlap sack and a box of gardening tools.

"Good morning, sweetie pie." Smith walked right past Wetzon and flung open the door to their garden. The young man had his hair pulled back in a ponytail, which trailed over the collar of his washed-out flannel shirt. "There you are. Wetzon, this is Philip, and he's going to get our garden ready for winter, aren't you, dear?" She closed the door on Philip without waiting for an answer, and brushed her palms together.

"You must have been reading my mind."

"We do those things quite well, don't we? And how did it go this morning?" She dumped her Burberry on top of the filing cabinet as if preparing for a quick exit.

"Before we get into that, you'd better sit down and ask me what Rona said."

"Rona?" Smith turned her chair around and sat down, crossing her long legs. "Oh, the drinkie-poo. Is it even worth discussing?"

"Smith, Rona's going back to Bliss Norderman. In fact, she's sitting there as we speak."

Smith's reaction was a low moan that began undulating into a shriek. "After all we did for her. Didn't you tell her it was a terrible mistake?"

"I did, but it's hard to argue someone out of a sexual tie as long as this one."

"Oh, for pity sakes. It didn't seem to stop her from moving initially."

"That was because of Brian. If you remember, they were moving together, then Brian changed his mind. Do you think he knew about Maglia?" She wasn't really looking for a response from Smith. She suddenly knew that Brian had been serious about moving to Loeb Dawkins because he'd found out about Maglia and Rona. He had to have given Maglia the check to buy himself out.

"Out the window. All that effort. Neil is going to try to get us to give some of the money back." She spun around and flipped the pages of her calendar.

"It's past ninety days. Let's try to stand firm."

"God will get her for this. There's always a payback in this business if you live long enough."

"Okay, let's put that crap behind us. Eliot has a fantastic operation, but he wants to pay us a flat fifty."

Smith was outraged. "That's a paltry five percent on a mil. Didn't you tell him we don't work that way?"

"I pointed that out to him."

"I *knew* I should have come with you."

It was Wetzon's turn to be outraged. "Excuse me? Do you honestly think his proposal would have been different if you were there?"

"Well, don't get so hot about it, sugar."

"I told him I'd discuss it with you, but his proposal was not appropriate. We worked out a sliding scale up to seventy-five k, but he wouldn't budge over that."

"Then we won't do it."

"I want to do it. He's got something special there, and he knows it. I think the gorillas would be impressed. Besides . . ."

"Besides?" Smith stood with her back to Wetzon, watching Philip work.

"Besides, if we don't agree, he's got Tom Keegen and Harold warming up in the bullpen. I've got to get back to him before lunch."

Smith turned in a fury, stamping her foot. "I've had just about enough of those two. Call Eliot. Tell him we'll do it, but only for old times' sake."

"Funny, that's what he said. Did you and little Eliot ever get anything on?"

Smith went into the bathroom and slammed the door. Wetzon laughed. She didn't know what made Smith angrier, Tom Keegen and Harold, having their fees capped, or Wetzon teasing her. Sighing, Wetzon called McConnell and told him they had a handshake deal. As if nothing had happened, Smith exited the bathroom fluffing her hair and humming, looking like the cat that feasted on the canary. Now what was she up to? The best thing was to confront her.

B. B.'s announcement that the market had moved up thirty-five

points in the first hour, and a feeding frenzy had begun, encompass-
ing not just the blue chips but even the secondaries, which had not
moved at all in recent months, blunted Wetzon's purpose. A hundred
and eighty million shares had already changed hands, and it wasn't
even noon. Max hovered behind B. B. in the doorway, curious.

"We're not going to get a hell of a lot done today. I can see
that." Wetzon nodded to Smith, throwing the ball to her. "We can
play catch-up today."

"Make a few calls anyway," Smith said. "You never know . . ."
She closed their door. "Is everything okay with Joan Boley?"

"I guess. I should call her." Wetzon picked up the phone and
punched in the numbers.

"Did you talk to Twoey?"

"I will." She listened to the ringing.

"You promised."

"I will. Don't nag."

"Humpf." She pulled her coat from the file cabinet. "I'm going
to get my nails done. How about we go together? You'll be spinning
your wheels here today. Anyone worthwhile is going to be too busy to
talk."

"I have to run up to the apartment and meet my contractor. Joan
Boley, please."

"Well, see you later, then." Smith sailed out of the office without
even waiting to hear about Joan Boley.

"Joan Boley." Joan sounded frantic.

"Joan, this is Wetzon. Is this a bad time?"

"Can't talk now, Wetzon. All the dogs are barking."

"Then I won't keep you. Another time."

Joan's "Thanks" was curt, but Wetzon took no offense because
she knew none was intended. This kind of market meant you had to
be quick or you'd miss something.

She took a cab up to West Eighty-sixth Street and got out next
to five minidumpsters parked in front of her building. Looking
around, she almost felt like a tourist. She missed her neighborhood
and her apartment. She was not a Village person; she was an Upper
West Sider.

George, the super's son, was filling in on the door picking up
extra money for college. He let her in. "I've got some stuff for you."

He went to the cabinet in the rear of the mailroom and returned with a load of what looked more like catalogues than serious mail. She was going to have to write to those direct-mail people to take her off the junk list. Maybe she could save a few trees in her lifetime.

After pressing the elevator button, she waited.

"Oh, I almost forgot." George handed her a manila envelope. "Ms. Reitman left something here for you."

"She did?" Wetzon took the envelope and got on the elevator when the doors opened. She hit the button for 12, undid the clasp, reached in, and pulled out five pages of computer printout. A word-processed note was attached:

Dear Leslie,

Couldn't reach you and I'm going up to Vermont for a few days. Figure this will get to you. Very interesting problem. If you look at the last twenty years, you can narrow everything down to one Gerald Gordon, one Jay Gordon, two Jeromes, and no Jerrys. If you look further, you'll see that Gerald was a chem major, undergrad. No grad. The Jay was business, with an MBA, last known address, Chicago. One of the Jeromes has a Ph.D. in philosophy and teaches at Rutgers; the other is a math nerd who works at IBM. Not a psych major among them.

Then I flipped the names, for fun. Gordon Jerome. That's my joke because this guy you're checking out has two first names. G. J. fits into your time frame, but his degree is in accounting. He's a CPA. Last known address is Wakefield Farms, Massachusetts.

Hope this is what you wanted,
   Sheila

59

·······

When Wetzon got back to the office, the phones were quiet. B. B. was out for lunch and Max was eating sunflower seeds from a little cloth sack and reading the *Wall Street Letter* as if he understood all the inside-the-business trade talk for which the weekly newsletter was known. She'd stopped at Mangia on Fortyeighth Street for a mozzarella, watercress, and sun-dried tomato sandwich on cheese bread and a double dose of decaf coffee. Now she opened a paper napkin and spread her lunch on her desk.

Smith was vivid in the garden, hands in motion, undoubtedly burdening Philip with a running commentary on his work. Smith always seemed to think she knew more about anything than anyone else did. Wetzon tapped on the window and got a brief, dismissing wave. *To hell with Smith*, she thought. *Here I was going to offer to share.* She sat down and ate her lunch, giving her thoughts over to her apartment.

Except for the kitchen, it had been essentially gutted. Louie's crew was still removing diseased and rotting plaster. Wetzon's barre and mirrors were packed into a corner of the huge living room along with most of her furniture. Her bookcases—out of harm's way, thanks be—were sealed under plastic. Everything was covered with drop cloths and more layers of clear plastic. A large portion of the living-room ceiling and the wall that the living room shared with the dining room were severely damaged.

But the essence of mildew was gone—all the windows were open wide—replaced by the cleaner smell of fresh plaster and sawdust. In the remains of her dining room, she was introduced to Jean, in gray painter's pants, working on a stepladder with a drill, her pockets crammed with tools, and Wendy, who was collecting chunks of plaster and cinder block in a big metal drum. They were Pillsbury ghosts in white breathing masks, shower caps, and goggles.

All the floor boards had been pulled up and covered with scraps of plywood, covered again with brown paper and drop cloths, so the floors gave and crackled under foot. "We'll be able to save the floor in the living room," Louie said, dropping her mask. "It'll need sanding and restaining." She was wearing overalls and an aura of plaster dust as she walked Wetzon through the destruction.

Wetzon was dazzled by the activity, but she felt again as if she'd lost a dear friend. Her apartment had died, and something new like this was difficult to adjust to. There was almost nothing left of her nest. There was almost nothing left of her life with Silvestri. If one were to believe in symbols, wasn't this an apt one?

She forced her thoughts back to the printout in the manila envelope hugged tightly under her arm.

"I know it doesn't look like much right now," Louie was saying.

"*Au contraire.* It's already an improvement from the mess I ran away from."

"Would you consider knocking down the wall between the living room and dining room? We can open up a lot of space."

"But I want my barre and mirrors on the remaining wall. Won't it look strange if it's all open? What if I have a party . . . ?" Although when had she given a party?

"Well, think about it. You can use a painted screen or a nice coramandel."

"Sure, Louie, spend my money."

Louie grinned. "Don't lock yourself in. You're got a great opportunity here. Change is food for the soul."

"Okay, I promise I'll think about it." And they left it that way. Maybe she should do something different, open up the whole space, open up her life. Change was food for the soul, huh? Well, she needed a spiritual uplift.

Her sandwich eaten down to the last crisp crumb, she sat twirling the cardboard coffee container, taking sips, thinking. She'd better call Twoey and get "Dickie" Hartmann invited to the party before Smith gave her more grief. Setting the phone between neck and shoulder, she punched up Twoey's private line.

"Goldman Barnes." This was the other Twoey, the trader. Wetzon could hear the furor of excitement and the shouting on the trading floor, where Twoey had his office, spill out over the phone lines at her. It never failed to turn her on.

"Twoey. Wetzon."

"Hiya, Wetzon. I'm jammed. Call me later."

"Twoey, wait. I want to put someone on the invite list."

"Call Maribelle." He was gone before she could say another word.

What the hell, she thought. *Makes it easier. No baroque explanations.* She called Twoey's assistant, Maribelle, gave her Hartmann's office number, and told her to issue an invitation.

That out of the way, she turned her attention to Sheila Reitman's note and the printout. Was it possible that someone had fallen through the cracks? No psychology Ph.D. at all? Jerry Gordon seemed like a fairly common name. Then there was the last thing in Sheila's letter. Gordon Jerome. Wakefield Farms, Massachusetts.

In her mind's eye she saw a small New England village with its center green and Civil War soldier statue, farms and homes separated by low stone walls. So why did the name of the village give her a jangle?

She picked up the phone and punched in the numbers for Massachusetts information and asked for the village of Wakefield Farms.

"We have no listing for a town called Wakefield Farms in Massachusetts."

She replaced the receiver. "Now isn't that strange?" she murmured out loud. "A phony address. He's a CPA, though, and CPAs have to be licensed." Oh, hell and damnation. Why was she getting hung up on a weird detour? She had enough on her plate without following trails that led nowhere. But it continued to plague her.

Ruth Abramson was a CPA. Ruth, a single practitioner, fastidious to the core, had been Wetzon's accountant since pre–Smith and Wetzon days.

When Wetzon got her on the phone, Ruth said, "Gordon Jerome? God, that's a familiar name. If he's licensed in New York, I can find him for you. Give me a couple of days."

Studying the printout, Wetzon saw that maybe she had narrowed it down too much. Maybe he got his Ph.D. in the '60s. Of course, that was it. In the late 1960s he could have gone straight through school to stay out of Vietnam. That would put him still in his forties now. Certainly, Jerry wasn't older than that, maybe even younger. But didn't a Ph.D. in psych have to do clinical work? Could he really have gone straight through for his doctorate? And hadn't he told Smith he'd spent two years in the army? In intelligence, no less. She shoved the printout and Sheila's note into her briefcase. When Sheila came home, she'd ask her to check back another ten years.

Meantime, she had to find out why Wakefield Farms was burning a hole in her brain. Marissa Peiser. Wetzon tried her office but was told Peiser wasn't available.

The phone rang almost as soon as she'd hung up, and Max knocked. "Paul Schlessinger for you, Wetzon."

"Who?"

Max read back the name he'd written down.

She rolled the name over her tongue, searching her memory. "All right! He's B. B.'s big producer." She reached for the phone. "Let B. B. know I'm talking to him, will you, Max?" She pressed the lit button. "Paul Schlessinger? This is Leslie Wetzon—" As of this morning she had something unique to sell him on. With surety, she began her pitch.

Schlessinger listened without interrupting, then said, "I've been here eight years and never made a move. They tend to take you for granted if you don't make noise. I may be moderately annoyed from time to time, but enough to make a move? I don't think so. I've been around long enough to know it's not any different anywhere else."

"Paul, look at the changing face of the industry over the last five years. Schiff, McConnell has a unique situation to offer. A highly unusual environment, designed for the top of your profession. And the perks are commensurate with your status." She was so engrossed in the sale that she only vaguely heard Max go out to the garden and call Smith to the phone..

"Well, that's all very interesting," Schlessinger was saying. "You're a great salesperson. You should have been a broker."

"Thanks, Paul. So what do you think?"

"Tell you what, you arrange a meeting with McConnell for me, Leslie Wetzon, and we'll see where it goes."

When she hung up the phone, she was on a euphoric high, all pumped up, larger than life, as when you do a turn on the stage and bring down the house. So she didn't see Smith at first, hadn't even noticed her come in.

"Wetzon! Are you listening to me?"

Wetzon turned, not even trying to brush aside the glow. "Congratulate me! I just got the biggest producer at Dean Witter to agree to meet Eliot McConnell."

"Congratulations. I just had a call from the Westport police. They dug a rifle bullet out of my shingle an hour ago."

60

· · · · · · ·

The scissors were sharp enough. Wetzon sat cross-legged on the kitchen floor, the *Journal* spread in front of her, guiding the scissors slowly through her hair, which hung like a curtain in front of her. An inch or two would do it. Ash-blond mowings began to pile up on the newspaper. Why not cut it all off? She flexed the scissors, poised, then dropped them as if burned.

On the kitchen counter next to the remains of a small pizza from John's, the bridal bouquet lived on. She got up on her knees and shook her hair out over the newspaper, which she then crumpled into a ball and hook-shot into the garbage bag, and made it. She was patting herself on the back when the downstairs buzzer sounded.

The small TV screen showed Marissa Peiser and, dammit, Ferrante and Martens. There went her evening. *Wrong! Cancel that*, she told herself in no uncertain terms. They were on her side, and someone was trying to kill her. She buzzed them in and opened the door.

When the elevator door slid open, she said, "Greetings," and waved them inside.

Peiser, made up and pulled together, had a peculiar look on her face. "What's wrong?"

"Oh, nothing much, aside from someone with a rifle taking potshots at me. Why?"

"You look different."

"Well, of course I do. Did you think I was a pinstripe? This is the real me." She looked down at herself, barefoot, in white midthigh leggings and one of Silvestri's gray sweatshirts, sleeves cut off; her hair hung loosely down to her waist. "Yeah, Alice in Wonderland."

Martens and Ferrante came right in and sat down at the table, not impressed with what she looked like, although Ferrante gave her a tight smile that translated into a leer. What did Peiser, who seemed intelligent, see in him?

"There's leftover pizza, if anyone's hungry," Wetzon said, closing the door. She was determined to be pleasant, to see this encounter through without losing her temper. "I'll make coffee."

No one responded. Peiser sat down.

"I understand from my partner that there was a bullet in the shingle. Can we assume it came from Wilson Boyd's missing rifle?" Wetzon filled the filter with coffee and, when the water in the kettle boiled, poured hot water into the container and pressed the on button.

"We can't assume anything," Ferrante growled.

Charming, Wetzon thought, and people told *her* to lighten up?

"You alone?" Martens asked.

"What does it look like?" The words came out short and curt. She had nothing against Martens. "Oh, hell, I'm sorry. I'm just a little tense." She set the box of cold pizza in the middle of the table. There were two slices left.

But Martens was making his tour of the loft and probably didn't hear her. Ferrante did, raising a smug eyebrow at her.

"If you're interested in renting it, I'll tell the owner." No one picked up on her sarcasm.

"Ms. Wetzon," Peiser said, then stopped and waited for Martens.

Wetzon poured coffee into mugs, set the mugs on the table with spoons, sugar, and Sweet'n Low, leaving her mug on the counter. She boosted herself up on the counter next to the coffee maker and faced the three of them, feeling infinitely better. Now they were all looking up at her.

"Were you able to trace the twenty thousand dollars?" she asked.

"Maglia had it." Peiser ignored Ferrante's frown. "He didn't deposit it because it was a third-party check. There would have to have been a lot of explanations. And he was still convinced he'd talked Middleton out of the move."

"Oh, give me a break. Brian gave him the check, so he must have been leaving. Well, at least that's something. Now Simon Loveman won't have his ass in a sling. Have you noticed that everyone's behavior in this is questionable ethically?"

"Including yours?" Ferrante looked pleased with himself.

"Fuck you, Ferrante," she said, and she liked the sound of it.

He laughed, and Martens smiled.

Peiser ignored the exchange. "You've got to help us out here. If someone is trying to kill you, you must know why. Do you have anything else to tell us?" Peiser seemed to be taking the lead in the questioning.

"Not really." She swung her legs back against the cabinet, holding the mug with both hands, sipping her coffee. "I've been racking my brain for possibilities. One really off-the-wall idea occurred to me because Dr. Jerry Gordon is always dropping his credentials into conversations. This may be plain old insecurity, or, conceivably, something else."

"Do you want to say that in English?" Ferrante took out his notebook and flipped over pages. He was really being a prick tonight.

"I think there's something weird about the two of them. Barbara and Jerry. She acts like a psycho, complete with mood swings and paranoia, and he's Big Daddy for everybody. Just a big, warm, sweet teddy bear."

"So?" Ferrante felt in his pockets for a pen, found it, pulled it out, and clicked the point out and in and out and in.

"So I heard that Barbara has violent episodes and attacks him, but I don't know how true it is." Not wanting to get either Sheila or herself in hot water, Wetzon didn't mention the computer information. And she didn't mention Mrs. Leonora Foley and her grandson, for reasons she couldn't have articulated.

"Any other detective work you want to tell us about?" Ferrante put his pen away and picked up a slice of cold pizza, folded it up like a package, and made it disappear into his mouth.

"Is Rona off the hook?"

Peiser shrugged.

"You let her go." Wetzon looked at them, one after the other. "She's still a suspect? You mean, you think she planted the gun herself?"

"You met her at the Drake Hotel yesterday afternoon." It was a statement from Peiser, not a question.

"How do you know that?" She smacked the counter with a fist, rattling the mug. "Are you following me, or her? What's this about?"

"Why did you have a meeting?" Peiser asked.

"She had something to tell me."

"What?"

"That she was going back to Bliss Norderman and Maglia."

"Why tell you?" Martens asked.

"Because I had the most to lose if she did. My fee. My firm placed her at Rosenkind, Luwisher. If she turns up dead, you'll know I or my partner did it." They were all staring at her. "That was a joke, in case you didn't recognize it. It was actually very nice of her to tell me. Most of the people I work with wouldn't bother. I'd just find out by accident that the broker had skipped."

"Sounds like the job," Martens said.

"Is that what you're here about?"

"We've been over everything back and forth, and we wanted to go through it one more time," Peiser said. "Just in case we missed something."

Wetzon groaned and took them through everything, only leaving out mention of Artie Metzger and Sheila Reitman. And Leonora Foley.

Ferrante put his notebook in his inside pocket and stood up, reached over and snared the last slice of pizza.

"Have you ever heard of a town in Massachusetts called Wakefield Farms?" Wetzon slipped off the counter and followed them to the door.

Peiser furrowed her brow. "Maybe. Can't place it. Why?"

"It just came up in conversation."

"Whose?" Ferrante said.

"Rona's." Rona, she thought. It hadn't come up in Rona's conversation, had it? Was that what was bothering her?

"I'll check it out," Peiser said. She paused at the door. "Don't meet anyone alone for a while."

"What does that mean?"

"Just that."

"I'm a recruiter. I am always meeting people alone, in secret, in confidence. You'll be wiping out my business."

"Is it worth your life?" Ferrante asked impatiently. "Stay in public places where there are a lot of people."

They got on the elevator and the door closed. Wetzon stood staring at the elevator. Sounds of arguing came up from the car as it traveled downward.

"Fucking waste of time." That was Ferrante.

And then Peiser's voice: "I don't agree. Keep it loose, but I want someone on her."

61

■■■■■■■

If there was truly someone keeping an eye on her, Wetzon never saw him. Wednesday and Thursday were lost in a haze of appointments and interviews. On Thursday, she'd heard from Ruth Abramson that there was no CPA licensed in New York State by the name of Gordon Jerome.

"Was there ever? Is there any way of checking? Tell me if I'm being too pushy."

"What are you looking for?"

"If I knew, it would be easy."

Halloween Friday rolled in, snappy cold, clear as the best fall days in New York. The minighosts and -witches would be out in force, accompanied by parents in the City version of trick-or-treat.

Smith was in a bitchy mood. She accepted Wetzon's happy-birthday wishes ungraciously and threw her card in the wastebasket.

"And I had such a lovely present for you, but I guess you don't want it."

Flinging herself in her chair, Smith fastened angry eyes on Wetzon, who stood before her holding a plastic plate on which a honey bran muffin sported a little lit candle in the center. "I hate this birthday, and you know it. Why are you torturing me?"

"Will you give me a break? Just blow out your candle, and I'll give you your goddam present." She set the muffin down on Smith's desk.

"Oh, very well." Smith came out of her slump and blew out the candle. "Now are you happy?"

"You look exactly the same as you did five years ago, better even. So I don't know what you're bitching about."

Whipping out her ready mirror, Smith stared deeply into it. She fluffed her curls with her fingers, then pointed to almost invisible lines around her eyes. "See these. What do you call these? Lines!"

"Everyone has them. They're laugh lines. *Laugh* lines!"

"You're really enjoying this, aren't you? There'll be a payback. There always is. Just wait." She smiled. "Okay, where's my present?"

Wetzon thrust a Bendel's box into Smith's grasping hands.

"I love presents." Smith opened the box and tore through the tissue paper, pulling out a silk scarf in streaks of pink, lavender, and yellow, fully fringed. "It's just beautiful, sweetie."

"Isn't it? My friend Rita Morgan designs a whole line of them for Bendel's."

"Well, she's really talented."

"Yes, and to think she used to be a stockbroker."

"No!"

Wetzon grinned. She loved needling Smith. "What are you wearing tonight?"

"A white sequined handkerchief."

"That doesn't leave much to the imagination."

"That's the idea, sweetie pie. And I suppose you're wearing your basic black?"

"Yup."

"You might treat yourself to something new."

"Nope."

"You could liven it up a little. It looks like a leotard with a skirt."

"How about silk underwear?"

"How about some big, gloppy strands of pearls?"

"What time is Twoey picking you up?"

"Eight."

"Well, be gracious and act surprised."

Smith did a cross-my-heart-and-hope-to-die. "Trust me, sweetie," she drawled.

"That's what scares me."

Smith left the office at midday for a massage and a facial, swearing she was ready for plastic surgery. And finally, at three o'clock, Wetzon put her pen down and quit. It was Friday. The market was very strong. Heavy volume. It was hard to talk to people. Brokers were watching their Quotrons for their trading clients, ready to take profits at an eighth- or quarter-point increase. They had to be in touch with clients, traders, and analysts; in the scale of importance on a day like today, the headhunter was down at the bottom, with the spouse.

She walked over to Grand Central and took the shuttle to Times Square, where she caught a number 1 train downtown. Children were in costume and makeup from school parties. Clowns predominated. Later, the masked monsters would make their appearance.

When she climbed up the narrow stairs at Sheridan Square, she had to sidestep a beggar who had planted himself near the top holding out a grimy cardboard cup. On Seventh Avenue, a man in a parked car made kissing noises at her. "Hey, babee," he called.

She felt herself tense up, then had the peculiar sense that someone was watching her, and it wasn't the beggar or the man in the car. She looked around casually, careful not to show she was looking, but saw nothing unusual. It was unsettling.

"Thank you very much," a bedraggled wino in a sombrero said to no one in particular. "Have a nice day."

"Jason, you're dragging your sheet," a mother told a little ghost.

Why should it unsettle her? Hadn't Peiser told Ferrante to keep an eye on her?

Still, it was a relief to get into Carlos's apartment and lock the door. The bridal bouquet drooped in its glass. She dropped it in the garbage and stripped down to her underwear, then did a slow, meditative workout at the barre, turning her thoughts within. Unless something happened to change how she felt, Alton would come home with her tonight. She wanted to be seduced.

And tomorrow? She bent forward on the barre, head to knee. Tomorrow she would deal with Silvestri, for better or for worse. She stopped in midmovement. For better or worse? What a Freudian choice of words.

By the time Carlos and Arthur arrived, Wetzon was dressed in her basic black. For Smith, she'd added two Chanel ropes of fat pearls. She left the door ajar and went back to the bathroom to finish her makeup.

"Birdie!" Carlos shrieked. "Where are you?"

She came into the living room, hands on hips. Carlos was wearing a hideous Sweeney Todd mask, and both he and Arthur wore black tie and white silk aviator scarves around their necks. "You are a nut case." Arthur looked like a bearded Fred Astaire, carrying a silver handled-walking stick. "Debonair, Arthur. Quite."

Arthur bowed and said in an English accent, "Charmed, my dear Wats—Wetzon."

"Enough of that. Let's have a look at you." Carlos took her shoulders and held her away from him, his eyes glittering through the mask. "I think I'll just have a wee bite of your neck."

She rolled her eyes at Arthur. "What did you feed him?"

Arthur laughed. Carlos whipped off the mask. "The girl has no sense of humor." He hugged her. "My Lord, you don't look any different."

"It's only been a few weeks."

"Well, at least you haven't gotten involved in a murder, so there's that to be grateful for." He gave her a hard look. "Right?"

"Would I lie to you?" She certainly didn't want to get into long explanations with Carlos, because he was sure to find fault, and she didn't want to hear it right now.

"Of course. And for sure. At least Silvestri used to keep you in check."

"I resent that. I am not some dopey little girl—"

"Don't get me started. Are you dressed?" Carlos demanded, sitting down in the living room.

"Don't I look it?"

"Well, come and sit down and tell Uncle Arthur and Uncle Carlos what's been happening." He patted the sofa pillow. Arthur sat in the club chair, looking mellow.

"Ooo, Uncle Carlos and Uncle Arthur, does oo hab a lolli for moi?" She flopped down beside Carlos.

"See, Arthur, that dirty business she's in has addled her brain." He kissed her forehead. "Tell about the apartment."

"It's going fine, but it'll be another two months at least before I thank you for the use of your hall."

"Good enough." He gave her a slow wink. "Who's the new man?"

"Alton Pinkus."

"Alton Pinkus?" Arthur's face registered surprise. Shock?

"Arthur! You know him?" Carlos hated not knowing everything. "Who is he? Wait a minute, not that union guy?"

Arthur nodded. Was he impressed? Or was he disapproving? She couldn't tell. She wanted her friends' approbation.

Wetzon looked from one to the other, cautious. "He's a little older than . . ." She stood up. "Do you think he's too old for me?"

"Birdie, it doesn't matter what we think. Is he good to you?"

"So far."

"Well, all right, then, Birdie. We won't put a hex on him, will we, Arthur?"

"Carlos, Leslie is serious."

"Arthur, Leslie may be serious. My Birdie isn't. Come back here and sit down." He patted the sofa cushion.

"You're bad." Wetzon shook her finger in his face, and Carlos grabbed her hand and pulled her down on his lap. "Have you sorted out everything with the cop?"

"He's a detective. And no, I haven't sorted anything out." She squirmed. "It's awful. Two men."

"Tsk, tsk. Two men. Isn't that divine?" He pursed his lips. "The girl's a slut, Arthur, don't you think?" Rising, he pulled her up with him. "It's almost seven. We don't want to miss anything. Get your coat, slut." He closed one eye and fluttered his dark lashes seductively, gave her a light slap on the rump.

Wetzon planted a kiss on his nose. "Listen, you very clever boy. In all your peregrinations, have you ever been to a place in Massachusetts called Wakefield Farms?"

"Well, hardly, darling. But it's right up Arthur's alley."

Astonished, she looked at Arthur. "You've heard of it?"

Arthur nodded. "It's a sanitorium where the rich park their booze and mental problems."

62

·······

"Wakefield Farms is just an upscale funny farm, Birdie. Don't you remember? Connie Janeway used to check herself in there to dry out."

Connie Janeway, who'd followed in Gwen Verdon's footsteps as the darling of dancing musicals. She remembered Connie Janeway, loaded up with booze and drugs, like a zombie on the stage toward the end of her contract. Then she'd go off and cool out at the funny farm in the Massachusetts hills. And that was Wakefield Farms.

Traffic was blocked off on Sixth Avenue, the main route of the Halloween Parade in the Village. Tradition had it that the parade would start on Sixth Avenue and Spring Street, travel north to Fourteenth and then east on Fourteenth to University Place and south to Washington Square, then turn north again and disband on Seventeenth Street. But there was always an extravagant finale—icing on the cake—and that was the costume parade on Christopher Street, the sometimes tarnished, often wacky, heart and soul of the gay Village.

On Sixth and Tenth Street, the crowds of oglers were already out in force. Across the way, Wetzon spotted Dustin Hoffman and a tall woman, just part of the audience.

A stunning black transvestite in a yellow lycra mini with Tina Turner hair sat on the hood of a Buick swinging long, graceful legs in black net stockings and gold stiletto heels.

People on the sidelines sported their own costumes: bizarre masks, skeletons dangling from earlobes, Indian war paint on the children. Bats danced from springs on a hair band worn by a woman in jeans next to the spot Wetzon and her friends had carved out for themselves along the edge of the sidewalk. A father carried a child in a rabbit suit on his shoulders. Some of the onlookers weren't even waiting for the freewheeling looniness and were trooping out on the street and joining the parade. A marching band from a Staten Island high school, each member in Lone Ranger masks, paraded by playing a barely recognizable "Ghost of a Chance."

The uniformed police were very much in evidence. There seemed to be one practically every ten feet, but they were not intrusive and appeared to be watching the parade. This was the blockbuster event of the year in Greenwich Village. The theme this year was world peace and sister- and brotherhood, but you couldn't tell by most of the outlandish costumes.

"Look at that." Carlos pointed to a huge, papier-mâché skull, which danced by nodding with dignity to a spattering of applause. Under its gaping jaw were four feet in white Reeboks. Just behind the skull was a float bearing an elegant king and queen in velvet robes and gold crowns, followed by an entourage of courtiers.

"Watch it, Leslie!" Arthur shouted above the noise. He and Carlos grabbed her and held on as the crowd surged forward to see the revelers and her footing became precarious.

The Gay Men's Chorus was followed by a float of hairy male hula dancers in grass skirts and balloon breasts popping out of skimpy halters. Then came Chinese coolies, American Indians, the Seven Dwarfs and a beautiful Snow White with a mincing prince and a fat, campy fairy godmother, like escapees from Charles Ludlum's Ridiculous Theatre.

While they were standing there, night had come on almost stealthily, and the streets were lit by the mercury vapor streetlights and the spillover from restaurants, which were clotted with people. Harvey Keitel and his wife, Lorraine Bracca, settled in next to Arthur. Under one of the lampposts, a drag Marilyn Monroe simpered for an amateur photographer.

After a table with a sign saying "The Ladies Who Lunch"— complete with four place settings and four robots sitting in feather boas and huge flowered hats—strolled by, Wetzon looked at her watch. It was quarter to eight. She tweaked Carlos's earlobe. "That's it for me, guys. I don't want to be late." She'd walk over to Seventh Avenue and catch a cab down to the Odeon, which was on West

Broadway in the section known as TriBeCa, the triangle below Canal Street.

"Where are you going?" Arthur took her hand, then laughed and pointed to the street where a man was dressed as a shower, complete with running water when a hand pulled a string. It was an only-in-New York costume, for sure.

"Down to the Odeon. Twoey Barnes is throwing Smith a surprise fortieth birthday party."

"Wouldn't you just know the Barracuda would have her birthday on Halloween? It gives witches a bad name." Carlos threw his arm over her shoulder. "Come on, Birdie darling, we'll put you into a cab."

"You'll miss the parade," Wetzon protested.

"We'll catch up on Christopher Street later." They edged out of the crowd, brushing past another Marilyn impersonator, this one on roller skates, wearing a long, red sequined sheath with a slit up the side. The skater rolled right into Wetzon, knocking the wind out of her.

"Hey, cool it, Marilyn," Carlos shouted.

Marilyn giggled and gave Carlos an ungentle push, which sent him reeling into Wetzon. Then she took off on her skates. She was gone in the few seconds it took them to recover.

"Can you believe that?" Arthur was pointing to the disappearing skater, talking to one of the cops, who then spoke into a walkie-talkie.

"Forget it, Arthur. There's a bitch in every crowd." Carlos had quite recovered. They all had.

Night was truly day in the celebrating Village. Horns blared. Music surged from the passing floats. Spotlights made eerie shadows of familiar buildings. The three retraced their steps on Tenth Street to Seventh Avenue. Turning back to the parade route for one last look, Wetzon caught someone looking at her. A derelict with a sombrero pulled down over his face, wearing ragged jeans and a quilted vest. When he saw she'd spotted him, he melted into the crowd. Chilled, she tugged at the collar of her trench coat. He was the same wino who was hanging out near the subway earlier. Surely he was too scary to be that cop watching her.

"Move it, Birdie." Carlos had gone ahead and had a cab waiting, door open. Traffic was rolling, but there was a lot of it because of the rerouting due to the parade.

Wetzon gave them each a kiss and a hasty hug. "Have fun tonight, guys. The Odeon on West Broadway and Thomas," she said, climbing inside. The driver turned. Her heart stopped, then she laughed. He was wearing a Freddy Krueger mask. "Very funny, ah . . ." She leaned forward to read his ID. ". . . Mohammed."

"Stay in constant touch," Carlos called as the cab pulled away. She felt a twinge of regret. If she went with Carlos and Arthur, she would never have to deal with Alton, never have to grow up, never have to make a decision.

The Odeon, with its big red neon sign, sat in the midst of a nineteenth-century business neighborhood, most of whose buildings had been converted to lofts and apartments for artists and writers and movie stars. Fire escapes dotted the front of many of the grimy buildings. Much of TriBeCa and its nearest neighbor to the north—SoHo —was part of the city's historic preservation, particularly because of the proliferation in this area of cast-iron buildings.

She had read somewhere that the Odeon had had another life as a cafeteria, and some of the art deco amenities still remained, the tile floor and the wood-paneled walls. A long bar of the same period was against one wall, and tables were crammed tightly almost one against the other. On normal days it attracted both a bohemian crowd from the neighborhood and a business crowd because of its proximity to the financial district.

Twoey had taken over the entire restaurant for the evening, which must have cost him a fortune. The guest list had settled in around forty people.

A small combo of a drummer and two guitarists was set up in a tight spot near the bar, and they were playing '60s rock music. On the wall was a mural in relief, picturing an old New York neighborhood. Men in pinstripes and ladies in everything from Carolyne Roehm to DKNY were clustered in small groups around the bar, drinking. The men were talking business, and it was obvious.

Wetzon checked her coat and scoped the room for Alton. She saw him at the far end of the bar talking to Neil Munchen from Rosenkind, Luwisher, but every now and then he would glance up, letting his eyes search the room. She felt a small, sweet thrill watching him look for her. She stood still, waiting. When his eyes lit on her, he smiled that warm, wide smile and reeled her in.

"You're looking dishy, Wetzon," Neil said, staring at her legs.

He was bronze as a lifeguard in his year-round tan. He must use one of those dumb tanning places. Remembering their meeting in Rockefeller Center, she wondered if he was seriously thinking of leaving Rosenkind, Luwisher.

She gave him her debutante smile. "Thanks, Neil." Maybe she shouldn't have shortened the dress as much as she had.

"She is dishy," Alton said, putting his arm around her, and Neil's face registered one of those surprised looks that said, *So that's the lay of the land.* Alton had not so subtly staked his claim. Immediately, it took the edge off her thrill. Why did men do that? It made women feel like a trophy of some sort.

"What are you drinking, Leslie?" Alton was holding a near-empty glass of bourbon. She could smell its syrupy essence.

"Amstel," she said, rewarding herself. But she'd stick to one. "Where's Gail?"

Neil pointed to his wife, who was talking with Janet Barnes, Twoey's attractive red-haired mother.

"Hey, Wetzon, how're ya doin'?" Dougie Culver, one of the managing directors of Rosenkind, Luwisher, sauntered over. Damn, now he would do his touchy-feely number, which he proceeded to do, running his hands up and down her back. She saw his face register surprise when he didn't feel her bra. Ha! She was wearing her silk teddy under the black dress.

She stepped away from him. "I'm doin' juss fine, Dougie darlin'. How're ya doin'?"

He had the grace to laugh at her put-on southern accent. "See y'all later."

"What a day," Neil said. He looked tired. He was sweating, and the restaurant wasn't that hot. He tilted the bottle of Beck's and took a long swig.

"The market close up or down?"

"Down a hundred."

"Down?"

Neil shrugged. "It was way up most of the day." He seemed nervous. Didn't look her in the eye. "The sell programs kicked in and the traders took profits."

"Everyone says we're in for a new bull market."

"Wetzon, when everyone says it, that's a sure sign it's over. I'd sell if I were you. I think we're in for crisis times in the markets. Like just before the Crash in '87. People are pushing the envelope, taking chances. When things blow this time, there'll be blood on the Street."

"God, that's depressing, Neil."

He grimaced. "Can't help it. There'll be more mergers, so it'll affect all of us." He took another swig of the beer. "I guess you heard Rona went back to Bliss."

"Yes. I'm sorry."

"It was probably a good idea. The guys weren't happy with the publicity."

"But she's been cleared."

"They'd always connect the bad stuff with her. She'd never have lived it down."

Alton was weaving through the crowd at the bar on his way back, so she had only a moment to pose the question. "Neil, how do you know . . . um . . . Dr. Gordon?"

"Dr. Gordon? I don't know a Dr. Gordon." He was looking at her blankly.

"Yes, you do. Jerry. Remember the day we met in Rockefeller Center? I saw you talking to him as if you knew him."

"Oh, you mean Gordie?"

"Is that what you call him?"

"Gordie. Sure. Gordie Jerome. Hadn't seen him in years. Why do you call him doctor? Is that a joke?"

"No. He's a doctor of psychology."

"My ass, he's a doctor of anything. He's an accountant, or at least he was. He got into trouble investing for clients. Nimble fingers and a great spiel. Funds disappeared. I don't think he was really bad, only careless. He wanted to be everybody's friend. He got sent up for a few years. Wrote to me from there, and I answered him. Some minimum-security place. Clinton, I think it was."

63

....

"Surprise!"

Smith clasped both hands across her breast and acted bowled over, the phony. Wetzon leaned back against Alton, feeling his heat and the solidity of him. Someone sturdy and reliable to lean on. If one wanted that.

When the strains of "Happy Birthday" petered out, Smith cried, "Oh, how could you all have kept this from me?" She blew kisses all around like a movie star in her white sequined handkerchief that passed for a dress. She was wearing the diamond grape earrings, and around her bare neck was something Wetzon had never seen: a wide gold mesh chain with a large pavé diamond clip. Now who had given Smith that?

Twoey was beaming, poor guy. He signaled to a waiter with wedged hair, holding a tray of champagne-filled tulip glasses.

"Tell us how it feels to be forty," someone called.

"Take down his name," Smith replied sweetly. Her eyes found Wetzon's. Wetzon shivered and set her beer down on the bar.

"What's the matter?" Alton was on the ball. He put his arms around her.

"Nothing. A draft, is all." Smith had murder in her eyes. Now she was on her way over, dammit.

"Alton, sweetie, how dear of you to come." She looked at them from under lowered lashes. "You two look very comfy." She shook Alton's hand. "As for you, sugar—"

Wetzon held up her hand. "Don't say it. That's a lot of beautiful jewels you're wearing."

Smith fingered the diamond clip, then the earrings. "Twoey is *such* a dear." She was looking around the room, smiling graciously, like a queen. "We'll talk later." She'd spotted Hartmann, and she left them quickly.

Alton set his glass on the bar next to hers and turned her around. "Say what you're thinking."

She put her hands over his. "I don't like parties." She was thinking that Dr. Jerry Gordon, radio psychologist, was really Gordon Jerome, ex-CPA, felon, and jailbird. Could he actually have had the chutzpah to change his identity—and in such an obvious way—stay in the same area, and get away with it? Well, he had, hadn't he? Until Brian Middleton. Brian must have found out. Or maybe he was in on it all along.

"Do you want to leave?" Alton's breath on her brow teased her hormones.

"Would you mind? No one will ever notice we're gone. It'll look as if we're going out for air." She gave him her coat check and went downstairs to the vision-in-purple ladies' room, where she remembered there was a phone. Her tiny shoulder bag had no address book or business cards. Information gave her the Central Park Precinct number, but she got a busy signal when she tried it. Next, the D.A.'s office.

"Can you call back, or can she reach you somewhere?" Peiser had stepped out for a short time.

"I'm traveling from place to place. Tell her I'm just leaving the Odeon, heading home with a friend. Tell her—" Wetzon dropped her voice to a whisper. "Tell her that Jerry Gordon is really Gordon Jerome, and he has a record. Tell her not to call me tonight. I'll talk to her tomorrow." She hung up quickly. Gordon Jerome must have been feeding business to Brian, and Brian was kicking back a portion of what he made. That must be it. Then that would mean that Penny Ann Boyd had probably been manipulated by both Dr. Jerry and Brian.

She climbed the stairs and worked her way through the crowd, shaking hands with Destry Bird, one of Twoey's partners, and a tall, thin model type with a blank look on her face. Destry's date. That's what they liked, men like Destry. Cardboard cutouts from *Elle*, no passion, no brains. Janet Barnes was standing alone at the bar, glamorous but not very happy. Wetzon waved to her. She'd love to have said to her, "Chin up, Janet dear, you'll have him back to yourself shortly."

When she reached the entrance, she did not see Alton. Was he waiting for her outside? She opened the door. A hand landed intimately on the small of her back. Alton's? The hand gave her a hard shove, and she staggered outside. The sidewalk was racing up toward her face. Then, just as abruptly she was caught and confined in powerful arms.

A man laughed. "You do take chances, don't you, Wetzon?" Richard Hartmann.

She struggled, but he held on. "Let me go. Are you crazy? Someone will see us." She tilted her head up to see his face.

"If they do, they'll just think we can't keep our hands off each other. Xenia will be *very* upset with you. And Alton won't be very happy." His lips brushed her ear, her cheek, her neck.

Behind her on the street she could hear people strolling by, laughing and talking, and all the while, the beat, beat, beat of the rock music issued from the party.

In that instant Wetzon knew that Smith had told him.

"Scared?" She didn't respond, but her heart was thudding at a thunderous clip. "Good," he whispered in her ear. "Stay scared." He released her. Shivering, she watched him straighten his tie. He smiled, his wandering eye looking over her shoulder. "I'm glad we had this little talk." He opened the door, adding, "One more thing. I wouldn't say anything to Xenia if I were you—" and returned to the party.

Go easy, Wetzon thought, *he could have killed me, but he didn't.* Maybe each time he'd stalked her, it was to scare her. Her heart was still beating double-time, but her knees had stopped trembling. *Damn Smith. She doesn't deserve me. I want to protect her and she exposes me. And herself.*

"Oh, there you are." Alton was coming toward her carrying her trench coat, which she slipped on but didn't button.

Wait a minute, she thought, even if Smith had told Hartmann Wetzon was onto his money laundering, it couldn't have been before Sunday. She closed her eyes. Was Hartmann left-handed or right-handed?

"Is anything wrong, Leslie?"

"How well do you know Richard Hartmann?"

Alton looked at her, a puzzled expression on his face. "Not well. Why?"

"Do you think he would commit murder?"

"Hartmann commit murder? Himself? I doubt it. If he wants someone dead, he knows enough of the right people to do it for him. Do you want to tell me what this is about?"

"It's nothing. Honest." Wetzon made a calculated decision. Smith would be safe with Twoey tonight. If Hartmann were going to kill again, he would have killed Wetzon tonight. Tomorrow she would tell Peiser that Hartmann had threatened her, and why.

"You're sure?"

"Just a little nervous." She smiled at him.

A haze enveloped the street lamps. The sky was rife with clouds, obscuring the moon. There was not one bit of wind. Only a fragile fog floated like an uncertain wraith. Lights glimmered from buildings.

"The air feels good."

Wetzon nodded. "Let's walk, okay? We can take West Broadway to Bleecker, then home." She put her arm through his, and her stomach chose that moment to rumble loud enough to be heard in New Jersey. She patted it with her free hand. *Quiet,* she commanded silently.

"I think you're hungry."

She grinned. "Probably. We're going right by John's. We can pick up a couple of calzones and reheat them."

They walked up through SoHo, past great windowed art galleries in old cast-iron factories and warehouses. Two children in witch costumes, followed discreetly by a mommy, came toward them leading a golden retriever in a clown outfit, including a pom-pommed hat. The restaurants along West Broadway above Houston Street were busy with people who'd come in to watch the parade. Italian, Indian, and Chinese aromas all mixed together. A waft of garlic floated out of the open door of Tutta Pasta.

"Smells good, doesn't it?" Alton's voice was husky.

She moved closer to him. Between them was the exquisite expectant sexual tension of the unknown. There was something wonderful about letting desire build.

They stopped at John's and picked up the calzones, which Alton carried, and headed up Bleecker toward Tenth Street, walking among revelers and exhibitionists. When they crossed Seventh Avenue, they became aware of the roaring sound, and looked at one another. And then unexpectedly, they were sucked into a wall of humanity, all surging up Bleecker toward Christopher Street. She'd forgotten the crazies came out in full force to parade on Christopher Street, the tacky finale to the Halloween Parade.

She was still holding tight to Alton, and he to her, but they couldn't hear anything over the clamor of the crowd, and the constant surging was pulling her away from him. "Please," she cried, but she was caught up in a writhing conga line. Alton was shouting something, but she couldn't hear him. She pushed back, fighting for space, and now she couldn't see him, could only feel his hands on her sleeve, and then couldn't feel that anymore.

Above her, on a fire escape, a spotlight lit Cleopatra, or was it Elizabeth Taylor? On the street, she was being crushed. She didn't dare trip or she'd be trampled. Faces contorted. No fun, no fun. Hands began to tug at her, pulling her toward the shops. "Alton!" Gasping for breath, she pushed again, getting help, and finally half collapsed in the entranceway of a shop. Li-Lac, the chocolate shop. She was on Christopher Street. Someone was holding on to her, tightly. Hartmann had followed her. She turned her head. It was the wino with the sombrero. She pulled away from him, but he wouldn't let go of her. *Oh, shit.* He was reaching into his vest. "No!" She was shouting, but she couldn't hear herself. She struggled to get away, back to Bleecker, no, maybe push forward to Hudson Street, but his hand gripped her upper arm painfully. She shouted, "Help me, someone." He was going to kill her. He had a gun.

Her life—it couldn't happen like this—she would be found dead, crushed, and no one would know what happened. The hold on her weakened suddenly; someone was helping her, tugging her away from him. And it was done so quickly, but in the process, she'd left him holding her empty raincoat. She was free, hand clasped with her friend's, another Marilyn Monroe look-alike. The crush was awful. Just masses of people pushing in every direction. And the costume parade continued to cheers, applause, and laughter. She scrambled to keep up with her savior. Where were they going?

Suddenly, they were alone. The noise continued, but the street was dark. "Wait!" Wetzon cried, skidding to a stop. She'd lost her purse somewhere. "We don't have to run anymore. I have to go back. My friend—" She was shivering in her skimpy dress.

Would Alton go to the apartment? What did all this mean? If she was looking for symbols, she'd found one. It wasn't supposed to happen. At least not tonight.

What was Marilyn doing? Taking her mask off. "Listen," Wetzon said, "thank you, but I was with someone. . . ." She stared at the face. The mask dropped in the gutter and lay faceup next to a beer can and a condom.

The face under the platinum hair was heavily made up, with false eyelashes. But familiar. Blue eyes. The body was squeezed into a red sequined dress with a long slit up the side. Legs in sheer hose, platform shoes with ankle straps. Marilyn reached into her swinging white leather purse with nail heads and took out a tiny silver gun.

"My God!" Wetzon backed away from her. "What are you doing? Who are you?" Her heart hammered in her ears. Behind them, the crowd roared.

"Look closely, Wetzon."

It was Jerry Gordon.

64

•••••••

"**Y**ou know about me. Brian told me."

"Don't do it, Jerry." Her hand flew up. *Idiot, as if that could stop a bullet.* "I won't tell."

"It's too late."

She moved, finally, adrenaline pumping, spun and dipped, a moving target, body fluid, lithe as a gazelle. The flash came; she felt the breeze the bullet made as it passed her. Must cross Hudson Street. Where to hide? It was too open.

Headlights bore down on them. A black sedan, muffler advertising its dying breath, roared up Hudson. Arms and head were leaning out of the car windows. Jerry was taking aim again, the little gun hidden in his hand, as if death came from his hand alone. The headlights pinned them. Then Wetzon broke again, racing across Hudson.

On the west side of the street, there was a playground behind a high iron fence. Forward and back, she found no opening. Panic rose like a deep freeze. She shook the fence.

Behind her, brakes screeched and someone yelled, "Fucking perverts," and someone else yelled, "Die, faggot." Skinheads leaned out of windows and shook baseball bats. Then with an explosive blast the car was gone, leaving the night to the high spirits jamming Christopher Street.

Looking back on Hudson where Jerry had stood taking aim, she saw nothing. The street was empty. Jerry was gone, and the revelers had begun to take up Hudson Street as their own. They, or the skinheads, had scared Jerry away. The thumping in her breast subsided slowly. There was safety among masses of people. A group,

their outsize masks silhouetted under the street lamps, came single
file toward her.

Hugging herself against the cold, she took a ragged breath. She
had to get home. Get to a phone. Get away from here. What had
happened to Alton? Would he be waiting for her at the apartment?
She crossed over where Christopher Street continued after being cut
by Hudson. What was that drab, grim archway? Like a black hole.
The PATH train entrance. The route to New Jersey. It looked abandoned. Darkness, steep steps going downward. She had no idea it was
here.

A sound, a faint sound behind her, heels crunching stones, then a
hand tight across her mouth, so tight she couldn't bite. Cold metal
against her forehead. She was being dragged back into the menacing
arch, the entrance to the PATH trains.

It couldn't end this way. Not like this. She wouldn't go like a
wimp. For her it would be kicking and snarling all the way. With
every ounce of strength she could muster, she bucked, kicking backward, her heels meeting his shins with the full force of her hundred
pounds of weight.

"Bitch!" Howling, he threw her against the archway. A deafening explosion, then the not unpleasant smell of gunpowder, replaced
quickly by that of singed hair. Chunks of cement crumbs stung her.
Her head burned. Something warm and wet dripped into her eyes.
Her hair oozed from its knot and slipped down her face. She pulled it
back, and it came away in her hands. Dazed, she tried to stand. She
heard someone say, "Why? Why?" The voice sounded like hers,
from a great distance.

He was standing over her, ludicrous in his blond Marilyn wig
and sequined dress. Big feet in platform ankle straps. Did he paint his
toenails? she wondered, slipping into hysteria. But he was talking.
What was he saying? "Because Brian was going to take everything
away from me. He told Tabitha and he told you. I didn't believe him,
Brian was such a liar, but I had to make sure. We had a deal. I sent
him clients and he gave me a cut. Then he decided *I* should pay him
to keep quiet. I was going to be rich and famous. He would have
ruined everything."

"What about Tabitha?"

"I didn't want to do that, but when I read the diary, I knew I had
to. It was only a matter of time before she told."

"You stole the diary and tore out those pages. Why did you send it back to me? You had what you wanted."

"I wanted to scare you off."

She raised herself on one elbow, felt the cold cement scrape her skin. Could she make it to the stairs? Had to keep him talking. "You mean Brian was going to tell that you're really Gordon Jerome, ex-accountant, convicted felon, phony psychologist, cross dresser—"

His face distorted. He ran his hands over his hips, balancing the gun precariously. "You were spying on me. I like dressing up. In some societies it isn't considered strange. Women wear men's clothes all the time."

He was right, of course, but forget about that. He'd killed two people and was trying to kill her. A bleeding heart would lead right to her own heart bleeding. She inched to the steps.

"There's nothing wrong with me. Barbie likes it when I dress up." He pointed the gun at her again, and she flipped herself over the edge of the first step. The gun clicked but didn't shoot. He became frantic, clicking, clicking. She rolled down two more steps. He threw the gun and it clattered, *bumptebump*, on the stone steps, then he grabbed her arm and pulled her kicking and screaming back up the stairs.

Pieces of hair hung in her face, matted with blood. He was choking her. Arms flailing, she fought back. She'd be a dead body on a slab in the M.E.'s office, just like Brian and Tabitha. "Silvestri," she gasped. A gray-blue film covered her eyes. Gorillas floated around her in the semidarkness. Jerry wasn't there anymore. She gulped rough, gasping breaths. Women's legs, some in lace tights, slim ankles, muffled voices. There was Jerry. He was backing away from the gorillas. Watch it! He stepped back over the edge and hung there for a microsecond, then pitched over backward. A hideous scream echoed up, then the sound of a horrid thud. And silence.

Gorillas bent over her. She could barely keep her eyes open. What a strange time to be sleepy. Blood stuck to her eyelids. *I'm a leaky hose*, she thought. She reached a hand upward and one of the gorillas reached out and clasped it, as if they knew each other. There were five of them. Women in hairy gorilla heads. They were comforting her now, stroking her. One of them propped her up, mumbling what sounded like "Leslie" through the hideous face. Wetzon was crying. "My hair, look, my hair."

"Police! Stay where you are!" A man's voice bounced around the alcove. The gorilla women straightened, fading into the darkness, giving Wetzon a clearer view of the speaker. It was the derelict in the sombrero. Two cops in uniform raced toward them.

Wetzon tried to stand, couldn't, sank back against the archway. Sombrero said, "Hey," and gave her a quick once-over.

"I'm all right, I think."

"Where'd he go?" He was peering down the staircase.

"He's at the bottom of the steps. Down there. He fell." She began laughing. "You can't miss him. You'll know him by his red dress." It was so funny, she couldn't stop. Smith's tarot reading had been only a little off. It wasn't a very powerful woman. It was a man in a dress.

One of the cops shone his flashlight down the stairs, moving it around, while Sombrero went down cautiously, gun up. People were running about, shouting, all around her now. The gorilla girls were gone. Or maybe, they had never been. A siren wailed close by, then stopped. Her eyelids were so heavy. One of the gorilla women had come back, was holding her hand.

Footsteps on the stairs, voices, cut through the fog. She was being prodded. "Leave me alone." They were cleaning her face with some sort of disinfectant, and it stung.

"Bag this."

She forced her eyelids open. Sombrero was dropping the little gun into an evidence bag. "She okay?" He got down on one knee and squinted at her.

He was holding a cat. "Is he dead?" She could hardly hear her own voice. Hands lifted her, held her when her knees collapsed. Sombrero twirled the cat on his fingers. But it wasn't a cat. She could see that now. It was a blond wig. "Is he dead?" she asked again.

"He wasn't there."

65

•••••••

"Ms. Wetzon." Something touched Wetzon's arm. The noise became horrific. Someone was crying. She heard moans.

Her eyes took their own sweet time about obeying her command to open. When they did, she saw she was in a hospital emergency room. St. Vincent's it had to be. It was closest. She was sitting, half leaning, head against the wall.

"Uh?" She moved her head, and the throbbing began. Touched bandage. Followed it with her fingertips down under her chin and back up again to her throbbing head. She rotated her head carefully to the left. Marissa Peiser was sitting there. "How did you get here so fast?"

"Detective Ferrante. He told me what happened. Said you refused to talk to anybody but me."

"I did?" Her mouth was parched. "Did they find him?"

"They picked up a man in a red dress in the PATH station in Jersey City. Martens went to check him out."

She was having trouble swallowing. "Can you get me something to drink? Black coffee?"

Peiser left her, and Wetzon began to focus on her environment. The emergency room was busy with the aftermath of Halloween—accidents, sick children, some mugging victims, one knifing. There were a lot of blue uniforms, most of them clustered farther down the corridor past where she was sitting.

Two men, both Hispanics in orderly whites, pushed a gurney

holding a patient up the corridor past her and into an examining room. The patient was attached to an IV.

Wetzon stood up. She was wrapped in an oversize hospital gown, and when she checked, no dress, no fake Chanel chains, no panty hose, just the black silk teddy, assorted bruises and scrapes and her shoes. It felt good to be on her feet. She stretched her legs. Where was there a bathroom? She started to walk, a bit unsteadily.

The orderlies came out of the room. Shaking his head, one said, "You see that, man? Jeeezus!"

"Yeah. Who got him?"

"Doc Levy."

They walked past Wetzon, taking no notice of her. Wetzon stretched again and did a plié. A little stiff, but not bad. What was that on the floor? Lying at her feet were two red sequins. What the hell? She bent to pick them up and slipped to her knees.

"You probably got up too quickly." Peiser was standing over her, holding orange juice in a clear plastic glass. She offered Wetzon her hand, and Wetzon dropped the two sequins in it. "What's this?" She handed Wetzon the orange juice, and Wetzon, still on her knees on the polished vinyl floor, drank it down.

"He's here." Wetzon got to her feet.

"Who?"

"Jerry Gordon. He was wearing a sequined dress."

Peiser stared at the sequins in her hand. "Go back and sit down. I'm going to find Ferrante." She went off down the hall at a fast clip and disappeared among the blue uniforms. Why weren't there any cops at this end of the corridor?

Go back and sit down? Those were fighting words. Wetzon tied the loose belt of the hospital gown and began to look into examining rooms. In the first, doctors and nurses were using all kinds of equipment, scrambling to resuscitate an elderly lady. In the second, a doctor was putting a bandage on a child's eye, while a worried woman in street clothes held the child still. Wetzon felt invisible. No one paid any attention to her.

She checked the corridor, more gurneys and hospital staff. No Peiser. No Ferrante. No cops.

Coming out of the third room Wetzon saw, then heard one of the Hispanic orderlies. "Doctor be right along, man." He pulled the curtain closed. When he saw Wetzon, he asked, "You know him?" There were red sequins on the floor near the entrance to the examining room. Wetzon nodded. He patted her hand sympathetically. "Doctor's coming soon."

She watched the orderly until he made a turn and she couldn't see him anymore. Then she parted the curtain and stepped in, creeping on tiptoe over to the person on the gurney, massive under a light blanket. The man gave a frightful groan. Wetzon came closer and was staring into Jerry Gordon's blackened and bruised face. His eyes opened, fierce blue bolts of anger, and his hand shot out and grabbed at her. She stumbled, lost her balance, and fell against the gurney.

"Didn't want to hurt anyone, Wetzon," he muttered. "They were going to hurt me. You were going to hurt me." Jerry sat up, pulling out the IV in the process, and Wetzon began screaming. His hand reached down at her, making grasping motions. She couldn't seem to get back on her feet.

A blur of white yelled, "Get her *out* of here!" Running footsteps, men shouting. A hypodermic needle made contact, and Jerry slowly sank back on the gurney.

"I was going to be a star," Jerry said, very clearly.

The room was full of blue, stepping around Wetzon. Someone said, "Put those damn guns away. This is a hospital."

"Come on." Peiser was helping her. "Lean on me." Out in the corridor, Peiser put her arm around Wetzon and walked her back to the chairs and sat her down.

"What happened to the rest of my clothes?"

"You wouldn't want them back."

"That black dress has seen me through years of boring parties. I'll miss it."

"I've got one of those, too."

"What's going to happen to Jerry Gordon? Or Gordon Jerome? Or Marilyn, or whatever he calls himself?"

"He'll get patched up, and then we'll try him for murder."

"Why did he serve time before?"

"As Gordon Jerome, he was a CPA who liked investing clients' money. But he wasn't good at it. He'd pay people off with new money coming in, but he couldn't keep up with it. He'd see a sure thing and borrow from his clients' accounts. He got four years, but only served two. He had a mental breakdown after his release from Clinton, and signed himself into Wakefield Farms as Jerome Gordon."

"Where he met Barbara. So he re-created himself as Jerome Gordon to hide that he was a convicted felon. He must have thought he was onto something when he saw how therapists work. He was really on the verge of becoming famous. Not to mention rich. Did he think that by eliminating Brian and Tabitha, and me, no one else would find out? A lot of people knew Gordon Jerome, CPA. . . . He'll plead insanity, won't he?"

Peiser shrugged. "He'll have a lawyer."

"Lawyer? Richard Hartmann, I'll betcha."

Peiser's face showed her distaste. "Do you want to go home?"

"Boy, do I! But I lost my date in the madness on Christopher Street, then my bag with the house keys, and my coat. . . ."

"Can't help you with your date, but . . ." The A.D.A. patted the seat next to her. "I think these are yours. Lenny had them."

"Lenny, I take it, is the weird guard dog you put on me?"

"How did—"

"Voices carry on open elevators. But you could have picked someone a lot less sinister." She looked at her watch. The hands weren't moving. It had stopped at ten-thirty. "What time is it, anyway?"

"Five o'clock."

"You mean Saturday morning?"

Peiser nodded.

Wetzon closed her eyes, tilting toward the right wall. "Peiser, you're not going to believe this, but five women in gorilla heads saved my life." And suddenly, as she was speaking, she knew who they were. She'd read about them. Not gorilla girls, but The Guerrilla Girls, a small, secret band of women in the art world who call themselves the conscience of that world. They went out in the dead of night in big, hairy gorilla heads, regularly papering areas of lower Manhattan with striking posters leveling charges of sexism against museums, galleries, critics, and white male artists. Louie. The one that said her name must have been Louie.

"Happy Halloween." Peiser stood up. "I'll get a doctor to check you out, and I'll come by tomorrow with Ferrante for a statement, okay?"

"Okay." Wetzon curled her feet up under her and closed her eyes. "Work fast," she mumbled. "Or I'll be asleep."

You didn't tell Peiser about Hartmann, she reminded herself.

And she answered herself, *I know. He's not the murderer.*

Okay, then what about Mrs. Leonora Foley and the money-laundering scam?

How can I blow him away when Smith is already involved with him?

Wetzon, her conscience scolded her, *do the right thing.*

Go away. Leave me alone. I'm tired of always doing the right thing. Besides, I can't do it to Smith. He'll trip himself up eventually, you'll see. . . .

"There she is," someone said.

"Hi." The doctor was kissing the palm of her hand, giving her goose pimples. Doctors didn't do that. She opened her eyes with difficulty. Then the doctor said, "Les."

Silvestri sat down next to her. She touched his jeans, felt his thigh tense. He was real. "You're real." He held his arms out and she crawled into his lap, lay her head on his chest. He smelled of coffee and after-shave. "Don't say anything, please."

He rubbed the nape of her neck, kissed it. "You're a mess."

"I asked you not to say anything."

"Couldn't help it."

"You should see the other guy. How did you know where to find me?"

"Don't get mad. I was keeping tabs on you through Ferrante."

"Damn you, Silvestri!" She tried to push him away. "I don't need you." Anger limped through her, generating energy, then subsided.

"You may not need me," he whispered in her ear, "but I need you."

A regal black woman in a white lab coat, stethoscope around her neck, arrived, flourishing a sheaf of forms. She wore a name tag that said "Dolores Bullard, M.D." "Okay, let's have a last look at you." Wetzon was taken into a tiny examining room. Head and bandage were checked. Blood pressure taken. Silvestri hovered like a mother hen. Dr. Bullard pronounced, "You're okay. Get out of here. Don't get your head wet. Come back in five days and we'll take the stitches out."

"Will my hair grow back?"

"It'll cover the scar."

Wetzon stole a look at Silvestri. He was thinner, and his eyes were that astonishing turquoise they turned when he allowed his emotions through. His cheeks were covered with dark stubble, and he looked tired. But face it, he still made her heart race. She discarded the hospital gown and wrapped herself in the trench coat he held for her.

Outside, Silvestri shook hands with Ferrante and Martens, was introduced to Peiser, then whisked her into his Toyota, which he'd parked in a towaway zone. Dawn gave the old buildings a rosy tint.

On Tenth Street, there was a parking place right in front of the loft building. A man in a suit was pacing back and forth on the sidewalk. *My God*, she thought. Alton. He stopped pacing, peered at the car, looked at her blankly, recognized her—all in a matter of seconds. He rushed to the car and opened the door. "Leslie! I've been so worried." His thick gray hair stood up on end and the seams on either side of his mouth were deeper. He was helping her out of the car, ignoring Silvestri.

Silvestri was pissed. He came around to the sidewalk and gave Alton a hard look. They were about the same height, and they looked one another over like bantam roosters, ready to circle. She felt in her purse for her keys and went into the building. They followed on her heels. No one was saying anything. They rode up in the elevator without a word spoken. *Oh, yuk*, she thought, *who needs this?*

She unlocked the door, left the keys and her purse on the trestle table, went right to the bedroom. Stepping out of her coat, she let it drop to the floor. Both men followed her and stood in the doorway watching. She tore off her shoes and, in her teddy, crawled into bed and pulled the covers up and closed her eyes.

The men stood there for a moment, then she heard them move into the living room.

"Who the fuck are you?" Silvestri barked.

"Alton Pinkus. Who are you?"

"I know who you are, for chrissakes. I mean, who are you to her?"

"I'll ask you the same question."

The door closed.

She lay in the bed. The sheets were cool and sensual. She could hear their voices rumbling. It was awful. Two men were fighting over her. That had never happened to her before.

Several seconds passed. No, she thought. No, it wasn't awful. Not at all. She smiled and pulled the covers up around her ears. She could live with it. She fingered the silk of the teddy, nestling down.

In fact, it was absolutely delicious.